MW01226173

"Finally! Our own s ...... ne of our own writers. Writing good gripping fiction is pure talent, but writing good fiction based on historical fact requires endless research; that Pryce has woven it all together in such a fascinating manner is true art. Her trilogy is bound to become an Okanagan treasure and should be introduced into our schools."

Jim Rheaume, Administrator, Retired
Regional District of Okanagan-Similkameen

"Only Elizabeth Pryce, with her deep Okanagan roots, could have written this in-depth trilogy! Her delineation of the characters, their backgrounds and the sensitive description of the country itself could only be brought to life by someone with a deep knowledge and love of this part of Canada. The reader is thoughtfully challenged by the philosophical statement of one character, 'Yes, one has to keep moving on, even when they don't want to.' This trilogy is required reading for anyone who would learn about and subsequently appreciate the fascinating history of the South Okanagan."

Dorothy Zoellner
Historian, Author & Educator
Editor, Okanagan Historical Society

"Pryce has blended historical reality with fictional characters and their lives. Her love for history is part of her heritage, with lyrical language and a wealth of knowledge picked up through stories shared by grandparents."

Leslie Plaskett
News Editor
OLIVER CHRONICLE

SKAHA RANCH

Vol. 3

ELIZABETH PRYCE

ACKNOWLEDGEMENTS

Recognition is owed to the late Dorothy and Doug Fraser, who reviewed the first draft and encouraged me to continue, and to the late Charles Hayes for editorial assistance on the second draft. Special thanks to A. David MacDonald and Robert Cowan for editorial assistance on the third draft; and to Gillian Veitch, editor of the final draft.

Grateful thanks also to my husband and our daughter, for their encouragement and faith in me to write the SKAHA stories.

Lines from "Rebellion" and verses from "As In The Bursting Bud", by Barbara Beldam, were published in her book May to December, 1979, and are used in *SKAHA RANCH,* with permission of her daughter, the late Patricia Leir. The comment regarding the freedom of the wild horses was made to the author by Okanagan pioneer, Sandy Brent.

COVER: Gillian Veitch: a derivation of original photos by the author.
Illustrations: Michelle Edge
Production: Gillian Veitch

Note for Librarians: A cataloguing record for this book is available from Library and Archives Canada at www.collectionscanada.ca/amicus/index-e.html
ISBN 1-4120-8400-8

Printed in Victoria, BC, Canada. Printed on paper with minimum 30% recycled fibre. Trafford's print shop runs on "green energy" from solar, wind and other environmentally-friendly power sources.

PUBLISHING™

Offices in Canada, USA, Ireland and UK

Book sales for North America and international:
Trafford Publishing, 6E–2333 Government St.,
Victoria, BC V8T 4P4 CANADA
phone 250 383 6864 (toll-free 1 888 232 4444)
fax 250 383 6804; email to orders@trafford.com

Order online at:
trafford.com/06-0155

10 9 8 7 6 5 4 3

INTRODUCTION

Often called *Canada's Pocket Desert*, the Okanagan Valley is filled with tall pine, sand hills, sagebrush and spiny cacti and has become the home of burgeoning cities, crowded subdivisions and communities. While this new life pulses along the beautiful lakes and channelled river of the valley floor, quiet, uncrowded areas remain in the flanking mountains. The rolling hills and flat land of the western White Lake Valley, where Skaha Ranch is located in this historical fiction, largely remain cattle range, shared by small estates.

The Llewellyns and McAllisters, and all the novel's characters are real only to this story. *SKAHA RANCH* is the final chapter in this Okanagan trilogy, with historical dates and events authentic to the best of the author's knowledge and research. All the characters in this book are fictitious and any resemblance to actual persons is coincidental.

Some of the publications pertinent to research for *SKAHA RANCH* are: Okanagan Historical Society Annual Reports; the Old West series from Time Life Books; Penticton, Years to Remember, edited by A. David MacDonald for the City of Penticton; Cattle Ranch by Nina G. Woolliams; Fifty Years - Three And A Half Million Cattle by Morrie Thomas; Ranching, Now, Then, And Way Back When... by Doug Cox; the Pioneer Days In British Columbia series, edited by Art Downs from BC Outdoors Magazine; Okanagan Sources, edited by Jean Webber for the En'owkin Centre; and The Salishan Tribes of the Western Plateaus by James Teit and Franz Boas. Many outstanding local and provincial publications, and personal interviews and photographs proved very valuable in the writing of the SKAHA stories.

E.P.

LLEWELLYN

*For the unknown paths are so many
and the known ones are so few... and
my soul is singing rebellion.*

Barbara Beldam
May To December

1

Thomas Llewellyn leaned over the railing of the S.S. *ABERDEEN*, and watched the waves churn away from the sternwheeler. A summer breeze whipped the water into lapping ripples, gently washing the shore and playing about the pilings of the wharf behind him. Ahead lay the windswept length of the great Okanagan Lake. Watching the water leap and roll, he remembered his mother's story of her first trip on this lake on the *PENTICTON*; it had been the last leg of their westward journey.

As the *ABERDEEN* moved down the lake, Thomas contemplated his future. This was not something he had often done, but now it bore consideration. He was leaving Kelowna and another term at Okanagan School behind and he had no desire to return.

Studies were not a fascination in Thomas' young life. The death of Queen Victoria in Britain after a sixty-three year reign, and the Boer War, fought in South Africa over issues never understood by Thomas, held no influence over which vocation he might choose, nor the direction he might take in his father's enterprise.

Of the Queen's death, he remembered his mother's shock as she read the sobering news in the VICTORIA COLONIST. The Queen had been expected to live forever. No one he knew had gone off to the faraway war between the Boers and the British. In the classroom Thomas had learned of Canada's history and place in world affairs. However, he had no idea where all that would lead him. What he did know was that he was expected, by those at home, to go somewhere important in life.

Advice from his father, Albert Llewellyn, always dealt with progress in life and was enhanced with the promise of an early partnership in the family concern, an enterprise which Thomas felt he was bound to inherit outright anyway. The story was the same each time he was at home. Consequently, he soon came to dread the visits to Skaha. He had even contemplated skipping and obtaining a summer job on one of the big ranches nearby.

But a timely letter delivered from the ranch's accountant, Ian Cartrell, to Okanagan School in early June saw Thomas heading home again for the summer. At sixteen, Thomas had come to realize that his father was more opinionated and overbearing as each year passed. After five years of living away from it, he was reluctant to return.

Thomas thought of the ranch foreman, Charlie Sandon, whom he liked, and Ian Cartrell, whom he disliked. He missed the teamster, Dick Foderow. The man had gone into United States to hunt the outlaw who had shot their neighbour, David McAllister.

Thomas smiled as he watched the waves lap at the ABERDEEN's side. He had always considered Dick Foderow a happy fellow to be around, therefore, it was difficult to imagine the man deliberately hunting another down to the kill.

In a few hours Thomas would disembark at the Penticton wharf. He was not impressed that his father ignored his mother's pleas and, each new term, ordered Cartrell to carry out the necessary school arrangements. Cartrell provided adequately for young Thomas, knowing that as each year passed Thomas came to dislike him more for his honest efforts.

On that same breezy June day in 1905, Ian Cartrell relaxed in the Skaha Ranch carriage, heading out of the White Lake hills toward Penticton. The clopping of the sturdy Morgan pulling the carriage over the hard-packed road held a comforting sound for Cartrell and he spent his time in reflection of his life at Skaha. Jason Whiteman, the driver, was the ranch blacksmith and had lived at Skaha all his life. He helped build the carriage they were riding in and had become its sole driver.

As they crossed the Penticton townsite and neared the lake, Cartrell wondered how the valley had appeared to the fur trapper, Rayne McAllister, when he arrived in 1834. Empty of settlers, Cartrell could only imagine what had drawn the trapper to make the valley his home, perhaps the beauty of the countryside and its sense of peace, or its reserved but congenial welcome by the trading Okanagan Indians. There were many possibilities should he choose to become permanent. Cartrell smiled when he thought of Two Way, the young Okanagan who grew up befriending the trapper, eventually helping to build Skaha Crossing. Two Way still lived in his small cabin beside Willow Creek.

While Ian Cartrell awaited the arrival of the S.S. ABERDEEN at the Canadian Pacific dock, he recalled his own arrival to the valley, amid the smoke and flames of his employer's dream burning to the ground. It had been a violent night. Albert Llewellyn lost his entire freighting business to arson carried out in revenge by an outlaw, and young David McAllister lost his house. That was the night Cartrell met the teamster, Dick Foderow. Cartrell smiled. He had grown attached to the young man and quickly came to hold him in high regard.

Cartrell contemplated the subsequent turbulent years he had spent on the ranch. More particularly, he thought about the young man he was to meet off the ABERDEEN. Thomas Llewellyn would, most likely, be in a dour mood and it would take all of his energies to lace their conversation with cheer and optimism. It was not easy dealing with his employer's rebellious son. No one found it easy, least of all the boy's father. Long ago Albert Llewellyn had given up on a peaceful relationship with his son and the burden had fallen to Cartrell, the ranch accountant.

As he watched the *ABERDEEN* ply the blue water, Cartrell thought of his future at Skaha. It was a fact that he would never leave the ranch; it had become ingrained in him to oversee the life of the ranch and its occupants through all their various troubles and successes. This would lead to strife in his own life. His patient wife, Belle, suffered a chest condition and, while he wished to spend time with her and their young daughters, time was often cut short by the demands of the Llewellyns. He lamented this loss, but could do nothing to ease it. Companionship for Belle came through Llewellyn's beautiful wife, Sydney.

While Ian Cartrell pondered his life, young Thomas Llewellyn contemplated the possible consequence of a poor showing at Okanagan School in Kelowna.

Ian met Thomas and greeted him cheerily. He was truly pleased to see the young man. When they returned to the carriage, Ian told him in a friendly way, "Your case is strapped on the back and Jason would like to get us home as early as possible tonight." Cartrell smiled. "We'll talk on the way," he added, nodding to Jason, who took up the reins and clicked his tongue. The breeze of the earlier hour had died and the summer sun bore down on them.

Unhappy and glowering, Thomas hastily stepped up into the carriage, lest he be left hopping alongside. "Is there something to discuss? You only repeat what Da says anyway."

"On the contrary, young man," Cartrell elaborated as the carriage was pulling away from the wharf, "they are not just your father's opinions, but simply some I share. As you grow older and know me better, Tom, you'll find that I am not always in accordance with your father."

"With my mother then?" Thomas' voice was suddenly full of defiance.

Turning slowly, Cartrell studied Thomas. "With myself," he replied patiently. "You'd do well throughout your life to keep your own counsel also. You've an axe to grind with your father, Thomas, but you'll grind it down to the powder of its metal and still find him standing over you."

Through the open window of the carriage Thomas watched the tug boats and barges at the dock; some moving in, others heading up the lake to Kelowna and Okanagan Landing. He knew that supplies unloaded from the *ABERDEEN* were being transferred to A & S

STAGE wagons and that his father's teams waited patiently in their traces to begin the haul south to the Okanagan Falls warehouse.

"Sometimes I miss Harrie," Thomas spoke reflectively of his deceased brother. "I think I resented him for most of our life together, but still, I miss him. I had a sister for about two or three days before she died." He looked across at Cartrell. "Did you know that? I often wonder what it would be like to have a sister around."

"It's not in your life, Tom, so don't waste time on it. Now, I'd like to know about your studies and how you came along this past term."

They left the town behind and followed the road through the tall pines and firs that blanketed the flats toward Dog Lake. The sun was extremely warm and the carriage held the heat. Cartrell loosened his collar and rested back against the seat.

Removing his jacket, Thomas said idly, "I don't know what I'm doing in that school, you know."

Cartrell stared calmly ahead at the narrow roadbed before them. "You'd best decide upon your father's business, study management and apprentice with me," he suggested. "Much as it goes against your grain."

"All this nonsense and expense just to run an orchard and look after some cows and load freight." Thomas sighed in resignation, pulled his hat over his eyes and sank back against the upholstery, locking Cartrell, his father and Skaha Ranch out of mind.

The bouncing of the carriage as it jolted over the road left little relaxation in the trip and Thomas longed for it to be over. He wished not to be worried about pressures and position in his father's business which should have belonged to Harrie, but now rested upon Thomas' young shoulders. By nature Thomas was not equipped for such responsibility, nor did he want it.

Cartrell, aware that young Thomas had shut him out, sat back and contemplated the matter of raising children in this day and age. He was a father twice over with a second daughter, Karen, born two years after Jennifer. It often occurred to him that total responsibility for their upbringing could fall upon his shoulders should his wife's health continue to deteriorate. He had grown accustomed to the difficult coughing spells and laboured breathing which Belle suffered. She needs to be reassessed, Cartrell decided. In the meantime, I've Thomas to deal with for another summer!

In the absence of his father, confrontation with his mother took place the following morning as Sydney glanced at Thomas' negative report from Okanagan School. His reaction to her disappointment was to challenge the direction he was expected to take in life.

"Why?" asked Sydney of Thomas. "Why don't you want all that your father and I have built here for you? We've given our life to it - more of our life than you know." Torn between husband and son, Sydney Llewellyn fought desperately to keep a balance. "You're home less than twelve hours, Thomas, and we're already at odds."

The air was still warm from the night before and, as she sat at the breakfast table in the large kitchen, Sydney raised a fan against the room's stuffiness. Loose strands of her honey-coloured hair waved teasingly about her ears in the breeze caused by the fan's movement, and her beautiful features were now soft in thought as she studied her son across from her. "There is in you, Thomas, a sad rebellion brewing, and I do not understand it."

Thomas wolfed down the eggs and toast before him. He was sixteen and always hungry. "Well, Ian was his usual predictable self when he met me, full of warnings if I didn't shape up." He drained the tall glass of milk, watching his mother over the rim. "How close are you to him, Mother?"

Sydney's voice was full of thought. "Thomas, without Ian, my life here would be next to nothing. You are sixteen now and able to see for yourself that things are not right between your father and me. Ian makes life bearable for both of us. It suffices for you to know that my way of life is completely beyond reproach!"

There was a desperate need in him to believe his mother. He loved her very much and could never forgive his father the affair with Alice Mason at Fairview. Quickly he rose from the chair, left the kitchen and crossed the yard, passing before Cartrell's office window without looking up. At the livery he saddled a horse, loaded his bedroll and a pack of groceries behind the saddle and rode off toward Sandon's cow-camp in the mountains.

The steady rhythm of the animal's pace, even the gnashing sound of its metal shoes against the rocks, was welcome comfort to his troubled mind. The mid-June sun beat unrelenting upon him. He pulled his hat low over his brow to shade his eyes and relaxed in the saddle. The rolling grassy hills before Thomas seemed to beckon and he booted his horse into a comfortable trot. By noon he had arrived at cow-camp.

Pleased to see young Thomas, Charlie Sandon grinned broadly. "Well, well, the absentee cowboy once again returns to the fold. And what good stores d'you have in your pack for us, Tommy?"

Thomas handed the saddle bags across to Sandon and hoisted the pack over his shoulder. "Some whiskey I stole from Da's cupboard, if that's what you're expecting. There's coffee, beans, bacon, ham. A tin of cakes and some sugar. I even got the eggs here without breaking them," Thomas added proudly.

Sandon chuckled, pleased. "Much of this high livin'," he joked, "and I'll be lookin' the size of your Daddy."

13

"Haven't seen him yet. Didn't hang around that long. Didn't want to raise his blood pressure getting through that first yelling match." Thomas lifted his bedroll off the horse, loosened the cinch, pulled the saddle and blankets off and placed them over the railing built alongside the cabin for such purpose.

Impulsively, Sandon caught the other's arm. "You got somethin' to tell me, boy? About your Daddy? Something's wrong?"

Thomas frowned. "Of course something's wrong!" he snapped. "Tell me what I do that's right for him." He dumped the pack and bedroll on the cabin step and picked up the lead from his horse. He strode angrily toward the corrals near the pond. "Good Lord it's hot, even up here."

Sandon followed and leaned against the corral rails in the shade, slapping at flies as they buzzed about his face. "What's stuck in your craw, lad?"

"I'm quittin' that school. I don't need it."

Sandon knocked the barrel of his pipe against a post and the near dead ashes fell into the dirt. "Have you given it thought, son? When I was your age an education wasn't there unless your mother could teach you. I just rode out one day with a good horse under me, an old rifle, a bedroll and some grub. Fifteen, I was-- your age. A boy could do that in those days. In your Daddy's time of school in Wales, youngsters finished most grades before lightin' out on their own. Now, you need your schoolin'. Just where d'you think your Daddy'd be without the benefit of Mr. Cartrell's education? He's more than just an accountant to your folks. He runs the whole outfit and he's a good friend, as well."

"I don't like him. I never did and I never will."

Sandon stowed his cooled pipe into a pocket and stared across the corral at Thomas where he stood brushing his horse. "Well, that's your loss and it's too bad, because he has a decent concern for your stubborn hide." Frustrated, he turned toward the cabin.

"I can work out here with you and on the ranch."

"You put in another year at school and apprentice with Ian. Then, you can come out here with me."

"That's a long time," Thomas called out.

"I'll still be around," Sandon called back.

Thomas tossed the brush into the utility box near the gate and caught up to the foreman on the trail. "What about the orchard and the wagons?"

"What about them? They're good money-makers. You're starin' at a fortune, so you go the route, Tommy. Don't throw it away because you're all mixed up inside."

As tall as Sandon, Thomas looked into the other's eyes and read concern there. The pains of growing up were hard to bear and often

Thomas found himself wondering how Harrie would have handled situations he now faced. Most likely Harrie would have gone along with whatever his father wanted. He felt Sandon's gaze on him. "It should have been Harrie who lived," he muttered. "He was Da's favourite."

Sandon reached out and caught Thomas quickly, solidly by the shoulder. Staring coolly into the defiant eyes across from him, Sandon warned, "Don't ever let me hear you cry like an ungrateful whelp again! Your father came over from the old country to build a good life in Canada, trusting in a son he hoped to have, to continue in his footsteps. He didn't cross that prairie in an old farm wagon, or climb over those mountains dragging mules behind him, then work himself near to death here for some insolent boy to throw away." He caught his breath and let go of Thomas. "Now, you keep that in mind. If I don't beat a bad attitude outta you, Cartrell will. Remember, I'm the lesser of the evils."

Throughout July, Thomas rode the range with Sandon. He made two trips to the ranch for supplies, deciding if his father wished to see him further, he could ride out to cow-camp and visit with all four of them residing there for the summer. Looking out upon the herds grazing in the meadows where he rode during those sunshine days of July, Thomas found it difficult to muster up affection for his father. His resentment at being sent away to school had become a harsh barrier between them. Often he sat atop his horse on the knoll above the camp and watched the cattle. At such times a small measure of pride stole through him, for he knew his father had built a fine herd in five years.

When he flushed stray cattle out of the thick willow and young poplar bush, chasing around clumps of sage and tall pines, the freedom he felt was exhilarating and he guarded it jealously. He learned to rope and pull wandering calves from bogs that waited like death traps in the higher mountain passages. With Sandon, he dug out three new water holes and equipped them with long wooden troughs. Higher up where bunch grass still grew tall and plentiful, they led pack horses loaded with blocks of salt for the cattle.

From atop a ridge one morning Sandon drew Thomas' attention to a grove of trees at the edge of a narrow creek. "Down there's where Dave McAllister got shot in a rustling duel of sorts. Him and young Dick Foderow against some Montana thieves."

"I think about that sometimes. Must've been some shoot-out."

"Only five years ago. It's remarkable in this age that a man should lose his life in somethin' like that. Twenty years ago shoot-outs were common all over the west, but somehow I always thought that it was a careless thing to happen to him. Such a waste. He ran a good herd,

15

McAllister did. It's part of your Daddy's now. Everything he owned, your Daddy set out to get, and that was quite a lot."

"Do you believe that Dick ever got the one who did the killing?"

"Well, I suppose Dick hunted down the other one alright. Followed a pair of light blue eyes, they say, clean across Idaho and Montana."

"Did he shoot him?"

"Heard he was goin' to walk him back to Canada, but I don't think so. That border is a kind of sanctuary, depending on which side your crime was committed."

Thomas' eyes were wide with curiosity. "Well, what happened?"

"Nobody knows for sure, unless Ian does and ain't sayin', and you're a inquisitive lad!" Sandon smiled, amused at Thomas' interest.

Thomas turned away from Sandon's teasing gaze and dutifully viewed the Shorthorn and Angus in the meadow before him. One animal appeared much the same as the other to him. However, he decided, he could learn. He recognized the teacher in Charlie Sandon. The business of cattle was the lesser job when he considered that he may soon be instructed on how to prune an apple tree or ordered to lift the lids on the bee hives distributed about Skaha's properties.

"I wish I wasn't always at odds with Da. Cross-purposes, Mom calls it," Thomas confessed thoughtfully to Sandon. "I don't even know anymore, what got it all started, but it's like my presence at home does nothing but aggravate him, not please him."

Sandon rested his crossed arms on the saddle horn. "Pickin' favourites in a family, especially between two boys, is a bad thing." He felt sorrow over his own words, for he spoke from the bitter experience of sibling rivalry.

"I know that I'll never measure up." Thomas' blue eyes were full of sadness as he gazed openly at Sandon. "I think things will only get worse."

Sandon shrugged helplessly. "It's your choice. Others don't make or break you. You do that yourself. I know it first hand."

2

August thunderclouds moved up from the southwest and hung low over Skaha Ranch. The smell of rain was heavy in the air. In the mountains and the valleys the grass had become tinder dry from excessive July heat. The country was in desperate need of rain.

As Albert Llewellyn rode his horse over the trail to Skaha Ranch and listened to the distant thunder echo in the mountains, he watched the darting flashes of lightning with some concern. He had just brought the stage in from Camp McKinney. He was tired and did not need a forest fire to tax his energies further that night. He knew Sydney planned a dinner party with the Cartrells, Heather Carmichael, Skaha's retired school teacher, and Harry Spencer, whom Llewellyn had recently hired as a blacksmith at his Okanagan Falls livery near Dog Lake.

As Llewellyn approached his house he saw Jason Whiteman assist Spencer's young daughter from the carriage to the steps of the house, and then drive out of the yard.

"Evenin', Albert," Jason called and stopped at the Skaha livery.

Loosening the saddle on his gelding, Llewellyn enquired, "Get everybody settled?"

"Bet your life! Spencers will stay in Dave's old house for the night."

Llewellyn nodded and strode toward his house.

Sydney met him at the doorway. She was beautiful in an array of soft blue materials. She was obviously pleased at presiding over the evening dinner. Albert tossed his hat atop the rack and watched his wife with renewed interest. He had not seen her so lovely, bright and cheerful in several years and he considered this carefully. Nodding a greeting to Belle Cartrell and Heather Carmichael, Albert strode across the room to where Harry Spencer and Ian stood in conversation, drinks in their hands.

Thomas sat alone at the top of the long staircase and watched the ladies assist his mother in serving dinner. Behind him on the landing, Cartrell's little girls, now five and seven, played quietly. The focus of Thomas' concentrated attention was centred upon the daughter of Harry Spencer. He guessed her age to be little more than his own. She had a fresh prettiness which reminded him of his mother.

Her name was Marjorie and she was not particularly aware of Thomas on the stairwell. The unsmiling countenance which he had presented at their arrival failed to invite further conversation from her. Having learned that he was younger than her, Marjorie Spencer had quickly abandoned his company for that of Sydney.

Throughout the meal Thomas continued to watch Marjorie. Her mother was dead, he knew. A glance at her father told him the man had already consumed too much wine, a favourite beverage.

His interest in the girl did not escape Cartrell, whose dark eyes missed nothing and, when the meal was finished, he found a moment to speak of it with Thomas.

"Meddling again?" Thomas bristled, turning away from the accountant.

"Let it be a warning that nothing short of a death in the family will keep you away from school, young man. You have less than a week left and your mother tells me you haven't a thing ready for departure." Cartrell's penetrating eyes burned into Thomas'. "You *will* be leaving, you know."

Thomas abruptly stepped out onto the veranda. Rain had finally begun to fall. Its freshness cleared the stifling, humid air, but not his angry mood. Thunder rumbled in the distance. Thomas remained outside listening to it until the farewells were finished and he was called to his father's den upstairs in the big house.

So Thomas mounted the stairs with some trepidation. A coal-oil lamp burned in one corner of the room, otherwise the interior was in darkness. Across the hall the door to his mother's bedroom had been left ajar. Llewellyn closed the door to the den.

Thomas stood before the wide panes of the windows through which he had surveyed the surrounding property so many times and through which he now gazed into the black night of rain. This was his father's room. Everything in it represented his father's achievements. It was not shared by his mother, nor was his mother's room shared by his father. Thomas recognized that lack of intimacy as a sad burden between his parents, all because of broken trusts. It served as a lesson.

Llewellyn lit his pipe, a habit he had developed, Thomas noted, since he had been home at Christmas. As Llewellyn lowered his tall, heavy frame into his favourite chair, Thomas noticed also how much weight his father had gained during the past few years. In fact, Thomas was suddenly aware of several changes which had taken place in his father over the last five years; the lines across his forehead and the puffiness of his face, the dark hair was much thinner and liberally laced with gray. And, the boy noticed, on the nights that he was home, his father retired much earlier to his bed in the den.

Suddenly without warning... before Thomas' startled eyes, and before a word had been spoken between them, Albert Llewellyn collapsed in his chair, falling forward to the floor. Thomas froze.

For one horrible, rigid, unbelieving moment Thomas stood fearfully rooted to the floor near the window. Then in a flash he reached down in an attempt to help his father up, picking up the pipe and stubbing out the burning ashes which had spilled onto the floor. Looking up at the door, he stared directly into his mother's astonished questioning blue eyes.

"I heard a thud," she whispered, anxiety in her voice. "I was afraid– Oh, my goodness, my goodness, Thomas!" Together, they got Albert to his bed. "Run and get Ian," Sydney cried, near tears as she placed a coverlet over him.

Thomas sped across the dark yard through the rain to Cartrell's house and called Ian to attend his father. Upon his arrival Cartrell ordered, "Go saddle my horse, Tom. I'll ride for the physician."

Cartrell assisted Sydney in making Albert more comfortable. "Whatever you do, don't let him get up. He must lay still. Give him only a few sips of water. I'll ride as fast as this abominable weather permits."

When Thomas returned, leading the readied horse, Cartrell instructed further, "Now, Tom, go down and get Two Way to come and stay with your mother. He's an old man but nonetheless knows how to handle every situation." Thomas put his slicker over his shoulders and once more left the house.

For a brief moment before departing, Cartrell held Sydney's small trembling hand tightly in his own and searched her pain-filled eyes. "The situation with your husband hardly warrants impassioned words of comfort, my dear. For once I'm at a loss."

Impulsively Sydney threw herself into Cartrell's arms. He held her there, tightly, pressing her face into his shoulder. Beyond the hallway the house was quiet. Outside the rain pelted down, bouncing heavily against the steps. During the anxious moment he held her close, Ian Cartrell finally admitted to himself the deep emotional love which he felt for this beautiful troubled woman.

"Be careful, Ian," she whispered. "Please be careful."

Moving a gentle hand over the soft waves of her hair, he tipped Sydney's face to look at him and met her eyes for a long moment. A rush of feeling seized him, and all the care and affection he had felt for her in the past now registered in his eyes for her to see. He knew that she recognized it. With great restraint he stifled the urge to bend down and touch her delicate mouth with his own, to forget that her husband lay stricken upstairs in his bed and that he had obligations of his own. The electric moment between them passed when Cartrell released her and moved toward the doorway. As he closed the door behind him, he heard Sydney's small sob of anguish as she turned and ran up the stairs to her husband's bedside.

Through the dark hours of night the rain beat relentlessly against

Cartrell as he urged his horse along the trail that led him south to the mining town of Fairview. He was soon soaked, despite the wide slicker, chaps and hat, but did not complain of the discomfort. He was simply thankful that Harold Stobie was in residence that night and not off doctoring in Camp McKinney, a boom town to the east.

Arriving in the mining town, Cartrell exchanged his horse for a fresh mount and paused long enough for hot tea. When he left with the doctor for the return trip to Skaha, the storm had settled into a steady downpour, rendering the journey almost as miserable as Cartrell had expected.

"Anymore disasters up your way," Harold Stobie called out to Cartrell through the bad weather, "you'll have to ride to Penticton for me. I'll be moving over before winter. Hang my shingle out there somewhere."

"Of course, since that old hotel burned, Fairview's dying," Cartrell called back. "No sense staying there."

They arrived at Skaha, where Thomas took their horses to stable. Shaking out their slickers, Cartrell and Stobie entered the house and were met by the Okanagan Indian, Two Way. The doctor, with his black medical bag in hand, went immediately to see Llewellyn.

Albert Llewellyn lay as Cartrell had left him, with Sydney remaining at his bedside. In the kitchen below, Two Way shuffled about in his worn deerskins and moccasins, preparing breakfast. When Thomas came downstairs, he enlisted the boy's assistance in setting out the food for Cartrell and the doctor.

Cartrell told Two Way, "I won't be staying."

Without smiling, Two Way ordered in his quiet way, "You stay. Thomas, find some warm blankets and get his wet clothes hung up. Then go to his house and bring some dry things for him to wear. Funny how it is," he murmured as he poured the hot coffee, "that young men know all the right things to do, but it takes an old one to tell them when to do it." His smile was smug. Because he had lived at Skaha most of his life and, with the trapper, had been its creator, Two Way felt privileged to give orders when necessary.

Thomas disappeared into the maze of rooms upstairs.

Two Way had lit the fireplace upon his arrival and the warmth in the parlour spread throughout the house. "You go in there now and wait for the boy," he told Cartrell.

When Thomas returned with a blanket, Cartrell said to him, "Your mother should have a woman in the house to help her now."

"My mother has always done her own work," Thomas informed him curtly, resentful of any intrusion into their private family life.

"I know, I know. But now I think she'll need assistance." Ian removed his shirt and trousers and wrapped the blanket around his chilled body. Thomas pulled a chair closer to the heat of the fireplace and Cartrell sank tiredly into it. "Sit down, Thomas," he suggested and waved a hand toward the nearby sofa.

"Two Way needs—"

"He'll manage." Cartrell stared at young Thomas, forcing Thomas' eyes to meet his. "I've known for a long time that you do not like me. As a matter of fact, you blamed me in little ways for putting you into that school. But then, I've been blamed for several things out of this household." He said to Thomas, "I want to tell you now, that if your father lives, he may never be physically active again. By the greatest stretch of imagination he may get along with a cane if he's lucky. I believe he has had a stroke, but we'll wait for professional diagnosis. Do you have the foggiest notion what this means for you? The kind of a relationship it forces you into with your father and with me?"

Thomas remained silent.

"I'm not about to leave this business. I'll die here, Tom, so you're stuck with me because you can't manage without me, which is precisely the way your father's own position stands."

Thomas refused to reply, although he knew Cartrell waited.

Cartrell did not smile. "You go up to that room now, Tom," he said gently. "Listen carefully to what the doctor has to say. Never from this night on do I want to hear you whine about how hard life is for you. To cry is to feel sorry for yourself and it is not you who has been struck down."

Two Way brought steaming coffee and a plate of bacon, potatoes and eggs to Cartrell. "Go to your parents now," Cartrell ordered Thomas. "Thank you, Two Way." He smiled gratefully up at the old Indian. "Bring one for yourself and join me, Two Way. I need your company and sage advice right now." The elderly Okanagan was well-respected in the valley and Cartrell was comfortable with him.

Upstairs, Sydney remained as the doctor carried out his examination. "I'm sure you know already, Sydney, that Albert has suffered a severe stroke. Just how damaging remains to be seen. He'll have some permanent slackening of the mouth, speech slurring which may improve with time and therapy." Harold Stobie leaned against the wall, closing his eyes momentarily. Weariness crept through his short frame. He felt all of his fifty-one years.

"Will he walk again?" she asked in a whisper of disbelief.

"I believe he might, but with some difficulty. He's a strong man, Sydney, with a body far too overweight, high blood pressure and all that. Nonetheless, he'll have an ardent will for recovery, I know."

Thomas entered the room, crossing to his mother's side. Sydney reached for his hand in comfort. It was the cold and trembling that surprised her.

"Well, young man," the doctor said. "You'll have some new responsibilities to face because of this night."

Thomas raised a hand to hide his trembling mouth and glanced across at his exhausted mother. In spite of Cartrell's warning, his eyes filled with tears he could no longer hold back. Apprehension over what the future might hold crept in. He pinched his eyes against the unsettling sight which his pale, paralysed father presented, laying still on the bed beneath the coverlet.

Sydney turned, put her arms around his shoulders and held him close. "This is the last time you will be my little boy," she whispered in a distressed voice. The white calcimined walls of the room enclosed them as Dr. Stobie prudently left them alone.

Thomas did not allow the tears to spill over his face. He hid his hurt and held onto his mother. After a time it seemed that it was she who drew solace from their contact.

Thomas Llewellyn was not destined to become an honour student and, although against his will, he returned to Kelowna in September. His visit to the ranch during the Christmas season was a tense, strained encounter filled with impatient rhetoric delivered from the side of his father's slackened mouth, and with exasperated sighs of impatience from his mother. Cold, dictatorial stares from Cartrell's black eyes and gentle warnings from Sandon only added to his anxiety.

Over the holiday, he spent as much time as possible at the barn and corrals with Charlie Sandon and with Jason Whiteman at the livery. At fifty-four, Jason welcomed the boy's help. Thomas worked with the hired hands in the pastures where sleigh loads of hay were hauled daily. The freezing wind which blew across the flats bit at his face and somehow lessened the pain of frustration and disappointment. He even took part in menial chores such as egg candling and packaging for transport, and milking and separating. Often he visited Sandon and the other cowboys in the bunkhouse; however, he never crossed the step into Cartrell's office.

Shortly before the Easter holiday of 1906, Thomas left the school at Kelowna of his own accord and boarded the steamer YORK, to disembark that afternoon at the Penticton wharf. There, he borrowed a horse from the nearby blacksmith and got himself over the road to Skaha just as dusk was falling upon the land.

He appeared at the ranch unexpected. He had terminated his formal education without consultation with his parents and therefore, was considered truant from Okanagan School, a situation which would be left to Ian Cartrell.

Thomas was acutely aware that Cartrell would now take greater control of his life. Following a period of learning at the accountant's desk, Thomas' father would then order him to work in the freight sheds in Okanagan Falls. There, reins strung out from the teams would be placed across his inexperienced hands, under the instruction of Leon Hicks. Such matters, he decided, would take care of the spring months, after which time he would be brought back to the ranch to ride range with Sandon.

Eventually he would be sent to Alfred Kennedy's world of orchard ladders, picking bags and apple boxes. Then, it would be quickly back to the ranch for fall roundup. Thomas soon realized his fate had been sealed by his own choice and by his father's stroke.

3

The Okanagan Indian, Two Way, had reached the grand age of eighty-five. Dressed in his deerskin jacket, breeches and moccasins, he still rode his horse into the hills, often alone. While travelling old, familiar trails he meditated and relived the past. Memories were gifts, he maintained. His friendship was appreciated by all who knew him.

One of Thomas Llewellyn's rewarding companionships was with Two Way. In Thomas, Two Way found as keen a listener to his stories as David McAllister had been. With Thomas, he happily shared the history and tales of his tribe; tales of waterfowl forays at Vaseux Lake, salmon fishing below the twin falls on Okanagan River and his life shared with the trapper whom he called Many Rains.

While riding beside Two Way one day, through the high grass in the lush hills of the White Lake valley, Thomas listened patiently to the old man's story.

"Nearly two centuries ago, it is believed by some that when the Spanish went north from Mexico into California," Two Way began, "they came further, by sea, to our coast, then inland. They travelled overland to that great plain your parents crossed. Our people called the Spanish horses medicine dogs. But then, you see what quickly happened? It did not take us long to get used to them and start stealing their bands of ponies away from them. Some of our younger braves started riding through the white man's camps, trying to scare them back to where they came from, but the white man was not to be moved. Soon we had to realize that the white man was here to stay."

"Do you resent us, Two Way?"

"No, but some of our people do; some old ones who have never lived with the white man. I lived with Many Rains. Young men and women of our tribes today do not bother themselves too much about whether they should or should not like their life changing as it is." The Indian sighed in resignation. "They just live with what is happening and try to keep their own traditions. I think someday that will change."

Astride his gelding, Thomas looked across the valley to the mountains of distant ranges. Below them grazed the herd of Angus and Shorthorns of which his father was so proud. In the distance a small band of horses galloped through the hills in and out of Thomas' sight, little dark specks darting across the blue-green landscape.

"Wild ones, those are," commented Two Way. "We chased their ancestors when we were boys, to prove our manhood to somebody, I suppose. There are several bands of those horses on both sides of the valley."

"Does anybody ever catch them?"

"Oh, yes! And sell them, too." Two Way's face broke into a broad smile. "The freedom of the wild mustang was the freedom I knew as a boy. To run where we pleased, stay where we chose and do what we wanted to do. No more, that kind of freedom." His voice was sad.

Thomas hung his head momentarily as though feeling guilt for an alteration he was not responsible for. "Two Way, do you like my father?" he asked suddenly.

Jolted from his reverie, Two Way turned his wrinkled brown face toward the young man and replied softly, "That is not for me to tell you. That is a feeling which belongs only to me, young fellow. I know you do not love him and I do not think you know why." The warm summer sunshine beat down upon them. Two Way pulled his hat forward. "There is one thing about your father, Tommy. He will keep trying to make a man out of you and you'll see the day you thank him for it." Two Way shrugged his thin shoulders. "Well, if he doesn't, Ian will do it for him. You have no choice in the matter."

"Pretty soon I'll be going down to the Falls to stay with Mr. Kennedy. Peach-picking starts next week and after that, prunes." Thomas felt quite glum at the prospect.

Two Way laughed. "Well, that won't take long. They are young trees with hardly much on them."

"I'd rather be up at Sandon's camp."

"Of course you would!"

"They're moving the cattle out to summer range in two weeks."

Two Way told Thomas curtly, "That's why you don't know anything about freight or fruit trees. You're always chasing after the cattle."

Thomas looked into Two Way's dark watery eyes and laughed merrily. "You're right, old man. You are always dead right." Kneeing his horse, he called, "Come on! Mama's new housekeeper should have something for us to eat and I'm hungry!"

Two Way watched them run, the boy and the horse in motion as one. He rides well, Two Way nodded, pleased to see it. Visions of himself as a young boy with his first pony, which his uncle had stolen for him, floated across his mind. He smiled and remembered the day he had crossed the river below the twin falls to show his new pony to the trapper.

Lifting the leather reins, Two Way jigged them once, and the horse stepped ahead onto the path along the hillside toward Skaha.

4

Believing in the power of expansion, Llewellyn had acquired twenty-five acres on the flats of Okanagan Falls and planted it to orchard. Each year he grew a ground crop of tomatoes in the panels between the rows of fruit trees. As his property bordered a substantial creek, he wisely installed a small waterwheel and flume for irrigation. He then moved Alfred Kennedy from the Skaha orchard and put him in charge of the new place.

At the outset Cartrell had been skeptical. "If everyone else decides to get into this business," he had told Llewellyn, "I can only suggest that you will quickly outgrow the local market. There's also the matter of extreme shipping costs."

To predict the lack of local market seemed ridiculous to Llewellyn, who felt the outlets appeared endless because of the steady influx of miners, and that some apples were being shipped to Alberta as a result of freight rate cuts. The cost per one hundred pounds was only eighty-five cents. However, the Prairie market which had normally obtained their fruit from Nova Scotia and Ontario, now received early produce from United States. This left little room for anything from British Columbia. Llewellyn had not fully realized this. He had only reckoned that, if freight rates remained low, he could ship his fruit anywhere at minimal cost.

Cartrell's skepticism soon changed to optimism and he pointed out, "The time may be ripe for development of the bottomland if a sufficient water system can be implemented." Trusting Cartrell's intuition, Albert had planted more acreage to pears and extended his irrigation system.

Several weeks later, Cartrell got on the subject again. "Penticton has gone ahead by leaps and bounds. There's even talk of incorporation. I think that soon the valley will undergo a complete transformation if a suitable irrigation system can be instituted; water not just hauled up by wheels, but moved by canals such as they employ in Europe."

Albert agreed, though he was astonished that Cartrell should be aware of what was going on in Europe. "Out here in the west," he said in a forlorn tone, "I always feel we're cut off from other countries. I've even lost touch with all places outside this valley. I have to admit that, if it weren't for you, I would know nothing of the Okanagan in its present day. That's how small my world has become since this stroke."

"On that note, Albert, you'll be surprised to hear that there is a fellow from up the valley by the name of Ritchie who is buying up properties on the hills along Dog Lake; not far from us, actually. Could be a community one day."

Llewellyn fell quiet in disbelief. "Obviously, I have not been paying attention to progress in the valley."

When Cartrell had gone, Albert rose from his comfortable chair in the upstairs den and leaned heavily on the cane held firmly in his good right hand. He thought of his son and the future of his business concerns. He walked unsteadily toward the large window to gaze pensively across the flats. He was proud of his accomplishments. Although he was unable to be in the thick of activity, he still controlled his holdings through Cartrell. Recognizing the limits his condition placed upon his life, and his almost total dependency upon Cartrell, Albert reaffirmed his conviction that despite Thomas' youthful age, the boy must be forced to accept more responsibility.

In mid-August Thomas moved from the log cabin on the range to Alfred Kennedy's new cottage on the orchard. His first experiences on the orchard were unhappy ones. He made little effort to adopt a positive attitude toward that type of farming. He was clumsy and seemed deliberately careless. Several times the short ropes came unhooked at the sides of the picking bag slung over his shoulders, allowing ripened plums to roll over his knees and bounce into the grass. Hoping no one saw the mess, he left them where they lay, crushing them beneath his boots as he moved around the tree refilling the bag.

But Alfred Kennedy noticed.

"Don't pretend you didn't dump them!" Kennedy admonished. "You get down there and pick up every damn one of 'em before you walk on any more. You got one hell of a mess here! It's not a funny situation!"

"It's not funny for me! I didn't ask to be down here doing this stupid work!" Thomas yelled as he crawled over the grass in search of what good fruit was salvageable.

Sighing in great agitation, Kennedy called back, "Do I look like I think it's a great game, havin' you down here? For cryin' out loud, all I need on this place is a spoilt, bumbling brat to look after!"

When two weeks had passed, Thomas found that he could no longer tolerate living under Kennedy's roof and, of his own accord, moved his clothes over to Rachel McAllister's residence beside the lakeshore.

Rachel, Duncan McAllister's widow, was the oldest surviving member of Skaha's founding family. As Rachel Hackett, she had arrived at Skaha Crossing with her parents in a wagon train and lived her life out between the Crossing and Dogtown. In widowhood, she remained in her son's house beside Dog Lake. After years of harbouring disappointment and bitterness over what her family had lost to Albert Llewellyn, she had developed a tolerant attitude and so welcomed Thomas with a warmer heart than she had ever extended to any member of the Llewellyn family.

As the weeks passed, Rachel enjoyed the young man's company around the house. Although she held her questions on his arrival, the following day she finally enquired, "Does your father know that you're here?"

"I doubt it," he replied carelessly, "but that Cartrell will sniff it out."

"And your mother?"

"She only knows what Cartrell sees fit to tell her." Pausing, he asked Rachel, "Mrs. McAllister, does it bother you to have me here? If it does, I can move over to Spencers." He had made several visits across town to the Spencer house and had found Marjorie's company most inspiring.

Rachel, wiser than Thomas gave her credit for, saw through his plan. "No, Thomas, you don't need to move." She patted his hand in a warm, motherly way. "Just come home nights and be at work during the days and we'll both stay out of trouble."

Thomas looked into her smiling eyes and they laughed together. But, as Rachel had anticipated, eventually Thomas failed to show up for the evening meal and was also absent from the breakfast table. She assumed that Cartrell had picked up the young man and marched him back to Kennedy. But one day when Kennedy turned up on her doorstep in search of Thomas, concern set in.

"Old Albert ain't goin' to like this," the foreman muttered impatiently, running a hand over his forehead and bushy eyebrows. Kennedy and Rachel stared at each other, sharing a growing uneasiness about Thomas' absence.

Across the townsite, Thomas lowered his head beneath the cooling ripples of the Okanagan River below the falls, and patted gently at his face. The water stung furiously against the bruises and cuts about his face. He turned to Marjorie Spencer. "There's got to be a hiding place here somewhere. I can't go back looking like this."

The girl sat on the grass beside Thomas where he lay stretched toward the river's edge. "Why don't you just go back to the orchard and start picking like you've never been away? You don't have to tell anyone what happened."

"Now that's real imagination. I'll still have to face interrogation like you wouldn't believe." He reached for his shirt and mopped at his sore, bruised features with the torn remnants. "If I give you some money, will you run up to the General Store and get me a new shirt?"

Long, dark red curls fell over Marjorie's slight shoulders and lay upon full breasts which strained against the cloth of her blouse. Wide hazel eyes stared into his from the regular features of her oval face. "You haven't got any money, sweetie," she told him cutely.

Thomas looked up at her. "What's your Dad going to say about you being gone all night?"

Unflinchingly, she replied, "I don't worry about things like that. He never misses me. My mother's dead, so he's lonely and drinks himself into a stupor most nights."

Thomas leaned back against his elbows and studied her. "Well, Marjie, why don't I have any money?"

"They took it off you. The guys who beat you up. They took your liquor, too." She giggled. "You're too young to have liquor anyway."

"I hardly remember what it was all about."

"They said your father kept a whore for a mistress."

"He doesn't. He's crippled. He doesn't even sleep with my mother."

"You told them he didn't have a mistress. You called them some rotten names and got your mouth bashed the minute you stood up." She smiled impishly. "You put up a good fight, you know, Tom."

"My face tells me that I didn't." He looked up at her and after a moment, suggested, "I did a little more than kiss you last night."

"Oh yes."

"How do you feel about what happened? You know—"

Marjorie Spencer stared into Thomas' questioning eyes.

"Well?" he persisted.

"You were very gentle. I know I was the first to lay with you," she said quietly without embarrassment.

Thomas Llewellyn was suddenly very still on the grass at the river's edge. In the distance he heard the clopping of a horse trotting across the twin bridges nearby but paid the sound no mind as he recalled the titillating dalliance with the girl beside him. Eventually he glanced awkwardly at Marjorie. "I hardly know you," he murmured. "I've only met you a half dozen times before last night."

Marjorie smiled prettily. "I'm not asking you to marry me, Tom. I'm merely talking about what happened, that's all."

A lengthy silence prevailed, broken finally by his question, "How old are you?"

"Eighteen. And you?"

"Nineteen," Thomas lied.

"You are not! About seventeen, maybe." Slowly she lay down upon the grass beside him, pulling him close to her. "It was good, what happened, Tom," she whispered. "I like you a lot."

The feel of her lips, warm and soft upon his mouth sent a yearning through him. As he reached to undo the buttons of her blouse, Ian

Cartrell's boot thumped to the ground beside them.

Thomas dropped his head onto his arm and stared at the polished, black monster in the grass near his face. Marjorie opened her dreamy eyes to stare up into the condemning gaze of the tall man in black who ruled Skaha.

Cartrell turned away from them, returning to where his horse waited. "Young man, I'll see you at Mrs. McAllister's house in ten minutes exactly," he called back in a commanding tone. Placing a foot firmly in the stirrup, he swung easily into the saddle and rode off around the bluff beside the tumbling waterfall.

It was intimidating for Thomas to face Ian Cartrell. He reasoned that confronting his father rather than the stern, stiff-backed accountant, would cause him less anxiety. He failed to give Cartrell credit for an understanding of the impulsiveness of youth, so was mildly surprised when the man asked him outright, "Did you do anything careless, as to cause some alarm, say, two months from now? We cannot have anyone tapping at your father's pocketbook for payment of escapades of drunkenness, brawling or anything else. If there are any unfavourable results from your antics of last night, they will be emphatically denied."

Thomas leaned against the wall of Rachel's kitchen, sullen and unsmiling.

From beneath a furrowed brow, black eyes bore relentlessly into Thomas' still gaze. "However, that may not be entirely in your favour, as your father will find a way for you to pay. You realize that, of course." The dark eyes bore deeper, leaving no doubt as to the truth of the warning.

Throughout the lecture, Rachel McAllister sat as if glued to her chair. Thomas received not a hint of support from her. Nor did he speak up for himself. There was no argument sensible enough to offer. So, after a few moments of utter silence in the room, Cartrell continued. "Now, get your things together. You're going back over to Alfred's house. You have bothered this patient lady long enough. You'll stay there until the apples are finished in October, then return to the ranch for roundup." He nodded his regards to Rachel and followed the smoldering, young Llewellyn outdoors.

Once outside on the steps, he turned to Thomas and viewed the bruised and swollen features. "Sooner or later, young fellow, I'm going to take you out behind the barn," he warned, "and give you a good shove along the road to maturity, so to speak."

Thomas was astounded. He straightened his back and stared coldly at Ian. "You, Cartrell?"

"Mr. Cartrell, to you." Involuntarily Ian's fist clenched open and closed again.

Thomas watched the hands, stunned at the strength which he

saw there. "I haven't given you good reason."

"You will."

Thomas leaned his head back, haughtily. "You want to do it now?"

Cartrell fixed a chilling stare in Thomas' direction. "It'll happen, I guarantee it. Now, get your tail over to the orchard." Cartrell left.

Before the week was out, Thomas was back with Rachel McAllister. Alfred Kennedy hardly cared and preferred the arrangement. Rachel was pleased. Her house was a lonely place since the loss of her husband, Duncan, and her son, David, and it was good to have the Llewellyn boy with her. She had little idea where her former daughter-in-law was; just that she had moved to the Cariboo country.

Although Thomas crept out of the house late in the evenings to spend several hours in the passionate embrace of Marjorie Spencer, he also turned up at the orchard each morning and even put in a decent day's work. No one could fault him. The complaints from Kennedy dwindled.

Because the trees were young, Thomas found no hardship in picking from a ladder once he had learned its correct placement in the tree. Whereas the metal and canvas picking bag had at first pulled heavily over his thin shoulders, leaving wide welts upon his sunburnt skin, its straps now settled comfortably into the groove created by the weight of the fruit. As well, his arms no longer ached from loading the wagon at the end of a long day. He became conditioned.

Fruit and tomatoes going to the mines were stored each night at Llewellyn's warehouse until the stage left the following morning. The rest was transferred to the barge which plied Dog Lake to Penticton. Llewellyn preferred water transport to road traffic, as the land route was rough and dusty, causing, he claimed, far greater damage to the softer fruits and tomatoes than the handling at the warehouse and dock did.

In September Thomas accompanied Cartrell to the packing sheds in Penticton. Thomas was amazed at procedures carried out there. Inside the huge building was a maze of enormous wide belts and high stacks of boxes. Whistles blew regularly, signalling schedules for the workers. All around him were people and noise and the sweet smell of ripe fruit. As soon as it was possible, Thomas got himself outside into the fresh air. There, he waited beside the horses for Cartrell to emerge into the sunlight.

Cartrell's irritation with Thomas showed. "You're impossible!" he snapped when he reached the horses. He waved an impatient arm toward the packing plant. "Instead of learning something in there, you disappear the minute I turn my back."

Stowing a roll of packing slips into the saddle bag, Cartrell stepped quickly into the stirrup and swung up into the saddle. He took his time settling himself comfortably upon the horse, fitting his boots properly into the stirrups, adjusting his coat and pulling on his black leather gloves before taking up the reins.

"They have perfected an automobile," he stated, calmer now, "and I would consider it thoughtful recognition of my years of faithful service if your father should see fit to purchase one." He spoke, of course, more to himself than to Thomas, for if an auto was to be had, it would be he who did the buying. "A matter of convenience; a reward, so to speak, for all the discomforts I've suffered on his behalf to administer his business and raise his son for him." Ready now for the ride ahead, he lifted a brow in Thomas' direction and asked, "Shall we return immediately to Skaha, or would you like a glimpse of the town and its particular entertainments first?"

"I'll discover things on my own."

Cartrell nodded. "No doubt. Did you learn anything at all today?"

Thomas reined his horse in behind Cartrell's and answered, "I learned that the less I have to do with orchards, the better."

Cartrell ignored the remark as he urged his horse southward along the tree-lined road which crossed the bottomland between Okanagan and Dog lakes.

Thomas remained a week at the ranch before going out to cow-camp. Whenever he was at home, his bedroom with its childhood toys stored in the closet where clothes that no longer fit him hung on the rod, appeared a pathetic reminder of a childhood which, he felt now, could not have belonged to him. He did not see his old belongings as representing anything happy. Life always had to be taken seriously. Harrie had been the one allowed to play, he remembered. Or, was it simply that Harrie had made it that way? How very different he and his brother had been. What had changed that? Harrie's death? Did his father bring out the rebellion in him? Glancing about the room, Thomas really wished his mother would clear out his juvenile junk.

A regrettable encounter with his father took place during the evening of his last night at home. When Thomas reached the top of the stairs, Albert was waiting at the door of his den. He motioned his son to enter. "Come in, come in. We should spend more time together, you and me."

Leaning heavily upon the cane, Albert watched Thomas for a long moment. He had not seen much of him lately and was surprised at how tall he had grown. He noticed the husky physique, the unruly sandy hair and the stubborn set of Thomas' unsmiling mouth.

Thomas entered the room. "I see you've not only found your voice, but your leg is much better now," he commented idly, realizing that for the first time he could easily understand his father when he spoke. Thomas was uncomfortable in the room. He was never invited into his father's den unless a lecture was in the works.

"While that may be a godsend to me, Thomas, it will hardly prove a blessing to you." Llewellyn sank into his chair.

Thomas glanced absently about the room, half expecting his mother to turn up in one of the corners. "How's that?"

Albert lit his pipe. Blue smoke curled into the room. "Although I can't harness and drive a team myself anymore to teach you, I aim to see that you learn. I now have the good fortune, as of two days ago, in having Dick Foderow back on board and it is he who will make the trips to Camp McKinney with you."

Thomas stood silent near the window. This was stunning news. He had heard nothing of Dick's return. "I'm surprised he's not in jail somewhere," Thomas murmured with a smile. "I heard he killed a man. How long do I have to travel with him?"

"All winter, if travel is possible."

Thomas leaned forward, surprised. "I don't believe you!" There was no mention of cow-camp for which he had eagerly readied himself.

"When you're finished, there'll be nothing you won't know about freighting." Albert Llewellyn smiled at his son and Thomas felt a little intimidated by the gesture. "In February you'll go back to the orchard and learn how to prune the trees." Llewellyn coughed in the depths of the blue haze created by the tobacco. "Don't think you fooled me all summer, young man. I know you stayed at Rachel's house. Eventually I was bound to find out. I don't intend to change that. Not for your sake, but for Alfred, whose been damned near on his knees to me to get you out of his hair. I've covered all your other activities, also. Nothing escapes me, Thomas. Your mother and Ian think they can fool me about you, but I have my own ways of finding out what's going on."

From Kennedy, Thomas decided, disliking the foreman all the more. He stared squarely, defiantly into his father's stern gaze. "I got beat up once over you," he said quietly.

"I know, I know, and it was stupid of you."

"Do you know why?"

"I'm not interested."

"They told me you kept a whore. That means paying for her house, buying her clothes, supporting her."

Llewellyn stiffened in his chair. Setting his pipe aside, he reached for the cane, rising to stand opposite his son. "That is a lie."

"It is not a lie, Da! I was stupid alright. I did call them liars, all four of them but, they were right. I knew that." Thomas began to pace the floor, uneasy and agitated by the turn of conversation. "I slept beside the wall of her room one night in Fairview, a long time ago now. I heard you in that bed and from then on I never respected you. You hurt my mother and I couldn't stand that." Without looking at his father, he added cruelly, "At this point, I doubt I even like you much anymore."

"Thomas! You're talking about a situation you know nothing about– your mother and me." Suddenly the corner of Llewellyn's mouth began to twitch. Every nerve in his huge frame seemed to jump beneath his skin and he suddenly felt nauseated. A tightening gripped painfully somewhere deep in his chest. "You'll regret this, boy. I'll see that you regret those words!"

"It seems like you must sit here every day, Da, moving a pin on a map. The map is your holdings and the pin is me." He turned and looked into his father's troubled eyes. "When you're gone, I'll sell everything but this ranch."

Llewellyn's face did not change expression. The chill remained in his body. Perspiration beaded his forehead. "You come from better stock than you're exhibiting. You have a great heritage in all ways of farming behind you. Thomas, I tell you, you wouldn't dare!"

"Watch me."

"Cartrell will not allow it!"

"Possibly Cartrell will do what I tell him when I own it all."

Llewellyn leaned against the wall and, raising the cane, swiftly struck Thomas across the shoulders and ear. Thomas spun with the blow. Hate leapt into his eyes. He could not believe his father had hit him. Llewellyn hobbled after him toward the door, attempting to strike him again. His weak leg hampered his movements and he swayed unsteadily as he flung the cane through the air. Anger blazed in Albert's mind and he yelled at Thomas in Gaelic, "Cuimhnich air no-- daoine o'n--"

"What the hell does that mean?" Thomas cut him off, spinning around in the doorway to glare at his father.

"I'm trying to tell you– that you are to remember– the men from whom you came in this family!" Unsteadily, he retrieved his cane from the floor. "Remember– who you– are!"

Stunned by the statement, Thomas huffed, not comprehending its meaning. He understood nothing in Gaelic and the sound of it now offended his ears. Impulsively, he screamed, "I hate everything that's you and yours and you can hit me all you want. It won't change a thing!" Dodging the cane held fast in his father's hand, he sped through the doorway.

Suddenly Llewellyn collapsed against the wall, sliding heavily to the floor. The cane left his trembling hand to roll away and bounce out onto the landing. His complexion whitened as a choking sensation clutched his throat.

Sydney flew past Thomas, tripping on the long skirt of her dress in her haste to get up the stairs, She reached anxiously toward her husband who was suffering an attack of some kind.

"I can't help how I feel!" Thomas shrieked and wheeled away from them down the stairs.

"You have no just reason, Thomas!" he heard his mother call after him. "What have you done to your Da! Oh my– Mrs. Davies! Alma!"

Ian Cartrell, who had been strolling with his family in the warm September evening, turned toward the barn. He and Belle had heard Sydney's words from the upstairs window and saw young Thomas run into the shadows of the livery barn. Cartrell knew that something terribly wrong had taken place in the Llewellyn house but also, that the housekeeper was there with Sydney. He sent his family home and went after Thomas.

Cartrell stood in the wide doorway of the barn, the light of evening behind him, and searched the darkness of the interior for Thomas. He heard the saddling sounds in the stable and quietly stepped up behind him.

Thomas leapt away, startled by the other's presence.

"You're jumpy," Cartrell spoke evenly.

"You snuck up on me!" Thomas snapped, reaching for a bridle.

"That's how it's going to be all your life, Thomas, when you least expect me." Methodically, he undid the buttons of his black vest and removed it.

Thomas held the bridle tightly in front of him, suddenly wary.

"Now, are you going to tell me what went on up there tonight or shall I beat it out of you?" Cartrell asked in an even voice. "I know something happened."

Thomas waited, and held his breath, stretching the fleeting seconds to their limit. He disbelieved what he saw. Cartrell was slowly rolling up the sleeves of his shirt. When Thomas looked across at the tall man's face, he realized that the man was serious. "What the hell gives here? You're three times my age!"

Unsmiling, unamused by the comment, Cartrell reassured Thomas. "Don't give it a moment's thought, son. I've drunk from the fountain of youth, so I'm a ready match for you. Now, put down that bridle. The time has come." With those words, an ominous quiet prevailed inside the barn.

Then, before Thomas could draw another breath, Cartrell reached into the stall, lifted him away from the horse and flung him upon the scattered shavings and hay on the floor. Gasping for air, Thomas rose but did not reach for a weapon as Cartrell half expected. They met directly. Young Llewellyn was no match for Cartrell. In a short time Thomas relived the horror of one month before; a beating that had taken four young men to carry out.

35

Cartrell was swift but Thomas had picked up a few defenses of his own. Striking back, he managed a solid slam below Cartrell's jaw, another into a shoulder and a gut-wrenching hold about the waist which dragged Cartrell to the floor. Cartrell rose. Thomas bolted from his knees, diving headlong into Cartrell's abdomen. Cartrell caught him once more by the legs, tossing him backwards. He then pounced on Thomas, pinning his wrists against the rough boards. Thomas heaved beneath Cartrell's weight but he could not throw him. He knew the struggle was over. Blood trickled from above his eyes, from his nose, and down over his chin onto the dry hay. His mouth was full of straw and the pain in his chest warned him of some injured ribs.

"Get off me, you bastard!" Thomas spat, attempting to toss Cartrell away from him.

Cartrell lifted Thomas' wrists and slammed them against the boards. Excruciating pain raced up Thomas' tired arms.

"Now you listen to me," Cartrell breathed above him. "I could tell you stories of cruelties I've suffered and carried out in the course of survival when I was no older than you, young man. Or I could show you some of them. Better yet, we could do without them altogether." Cartrell waited and caught his breath, for the strain of the fight had been more taxing on him than he realized.

Thomas did not reply, remaining sullen and furious on the floor.

Cartrell continued, "Don't ever think you'll get the upper hand on me. The man doesn't exist that can. I learned my tricks from rebellious ones like you whose lives I didn't give a damn for. But you? I watched you grow up, wishing I had a son." Ian Cartrell sat back then, against his heels in the dusty straw, with a cautious eye trained on Thomas. "You don't know what I'd give for a son and it's my rotten luck that you're the closest I'm ever going to get to it." He ran his hands through his hair to smooth it back. "Think about that."

Cartrell rose to his feet and brushed at the dust and shavings which clung to his clothing. The white shirt he wore was spotted with Thomas' blood. Removing it, he strode outside to the yard water pump. Working the handle, he spilled water into the trough and dropped his shirt into it. He heard Thomas come up to stand beside him. Cartrell pushed Thomas' throbbing head beneath the flow of cool water.

"Throw in your shirt," he advised. "That same idea could apply to your dealings with me in the future. This unholy situation has got to end or you'll kill your father."

Thomas lifted his head, shaking the water from his mop of sandy hair. "And my mother?"

Cartrell met Thomas' eyes directly. "You're suspicious of me, aren't you?" he confronted.

"Absolutely."

"Well, continue to be. It'll keep you on your toes, so to speak."

For the first time in many months Cartrell bestowed a smile upon young Llewellyn, who leaned forward to rinse his torn shirt, avoiding the other's penetrating gaze.

Evening descended upon them. Lamps had been lit in the few houses still occupied at Skaha. In the distance crickets and frogs began their nightly chorus. On the horizon a September moon rose to illuminate the flats. Soon the yip-yipping of coyotes would be heard, as often happened when the moon was full.

Deeply troubled by the fight, though suffering no serious injuries, Thomas packed his bedroll and clothes and left the ranch at dawn the following morning. An hour later he raised the knocker on Rachel McAllister's door and announced that he would need board and room for the winter months ahead. Because she had developed a fondness for young Thomas and some understanding of his troubles, Rachel leaned forward and kissed him gently on the side of his face, mindful of the swelling.

5

Passing along the valley from Camp McKinney to Penticton in the second week in October, Dr. Stobie made his usual call at Skaha. He rode amongst the trees along the river, swinging up onto the time-worn trail created by generations of Two Way's family. His thoughts strayed to Albert Llewellyn and Belle Cartrell, and the deteriorating state of their health.

All around him the hillsides were ablaze with brilliant fall colours. Lovely, wide patches of yellow, red and orange dotted the landscape, reminding the doctor that soon winter would blow across the flats and, that the older he got, the less he felt like subjecting himself to the oft-times vicious elements.

The sad state of Albert's condition was certainly not what Harold Stobie had expected to see. He voiced his surprise to Sydney, who denied any incidents that would have caused distress. "Well, I'll go across and look in on Belle while Mrs. Davies sets the tea for us."

As he climbed the steps to Ian Cartrell's small office, he was greeted and offered a chair.

Cartrell removed his glasses. "Jason has seen to your horse as usual. How do you find my wife?"

"First, I must say that it is a relief to see you in good health. This place demands at least one able body. As for your wife, she is not a well woman and I have my suspicion. I believe it's time for further tests as I find new disturbing symptoms."

"I see," said Cartrell, soberly. "Well, we'll not have any more children. It is apparent that I'm to go through life without a son, perhaps for sufficient reason, which has recently occurred to me."

"That is?"

"That the Llewellyns have an immature, spoilt brat whose rebellious nature needs the firm hand of one not related to him."

Harold smiled. "Now, about Albert," he began. "Certainly something happened recently. I believe it is his heart. He's gone down. Were you there?"

"I was not present either time, but it seems he's alone with Thomas each time an attack has happened. However, I think the boy is completely blameless."

"Well, it's possible. Anxiety and inactivity. He'll rally 'round alright. He has determination beyond belief, but he'll be susceptible to other conditions such as pneumonia."

Stobie and Cartrell went to the Llewellyns for afternoon tea, later joined by Belle and her lively daughters. When the doctor had departed Skaha and Ian had seen his wife and daughters home, Sydney emerged to walk with him on his return to the office.

She confided, "He'll never walk again. I feel it here, in my heart."

"Nonsense," Cartrell scoffed. "Just hook that cane on the bedpost and let its sheer inactivity provide the inspiration and challenge of therapy."

Sydney laughed, the delightful sound of it reaching out to Cartrell. "Oh, Ian, you are a good person to be around! Your quick wit does so revive one's spirits." She smiled up into his eyes. "Truly a joy for me!"

"Hmmm, in many ways," he teased. "You've only just tapped the surface, my dear." Cartrell smiled down at Sydney.

"If I didn't know you better, Ian, I'd say that was a very provocative remark!"

Watching her lovely, bright face framed by the loose sweep of golden hair, he told her, "You don't know me at all, I'm afraid." Turning Sydney by the shoulders, he directed her toward the pathway to his house and ordered, "Now, keep your promise to Belle and take the girls for a long walk. She's in desperate need of rest and it'll do wonders for you, as well."

For a long while Cartrell remained at his office window, watching the women talk, and then Sydney took up the hands of his daughters. There was no longer a will within to hide his feelings for Sydney. Years before he had felt sympathy for David McAllister and the struggle in his affair with her. No man could turn away from her. The more often he allowed thoughts regarding Llewellyn's intimate relationship with Sydney, or lack of one, to roam about his brain, the more Cartrell became troubled by his own desire. He carefully kept his wife outside his problem. His love for her had somehow become simply affection, but of a special nature, born of a need for a contented hearth.

Certainly Belle had fulfilled his hopes as best she could. Cartrell was one of the very few men of his time who realized there was no profit in blaming his wife for lack of a son. Obligations toward Belle and their daughters were always met. Duty was a natural ingredient in Cartrell's character. It was his heart that he lately found difficult to deal with. Watching Sydney now, he recognized his driving concern for her welfare was born of a selfish passion to have what was not rightfully his.

As Sydney walked into the trees lining the pathway and out of his sight, Cartrell turned away from the window. Placing the thin arms of his glasses over his ears, he attempted to concentrate on the mountain of paperwork awaiting his attention.

Thomas' residence with Rachel McAllister became so extended, lasting throughout the autumn months of 1906, that he no longer considered the ranch at Skaha his home. The conflict that seemed to rage within him and ravage the lives of those who touched his, were not easily quelled by his father, his mother, or Cartrell; nor by his own measure, for Thomas lacked self-motivation and confidence.

The aging Okanagan Indian, Two Way, was the only person who could calm the anxieties under which Thomas laboured. Through the autumn, the two often met at the Falls General Store and spent time together chatting in the shade, upon the nearby bench, or strolling in the bright sunshine along the shore of Dog Lake. Two Way, generally lost in nostalgia, would recall similar times of struggle, but of different issues, during his own youth. He listened with patience to Thomas' complaints and provided answers to his searching questions.

On a cold December day one week before Christmas, when frost had seized the ground without the warming benefit of snow, Two Way rode out of the mountains in the Llewellyn carriage with Jason Whiteman. The carriage did little to protect the old fellow from the winter chill and he huddled deep into a thick Hudson's Bay blanket. He kept his moccasined feet planted firmly against the warmer on the floor. Dark eyes peered from beneath bushy, white brows in search of Thomas, whom he expected to find loitering about the store. A smile suddenly creased Two Way's leathery face and he motioned for Thomas to enter the carriage and sit beside him.

"It's cold out there. Not much better in here but, no wind," Two Way said upon greeting.

Thomas was astonished at the Indian's presence in town. "Two Way, what are you doing down here on a day like this?"

"I am glad to see you." Pursing his thin lips, Two Way mentioned, "You do not come home to see us at Skaha anymore."

Thomas slumped against the upholstery of the carriage wall. "Well, it's not like going home, to a real home. The only ones I miss are Charlie and my mother and you. But Mother comes down to Mrs. McAllister's, so I see her then."

"There's talk up there that Ian Cartrell may move down to Dogtown," Two Way informed Thomas. "Although I don't believe that will happen."

"Two Way, they don't call it Dogtown anymore."

"Really!"

"It's Okanagan Falls and has been for a long time."

Two Way's eyes widened. "It used to be Shoshen-eetkwa. Well, Ian needs to be closer to these important enterprises located down here."

Thomas laughed miserably. "All the better to watch me, my friend."

"Perhaps that, too." Two Way looked hopefully into Thomas' eyes. "Do you like the orchard now? You did not go with Dick, like a good boy, on the freight wagon?"

"Not for long, just to spite Da. He shoves me around on his map up there wherever he wishes. He forgets that I'm human. I live and draw breath and have a mind of my own,"

"That is for anyone to conclude easy enough!" Two Way laughed.

"Well, Two Way," Thomas began seriously. "Every time I used to visit him, it was never, 'how do you feel about it' or, 'why don't you like the idea of fruit farming?' Does he ever call me *son*? For God's sake, Cartrell does that for him. Just once, he could ask me what I want to do."

Two Way smiled indulgently. "You don't know what you want to do. In the old days a son followed his father, especially if that father had built a little empire." Two Way watched Thomas' expressionless profile. "To follow was a matter of appreciation for enjoying all the comforts in life and never having laid out a penny for it."

Thomas' eyes widened at this statement. "Boy, d'you sound like old Cartrell!" He frowned in Two Way's direction.

"I wonder what made everybody think that Harrie was the rebel of the family." The wise old Indian spoke idly, more to himself than to Thomas. He knew all his advice fell upon deaf ears beside him, so wasted his breath not a moment longer. "I came down to do some visiting and get some food today," he said, "so I better go do it. Help me out of here."

Together they appeared from the carriage and Thomas walked to the doorway of the store with Two Way.

"I would ride back with you, Two Way," Thomas told him honestly, "but I got a lot of things to do."

"Such as? Young people always have a lot of nothing to do." A smile played about Two Way's mouth. He knew he had developed a caustic tongue in his advancing years, however, did not curb it.

"Just some things–"

"You don't have time for others now. Someday when we are all gone, you'll wonder why you didn't make time," he accused mildly, and raised a hand against any reply Thomas might have offered. Two Way went into the building to stand beside the warmth of the wood heater in the far corner.

Thomas watched through the steamed-up window as the old Indian was warmly welcomed by others there.

Thomas pulled the collar of his jacket around his neck and walked away. What did he have to do? Why could he not spend an afternoon with Two Way and ride back to the ranch? Thomas knew that his mother craved visits from him but there was always his father present or, if not him, Ian Cartrell hovering near. He turned, instead, along the road toward Marjorie Spencer's house.

From the distance of Skaha Ranch, Cartrell could not attempt to keep pace with the younger Llewellyn's activities in Okanagan Falls, Penticton and other points north and south, all easily accessed by new roads. The Christmas and New Year season passed with only a brief visit from Thomas. On the morning of Easter Sunday, Cartrell rode down to Rachel McAllister's house and, piercing the woman's conscience with his black eyes, extracted a shaky confession from her that the young man was not often at home with her. Where did he stay? Rachel could not tell Cartrell. What did Thomas do for a living if he was not there? She could not tell him that either. How had he managed to fare through the wintertime? She knew nothing.

Alfred Kennedy's solution was simple. "That boy's got a lot of wild oats to sow, it appears. Don't know why you don't just take the collar off, stand back and let him go. He'll come home one day, tail 'tween his legs."

6

Throughout 1907, the playground of Thomas Llewellyn and Marjorie Spencer ranged much farther than Cartrell imagined; from Rock Creek to Kelowna, turning up a few times as far as Kamloops, which was now a large and busy cattle and railway centre. They travelled on horseback, by steamer and railway. When they had money, for Thomas was often lucky at cards, they lived in hotels. When it had all been spent, they slept in railway boxcars, or in sheltered spots on beaches during good weather, and hunted for employment.

They worked at odd jobs: he, as a teamster for three dollars a day and she, as kitchen help or waiting on tables. For a time they picked hops to be shipped to distilleries from a farm near Vernon, working alongside Colville Indians who annually migrated from Washington during the picking season. There were even a few Mexican families. Thomas thought it strange that they should be so far north. They were a happy people and worked well enough. In the evening they played fast music and sang and danced between the tents of their camp.

Thomas and Marjorie mixed well with everyone. They enjoyed being around the Mexicans and learned to dance to the fascinating, rhythmic music played on violins, concertinas and guitars, while the Indians watched in stony silence.

Albert's orders to Cartrell were to impose strict regulations upon his son; but, if Thomas could not be located, no rules could be set down. Cartrell smiled sourly over the out-of-control situation into which he had been thrown. By their silence, Thomas and Marjorie were safe from everyone.

To Albert, Cartrell could only offer weak assurance. "He's doing what is called 'growing up his own way', the trend, it seems. We're not going to change things now, but at least the constable is not on our doorstep."

A final inner reckoning was to surface in Thomas on a warm, quiet Autumn day when his path unintentionally crossed that of Cartrell's in Penticton.

Thomas leaned against the deck rail of the *YORK* as it docked at the Penticton wharf. Marjorie Spencer was close beside him.

"Are we going to go back farming now?" she asked with a giggle.

"No, that's no fun."

"You're spoilt. It'll be winter soon, and then what? You're

deliberately provoking your dad and you know it!"

"I enjoy life like this!" Reaching out to catch her close, he laughed, "So do you, little girl!" When he looked over Marjorie's shoulder to the crowd gathering on the wharf, he suddenly stilled. Standing off to the side, distinctly conspicuous, was Ian Cartrell, tall and straight, watching him. He quickly released Marjorie and whispered, "We'll leave this boat separately and meet at the hotel in an hour. There's trouble waiting for me on the dock."

Passengers disembarked and melded into the waiting crowd. Thomas strolled casually toward Cartrell, hand in pockets, with a nonchalant grin upon his face. "Minding Da's freight are you?" he enquired contemptuously.

"I thought that is what you might be doing."

Casting an eye toward the freight being loaded onto A & S wagons, Thomas replied, "Thought I'd keep an eye on it, alright."

"Since we're here, can I interest you in something to eat? I've missed a meal already today." Looking around, Cartrell asked, "Where is the girl?"

"She has a friend here she's staying with," he lied.

"I have news of your mother, Thomas."

Thomas' head swung around.

"She is ill." Cartrell motioned Thomas to walk with him along the shore. A brisk breeze had suddenly blown up, coming at them off the water. His silence failed to exercise the calming effect upon Thomas that he had hoped for. "Her need to see you is great, Tom. You are really all she has, the way things are with your father."

"She has you."

Cartrell ignored the implication. "Your mother is a sad, lonely lady with no real normal enjoyments in her life. You could be a source of great happiness to her, if you had a mind for it. She is now nearing forty. Life takes on different meaning as one gets older and, at a time when she should be enjoying all that life has to offer, she lives with restrictions of the greatest order upon her. She is trapped at Skaha where she sees no one and rarely comes to Penticton and does not even enjoy a harmonious relationship with her husband."

Thomas glanced around at Cartrell, keeping in step beside him. "I'm supposed to change that?"

"Your mother is becoming very depressed. Dr. Stobie has been to visit and talk with her, but it helps little. There have been cases with pioneer women, I can tell you, where they have destroyed themselves. I mean suicide, Tom. Your mother is just as vulnerable to such extremes as any other woman." When he detected no visible change in Thomas' expression, Cartrell added pointedly, "The pleasure of your company more often would alter a darkened outlook considerably; save a life, so to speak."

44

During the minutes that ensued, a strange fellowship crept over them, compelling Thomas to turn and look directly into Cartrell's dark, searching eyes and smile at the man.

Cartrell ceased his steps, sensing a change. He spoke softly. "Come home with me, Tom. Now. We miss you."

Thomas remained quiet for some time, then finally replied sadly, "I can't. I really can't just yet."

"Have you asked yourself why? Have you actually looked for the truth of the matter with your father?"

Thomas stared across the wide expanse of water. The gentle wind tugged his fair curly hair into miniature knots. "I know why."

"I don't think you do; you will not accept part of the blame. You're walking a blind alley, son, and there's nothing but darkness there. You take a look down it, Tom. It's empty at its end."

Thomas lowered his head, watched the small ripples of water lap at the sand near his boots and did not reply. His feelings were very mixed.

Briefly Cartrell reached out and touched Thomas' coat sleeve. "You have shut us all away from you, Tom. Don't pull away too far. You are not alone in the blame."

He left Thomas on the beach. From a distance Cartrell watched the young man stroll the length of an empty wharf on the west side and sit down. He waited in the carriage for a long while, keeping a clear view of Thomas' movements. There were none; he simply remained alone on the pier. Eventually, Cartrell took up the reins and drove off across the town. There was no doubt in his mind that Thomas would come to a conclusion before the night had passed.

By the time he had arrived at Skaha Ranch four hours later, Cartrell considered a change in Thomas' attitude a certainty, and he mentioned it to Albert that evening. "He'll be at the freight shed by tomorrow morning. I guarantee it."

"Did he say that?"

"It was by chance I met him. I believe the good Lord played a winning hand today for all of us."

"That's all you have to say about it?" Llewellyn sneered. "That God plays cards!"

"Albert," Cartrell sighed wearily. "You're growing bitter, and you've built up resentment over your health, which you tend to take out on him. You aren't without fault, neither is he. My advice, if you care to hear it, is to leave him alone now. Let him find you in himself; and I mean you, as you were twenty years ago. Thomas needs to learn by his own experiences, just as you probably did."

"Is that the end of your educated analysis?"

"Rest assured, the last I'll ever speak regarding your son. My services to you over the past dozen years have gone far beyond normal duties." He was weary of the subject of Thomas, weary of Albert's pettiness, and wished to be quit of it. "I have only one obligation left to carry out– to bury you, when you go."

Llewellyn snorted impatiently and, positioning his cane upon the floor to rise, he snapped, "Get out!"

When the door closed, Albert reached for his binoculars, placed them against his face and searched the flats of Skaha Ranch. In a moment he lowered them, allowing them to fall carelessly into a chair. In resignation he covered his slackened face with his good hand and leaned against the wall in despair. Tears overcame him. It was the first time since childhood that Albert Llewellyn wept. He had gained so much in his time and now, it seemed, lost everything.

Never having come to terms with his paraplegia, Albert found it difficult to believe that others had. He realized long ago, that the reins of control over his holdings had been taken up by Cartrell, and admitted the man's capabilities. Even the deep sense of loss over the death of Harrie, which had never subsided, somehow seemed not so tiresome suddenly, if Thomas was indeed about to return.

Yet above all other matters, it was the empty, condemning relationship that continued year after year between himself and Sydney which hurt the most. He knew himself to be at fault. He had failed miserably in his care of her emotional and physical needs. She had been young and beautiful, admired by all who met her and, he knew, adored by a few. Had she not stood stoically beside him through their life together? She had worked long hours for the benefit of the family's comfort, until she dropped exhausted onto her bed at night. Indeed, her losses had been equal to his: Bronwen at birth, then Harrie from a rattlesnake bite.

His thoughts tumbled madly and Albert knew it was unacceptable that he should have turned away from her. Distraught and buried by the sudden onrush of emotion, Albert sank to the floor beside the cane and binoculars and wept bitterly for all that he had won and lost in life.

7

In the late 1860's, before Albert Llewellyn's time, cattle were first herded across the International Border to feed the growing Cariboo gold mining population. Mixed ranching had already begun in the Okanagan Valley. Its success defied the early west's traditional belief that where there were cattle there should not be sheep.

Early west range wars had been fought over sheep, their constant bleating, their musky odour and the amount of good cattle rangeland required to support a large herd of sheep. However, it soon became apparent to the early pioneers that sheep were more profitable in some ways than were cattle. They supplied the pioneer's need for not only food but clothing and ready cash as well.

Where the trapper McAllister had profited from furs in the streams on the east side of the valley in the mid 1800's, Hampshire Down sheep ranged at large by 1907 in the eastern meadows above Vaseux Lake.

Ian Cartrell visited a ranch on the east side in late winter during the lambing season, where ewes were being watched by the hired sheep herders. The first few weeks of a young lamb's life, he was told, were the most critical. Lambs born to dry mothers, if no foster mother was available, often had to be fed by bottle with a mixture of molasses, milk and water.

Cartrell made a second trip to the east bench later in the springtime when shearing began. Dressed in overalls, rubber boots and leather gloves, the men threw themselves into the cumbersome, sweaty work with a vigour that astounded Cartrell. At the end of day, several hundred sheep had been shorn of their thick wool.

Following shearing, the sheep were dipped in a warm mix of sulfur and medication to kill lice or ticks and to heal any skin abrasions or ailments. The vat used was a long, narrow trough about four feet deep. Cartrell positioned himself at the side of it to see the complete procedure. The sheep were placed in the trough, dipped completely and allowed to scramble out over the ramp at the other end. In the process, the meticulous accountant was thoroughly splashed, and disappeared from the wet, busy scene while wiping at his clean suit.

With this procedure complete, the herd was ready to be moved out onto the eastern meadows where they would be held from June through October. Assisted by trained Border Collies, the herders guarded the flock against such predators as wolves, coyotes and bears.

All this, Cartrell dutifully reported to Llewellyn, adding, "If we don't raise the little beasts ourselves, at least we have the means of shipping the wool out of the valley."

"If we do go into sheep," Llewellyn considered aloud, "my concern is the rangeland. I know first hand from having tended them when I was a youngster, that crowded sheep held too long in one area eat the grass clean down to the roots and even pull them up." As well, he knew, their sharp, cloven hoofs would trample any plant life left.

"What I am saying," Cartrell continued, "is that we don't need to get into the actual farming of the breed, but do the transporting for the rancher."

"How many ranches have sheep here?"

"There's one spread over in Marron Valley and another in the Similkameen. Between the three, there must be five to six thousand sheep."

Llewellyn nodded. "Get their contracts, then. The way things are looking at Camp McKinney, if any more of those mines close, we'll be down to one trip every two weeks. Fairview died. We're left with the Similkameen trade, and Dick has two drivers and himself to keep on the road."

"Bear in mind, the weight is different and the price is different," Cartrell cautioned. "At thirty-five dollars a ton to the mines, you were ahead."

Llewellyn sighed heavily. "My God, how swiftly things do change," he murmured sadly, feeling totally out of touch with the general pulse of life in the valley.

Dick Foderow was an easy-going individual, a favourite with everyone in town including Rachel McAllister, who often distanced herself from those associated with the Llewellyn businesses. Dick had moved back to the Dog Lake town with his wife, Fern, whose quiet, unassuming manner endeared her to all.

Thomas could not help but fall under the Foderow spell of patience and easy manner. He began to follow Dick everywhere, much as Dick, at the same age, had followed David McAllister. At nearly eighteen, Thomas had grown to six feet and had developed a husky physique. When he could tear himself away from Marjorie's arms, Thomas could be found at the freight shed, where an old and tiresome world now seemed reasonably exciting to him.

The C.P.R. had extended its line west to Midway in the Boundary Country by 1900, facilitating shipping of ore from Camp McKinney to the smelter in Nelson. Despite that convenience, some of the mines had closed and it appeared as though others might follow. So after more than a decade of transporting goods to the Camp, the A & S

STAGE freight business was hanging on by a mere thread.

In early February of 1908, Dick Foderow, with Thomas, loaded the largest of the A & S STAGE wagons with over two ton of mine machinery, lumber, miscellaneous equipment and supplies for Camp McKinney. As well, they were to stop at the Volholven dairy south of Vaseux Lake for fresh products.

"I thought all the mines were closing," Thomas suggested as he helped Foderow. "Most of them anyway, according to rumour."

"There's still a few shipping gold out. What do we care, really? If there's someone willing to take a chance on a vein in the mountain, it's our business to get the equipment they need up there on time."

Travelling was slow over rutted roads. Four teams pulled the heavy load, moving south along the bench above the meandering Okanagan River, then dropping downhill at Vaseux Lake. By noon a dark sky brought snow and, although Thomas felt apprehension over the trip, Foderow remained confident.

At the great overhanging rock of Vaseux they were abruptly halted. An enormous pack of snow had dropped over the cliff and partially blocked the narrow roadway. Consequently, having had to unhitch the lead team, rig a scraper from materials slated for the mine and clear the road of debris, they did not arrive at the Volholven dairy until well after dark. At the farm the teams were cared for, while Foderow and Thomas wolfed down a hearty meal.

Helga Volholven was overjoyed to see young Thomas again, fussing over him in an affectionate way; Thomas was happy with the attention. Helga and Gus, had travelled west with his parents to Skaha. All his life he had been cared for by them. He met their enquiries of those left at Skaha and told them about his father's worsening condition.

In the dark hours of the early morning, with a bitter cold breeze moving against them across the pastures, the men loaded large metal containers of milk and cream, and wooden boxes packed with butter, cheese and eggs.

At their leave-taking Gus Volholven waved farewell, calling, "Give my best to your folks, Thomas. And take care of yourselves, you two!"

Soon the teams were out of sight, the large wagon wheels crunching noisily against the hard-packed snow.

Steep grades between Wolftown and Camp McKinney were barely passable in places. The stretches were slippery and required Foderow's total concentration and caution. Several times Foderow handed the sets of reins to Thomas and climbed down from the box to lead the labouring Percherons along the snowy slopes. The special rapport that Foderow seemed to share with the teams did not escape Thomas and a slight twinge of envy gripped him.

When they were once again together on the wagon bench, Thomas asked, "Why did you come back to this? It's hard work, being winter and all."

"Because I have to do what I like best, or it's all for nothing you know. When I was a young fellow like you," Foderow remembered, "Dave took me on my first trip. I went on many with him. One night we had an accident below Fairview. He was a good teamster and it wasn't his fault, nor mine, but it took everything out of him. Things weren't the same after that for him."

A pause followed. Finally Thomas asked the question burning within him ever since he had learned of Foderow's return. "What about the shoot-out? They say you got the one that killed McAllister."

Foderow fell silent on the seat beside Thomas, smoothly working the reins as the teams pulled into the snow-bound camp at McKinney.

Without willing them, images crept through Foderow's mind of a windswept Montana winter landscape where he lay hidden in the brush, with binoculars to his eyes, as riders passed below him; of staring unflinchingly into light, blue eyes that glared threateningly back at him in a smoky Miles City saloon. These vivid images, and others, lived in the teamster, almost refusing to be buried.

But, lately, because he had returned to the Okanagan and the pleasant life he had shared with McAllister, Foderow had been able to put a frustrating anger behind him. He found he could dare to reminisce with Cartrell. In occasionally sharing memories with Sydney, it became easier to put the hurt and lost time in his life behind him.

However, the young man beside him had just raised an intruding question so pointedly, that a resentment over the invasion into his long-held silence on the matter caused Foderow to immediately bristle. He had wrongly shared a few thoughts with Thomas, he saw now, and vowed to never let sentimentality grip him in the others' presence again.

It was a hard moment for the teamster and to get away from it, he prepared to leap to the ground. "Well, you know how rumours go," he said stiffly. "They grow, and grow--" Foderow jumped. "And grow."

Thomas stared down at Foderow as he reached out to shake hands with the miners now emptying from the Cariboo Hotel to greet them. He smiled. I'll catch him off guard someday and he'll tell me. He climbed down from the wagon seat.

They remained at Camp McKinney for four days, trapped by the weather. Finally, as the weather permitted, they returned to the valley with the trip out not any easier than the going in. Although Thomas broached the subject of the American outlaw again, Foderow kept his privacy on the matter. Thomas remained as unenlightened as when he had departed home.

At the end of February, Cartrell sent Thomas, once more, to the orchard, where Alfred Kennedy proceeded to teach him how to prune a fruit tree. Cold days faced Thomas each morning as he took up the long-handled pruning shears, special handsaw and clippers, and followed Kennedy through the snow-covered orchard.

"You have to let the light in," Kennedy informed Thomas. "If you leave things bushy and cluttered in the middle, no sun'll get down in there, and the fruit won't ripen. Open the tree up, let it spread out and live. Flatten off the tops. Nothing looks nicer than to glance out from a window and see row upon row, all the same conformity."

During the thinning of the apples in the springtime, Kennedy demonstrated swift techniques. "Break the clusters. Nothing's going to grow to any size at all if you let them crowd into each other. They need space to grow in-- just like you claimed you needed."

Thomas snorted at the remark. He hardly likened himself to a growing apple. However, if Alfred Kennedy considered the produce as near human, who was he to differ? Certainly, Thomas knew it was to everyone's benefit that the man operated both orchards, for fruit from the Llewellyn farms was considered top of the class.

"I hope you've been listening, young man," he heard Kennedy say. "It may be that in the future you won't be doin' the labour anymore than your Pa does, but how're you goin' to know who to hire for a manager if you don't know what he can or can't do? You have to understand exactly what the applicant's capabilities are and, in order to know that, you have to understand every aspect of this type of farming."

Thomas smiled at Kennedy who, though shorter and stockier in build, stood authoritatively before him, and conceded amicably.

Up at Skaha, he reflected with yearning, calving time would soon be finished. Then there's branding and moving the cattle out to spring range. Thomas longed desperately to be with the cowhands there, but Cartrell remained adamant that he stay on the orchard until July. It was a matter of self-discipline, Thomas realized, for he had come to learn most of Cartrell's motives. He considered it fortunate that Cartrell harboured a dislike of sheep, for right now, he mused, he might well be up to his ears in wool.

On Marjorie Spencer's twenty-first birthday, Thomas went down to a tar-papered shack near his father's orchard on Shuttleworth Creek and purchased a small bottle of wine made from elderberries, a tangy berry which grew in attractive clusters on bushes along the river.

When he reached the Spencer home across town, he took

Marjorie's hand and led her to the bluff above the town. There, long ago during his many forays through the tall pines to assess his personal losses, Thomas had come upon an abandoned cabin. He had mended the door, covered the open windows and nailed the bed together against the wall. He ambitiously cleaned the dirt floor of small brush, piles of cones and other materials packed in by rats, thereby ridding the place of the offensive odour of rodents. The cabin quickly became a hideaway for Thomas and he was reminded of the old Bean cottage of his childhood. There, he and Marjorie had kept to themselves throughout the past two years.

Together that night in the faint July moonlight, Thomas and Marjorie sat upon their bed and drank their wine and kissed, and were very happy. Thomas felt that there was no more he could ask from life than this. But, Marjorie had taken a serious look at the pattern of her life and found it very lacking and out of control. She was after all, two years older than Thomas, and pondered why she remained with him, instead of seeking marriage with someone older. Further, a problem had developed and Marjorie felt it was a certainty that Thomas Llewellyn would never be allowed to marry her. She had been forced to make a decision.

Eventually they removed their clothes and lay down together on the crude bed; Thomas tenderly kissed her face and neck and breasts. Her slight body was soft and warm beside his. Her lips moved against his shoulder. "I want to love you perfectly tonight, Tommy," she whispered with sadness in her voice.

Thomas smiled down into her pretty face, framed by long, red tresses spread over the thin blanket on the bed. "You love me perfectly all the time, Marjorie Spencer. What d'you say we get married and make everything right?

Her soft fingers stroked his chin and neck. "What would your father say? We might have a baby and then what? Bad blood, they'll tell you."

Thomas frowned above her. "Don't joke like that. To hell with my father, and Cartrell," he whispered angrily. "We'll get married if we want to. It's that simple."

Marjorie smiled indulgently. She had long ago learned that nothing was simple in life. There was no kind of circumstance easy to live with or often even acceptable. Thomas' hands caressed her as he kissed her. Marjorie closed her eyes and sighed. These first moments of tenderness and touch were the sensations which she craved. She held Thomas close, while in her womb a tiny life stirred.

It rained throughout the night and in the morning a heavy mist hung over the river. Two workmen loading lumber on the dock north of the waterfall, discovered a body. It lay caught between the pilings beneath the deck, exposed to view because it had become hung-up by a sweater snagged on the protruding spikes.

Sorrowfully, they recognized Marjorie Spencer.

Immediately they brought her body up to the dock. The coroner and constable in Penticton were sent for. Her father was notified, however, as Harry Spencer was too drunk to come out of his house, a rider was dispatched to Skaha to notify Ian Cartrell. The message suggested that young Thomas might be held accountable, that there were witnesses to the fact that Marjorie Spencer had been last seen in his company.

Dick Foderow found Thomas in his father's orchard and took him aside. "Got to talk to you, Tom."

Thomas shrugged.

"When did you get home last night? You look terrible this morning," He suggested, "It must have been a long night."

"It was a long night. Why?"

"Where did you leave Marjorie?"

Thomas frowned, disapproving of the intrusion into his privacy. "At her house. Why?"

Foderow looked across at Alfred Kennedy, then back to Thomas. "Tom, this is serious. Two guys down at Madden's old pier found her body floating under the dock this morning."

Thomas' mind reeled. Suddenly confused, then stunned at such shattering news, he could only stare at Foderow. "You're lying. Tell me you're lying to me–" His heart raced. His knees threatened to buckle.

"I ain't lying to you. For God's sake, Tom, would I lie about a thing like this? What's also bad, is that you were the last one seen with her."

Kennedy glanced up at Thomas, shook his head in disbelief of all that he had just learned and walked away through the trees. Foderow led Thomas out of the orchard. They crossed the townsite toward Rachel McAllister's house. As gently as possible, he enquired, "Were you drinking? I mean, drunk out of your minds, wandering around an' so on?"

"What the hell does it matter!" Thomas cried, weeping inside. Fear clutched at his brain. "I'm goin' to get blamed anyway." My God, Marjie, Marjie– why? He felt his heart breaking and his eyes filled.

"At first, Tom, for sure. It's proving the innocence that becomes the problem." Foderow watched Thomas closely. He felt sympathy for the young man, for he truly believed Thomas incapable of taking another's life, accidentally or otherwise. He noticed tears welling in Thomas' eyes, though they did not spill over. I'm sure he loved her in a way, Dick told himself. I can't help but wonder why she did it. Reaching out, Foderow touched Thomas' shirtsleeve in reassurance.

Thomas looked across into Foderow's understanding gaze. "I need Ian Cartrell," he whispered. "I need Cartrell–" A feeling close to panic was catching hold of him and he recognized that it would not subside until he felt the security of Cartrell's presence near him.

Foderow placed a reassuring hand on Thomas' shoulder as they continued to Rachel's house by the lake.

When Cartrell returned to Skaha that evening with Thomas riding beside him, the constable was waiting for them. Cartrell swung down from his horse and tossed the reins to one of the ranch cowboys.

Cartrell spoke to the constable; not because he wanted to, but out of necessity. For reasons he could not explain even to himself, he bore a distrust of all peacekeepers. "You boys don't waste a minute, do you? Always get their man, the Mounties do, and I suppose you Provincials fancy yourselves of the same ability." He climbed the stairs, entered the room and lit the gas lamp. He placed his hat and gloves on a shelf and motioned for Thomas to sit down. Locating his spectacles, Cartrell hooked them over his ears and began scanning the paper handed to him by the constable. He glanced up. "Are you new? I've not seen you hereabouts."

"Name's Gantry," the constable replied calmly. "If we can all get settled down, I have a few questions to ask."

"I'm sure you didn't ride all the way out here just to watch us glower at one another." Cartrell flipped the paper aside.

Outside, evening shadows had fallen across the yard, casting eerie dark shapes against the buildings. Thomas looked through the window beside him and was not comforted by the sight, so settled, instead, to listening to the constable's strained breathing. He's horribly overweight, Thomas thought, like Da. It was a relief to think about something else beside the daunting circumstance that he had been cast into.

Cartrell's voice broke the silence, "For the moment I've seen fit to keep this incident from your parents, Tom." He turned to Gantry. "I would appreciate it if this can be handled completely by myself. Otherwise," he leaned back in the chair, looking directly at Thomas, "you may send a sick man to an early grave and cause a fine lady a nervous breakdown. If need be," he added, glancing again at Gantry, "Mrs. Llewellyn can be informed, but I'd rather not either of them."

"I don't want to see them," Thomas said quickly.

Gantry spoke up. "It would seem unavoidable. There'll be a court appearance and so on."

Cartrell leaned forward and studied Constable Bob Gantry through narrowed dark eyes. "Don't tell me you think he's guilty. I know damned well he's not! It's not in him to kill anyone, by drowning, or any other way."

54

Gantry straightened in his chair and barked superiorly, "The killer instinct lurks within all men!" He had allowed the wily Cartrell to best him and he was suddenly disappointed with his own response.

"That's crap, Gantry, and you know it. Now, let's get down to business. Tom'll tell you where he was and what he did last night. You'll write every word down." He motioned for Thomas to speak up.

From her bedroom window above the yard, Sydney Llewellyn saw the light hanging from the ceiling in Cartrell's office. Its brightness shone through the windowpane to illuminate the steps. She strained her eyes in an attempt to make out the figures seated in the room, but could not recognize at the distance who they were. She knew two men were with Ian, for someone had led two horses into the barn and one remained tied at Ian's doorway. Finally she gave up watching and retired to her room across from Albert's.

Presently Bob Gantry hoisted himself into his saddle and rode away from Skaha. Cartrell and Thomas were left to stare at each other.

"I'm not staying here," Thomas announced in a moment. "I'm going down the hill to Mrs. McAllister's."

"You could stay in the lodge. There's only Holinger there. The rest are up at cow-camp."

"No."

"Will you be alright, then?"

"Of course I'll be alright! I know the trail and her place is where I live!"

Ian Cartrell reached out against Thomas' sudden anger, placing a cautioning hand upon his arm. "Take care of yourself then," he said quietly, patting Thomas' arm reassuringly. In a moment he left his office and walked down the path to his own home. His steps seemed slow.

He's tired, Thomas thought, while walking to the livery. I'm making old people out of everyone around me. He saddled his gelding and left Skaha, using Two Way's trail over the hill. It was midnight of a warm summer evening.

Cartrell refrained from stopping at the Llewellyn house for several days, lest he let slip that serious trouble was afoot. Each day Sydney watched him pass by, head bowed, eyes focussed on the path ahead. On the fourth day, as she stood in the porch at the back of her house, rocking the boat-shaped washing machine full of clothes, she waited. When she saw Ian going along the path, she ceased her chore, left the porch and hurried across the yard to meet him.

"I need to know what's wrong, Ian. I can sense a problem," she pleaded, searching his face for clues. "Is it Thomas?"

"My dear," he assured her. "All problems that exist here rest on the shoulders of us men. Women do not bother their minds--"

"Ian!" She chewed nervously at her bottom lip. "Don't treat me like a child with all that 'men' stuff."

He halted and stared at her a long time. Then, against all his sane, rational judgment, Cartrell took his next step, knowing he was letting go the careful reserve he had built up through twelve years, respecting this woman's wonderful presence in his life. He smiled. "You haven't been riding in a long time, Sydney. Let's change that," he suggested quickly.

"I can't leave Albert."

"Yes, you can. Let that housekeeper I found for you earn her keep."

"You're avoiding an issue. You're impossible!"

"I certainly hope so," Ian grinned and, taking her arm firmly, insisted, "Ride just as you are. No riding hat, gloves or anything else. We'll go right now." He started away toward the livery.

"But-" she looked down at her skirt.

Ian laughed and called back, "Horses don't care what you wear!"

Cartrell saddled their horses himself, waving Jason Whiteman away. Together beneath a brilliant sky, they rode toward Twin Lakes (Nipit Lakes) and climbed an ancient Indian hunting trail which led to the windswept ridge above Skaha. Cartrell informed Sydney of the difficult time Thomas was facing and watched her expression pale.

"He may go to court. At the least there'll be a hearing. I'll try to settle the matter out of court, because the boy is innocent. Anyone can see that. However, the law tends to relish formalities. Then, there's the news version, once they get hold of it."

Before long they rode out of the grove and into the open. The sky was very clear and blue. The view of the White Lake basin, its rocky ridges and bluffs, and Skaha Ranch below was wide and spectacular.

Sydney, now in a much happier mood despite the troubles of her son, turned her face upward to the warm sun. "Oh, this is beautiful, Ian. We do live in the most gorgeous place."

As he dismounted, Cartrell caught her smiling at him. His heart capitulated. "Indeed, we do," he replied calmly. Reaching up, he assisted her from the saddle. Her long gingham skirt danced about her slim ankles as she hopped over the rocks to the rim of the ledge. "Come back!" he called anxiously. "I can't have something happening to you next!"

Sydney returned and stood before him, her serious eyes searching his. Rays of sunlight, in a lovely reflection from the bright sky above them, seemed to waltz across the soft waves of her honey-coloured hair. Her eyes, when they looked into his, sparkled as though touched by dew.

"Whatever would I do without you, Ian," she whispered. "You have become a perfect extension of myself. You worry about me, care about–" Her voice trailed.

Cartrell smiled, fully aware of the implication of her words. Then impulsively, he leaned forward to kiss her lightly at the corner of her mouth. Involuntarily, Sydney turned her head and suddenly the kiss was altered. Cartrell's mouth became soft and gently demanding upon hers, as he was suddenly caught up in the dream which he had believed would never happen.

Sydney's response was instant. She moved without hesitation into his arms. Ah, the sweetness of a kiss, she sighed. The longed-for, needed feel of a man's encircling arms and a body so near to her own! Her every nerve sang with pleasure and, reaching up, she clasped his shoulders tightly as his strong arms pulled her against him. She revelled in the touch of his sensuous mouth upon her face, her neck, her throat, and allowed herself to yield to every thrill of this unexpected encounter. It had been so long and Sydney craved a man's gentle touch.

No tender words were spoken. No hurried promises made. Only passion existed between them. Cartrell led her out of the sunlight into the trees, to the privacy of Nature's blind. He spread his jacket over the grass and she lay back upon it. She was beautiful in her anticipation of him and he watched her face, savouring every expression as he began to undo the buttons of her dress.

Later, when she lay against his shoulder, content and quiet, she whispered to Ian, "Did you plan this?"

"From the first moment I saw you."

She touched a fingertip lightly along his chin. "Should I trust that?"

Cartrell smiled. "Always."

She turned her head to face him. "Ian, I think I have fallen in–"

"Shhh," he whispered, placing a finger over her lips. "We cannot say those words to each other– yet," he told her seriously. "Everything in life takes time, my love, as does this." Releasing her from his arms, he rose from the ground. "Now, as much as I dislike the idea, we must return to Skaha." Assisting Sydney to her feet, their eyes met, but still no words of affection were spoken. An infidelity had been shared and neither wished to speak further of it.

It was near dusk when Cartrell and Sydney rode into the livery yard. Llewellyn witnessed their arrival from the wide window of his den, the binoculars at his suspicious eyes. On questioning Mrs. Davies, he had learned of the hour at which they had departed. He turned to meet his wife's astonished gaze as she bound quickly to the top of the stairs.

"Albert!" Sydney's hand flew to her throat.

"Yes? You didn't expect me here? I don't sleep forever, you know," he informed her coldly, bitterly.

Quickly Sydney fled around the banister, across the landing to her room, carefully bolting the door behind her. Cherishing this private moment, she recalled again Ian's tender, loving touch.

Llewellyn closeted himself within the isolation of his den and, suffering a tremendous sadness, felt this day that his wife was finally, unfairly lost to him. With a lonely heart, he leaned against the wall and could not prevent a terrible sense of desolation from descending upon him. The moment was so gripping that it threatened to overcome him and, for several minutes, Llewellyn barely remained in touch with his surroundings. When the weakness had passed, he groped toward his chair, falling into it. He threw the cane to the floor. Overwhelmed by an incredible sense of loss, Albert Llewellyn sat in the cold isolation to stare absently at the white, calcimined walls of his room.

8

The second week in August Thomas Llewellyn appeared before Judge Michael Ridell, a perceptive individual, of medium height, draped in a traditional black robe. The Judge, Ian Cartrell, Thomas and the Court Clerk were the only ones present at the hearing.

Thomas' statement to the constable was reviewed by the Judge as he watched the young man with a discerning eye. Thomas exhibited none of the expected uneasiness or agitation, no traits of the guilty. If anything, Judge Ridell noticed, he appeared confident and relaxed. It's obvious, he decided, that Ian Cartrell has a great deal to do with the boy's welfare.

Keeping his attention directed toward Thomas, he enquired, "Why do you suppose a healthy, happy young girl would do such a thing as drown herself when, as you say, you believed she would someday marry you?"

Thomas glanced cautiously across at Cartrell. Until now he had not breathed a word of the suspected circumstances and was not entirely sure that now was the time to begin. He wished, too late, that he had been honest with Cartrell and had confided in him properly. He blurted awkwardly, "I think she was going to have a baby."

Instantly Cartrell sagged deeper into his chair, raising a hand to pinch his eyes shut, to blot from his tired mind that which he had just heard, a suspicion confirmed.

Judge Ridell leaned forward, placing an elbow on his large oak desk. "You didn't know this for certain?"

"No. Yes. Well, not really. I wondered if it had actually happened– Your Honour."

Beside him, Cartrell's brain reeled. Oh, my God, he swore silently. If it had actually happened! What intolerable immaturity!

The discussion continued between Judge Ridell and Thomas without intervention from Cartrell. The word 'drowned' had become painful for Thomas to hear, especially when he was still struggling to believe the tragedy had actually occurred. Thomas learned of a letter about the baby from Marjorie to her father, an apology for any embarrassment he may suffer. He heard of a medical report that confirmed her condition.

Judge Ridell cleared his throat, the sound crackling through a momentary silence. "You were the last one seen with her, young man. Circumstances led to you. It is Mr. Cartrell whom you must thank for our indulgence the past two weeks. He accepted you into his custody and, I understand, voluntarily placed no restrictions on your movements. That was putting a great deal of faith in your behaviour, which I understand has shown considerable irregularity in the past. I'm sure I do not know everything about you, young man, but I'll be tolerant. At this time I will tell you that I do not expect to see you before me ever again, for any reason. I believe my meaning is clear. You are free to leave this room." He gathered up the papers before him, tapping them against the desk top. "Thank you, Mr. Cartrell. Good-day."

Thomas withdrew from Okanagan Falls, from all his old haunts in Penticton, from Rachel McAllister's quiet abode, and turned instead to the vast mountain ranges of Skaha's cow-camp.

Although life at home with his parents presented an awkward existence when he remained overnight there, the compensation of working with the cattle, the stimulating association with the cowboys, and the fun he had with horses and lariats, helped for a while to make up for the lack of a social life as he had previously known it.

The indignation and resentment he felt regarding Marjorie's decision to end it all, would remain with Thomas always. He saw it as a thoughtless action which proved a lack of faith in him as a responsible person who could cope with marriage and family. Although he continued to feel love for her, he considered the act of taking her own life a terrible injustice against him. In choosing to end her life, and with it that of their baby, Marjorie had removed from Thomas the stability and affection which he craved to give; the same of which he was now deprived. He felt quite dead.

Thomas' emotions reached a new depth and his final analysis of all the circumstances proved critical of Marjorie. He never questioned his ability to provide for her and the baby if they had lived, only that she had cheated him of the opportunity.

Cartrell's incredible intuition warned him of an unhappy situation brewing and his manner with Thomas took on additional severity.

Over the remaining weeks of August Thomas grew uneasy. One day he confided in Two Way, "I feel the trap being set."

Two Way sat in the sun on the step of his cabin braiding his long, gray hair. He smiled indulgently. "Traps are set only for furs."

"No, Two Way, you don't understand."

"I don't?" Shaking his head, he wondered aloud, "Why do young folks think old men have never lived through what is supposed to be understood by them?"

Thomas ignored the remark on the basis that the old Indian seldom lent the appearance of having dealt with difficult times. "I feel boxed in. I can't go anywhere but Cartrell's with me. I eat all my meals here or in camp, sleep here or in camp, and work seven days a week. Sure, I have everything I need in life, except other people close to me. I didn't mind being alone at first, but now-- I know there's lots of fun to be had with the guys on the ranch, the horses and barrel racing and all, but it's not the same. I had freedom before. Now I have none." Thomas stared into Two Way's widened dark eyes. "Do you understand what I mean, Two Way? I think I'm outgrowing this place."

"I think you are not appreciating this place, that's what I think." Again, Two Way smiled, for he really did know the turmoil and confusion which could rage within a young man. He had been witness to indecision in many men and its resulting damage to others.

But it was true. Thomas seemed to live in an isolated world; a lack of social stimulation and friendship with those of his own age was evident. One evening he spoke to his mother of the stagnant situation in which they all resided at Skaha.

"Don't you see what's happening to us? We're growing into each other," he stated, fervently hoping she was listening. "There are eight families who live up here and most of them work for the ranch. There's hardly anyone left. Even Miss Carmichael's moving to Penticton because this town is dying." Watching Sydney's face for some reaction, he continued, "The fellows go down to the hotel or up to Penticton every Saturday night, but do I? I sit and listen to Da reminisce with old Two Way and watch you knit! Nobody my age lives here and Ian blocks the exit."

Sydney attempted to explain. "He feels that you carried on enough in two years to make up for ten. Sort of sowed your wild oats early. He–"

Thomas was astonished and bolted upright on the couch to stare at her. "Why does he matter? Why are you letting him run our lives?"

"I'll tell you, Thomas," Sydney spoke with stubbornness edging her voice, "without Ian, you would have nothing. I would have nothing, and your father would have shot himself long ago." She was not attempting to be dramatic; simply pointing up some truths.

Thomas was not impressed by truths. He watched her pick up the long needles and wool, and begin to knit furiously. "I think he means more to you than you are admitting to me," he said coldly.

From behind Thomas, at the doorway where he had arrived unannounced, Cartrell's stiff voice interjected, "You will apologize to your mother, Tom." Black eyes stared from beneath a frowning brow, sending a stern warning across the room.

Thomas spun around on the couch, then turned again to confront his mother, "Everywhere we are, there he is, minding our business."

"It so happens," Cartrell elaborated calmly, "that I just came from your father and overheard your abominable insinuation."

"Perfect timing," Thomas snapped irritably. "A necessary ingredient to keeping the milestones of our lives in proper balance, so to speak!" he mimicked, leaping to his feet. The parlour door slammed behind him, threatening its hinges and emphasizing his exit.

Tenseness reigned between Ian and Sydney. He attempted to meet her eyes, but she would not raise them to his. She was embarrassed, hurt and distracted.

"I'm sorry," he spoke softly near her. "I wish it were the case, though. I need you, my love, and I know you need me."

"Ian, please– I suffer sufficient shame already whenever I meet Belle and every time I look at Albert. I remember so well how he used to be and my heart often aches for him." Sydney hid her face in the palms of her hands, a pitiful vision of despair to Cartrell's saddened eyes. Her shoulders began to shake and quickly the tears slid from between her slim fingers to be absorbed by the bundle of wool in her lap.

Cartrell felt helpless. He raised his arms toward her, then dropped them to his sides. "If God had been fair," he murmured softly, "He would've had us meet before He complicated our lives otherwise." No sooner were the words spoken, than he knew they were wrong. "Sydney," he knelt before her. "You and I were meant for the same hearth from the start. Your marriage was in the way for me in the beginning, then mine; and then there was Dave. This is a strange time to tell you this, but I love you, dear heart, more than anyone else in this world." Cartrell's eyes mirrored the sadness he felt at the infidelity he furthered.

Sydney remained withdrawn from him, as though she had not heard his bold confession.

After a long pause, Ian whispered, "Goodnight, my dear," and left her, perceiving that he had not eased her apprehension at all.

Sydney's last diary entry of 1908 bore all the signs of a will slowly fading. Silent pleas existed for a reconciliation between father and son and above all, for her own will to resist the overwhelming power of Cartrell's deep affection for her.

"I have loved the men in my life in different ways," she wrote. *"My father and brother, husband and sons, and yes, David; but none, I now realize, have I loved more than Ian, who has been*

to me, through these years of unrest and toil, the very life and breath of my existence."

Having put her thoughts, so personal, to paper, Sydney lowered her head onto her arms against the desk and wept for the sweet, tender moments of early marriage with Albert, for the marvellous dreams they had spun together, and for the union that had given birth to three children - the marriage which she now, in her loneliness, sometimes casually dismissed.

9

The profound regret of a fruitful life long lived is that at some time it must reach its end. His gentle manner and the practical wisdom imparted to both his people and the white generations was indicative of how the Okanagan Indian, Two Way, lived his life. It brought recognition and respect to his controversial promotion of harmony and co-existence.

Realization that the end of his life upon these hunting grounds was drawing to a close, came to Two Way with the quiet dawning of a beautiful September day. To him, the spirit of his forebears, his sister, Nahna, his wife, Waneta, and their babies and, strongest of all, the spirit of Many Rains seemed to beckon him to their permanent abode.

With the sun's brilliant rays casting their early morning light across the grassy mountain paths, Two Way's moccasins tread the time-worn trail for the last time to the cliff above the rolling waterfall. With his wrinkled brown hands cupped together in his lap as he settled against a tree, he allowed his memories to transport him back in time. The brilliance of the sun, the vast ranges of the valley, and his village at the end of the lake had held significant meaning for him throughout his eighty-eight years. Meeting the trapper while in his youth had led to many years of happy companionship.

When the day was drawing to a close, Two Way wrapped a wide deerskin robe painted with a mythological coyote on the back close around his body. Choosing the protection of a prominent rock, he sat down upon the soft grass at its base, crossed his ankles and pulled the robe over his chest and knees. He wished to rest a little longer before returning home to Skaha. He raised his tired, watery eyes toward the cloudy sky and listened to the rhythm of the falls below. The warm comfort of the hide about his thin body kept away the September evening chill. Here, in the safe closet of Nature's lovely endowments, the Okanagan Indian, Toohey, always known as Two Way, closed his eyes and drifted toward a final, restful peace.

At midnight, riding up the trail toward Skaha, Thomas came upon the body and the Okanagans who had arrived to attend it. In the darkness he strained his eyes to watch four men place supple poplars upon the grass, binding the pieces together with thick deer thongs. Pulling Two Way's robe around his lifeless body, they lifted him gently onto the stretcher. Then the four Okanagan men moved slowly down the trail leading to the valley floor. Aware of Thomas' presence, they chose to ignore him. Not even did they acknowledge him when, in their passing on the trail, Thomas enquired gently, "How did you know?"

Through the night, the woods stood silent. No breeze tossed the falling leaves about. They drifted silently to their natural compost. The usual prevailing chorus of water-life in the ponds, lakes and streams in the mountains was conspicuously absent. Browsing deer, wandering bear and other wildlife paused to regard the stillness. Inquisitive, as though sensing a difference, a beaver waited a moment on the river before diving toward a watery hutch. Not even an owl hooted. It seemed that it would remain that way forever.

Then, as if by signal, a coyote rose from the cover of darkness into the dawn, and sent the long quavering cry of his brothers to echo between the mountains. From the hills across the valley, the consistent beat of drums rode faintly on the air.

After three days, when the drums had ceased their message, Cartrell, with Sydney and Thomas inside, drove the carriage out of Skaha's yard, across the flats and down the winding hill above the lake onto the benchland home of Two Way's family. Upon their arrival, as though they had been waiting for these special visitors, one of Two Way's nephews raised his arm to the sky. A long, persistent call passed from his lips.

Two Way's body, now wrapped in a beaver robe, was lowered upon its side, in the open grave. The sandy soil was replaced into the cavity. A slender pole was then erected at the head. Trees near the gravesite displayed the hides of two horses slaughtered for the feast that would follow the burial. Now dressed in their finest head-pieces and tunics decorated with quills, the four braves who had carried Two Way's body home placed a canoe over the fresh mound. After a time, the Indians moved away to the yard where the feast had been prepared. The ancient tribal rite was finished.

Ian Cartrell reached for the reins of the team. Thomas remained quiet and Sydney had become ill. Cartrell watched her face and was reminded of how quickly Belle could be ill over anything out of the ordinary. "What is it, Sydney?"

"It's those hides! How can they kill their horses for something like this?" Indeed, she appeared very pale.

"The slaughter wasn't for sacrificial reasons, but for meat at the table," he informed her, in an attempt to ease her mind; but he only succeeded in worsening the matter. "It's a custom, that's all, and you probably witnessed the last of its kind today. They're becoming more modern and this special ceremony was only because it was Two Way who died."

"All the same, I'll never understand these people," she murmured, dabbing a lace handkerchief to her damp brow and upper lip. "It's barbaric. I don't blame Belle for not wanting to come with us."

"What's so different about it? Don't we dehide the cow, ring the neck of the chicken and scrape the pig?" Cartrell smiled.

"Oh, Ian! Really!"

Thomas interrupted. "Ian, you can let me out down here. I'll walk up to the ranch tonight."

Cartrell pulled against the reins and the carriage jerked to a stop. "Remind me to approach Albert about a motor car. In this day's need for increasing speed, it's damned ridiculous to not own a vehicle with four wheels, a motor and a steering control."

Thomas stepped down and the carriage was pulled into motion once more. It bumped across the twin bridges over the falls and along the hillside above Dog Lake.

In the spring, Thomas, during a particular time of loneliness, went to see the old Indian's grave and noticed that the mound had sunk, but the barren pole remained. That evening he told his mother, "No name or date; nothing's recorded on it. It's like Two Way never lived." He felt very sad about that.

Llewellyn mumbled, "Everybody knows it's Two Way's grave."

"I don't suppose anyone knows when he was born," Sydney noted idly. "I wonder if Duncan even knew."

However, David McAllister had known through his father. When Thomas mentioned the matter to Dick Foderow, the teamster informed him, "I was riding with Dave one time and he said the old man was seventy-nine then, the year that Dave got shot."

So the dates were established on the width of a cross. With the approval of Two Way's family, Thomas had painted on it "Indian Two Way 1821-1909". No one since the trapper McAllister, had ever asked Two Way his real name.

10

The automobile, as styled and operated in the early 1900's, had come a long way since two Englishmen took out a patent in 1619 for a carriage powered by strength other than the horse. Called the 'horseless carriage', it was improved in reliability and safety to sufficiently launch it into astounding popularity in the twentieth century.

The product of Henry Ford's imagination, which arrived at Skaha in early October, 1913, puffed and boomed its way across the flats into the sharp view of Albert Llewellyn's binoculars. Everyone who was on the ranch that day heard the approaching mechanical contraption and rushed out of the buildings to greet Ian Cartrell as he crossed the bridge over Willow Creek, braking to a stop in Albert's yard.

Eventually Thomas, astride his horse, came into view behind Cartrell, leading the accountant's mare. Llewellyn lowered the glasses, remained unsmiling and looked down to the yard from the wide windows of his den. He saw his excited wife rush out with the others to view the new motor car. Their mobility was an enviable thing for him to watch, though he knew they were hardly to blame for his lingering confinement and were scarcely worthy of the contempt he bore them.

For a while, he stared unemotionally down at his latest purchase and considered its possibilities. He would now be able to live a more active life. He knew the benefit Cartrell would derive from the automobile. Time spent in travelling would be cut in half. Llewellyn envisioned trips for himself down to the orchards, the freight sheds, even up to Penticton if he had a mind. The doctor must be consulted, of course; but Llewellyn foresaw no drawback to his re-entry into the industrial scene, so long as the capable hands of Ian Cartrell controlled the vehicle. In fact, he quickly decided, he would make that a permanent rule.

When Sydney returned to the den, he informed her, "No one but Ian is ever to drive that thing. No one!"

"I'm sure no one wants to, Albert. They all appear to be half afraid of it." Her cheerful giggle echoed against the high ceiling of the room and Albert smiled at the sound of its merriment.

Indeed, the cause of the activity in the yard below, although it indicated progress, also left room for doubt. The reliability of the machine was an issue, when compared to the remarkable endurance of the horse, and one of the ranch hands in the crowd asked Cartrell, "What happens when the fuel runs out? We don't have a supply here."

"We will have to store it in a barrel somewhere on the ranch. A truck from Penticton will bring it out."

"And if it breaks down?"

"There's a mechanic in Penticton who has a repair shop and says he knows everything about motor cars," Cartrell replied to the small attentive crowd. He moved possessively about the machine. He was extremely pleased with the new addition to Skaha. It was time, he felt, that they had a vehicle on the place and he believed that Llewellyn owed him this one convenience.

While the arrival of the new motor car was timely for Cartrell and afforded Albert a new lease on life, it was viewed as something near a godsend by Thomas. He considered it a huge advantage to be able to get off the ranch and downtown over new roads in less than an hour. The fastest he had ever covered the distance to the lakeshore village was over Two Way's old trail at an easy trot, well over an hour.

Excursions in the automobile so brightened Llewellyn's life that, in the spring of the following year, he purchased a McLaughlin-Buick. The Ford was given to Charlie Sandon in compensation for his unquestionable loyalty. Complete with an overhead cover, protective windshield, brass trim and bright lights, the Buick was an impressive vehicle to own. Proudly, now, with Sydney beside him and Cartrell at the wheel, Llewellyn could ride with little discomfort all the way to Penticton for a day's outing, allowing Sydney to enjoy shopping and an evening dinner at the hotel.

Often Sydney joined them on their trips down the hill to Okanagan Falls to spend time with Rachel McAllister. Sometimes she strolled the beach with Thomas when he was there to work at the freight shed.

During one trip, when she had shared memories of her childhood in Wales with Thomas, who could not envision life in a country other than the one in which he had lived all his life, her thoughts took a more serious turn.

"The water is calm here. Do many swim here? Do you?"

"Sometimes. I have a hard time getting into the water that killed Marjorie."

"Oh, Thomas, that seems so long ago now," Sydney sympathized. "Well, I think I should like to purchase a bathing dress and try it. At forty-four and with a new car in the yard, life has come to have meaning again for me, Thomas." She watched the sand around her bare feet. "Isn't it odd how the sand shifts and fills in one's footprints? Life is much like that, you know, Thomas. When we are gone from this earth, someone else shifts into our place and it quickly seems as though we had not existed at all. Your father's life and mine have been separate for many years now. Neither one of us can remember when that began, or what really set it in motion. It was something that just happened to us, without our realizing the beginning of the end."

"Will you miss him when he dies?"

"Certainly, and I've no doubt that he would miss me were I to go first; but the strengths of togetherness that bound us in the beginning and brought us finally to this valley are no longer there. So, the 'missing' will not be the same." She dabbed a handkerchief at her brow. "Goodness, but it's getting warm." She smiled up at her tall, fair-haired son. "I do love you, Thomas. Whatever happens in our lives, please remember that I love you. Always."

"Yes, Mother, I know that." She had caught him off guard. "I've always known that," Thomas replied quietly, perplexed at her sudden change of mood. How can I tell her, now, that I've thought of enlisting. She hardly seems aware that there's a war brewing in Europe. He had listened to Cartrell and Dick discussing it and was aware that Canadian men were already enlisting. The VICTORIA COLONIST was always headlined with details. But in their home, his mother never mentioned it, never listened to the news on the battery radio in his father's den. Was it that she feared he might leave? He walked beside her in silence, listening to the water lap onto the sand beside them.

Assessing the growth and changes at his Okanagan Falls orchard, Llewellyn felt very pleased and commended Alfred Kennedy on his efforts toward improvement. Of his three foremen, Kennedy, Foderow and Sandon, he got along best with Alfred. The man minded his own business and operated the orchards successfully.

Sitting in the car parked beside the huge cherry trees one day, he could hardly believe their height. "Good Lord!" he smiled upwards to Kennedy from the car window. "They're awful damned high." Suddenly his attention was drawn to new plantings, already three years old. "What is this?"

Kennedy informed him, "Three years ago we ordered newer varieties in apples and extended the orchard another two acres. If you remember, we had this in tomatoes." He snapped the suspenders of his trousers against his chest, feeling a certain importance in the development of Llewellyn's holdings. "An increase in the demand for fresh fruit changed all that. Last year was the end of the ground crops."

Llewellyn's hand tightened over the curve of his cane where it lay against the seat of the car. He glanced suspiciously across at Cartrell, mentally assessing the loss in revenue from ground produce.

"You knew, Albert," Cartrell reminded him calmly. "You made the decision."

Llewellyn thought about it, idly stroking his mustache. It irritated him that he would allow things like that to slip his mind. "Of course, of course."

Standing beside the vehicle, Cartrell studied the man inside. It was obvious he was enjoying this excursion. The warmth of the summer sun and the fresh air, accompanied by all the sights and sounds of his industries, rejuvenated Albert.

Nonetheless, the end had begun for him, and Cartrell began to notice. Throughout the spring and early summer of that year, 1914, Cartrell watched the weakening, paid special attention to decisions made by the man, and attempted to shield Sydney against the inevitable.

Lying comfortably beside his wife one night, Cartrell told her, "Now that it's actually happening I can hardly believe it. Albert's definitely not himself lately. His memory is getting difficult to deal with. It causes him to be so contradictory that even I must argue insistently at times with him."

Late into the night he pondered the eventual passing of control of Llewellyn's holdings into his own hands, and the man's beautiful wife in widowhood. While he talked, Belle heard nothing, for having taken the required medication to quell the pain in her chest, she had drifted off to sleep beside him. When she failed to respond, he leaned up on an elbow and, in the moonlight illuminating the room, allowed his gaze to linger over her relaxed face. He was startled to notice how pale, almost gray her skin appeared. She seemed very still suddenly. Cartrell rose to his knees on the bed and shook her gently.

Belle's eyes flew open in surprise.

"You frightened me. I thought for a moment– are you alright?" he asked, slightly shaken. "You look positively unwell."

Belle did not smile; in fact, her expression remained unemotional as she answered curtly, "I've been ill many times, Ian dear, and my appearance has completely escaped you." Her brown eyes appeared large to him as they stared coolly into his.

He frowned, troubled, and lay down beside her once more. "I can hear your breathing quite easily– raspy, to say the least. I can hear it–"

"A rarity, I must say," Belle interrupted. "You're seldom beside me for long." She smiled wanly, curling her thin body close beside him. He reached out, patting a comforting hand upon her hip and drew her nearer.

"Dr. Stobie will be out tomorrow," he informed her, gently kissing her forehead. "He's to see Albert, so he'll be over here as usual."

The prognosis was that Belle should be admitted to the small hospital in Penticton for re-assessment. "There's no doubt in my mind," Stobie told Ian sadly as they walked across the yard to the office, "that your wife is now suffering from tuberculosis and must be removed from the family immediately."

Cartrell was not entirely surprised at the statement. It confirmed his long-standing suspicion of the disease. He invited the doctor upstairs to the small apartment to have a cup of tea and a rest before returning to Penticton. Although Harold Stobie travelled by car, as did many in the area lately, the trip out to Skaha made a long day for a man of sixty years. He had hoped to retire from medicine but the lack of young doctors in the area, due to enlistment in war service, forced him to remain in practice.

With Belle's departure at the end of July, Cartrell was forced to concentrate on the care of his two young daughters, now sixteen and fourteen. He did this by installing them temporarily in the Llewellyn household under the motherly eye of Sydney.

Belle's absence from Skaha and Albert's failing health were instantly overshadowed by the stunning news of August 5th.

England and France declared war on Germany. Suddenly war news was heard everywhere; on the radio, in all the town shops, in every conversation, in every home. Newspaper headlines read, VOLUNTEER, SERVE KING AND COUNTRY.

In less than six months, in Penticton, steamers were pressed into extra service to transport troops up Okanagan Lake to Vernon where the 30th B.C. Horse was located. Proceeding overseas they became the 2nd Canadian Mounted Rifles, serving in a conflict which historians would record as The Great War.

The Buick, as apparently all automobiles and machinery were slated to do, fascinated Thomas. Disregarding his father's orders, he drove the car whenever he chose. After all, he had been driving the old Ford which Sandon now possessed, gaining experience. On a cold January day, Thomas hopped into the Buick and drove away from Skaha.

Although the weather had cleared and the snow had ceased,

winter had settled in. Thomas spent the day in Penticton with old school chums from his Kelowna days, who had enlisted in the Army and were preparing to leave for Vernon. Talk of war in Europe was all around him in town, and in the newly built Incola Hotel where the young men gathered, drinking beer. It left him feeling inadequate and alone, as there were only two others among his friends remaining behind. It was a depressing realization, and Thomas dealt with it by ordering one round of beer after another.

When the good time drew to a close, Thomas climbed into the car and headed out of town toward the long, winding hill to the bench above Dog Lake. He did not, at first, realize he was losing control. He could not see the ice, but knew suddenly that it was there. In an instant the car veered to the side of the roadway, turning and sliding backwards, pausing for a moment, then dropped into the ravine below. Flung from the automobile, Thomas was tossed into darkness against boulders and brush. The vehicle rolled and tumbled through the trees over the frozen sage, to finally settle at the bottom of the draw, its wheels spinning crazily in the air. In the cold and snow, unconscious, Thomas lay where he had fallen against the rocks. His head rolled to the side.

At dawn the next morning Cartrell set out in Sandon's car in search of Thomas and easily located him. With considerable difficulty he got Thomas to the hospital, having to haul his injured, limp body up to the roadside and into the Ford.

At Skaha, Albert raged from his bed, the chair, the den. Everywhere in the house his voice could be heard. When Cartrell delivered Thomas home four days later, it was to the ranch bunkhouse.

"No sense taking you over to the house, upsetting everyone," he told Thomas testily. "You can look after yourself here. You've got one good arm. Put it to work. Keep the snow pushed from the walkway, the horses groomed and so on. You're lucky you weren't killed, you know." Cartrell's voice registered his disappointment in the young man. The last few years had shown Thomas to be fairly responsible in freighting, as well as in ranch matters. Cartrell felt let down.

Llewellyn refused to speak to his son. Sydney showed reserve toward him. Cartrell exhibited impatience while Thomas passed the winter idly. However, by March his left arm and shoulder were well healed and he worked with Sandon during calving time on the ranch. His conversations with Cartrell were curt and to the point. He sensed compassion in Sydney's voice whenever he visited her, but also her disappointment. No communication was to be had with his father.

Then one day at the end of May, Thomas disappeared.

72

11

Ian Cartrell did not bother to search Thomas out, contending that bad news reached one's ears soon enough. At the time, Cartrell was caught up in the preparation of getting the Llewellyns to Penticton, for a significant event was taking place there. It was the arrival of the first train into the south valley.

As Sydney carried her overnight case down the stairs to the hallway, she said to Cartrell, "Ian, are you sure there'll be rooms for us? I can't believe that at long last that train is getting into town. I think I read in the HERALD, that it would make several runs a week." She halted before the wall mirror to adjust her hat and secure it with a long pin. "Imagine the accessibility to the coast."

Beside her, Albert, leaning on Ian's arm, grumbled, "Don't know why that's important to us. We've no need to go there," and heaved a sigh of relief at having made it to the bottom of the stairs without incident.

Sydney pouted slightly, "I do wish that son of ours would've shown up to go with us. There'll be a wonderful celebration and he'll miss it."

"I doubt it!" snapped Llewellyn, struggling down the outside steps. "The only thing he misses lately is a work day."

Cartrell got them into the old Ford and off to Penticton on that bright and glorious early morning of May 31, 1915. Once they were settled into their rooms at the Incola Hotel, Sydney and Ian left Albert to watch the ceremonies from the veranda of the hotel. They joined the enthusiastic, impatient crowd which swarmed over the newly laid steel tracks of the Kettle Valley Railroad. At the C.P.R. dock, the sleek *S.S. SICAMOUS* was preparing for departure.

The beautiful new white swan of the lake, the steel-hulled *SICAMOUS* had been launched the year before and carried out daily runs between Kelowna and Penticton.

Ladies dressed up in their best suits, attired with gloves and wide hats covered with fine net, and men wore handsome jackets, ties and top hats. They waved goodbye to departing soldiers on the *SICAMOUS* and talked of the tremendous advantage of the railroad and the transportation link to the Okanagan.

Sydney allowed herself to be caught up in the excitement. Her eyes took in all that was possible and sparkled with pleasure. She revelled in the exposure to life outside her reclusive world at the ranch.

"I don't believe how fast Penticton has developed!" she called to Ian. "It's absolutely wonderful to be here! And look, Ian– that beautiful new boat. I'd not seen the *SICAMOUS* until now." With wide, staring eyes, Sydney whispered, "She is magnificent."

Cartrell could not take his gaze from Sydney's face as he stood, relaxed, hands in his pockets, watching. An understanding smile played about his mouth. Near the train station, a band played a rousing march, and Sydney clapped her hands to the rhythm. She needs this more often, he thought. She's finding out how alive she still is.

Sydney turned and looked fully into his eyes. Her face was bright, happy, smiling at him over her clapping hands. A surge of love for her rushed through him.

Then suddenly he saw her smile fade, her hands still, and she fixed her gaze toward the *SICAMOUS*. Then she rushed, pushing between the spectators, running toward the wharf. "Thomas!" she called frantically over the crowd. "Thomas, what have you done? Oh, dear Lord, what have you gone and done?" People bumped against her; stared at her. Some made way for her.

Cartrell bolted after Sydney, hampered in his pursuit by the milling, waiting crowd. As he reached out and caught her shoulder, he looked up to see Thomas standing, in uniform, on the middle deck of the boat. "Oh, thank God–" he breathed. "At last!" He tried to hold on to Sydney, but she pulled away. "Sydney! Don't! Leave him alone." He caught her arm and spun her around to hold her against him. "For heaven's sake," he whispered close to her, "let him go– let go–."

"You don't understand," Sydney cried, fighting to be free of his restraining arms. "He may go to war."

"Definitely." He clasped her more firmly.

"But I may never see him again!"

"A harsh reality, Sydney."

Sydney ceased her struggle and, past his shoulder, watched the boat move up the lake. "He's my son," she whispered plaintively. "I've lost them all now. All of them– gone."

Cartrell tried to get them away from the pressure of the crowd that now watched in curious interest. In the struggle, her hat was knocked to the ground. Someone picked it up and handed it to Cartrell, who shoved it under his arm where it remained crushed. "Sydney, get a hold on yourself," he demanded of her. "You're losing your grip–"

"I'm losing my son!" She broke free of Cartrell and, with tears sliding over her cheeks, walked alone toward the Incola Hotel.

Cartrell followed at a discreet distance to attract no further attention, and to leave her the privacy she so obviously wanted. He turned to watch the S.S. *SICAMOUS* sail into the blue distance of Okanagan Lake and derived a certain reprieve in its carrying the younger Llewellyn away from them.

As a warm spring breeze blew off Okanagan Lake, Thomas stood on the deck of the beautiful sternwheeler, to quietly depart the valley. Thomas' heart was very heavy. He had come to feel unacquainted with himself. To assess who he was as a man of twenty-five, frightened him. He recognized his frailties; he had no definite goal in life and little motivation to change things. Until now.

Standing on the deck of the luxurious boat, he had no one to wave goodbye to, no one to wish him a safe return; in fact, no one to even realize that he was leaving. He had not noticed his mother push her way through the crowd gathered on the lakeshore. He found it difficult to believe that he had actually taken the positive step of enlisting and leaving home. He had felt loneliness many times in his youth, but the sudden isolation that assailed Thomas Llewellyn at this profound moment was unparalleled by any emotion he had known in his life.

In the bright sunshine the great white swan moved against the waves up the lake.

When Sydney received the post from Cartrell six weeks later, she gasped, placed a trembling hand to her chest and sank onto the sofa in the darkening parlour. "Really Ian, whatever would make him– He says he's in the Cavalry."

Cartrell smiled as though understanding Thomas. "Don't put it down, my dear. It was the only course left to him."

"Can't we do something to get him out? I mean, we have a large ranch here, and other businesses which need him." Her heart raced anxiously. Cartrell watched a flush creep into her face.

"Sydney, be rational about the situation. There is no more a need for Thomas on the place, rebel that he is, than there is for another toad down at the pond. When he returns–"

"If he returns!" she wailed, tears trickling down over her flushed and burning cheeks. "If! We are at war! Don't you know that?"

Cartrell was patient, though he paced the Llewellyn parlour floor in an agitated manner. "When he returns, there'll be need for a man here, not a boy, and I'm placing sufficient faith in our defense department to do a job that we could not."

Following a lengthy silence, during which even the air in the room seemed to hang still, Sydney sighed in resignation. "Well," she asked wearily, "how do I tell Albert?"

Cartrell glanced down to the sofa, where she sat wringing her hands on her long skirt draped sedately over her knees to the floor. "Do you want me to?"

"Ian," she perked up quickly. "Would you please? I can't bear the tortured look that comes into his eyes whenever Thomas' name is mentioned."

Raising a brow at her statement, Cartrell reflected aloud, "More likely it's a reflection of the killer instinct you're seeing."

"Ian– you know he regrets the loss of Harrie still, and always will. Because of it, he's placed a terrible emotional burden upon Thomas." In a sad voice, she added, "In a way, he drove our son from home."

"Well, Thomas has more than repaid him, it seems."

"Please, Ian!" Still twisting her slim fingers together nervously, she whispered, "I hate to admit that things should have been very different, that Thomas was wrong in all the things he did to upset us. I just wish–"

Cartrell leaned toward her, bracing a hand against the sofa arm. "Sydney," he said seriously, "take heart in the fact that you are not alone with heartache. With this letter, you have just joined the majority. Almost every family in the valley will eventually have a husband, son or father in the conflict overseas. You will not be alone."

Indeed, Sydney Llewellyn would not be alone.

In December, Ian was summoned to the Penticton Hospital to a consultation with Dr. Stobie, who remained in attendance of Belle. The diagnosis was devastating. Because one was not required to be gentle with the tall man in perennial black, Stobie put the news to Ian bluntly. "Because it's tuberculosis, Ian, we have to permanently remove her from your home."

Cartrell stared across the desk at him. "Harold– the girls–"

"She'll have to be moved as soon as possible to a sanitarium," he informed Cartrell. "We can no longer have Belle bouncing back and forth from here to home, endangering everyone in contact with her, and herself, further. From time to time you will all have to be tested."

Cartrell was upset and showed it. Harold Stobie felt very sorry for him, and sad to be dividing a family.

"Now, the nearest is at Kamloops, which is not bad at all," he continued slowly. "I believe in being completely honest with you, Ian. Don't ever hope to have your wife at home for a very long while, if at all. You will have visiting privileges, of course. We'll do all we can to make her comfortable, but we both know that TB is an unrelenting disease."

"It hardly seems fair," Ian murmured sadly. His mind had become crowded with visions of Belle as she first arrived at Skaha; she had courted him, not he, her, and she cared for him and their daughters tenderly. He loved her, of that there was no doubt. At this time, his affection for her ran very deep. He could not recall when their life together had begun to change, but altered, it was. Perhaps the breech lay with Belle's resentment over her bad health, his good health, and certainly the attention demanded of him by the life the Llewellyns lived.

Slowly Cartrell rose from the chair, placed his hat over his dark hair and reached for the doctor's hand. "Thank you, Harold. I don't like what is happening, but I know you're doing the best you can for all of us."

"Where are the girls?"

"They're with Sydney sometimes, but mostly at home with me. They are in school at Penticton where they stay with Heather Carmichael during the week."

"They'll have to be tested, you know. So will you, Ian."

Cartrell nodded and stepped out into the brisk winter weather with a heart full of sadness.

Belle Cartrell would be transferred to the sanitarium at Tranquille near Kamloops in January, 1916, as soon as the festive season was over. The girls, Jennifer and Karen, spent what everyone was predicting would be their last Christmas with their mother.

It was a traumatic, heartbreaking time for them. Their mother had been their most constant companion, always attentive and caring, comforting in their childhood hurts, and understanding of their little problems as they developed into young women. They had watched sadly as Belle paled through the years of their lives, from the beautiful, cheerful lady, always immaculately dressed and fussy about her appearance, into the unhappy, complaining, weakened patient that she had become. It was difficult for them to understand frailties in life and the relentlessness of the disease which was taking their mother from them. Throughout that Christmas season they were, for the first time, beginning to feel the emptiness that their mother's absence would leave in their home.

For the first time in several years a sense of peace reigned between Ian Cartrell and his wife, enhanced by the liveliness of their pretty, young daughters and the excitement of the festive season. They enjoyed visits from Sydney, who brought baskets of cakes, cookies and a large plum pudding. Fern and Dick Foderow remained for morning coffee during one of the teamster's trips with extra Christmastime supplies, mail and gifts. Alfred Kennedy arrived for a rare visit with his niece, and resided with the Llewellyns out of fear of the disease.

Cartrell was grateful for everyone's contribution toward a happy holiday season; however, there were occasions when he fell into spells of sorrow over his loss, and remorse, but he was quick to recognize it as self-pity.

Following the Penticton school's Easter holiday, Cartrell removed his daughters to Kelowna to a fine boarding school where they would obtain their remaining education. There, they would also receive the benefit of social refinements that the ranch and Okanagan Falls did not offer. In their teenage years, the change of residence was not as traumatic as it might have been at an earlier age. While Jennifer and Karen were sorry to leave the close association shared with Sydney, they looked forward to new friendships in Kelowna, a larger city than Penticton.

Life at Skaha, Cartrell concluded, was settling down.

12

The spring season began with rain and continued with rain until the end of June. At the meadows a disaster was taking shape. One warm day Cartrell saddled his horse and rode into the draw on the eastern slope of Skaha, suspicious of the tumultuous affect that hot weather could produce. He was astounded at the threat before him. Water overflowed the causeway, wearing away the supportive soil on top of the rock and timber, leaving bare an inadequate structure unable to contain the body of water currently building in the lake behind it.

Streams broke through at each side of the dam and flowed into the ravine. The overflow spilled gently onto the southern flats. Cartrell realized that when it reached its limit, the stream would change course and race toward White Lake.

Everywhere around where Cartrell stood remained a thick snow pack; his horse was up to its knees. Above him in an opening sky, lately relieved of rain clouds, the summer sun blazed. The heat predicted terrible consequences. Leaning over the horn of his saddle, he pinched his eyes closed against the all-too-clear vision of a major flood.

The dam was over twenty years old, having been constructed when Llewellyn needed irrigation for his orchard. Poorly constructed, it should have been rebuilt, Cartrell knew, and blamed himself for his lack of attention over the years. But was he really to blame? Had Llewellyn ever mentioned the dam? Sandon passed the site regularly, and sometimes even set up fencing camps near it. Nonetheless, it remained clear that a flood was imminent. Everyone would be affected.

Cartrell went to Charlie Sandon.

"If you get some teams to work up there, Charlie, deepen the channel near the bottom and build a wall on this side, you could force all the water southward before something serious happens. You got enough men here to do it."

"That's a good suggestion, but no easy job with all that snow and frozen ground, you know," Sandon informed him curtly, feeling that the accountant was treading outside his own ground. Sandon bristled. "I'm about to push the cattle out to summer range on those south flats. It's got some bogs now. We don't need additional water out there. Let it come down to the lake."

Cartrell stared at the man. He did a quick, critical appraisal of

Sandon. The man must be getting on in age by now, tired of matters here perhaps. "I'm damned if I want a flood down here. Get some trees and boulders against it up the draw. I know nothing's going to save us from getting some of it, but we don't want it all. I know we can send most of it off to the south," Cartrell insisted. "Push the cattle west. The water will not go west." Of course, he could order Charlie to do it.

"If you can veer it off, you're a bloody magician," Sandon snapped testily, turning to leave. "When that lake up there gives out, which I don't think'll happen, you better run like a son-of-a-bitch, Ian, 'cause no matter what you build to divert the water, it ain't never goin' to go where you want it to. That's my last word on it." He huffed. "I'll move my cattle where I want."

Cartrell sighed, partly in bitter resignation, but also out of impatience with Sandon. "Instinct tells me you're partly right, but I have to try." He removed his glasses and, tipping the chair back against the wall, sat in deep contemplation, twirling the glasses between his thumb and fingers. "Charlie, get your men and teams together. We're going up there tomorrow."

Any chance to avert the looming disaster was removed from them during the night. The intense daytime heat and a downpour of rain in the early evening brought the dam down. It cascaded along the ravine, breaking out across the flat in minutes, filling the lake. It was the destructive monster that Cartrell knew it would be. Boulders rolling with timber slags crashing against the buildings. Bean's original cabin, the livery barn, corrals, McAllister's tack shed, and the abandoned general store all succumbed to the power of the flood's tremendous force.

The few residents of Skaha were jarred from their sleep by the outfall as it roared its way down from the ravine, dumping its massive flow upon the flats. The swirling sounds of rushing torrents tore around the remaining buildings and out across the fields and pastures.

Upon its crest rode small outbuildings; cattle, pigs and chickens struggled to survive. Horses screamed within the confining stalls of the livery, some breaking loose as part of the old building collapsed. As if in a final lash, the tide forced Llewellyn's new Buick from the collapsed barn, tossing it over onto its hood and leaving it upside down in the mud. Destruction was everywhere on the ranch.

The rain continued as the meadows emptied.

In the quiet aftermath, Cartrell trudged gloomily through the water and debris toward Llewellyn's residence. Muck splashed over his high rubber boots onto his trousers. With the rain, the morning sky was dark and foreboding. The structure housing his office and apartment remained on its footings, but the wide step had been torn away. Llewellyn's house was lower, but still better off than some of the original buildings. The veranda, ripped apart, had allowed the rush of water into the entrance, spilling over the main floor. Cartrell climbed the inside stairs with Sydney, entered Llewellyn's den, and took up the binoculars.

The devastation he saw was unbelievable. Like his own house, most of the log buildings of earlier decades remained upright, but bare of their steps and porches, with some windows shattered. Llewellyn's livery was partly collapsed. The car was overturned. The carriages of earlier decades were on their sides. Some of the horses wandered aimlessly about, others had disappeared into the hills. Cattle were bunched on the lower knolls.

Cartrell focussed the lens to watch Sandon and two cowboys disappear into what was left of the livery. Suddenly he lowered the glasses, glanced down at Sydney, then raised them to his eyes once more. "It can't be," he whispered. ""They just brought a body out of the barn."

When Cartrell arrived at the scene, he discovered that it was Holinger. Still clutched in his hand was the knife which the elderly blacksmith had used to cut the ropes off the trapped horses. Cartrell covered his eyes and felt sorrow over such devotion."Why did he try? An old man—"

Beside him Sandon answered curtly, "You don't know how he felt about horses, and he knew that the lumber wouldn't hold up. These boards ain't like the old logs. There's no strength in them." Staring down at Holinger, he added sorrowfully, "A beam fell on his head and the rest collapsed on him."

Cartrell was saddened. The old blacksmith had been at the ranch a long time, when it was just a crossing. Skaha would seem very empty now, with his passing, as it had when Two Way left them.

Visions of reconstruction and the expense to rebuild the ranch threatened to overwhelm Cartrell. He told himself that he must be getting old to shrink in the face of such a task; but fifty-four could hardly be considered old, he knew, and he had never yet turned away from responsibility. Still, he reflected, it would be an enormous help if he were not saddled with the older men with whom he must share the burden. What I wouldn't give right now, he wished forlornly, for a fresh, young face in the picture.

For the first time since Thomas' enlistment, Cartrell wondered where the young man was, and if he was well.

A common residence was set up at the lodge after it was cleaned.

Amazingly, the little church remained undamaged despite the fact that its location was adjacent to the creek. Cartrell preferred not to consider it the miracle Sydney did.

"Preserved," she had declared, "by the hand of God", to which Cartrell replied, "More likely because it was located with its back against the tide, upon a cemented rock foundation."

Wagons of supplies organized by Dick Foderow were hauled up to Skaha. The teamster remained behind to assist in the clean-up. The work continued to be slowed by persistent summer rains, driving Cartrell to near madness and Sydney into exhaustion.

After the solemn burial of Holinger in the graveyard on the rise east of the ranch, reconstruction quickly began. Suddenly the lodge was filled with extra hired hands. Pickle Bill complained, although happily enough, about the extra cooking. Alongside other women, Sydney cleared the buildings and cleaned furniture, walls and floors. Salvaging clothing, she rubbed until her fingers were raw against the scrub board, and rocked the tub of her washing machine until her arms ached. Dishes and cooking equipment were dug from the mud in some places, but most personal keepsakes were either lost or ruined.

Eventually, homes were once more livable. Cartrell worked twenty hours a day, while Llewellyn watched the activities through the Jena lens, with a mind as unwilling as his body had become.

Wagon loads of lumber from the mill on the flats of Dog Lake appeared at the ranch. Teams pulled scrapers over the drying land. Boulders and trees were hauled away and the ruined timber put to the torch. A pall of smoke hung above the valley of the white lake. In the mountains, the dam was rebuilt, and the creek bed was cleared of debris and then deepened, leaving a channel of rocks through which the normal flow meandered southward.

The summer was filled with frenzied activity. Cartrell informed Sydney, "You're going to have to stay at the office all the time for awhile. I cannot manage everything. The new car will arrive soon and, I do believe," he chuckled, "I'll be forced to teach you to drive the thing."

"Impossible!"

"Why?"

"It's not ladylike for one thing and—"

"That's old fashioned and you know it, Sydney."

"Albert would never allow it."

Cartrell looked directly into Sydney's eyes. "When did you ever do what Albert told you? Now, drive the car you will, dear heart, because I need you to learn." The matter was settled. Beside her, he told her softly, "To be a driver and a secretary are not the only reasons I need you near me. Apart, we are slowly destroying each other."

"Together, Ian," Sydney replied emotionally, "we destroy two others."

In October, Cartrell and his daughters travelled to Kamloops for a week-long visit with Belle. The disease was slowly exhausting Belle's strength. Her appearance hardly resembled that of the bright, saucy Southern woman he had married. Her vitality and the youthful lines of her face and body had been a winning asset for her. Now her thinness produced a gaunt, wasted form, and Cartrell's heart ached for her loss. She looked appallingly old and tired. The raking sound of her cough made him vow not to bring the girls to visit their mother again. Cartrell returned to Skaha very upset.

The new car, another Buick, arrived in April 1917. Sydney refused to take instructions until July, when the rainy season was over with and the ground was dry. The weather co-operated.

As Sydney slipped into the driver's place in the car, Cartrell instructed her, "Just keep a good grip on the steering wheel. Any little rock or rut will pull the car all over the road. So hold tight. You know about the throttle and about the brakes. Go ahead now."

"Except," she reminded him, "I cannot turn the crank. That abominable starting contraption takes a man's strength."

"Sydney," Cartrell smiled affectionately, "assistance constantly hovers at your elbow. Where there's you, there is always a man nearby to help."

"All the same, I'd feel awfully stupid if I were left stranded."

"Let me assure you, that will never happen! Now take hold," he suggested, "and we'll spin about the ranch and thrill everyone with your ability."

As Sydney motored along the roadway toward the lodge, a group of cowboys gathered outside on the steps and vigorously clapped their hands, whistling and waving their approval as she and Cartrell passed by.

"What did I tell you?" Cartrell grinned. "Admirers everywhere. A fan club already and you're not even off the ranch."

Sydney pursed her lips together. "You're making fun of me!"

"Would I do that?" he teased.

Sydney stopped the car abruptly and, in so doing, stalled the thing.

Cartrell pinched his lips together and scowled in her direction. "Now, why did you do that?" he asked slowly, trying to curb his impatience.

Sydney bit nervously at her lip. "Sometimes Ian, your humour hurts. You think you're funny, but you're really not!"

"What did I say wrong?"

"You know you made fun of me!"

Cartrell reached over and covered her trembling hand with his. "Sydney, what has brought this on? My humour never hurts you." His voice was soft and gentle. "It seems that you've lost your sense of wit."

Sydney withdrew her hand from beneath his. "I never had a sense of wit and you know it."

Leaning back against the leather upholstery, Cartrell watched Sydney thoughtfully. The breeze had blown her honey-coloured hair into loose strands which fell carelessly over her ears and along her slim neck. Beautiful until the day she dies, he thought. It is the wasting away which causes her irritability. All the needs of the human mind and body are denied her, and the weight of that denial is slowly pulling her down. "Sydney, dear heart–" he whispered.

Turning quickly, she met his eyes. "I want to come to you–"

"Then do."

"And you?"

"You know I wait," he replied softly. "You know–"

Sydney fell silent beside him. There was no need for words between them. Each was aware of what the other felt; it did not have to be told. In time, Cartrell stepped down from the vehicle and walked around to the front. Loosening his vest and rolling up the sleeves of his white shirt, he began to swing the handle of the metal crank. The car started and spluttered into a consistent hum while Cartrell climbed back in. "Sydney, it's time to drive us back home," he told her gently.

In the middle of the night when she could not sleep, while memories plagued her conscience, Sydney reached for her diary and wrote:

"His wife is dying and my husband awaits the same. Forgive us Lord, for what Ian and I begin this night."

Then she dressed and quietly left the house.

When Cartrell opened his door and saw her - for he had waited for her - his desperate need of her and his loneliness suddenly overwhelmed him. He reached out and clasped her tightly against his chest, and buried his face into the soft lengths of her hair on her shoulder and neck. A sense of great happiness seized him.

In July, Cartrell was invited, on Llewellyn's behalf, to attend a meeting of South Valley Development, an association newly-formed by several prominent businessmen. Its purpose was to make arable tracts of land available to men wishing to take up farming in a small way. Albert Llewellyn's property, the vast triangle between Marron Valley, Twin Lakes and Fairview, caught the attention of the developers involved.

Following the meeting, Cartrell climbed the stairs to Llewellyn's den with news of a large undertaking. Alma Davies brought them coffee and fresh cinnamon rolls and, when he had complimented her, he turned his attention to Albert.

From a hunched position in his chair, Llewellyn snapped, "A meeting about what? Did you tell me you were going to a meeting?"

Llewellyn was in a miserable mood, the accountant realized. "It has simply slipped your mind, Albert. Now, they are interested in acreage for small ranches and hay fields where, of course, there is available water. Natural springs have to be relied upon. There are several good-sized lakes in this valley. We already have a fair system for the ranch. For certain areas on this bench, irrigation could be controlled by flumes."

Setting aside his empty cup, Cartrell added, "In a nutshell, they want a fair piece of your range between here and Fairview. There's hundreds of acres of flat and low rolling land that could be made more productive than it presently is." He paused a moment, thinking. "Now, for that community called Kaleden along Dog Lake, where they're planting orchards, they've implemented an irrigation system by building a proper dam in the hills north of us."

Llewellyn leaned so far forward in his chair to stare at Cartrell that the accountant feared he would fall over onto the floor. His face was red and appeared bloated. "I don't care what's going on somewhere else. What am I to do with my cattle? For every one of those acres, I have quality beef depending on them."

Cartrell mentally assessed Skaha's herd of over four hundred Shorthorn, Black Angus and Hereford; it was a mix of McAllister's herd and Llewellyn's. Long ago, the original Durham of the trapper's herd had been weeded out and replaced with more substantial breeds. "You actually have excess land, Albert. You could decrease your stock; specialize in just one breed."

Llewellyn sat aghast in his chair. His head ached furiously, causing him great discomfort. "What're you telling me? Decrease, you say?" he snapped. "I spent a lifetime building everything, and I'm told now by some fresh upstart, to get rid of it all?" He broke into a coughing spell, spluttering and gasping for breath, and spitting noisily into his handkerchief.

Cartrell closed his eyes against the repulsive sight and sounds.

"I'm not a doddering old fool, I remind you, Ian, that some hot-shot

developer can come here and say 'Out with you, I need your land!'"
He rubbed at the back of his head, willing away the pain which
bothered him. He realized that with his consent to their plan, he
perpetrated further, the end of Skaha, the town.

"Albert, nobody's telling you to get out, just to get serious. The role
of the large landowner and cattle baron in this valley is diminishing.
The downsizing of the Ellis Ranch proves that. You could perhaps do
better specializing with less numbers, than keep a whole lot of mixed
breeds using up the grass, some of them producing nothing. There's
a new type of ranching, farming–"

"I don't believe you!"

"All you have to do is turn your binoculars away from your
backyard and my office once, and look at the barren hillsides that
make up your range, and you'll see the results of overgrazing. You're
not alone in the blame. Dave McAllister was, too. So are many other
ranchers." Cartrell sighed heavily. "Who would've thought years ago
that the sea of tall grass which attracted all of you to this valley,
would become the thing that undoes you - a land of dry, broken
stubble that happened, though it's hard to believe, in only a few
decades."

"You're exaggerating," Llewellyn accused angrily.

Cartrell leaned forward in his chair, meeting Llewellyn's eyes. "Can
I explain something to you, Albert, about your own condition and the
situation it imposes on others?"

"You will anyway," Llewellyn sulked and turned away, leaving the
best side of his face to Cartrell's view. The thick panes of the window
reflected the stifling heat of the day and the room was very warm.

"My concern is in your best interests," Ian told him.

"That's questionable."

Ian Cartrell sank against the back of his chair, covered his eyes
and wondered why he bothered. When he looked up, he slowly
scanned the room. He saw his employer's life recorded in every
corner - the wood carving of a pair of Percherons and a freight wagon
done for him by the blacksmith Holinger. The black Jena lens
purchased for gazing over the flats of Skaha and through which the
man had dreamed his dreams. At the end of the long room, in a
glassed cabinet, were three rifles which had been used by the
teamsters on the freight wagons. In a corner hung a fine leather
chest band filled with shells. Other notable memorabilia hung on the
walls. Cartrell glanced again at the guns leaning against the plush
upholstery of their polished cabinet. An uneasy feeling crept through
him. He brushed it aside momentarily and cleared his throat to draw
the other's attention.

"Albert," he began. "It's really a matter of whether you want to go on like this, or even how long you can. Your stroke shifted everything to Dick Foderow and myself. Sandon's an old man now. Kennedy wants an orchard of his own. I'm overloaded with work. Sydney's at a breaking point. I know Mrs. Davies takes care of you, but the real burden is on your wife. We are not getting any younger."

"If that goddamned war ever ends, Tom'll bc home to take over."

"He may someday shake our world up, but not in the manner that you hope. I doubt that he'll settle down much. I could be proven wrong, mind you," Cartrell mused and prayed that would be the case.

Sydney arrived with fresh coffee and, though uninvited, took a chair in the corner near the door.

Leaning forward in his wheelchair, from beneath a knitted brow Llewellyn's watery eyes stared accusingly into Cartrell's. "So tell me-- what do you want me to do? Die?"

"First of all, get it out of your head that any land company is out to steal your property. Your problems--"

"Which I don't have," Llewellyn interjected.

"--your problems can be shed to the advantage of others, in that selling off some of your range, decreasing the herd, bringing it all back into perspective once more, seems sensible." From the corner of an eye Cartrell watched Sydney's growing interest in the conversation; saw doubt move into her eyes. "Think about it, at least. You could build a house downtown," he continued. "You'd be close to the freight sheds and other people. Tom likes the ranch. Alone up here, who knows how he might turn out. When he returns, let him manage it. Lease the orchard to Alfred. With the freight and the ranch, you still have ample income. You can afford a new house and keep Mrs. Davies, as well."

Silence prevailed in the room for a long, tense moment. "Something else that you should realize, Albert, is the prominence the automobile is gaining in these parts. In time you will have to consider serious changes in freighting." He glanced in Sydney's direction, but did not meet her open, enquiring gaze.

Sydney coughed delicately to catch Cartrell's attention. "What are you saying, Ian?"

"That the truck will soon replace the freight team."

"No, not that. About selling--"

"I'm telling Albert that his situation, and yours, can be made a little more comfortable if he wishes. An interest has been shown in some areas of your rangeland between Twin Lakes and Fairview." Turning toward Albert, Cartrell informed him, "Tomorrow I'm going up to Kamloops. Think about it while I'm away, Albert. Talk it over with Sydney. You don't have to make changes instantly, but it's something to consider when Tom returns." With hesitation registering in his voice, he elaborated, "If you don't make the changes you want now, he'll do them for you and probably not in the way they should be made."

Llewellyn caught the warning and laughed bitterly. "That is a fact." His voice was hoarse and he sounded very unhappy. "I might sell the orchard before he does it behind my back, but I'll not move away from here and give you free rein with everything else."

Cartrell rose and stood beside Llewellyn's chair, tall and straight. He appeared intimidating to Llewellyn. "You gave me a free rein the night you had your stroke, Albert. There was nothing else you could do. I've never advised you wrongly and I've always conducted your business in your best interests. So don't talk foolishly to me now about free rein and distrust." Abruptly, Cartrell picked up his hat, turned on his heel and left the room.

Sydney bolted from her chair, gathered up her voluminous skirt and flew out of the room after him. "Are you angry with him?" she asked hurriedly. "I wouldn't blame you."

As he went down the stairs ahead of her, Cartrell turned slightly and suggested, "Sydney, I advise you to get rid of those guns in Albert's room." He pulled his jacket over his vest and did up the buttons. "Get Dick to come up and take them away."

"You really are angry with him for some reason." Her eyes were wide, wondering, as she quickly followed behind him.

Cartrell shook his head. "Not with him. Not with anyone, really. Just with circumstances."

"I know he doesn't want to sell anything."

"He doesn't have to."

"I don't want to move either, Ian." Searching his dark eyes when they reached the bottom of the stairs, she caught his arm and questioned, "Why do you want me to move?"

"I don't."

Sydney frowned. "Well– I don't understand, Ian."

"Another time, I'll explain, Sydney."

Anxiety showed in her face. "I didn't know you were going to Kamloops so soon again." She reached out to hold the door open when he had passed through to the new veranda.

Cartrell fell quiet for a moment. Then searching her eyes deeply, compelling her to look into the depths of his own, he told her, "I've had news, late yesterday, that Belle has passed away."

Sydney's hand tightened against the edge of the door. She struggled to absorb his words.

Cartrell stepped back into the hallway. "Sydney, it's awfully hard for me to explain how I feel at this moment." His voice was steady. "My wife, who was a good wife, has just slipped away from me and

I feel a great deal of sadness about that. Yet, I stand here as totally in love with you as when I first saw you at Skaha, and I remember only the sweetest moments I've shared with you." Slowly he placed his hat upon his head, fitting it in place. "Strangely, you've been the only woman I've held truly, in a special place in my heart, even though I know I'm one among a few in yours. I should resent that, but I don't."

When he noticed quick tears spring into her hurt, blue eyes, he reached out to gently brush them away with his thumb. "I did not say that to hurt you, dear heart. Sadly, your Lord saw fit to give us partners who needed our strengths. With your faith, maybe in the end, He will give us each other."

In the stillness, Sydney's whisper was choked with emotion. "We have each other now."

In the privacy of the narrow hallway, Cartrell leaned down and held her face tenderly between his hands. "It is not enough," he whispered, brushing her lips softly with his own before departing.

The poignancy of the moment was broken with the quiet closing of the door. Sydney leaned against the wall for a moment to gather her thoughts. Then quickly she darted to the window to watch Cartrell as he walked away from the house and across the yard to his office. She noticed the slight stoop to his tall figure. "The weight of all our lives–" she whispered to no one. All the decisions our existence causes rest unfairly on his shoulders, when he has so much of his own. Has his love for me now become a burden also?

Across the distant fields Sydney could see the trail of dust which signalled the arrival of Dick Foderow on the freight wagon. Beneath the hot summer sun, Charlie Sandon rode out from the forest, arriving at the ranch for supplies for cow-camp. They met on the trail, Sandon and the teamster, and exchanged greetings.

Cartrell stopped, watched them for a moment, then climbed the steps to his office. He felt very sad and wished not to be caught up in conversation with either man.

Sydney turned away from the window. "Albert?" she called as she gathered her skirt to prevent stumbling, and ascended the stairs to the den. "Did Ian tell you that Belle has died?"

Llewellyn glanced in her direction. "No."

She looked down at her husband in his chair. "Doesn't that tell you something, Albert? That Ian places our problems before his own, always? He is going to Kamloops to bring her home for burial."

"He should've told me," Albert mumbled, not really caring that Cartrell had not mentioned the death. He could not recall Belle, so casually dismissed the subject of her passing. There were more important matters on his mind at the moment.

As Sydney watched her husband push himself around the large room in the wheelchair Cartrell had been able to obtain for him, she was struck by the lack of compassion he exhibited, the self-centeredness which he had lately shown.

"Albert?" she asked slowly. "Do you remember how it used to be with us? How happy we once were? And the life we shared in the beginning?"

Llewellyn rummaged through the papers in the drawers of his desk, mumbling to himself, "I wonder when that damned Tom'll get himself back here. We sure as hell need him on the place. I need firmer hands on the reins."

Sydney frowned. "Albert– what are you looking for?"

"My will."

"Your will? Well, it's with Ian, of course, for safekeeping." Sydney turned away. Behind her the shuffling of paper and slamming of drawers continued. She felt weary of everything.

Through the window she watched a hawk circle above the outbuildings of the ranch. The sky was clear, a brilliant blue cap above a warm, cozy valley. She wondered where her son was, and what the world was to him at this moment. She read the local papers regularly for the news about the war, but often reports were late or conflicting in content and did not adequately inform her of the exact turn of events, or hint of her son's whereabouts.

Come home, Thomas, she pleaded silently. No one needs you more than me.

13

Thomas Llewellyn was a tall man, standing six foot two. His body had filled out, becoming taut and muscular. Though of fair skin, he had tanned deeply from constant exposure to weather. His eyes had become searching depths full of thought; his mouth, less pinched with resentment, now more sensitive. Wounds to his left shoulder had healed and pained him rarely. As he lounged against the upholstery of his seat on the train, the constant clickity-click of the wheels of the railway coach against steel track soothed him toward sleep. It seemed the trip home was passing slowly.

The train carrying returning troops from overseas had left Halifax three days before and to Thomas' reckoning, they were not yet half way across Canada. He watched the colourful, fresh April-spring landscape swish by. Sometimes quick flashes of gunfire, crumbling towers, narrow damp trenches and broken, distorted bodies assailed his mind, momentarily blotting out the pleasant scenery before him. Unexpectedly at times, these unpleasant memories thrashed about his brain, but he was usually able to push them aside. In their place, he allowed thoughts of his mother, the ranch and even Cartrell, to roam. He recognized that loneliness, his old enemy, still lurked within and, that the years away at war had not changed that.

He got up and walked to the end of the car, stepping out onto the small railed platform. The air was refreshing. Presently another soldier joined him, lighting his cigarette. He offered the packet to Thomas.

"One habit I never picked up. Thanks anyway," Thomas smiled.

The packet was stowed away and the young man leaned against the rail beside Thomas. "Seems strange to be away from it; back on home soil."

"It'll seem stranger to be at the ranch when I get there."

"A fella wonders if he can actually pick up where he left off, or if somebody's taken up his place." He turned toward Thomas and extended his hand. "Name's Rick Dietrich."

"Tom Llewellyn."

"From Williams Lake. You?"

"Penticton. A ranch just south of it."

"Wife?"

"No." Visions of Marjorie Spencer floated across Thomas' brain. "Never got that far," he replied solemnly.

"Well, I got me a fine little wife to introduce," Dietrich boasted, his grin as broad as his face. "Her sister-in-law to boot. Don't know how Mom'll take to two other women about the place, but it won't be for long I hope. Mom's not exactly a welcoming person. She doesn't cotton to too much interference in her way of life. We live on a ranch too, so maybe it's big enough to keep us out of each other's way." He laughed at his own words but, nonetheless, felt a concern about his mother's reaction. "In one of her letters to me, she wrote she didn't want me bringing home one of 'them war brides', and now that's exactly what I've gone and done!"

Thomas glanced across at Richard Dietrich, who was almost his height. "You hardly seem old enough to be married. And your sister-in-law?"

"The wife's sister-in-law, actually." Dietrich dropped his cigarette butt and stepped on it, snuffing it against the steel floor. "War rushes things, you know. At twenty-two, I'm married. I know I'll never regret it. Joanie's a wonderful girl. This is a big change for her, coming here, but at least I was able to come with her. Met her in a hospital in England last year after I got a foot blown off. Stuck right along with me she did, so we up one day and got married."

Thomas' reaction was to glance down at Dietrich's boots. Of course, he thought, embarrassed, I'd never be able to tell one is missing. "Nell– the sister-in-law, is a widow," he heard Dietrich say, then add, "Well, be seeing you. Nice meeting you."

"Yeah, same here."

"I'll introduce you to the womenfolk inside if you're in the mood for visiting. Next car up." Dietrich disappeared into the interior of the coach as the train continued to move across the widening landscape. We're getting close to Winnipeg, Thomas decided. A happy chap, that Dietrich. A German name. I wonder how much guff he had to take because of it.

Returning to his own car, he settled against the seat. Beside him a corporal shuffled a worn deck of cards. Low rolling hills, greenery of the late spring season, farms and small Manitoba villages passed before his eyes. Was this the path into the unknown, that great road to the far west that his parents had travelled thirty years before? How well he knew their story! His father had many times reminded him of hardships suffered; the beginnings, the sacrifices, and the labour. One would have thought his father had reached the peak of his success entirely by his own measure.

His mother had told their story in a different way. Her moments of nostalgia brought memories of the ocean crossing, the wagon they had travelled in across an empty prairie, the great mountain pass with enormous glacier-clad peaks, and wide green fertile valleys through which ran the rivers of the land. A dreamer's landscape perhaps, an artist's painting, a writer's story; but when told by his mother, the scene was brought to life, and he could sense the will in her to make her world completely right. Was it possible that those days were the happiest she had known with his father?

It amazed him that the journey he had made with his parents, which had taken many months of hardship, could now be travelled by him in a mere six days of comfort. There was no one there he could share the story with; the other men would hardly believe that he had crossed the continent in a covered farm wagon and climbed a mountain pass in a saddle, curled in his mother's arms.

How much had his parents changed in the three years he had been away? What did they expect of him? They would anticipate something, it was certain. How would he see Skaha now? It hardly seemed believable that the demise of his small town had taken most of the years of his youth to happen, when in Europe, he saw whole cities reduced to nothing in less than one week. Thomas looked out at the prairie in deep thought, barely aware of the car crowded with boisterous soldiers passing the time with cards and song.

At Winnipeg the train was delayed four hours. There was a derailment somewhere, they were told. Soldiers and civilians converged upon the gateway city. As Thomas stepped down from his coach, he was met by Richard Dietrich. With a natural warm exuberance, Dietrich presented the women accompanying him.

"Pleased if you'd join us, Tom. This here young lady's my wife, Joanie. This is her sister-in-law, Nell Windsor. Ladies, I give you Tom Llewellyn." Dietrich waved his arm outward in an elaborate flourish, to Thomas' embarrassment.

Thomas nodded, took the warm hand of Nell in his and, without smiling, replied simply, "Hello, ma'am." He knew they were being paired by Dietrich, but he did not feel put upon because of it.

The woman, he noticed, was tall and slim with fine, regular features; not pretty, but of average good looks. Her face was surrounded by an abundance of dark, wavy hair. She favoured him with an engaging smile, which told him to make the best of it. Actually, Thomas decided, he did not mind. He had four hours to kill and the idea of spending it in her company seemed very appealing.

They strolled along the city streets, looking through the busy shops and purchasing lunch to take to a nearby park. While Dietrich and his wife fed the noisy waterfowl at the pond, Nell sat upon the grass. Thomas sat down beside her. How did one begin? I'm horribly out of practice. With Marjorie, knowledge of her had simply happened. Be direct, he told himself, and henceforth asked, "Why did you come to Canada? Here, you have no one to begin with. I know you're a widow."

"I can't answer that. I simply made the decision and purchased passage." His abruptness failed to bother her. She was used to it, for she had learned that most men were abrupt, simply by nature. In return, she pried, "Why are you not married already? I mean, before the war. I'm sure you must be nearly thirty."

Thomas grinned, raising his hands in mock defence. "I wasted the years of my youth embroiled in rebellion, aggravating my parents and Cartrell, and everyone else for that matter." He stretched out upon the grass, linking his hands beneath his head. Toward the sky, he said quietly, "However, I suppose it's really because she died."

After a moment, Nell Windsor whispered, "I'm sorry."

Thomas rolled his head to one side to look at her. "And I'm sorry about your husband. It sort of puts us in the same basket, doesn't it." He met her brown eyes and held them. He enjoyed the fact that she had been watching him all the while. He felt strongly attracted to her and did not deny it.

"Who is Cartrell? You mentioned him."

"My family's business manager. The boss of the place since Dad had his stroke."

"Stroke?"

"I got the blame for that, too."

Suddenly Nell giggled, a delightfully girlish sound which thrilled Thomas' heart. Her smile was bright when she told him, "Strokes aren't caused by people. They happen for medical reasons." She turned on the grass, stretched her legs out before her and leaned back against her elbows."

"Try and tell Cartrell that. What're you going to do when you get to Rick's?"

"Get work as fast as I can and move out on my own, of course." She became pensive. "The last thing I want is to be a burden on anyone. Rick is a fine person. Means well. Life is a breeze to him. He doesn't think of complications. The fact that he has one foot missing means little. He simply replaced it with a false one and walked on. He sets an example for me, that there is something, some special corner in this world for everyone." She smiled down at Thomas. "I'm boring you."

That had to be the last thing she was doing to him, and he told her so. Thomas wanted to reach out and hold her hand in his, to allow the obvious warmth of her personality to flow through him and mellow his narrow, guarded self. Watching her, as she sat tugging gently at the long grass around them, he thought, if she smiles at me once more, I'll reach up and kiss her. To his disappointment, Nell rose to her feet and brushed the loose grass from her skirt, indicating that it was now time for them to be back at the station. As they boarded the train, Thomas thanked her for her company. She had completely captivated him, he admitted and did not want their new friendship to end.

During the evening Thomas made his way to the car where the Dietrichs and Nell were housed and asked Nell to accompany him on the platform. It was cool, so she bundled herself into a warm coat and stepped out into the night with him. The steady wind produced by the train's speed tugged at them and he put his arm around her, drawing her close. She moved nearer willingly, wordlessly, recognizing the attraction which they had avoided earlier in the day.

She had known the joy of love with her husband, suffered the sorrow of loss, and cried the tears of loneliness and despair through two empty years. What this new man's life had been before, Nell had no way of knowing, but she quickly realized that this was no young, foolish romance which would begin and end with their journey across the continent. There was something about Thomas being beside her which let her know that. She felt comfortable with him, even though they had met only hours before.

Tall and slim, she fit nicely beside him. When he turned and kissed her on the mouth, she responded with a natural longing for an intimacy denied her. He took her arms, placed them about his neck and held her face between his gentle hands. No words were needed, no explanations offered, no reassurance necessary. The women in his life had been few, for his hesitant approach toward them had done little to encourage relationships. Now, long-buried response flooded him as his mouth found hers again and again, and he understood her longing.

They remained together beside the railing as the train clicked through the night. The wind blew her soft, silky hair across his face, and suddenly Thomas whispered to her in the dark, "Will you marry me in Vancouver?"

On the chill, night air rode her faint, but happy reply, "Yes. Oh, yes."

Upon his return to the Okanagan, Thomas was shocked to find his life empty of Charlie Sandon and Rachel McAllister. They had been his lifetime associates. It was impossible for him to believe that the deadly influenza reached into such little corners of the country as Skaha, even though he recognized they were only two of many thousand Canadians who had lost their lives to it. Without Charlie Sandon, Thomas was bereft of a comfortable return home.

As Thomas walked with Ian one evening, toward Cartrell's house, he lamented, "Not to be met by Charlie at the gate is like looking down to suddenly see one of your hands missing. I grew up with that man holding my hand."

"And here, all the time I thought it was me who did the holding," Cartrell chuckled.

"You did the leading."

"Well, I must say you took your time at returning. Most of the local chaps were back some time ago." Glancing across at Thomas he added, "But of course, you stopped off to get married and try to settle elsewhere." Cartrell smiled. "I can't imagine you proposing marriage within a few hours of meeting. And getting married within days!"

Thomas looked around at Cartrell. "Does that put you out?"

"It does surprise me. There is such a thing as a telephone now, you know. A message could have been left for us at the store downtown."

They had reached the small veranda of Cartrell's house. Thomas halted, placing a restraining hand on the other man's arm. Meeting Cartrell's eyes directly, for he was the same height, Thomas asked testily, "Us?" His pause was a brief one. "Actually Ian, what does it matter to you? Why do I always have the feeling that I must account to you, notify you first or even at all, of everything that goes on in my life?" The moment was not particularly tense.

Cartrell's eyes narrowed, but did not waver. "Because you are the son I never had," he said boldly. "I've told you that before. When your father suffered his first stroke, the concern of your welfare, and your mother's, was instantly shifted to me. Your mother never questioned it."

"For heaven's sake, she's never questioned anything you do, and that irritates me. She should," he said through tight lips, "instead of always just drifting along."

"Why?" Cartrell remained calm. "Am I destructive to her?"

Thomas watched the other man for a long, rigid moment. He could not readily answer. Suddenly he realized something which he now supposed that he must always have known; that Cartrell, through all these years, had breathed into his mother the life which his father had slowly taken from her throughout their turbulent marriage. In silent resignation, Thomas stepped aside to leave the yard.

"Tom! Answer me," Cartrell commanded gently from the shadows of the veranda. "With honesty."

In the stillness of the evening, Thomas stated slowly, knowing that he was not wrong, "I believe my mother has always loved you in some way, Ian, from the very beginning. And seeing her now, I can't say as I'm right to disagree," he admitted.

"Come on in," Cartrell suggested.

The two men entered the dark house. Cartrell lit a lamp, placing it at the centre of the table, and indicated for Thomas to take a chair.

"Now let's abandon talk of flu and marriage," he said flatly. "And strive toward working together since we have no other choice. I no longer involve your father in decisions as his mind is often so atrociously vacant that it's not worth the frustration he causes me. The state of his health is deplorable and Harold Stobie says he doesn't know what kept Albert from surrendering to the flu last year. I'd like to know in time, Tom, what your plans are. The burden of the freight, the ranch, and orchard management now rests on your shoulders where it belongs."

Cartrell went about making coffee for them. "We have a labour problem developing, because men like yourself returning from overseas are taking up on new land, going into business for themselves, or remaining in the cities. The Indians are becoming independent, working their own land and, like you, getting back from overseas. There is an over-grazing problem and we have to decrease the herd and practice better range management to solve it."

Thomas interrupted. "Add to that, that we also have an orchard to get rid of."

"In anticipation of that being your first move, I have discussed the matter with Kennedy, and a price has been tentatively agreed upon. It rests between you and your father, whether you sell it. You do not have power of attorney yet. I do, with your mother."

"What's stopping you then? Sell it!"

"I am reluctant to dispose of lucrative properties. To get rid of over-grazed rangeland that you are no longer using is reasonable," Cartrell explained, "but to dump a paying project doesn't make sense. Regarding the freight, Dick and I have talked about buying a truck or two. It's a move you'll soon have to make."

Thomas considered the possibility for a moment. "A fleet of trucks," he murmured, the idea clearly appealing to him. "There's no such thing as a wagon and team in the east anymore, only in remote areas."

"I would believe it." Turning to the younger man, Cartrell spoke very seriously. "You are a fairly well-off man, Thomas Llewellyn. Not over-much, but comfortably so. However, it's all in property, and a man can become property poor if he's not careful. I'm only fifty-six years old, so I've a lot of years left in which to help you, but it's really up to you to keep it going. I'm trusting your interest in the place is at its best. You can begin by allowing your mother to teach Nell something of the office, so she can retire to a well-deserved rest. She's carried quite a burden and she's beginning to feel the strain."

Thomas resented the possessiveness in Cartrell's voice. He turned toward the window and stared out to the darkening horizon. He contemplated the future and concluded, a little to his relief, that it was already planned for him. God has decreed my pathway in life on two occasions, he told himself, when He took Harrie from us and allowed me to survive the war.

14

The valley was rapidly changing in scenery and pace. Mechanical technology, rapidly expanding industry and population increase demanded alteration and development. Skaha was not exempt. Thomas sold the thirty-two acre orchard to Alfred Kennedy, who welcomed the independence it afforded him. The southern-most acres of rangeland were purchased by several returning veterans.

The first Provincial Bull Sale took place March 26, 1919 at Kamloops. It drew Cartrell's attention and he decided that Thomas should be in attendance in the spring of 1920. As it was beyond Cartrell to judge a good productive bull from a freeloader with any amount of accuracy and, as he lacked confidence in Thomas' assessments, he called in a recognized examiner. Five bulls were selected from Llewellyn's herd. With winter behind them and the selection having been made, the trip got underway.

Thomas enjoyed the feeling of freedom he was experiencing, though was still acutely aware of Cartrell's dogmatic determination at the helm. Everything Thomas craved in himself, he recognized in Cartrell.

Two cowboys from the ranch, John Strickland and Bud Smith, accompanied him on the trip. They had been on the place since Luke Dalhousie and Jim Roper left, when David McAllister died. They were knowledgeable and had behind them more years of experience than any of the others on the place. Thomas needed that kind of support.

Winter's chill still hung in the air but, with a promise of an early spring aboard, Skaha's old bulls were, with luck, held together and driven down from White Lake to Penticton. They were then loaded into a railway cattle car and transported by barge up Okanagan Lake to Okanagan Landing. Travelling by rail from the Landing, they finally reached their destination at Kamloops.

The bull sale had only one year behind it when Llewellyn, Strickland and Smith attended. The first sale had taken place at the C.P.R. stockyards in Mission Flats, located on the west side of the Thompson River. Strong, high pens contained the mean-tempered range bulls. They were ungroomed, with horns not trained. To train a young bull's horns to grow downward instead of outward, weights would be placed over the tip until the proper slope of the horn was achieved. The danger of injury was thereby reduced. However, the interest of most cattlemen was in quantity, rather than quality. That attitude would change as the industry developed.

The newly-built Agricultural Hall in Riverside Park on the banks of the wide Thompson River, was the chosen centre for the March, 1920 sale. Due to the angry nature of most of the bulls and disruption during the previous sale, it had been ruled that all owners handle their own animals in the ring. That meant that the Skaha men would have to bring the bulls out by halter. Lengthy practice sessions had been carried out at Skaha between Thomas, Strickland and Smith, and the five ornery bulls.

Moderately satisfied, the iron-muscled Strickland commented, "Well, we'll never win a best behaviour award, but I do believe we'll get the bastards into that arena when we're s'posed to!"

At the sale, Thomas associated with ranchers from the enormous Douglas Lake Ranch, and with others whose spreads were far greater in size than Skaha would ever be. Information gleaned from their conversations would inspire ambition in him.

Away from Cartrell, Thomas enjoyed the vanity of other men addressing him as one of themselves. At the sale he saw Angus, Hereford, Shorthorn and some Red Poll judged. He learned the importance of proper breeding, size and conformation in a good bull. Range management and ranch development was discussed. Thomas listened and learned; he came to realize how poorly-stocked and unorganized Skaha had become under his father's management. In the beginning, he knew, his father had kept up with changing times, but his poor health had caused his interest to wane and finally disappear altogether.

Cartrell was relatively free of it. The man had not professed to be a cattleman, nor a teamster or a horticulturalist; only an accountant. He realized that it was Cartrell's efficient way of handling all business and family affairs that had kept Skaha afloat.

The training that the Skaha men had done in handling their bulls about the corrals, failed. As the independent Herefords were being brought into the ring, a powerful eighteen hundred pound ten year old broke away, crashing through the gate. The sudden disruption quickly spread. Wild-eyed, excited bulls broke into the arena, butting against walls, rails and gates, while cowboys tried to gain control and get them out of the pen. Strickland leapt toward the spot where he had last seen Thomas, only to find the Skaha boss on the ground. Impatiently, he crossed the pen.

A short, stocky man in his late fifties rested back on his heels near Thomas and stroked his tapered beard in amusement. "He'll be alright," he pronounced. "Just stunned a little."

Strickland looked across at him curiously. "You a doctor?"

"Naw, just an old construction boss who likes watching cattle sales."

"What happened?"

"Got himself booted with a horn and stomped on a bit."

The two men got to their feet, helping Thomas to his. Strickland clenched his teeth in disgust and stated, "From now on everything that grows horns at Skaha, gets those horns removed."

Thomas nodded agreement and rubbed at his right side. "Feels like a rib or two got it."

The stranger introduced himself. "Name's McGovern," he said, extending a friendly hand. "Terrance McGovern of McGovern and Watt Contracting." Winking an eye in Strickland's direction, he advised Thomas, "You'd do better to get out of the bull business and into construction."

As Thomas placed his hat upon his head, his glance about the place told him that Bud Smith and others had finally contained the aggravating beasts, and the auction was again underway. Turning to McGovern, he smiled, showing interest in the man's suggestion. "By construction, you mean road building, bridges and so on."

"Of course! 'Course!" McGovern replied enthusiastically. "If I were you, I'd let your boss look after his own bulls and go with something a little less ornery."

"I *am* the boss," Thomas stated firmly. "Those are my bulls."

The construction man's glance took in the Herefords being led about the ring and shrugged. "Well, McGovern and Watt," he repeated, reaching out to shake Thomas' hand again. "If you decide to leave it all behind, there's an offer."

Thomas paused a moment before leaving the pen. He had never heard of the company. He frowned. "Do you live here?"

"Vancouver. Visiting my daughter in Oliver."

Nodding acknowledgement, Thomas replied seriously, "I live just northwest of Okanagan Falls. Your offer's something to think about."

He silently warned himself; regardless of how happy I am at the ranch, I still have a yearning to move onto something new. Why? With Nell and all– My God, I don't believe I might actually consider such a choice!

The day was beginning to get warm, even though it was still only March, and Thomas began to sweat. It's not so easy for me, he lamented, to just leave everything behind, even if that is what I'd like to do. Mopping at his face, he knew the warmth came from anxiety, not just from the sun overhead.

Llewellyn, Strickland and Smith returned to Skaha with three new Hereford bulls. Strickland had weighed in heavily on the selection, as experience told him what the market required, and what Skaha's decreased herd lacked. Thomas was surprised with the pleasure shown by his father when the bulls were paraded before the Jena lens, and also with the limited praise from Cartrell.

During May the new calves were branded and turned out onto spring range. The days in the pasture and corrals were long, dry and dusty. The stench of burning hide and wood smoke hung heavily on the warm, spring air. All his life Thomas had been familiar with these odours and had never found them offensive. They were part of a life that he enjoyed. The number of cattle turned onto the summer range was less, by sixty, than in years past.

In a concentrated effort to restore the rangeland to its original lushness, some of the productive cows had been sold to local ranchers, with dry cows having gone to sale the fall before. Over-grazing had been one of Albert's lesser concerns, consequently becoming the ranch's greatest problem. As well, a devastating plague of grasshoppers reduced the value of remaining grassland. At the ranch, the fields were turned back to pastureland when haying was finished, in an attempt to glean what little feed might be left.

The following year beef prices dropped by half. Thomas sold the remaining southern rangeland, thereby reducing the ranch size considerably.

"Did you have to sell so much?" Albert barked from his bed. "You have no idea what I paid for that in the beginning! I can see I was a fool to trust your judgment!"

"Dad–"

"Da, to you. I'm your Da," Albert muttered.

Thomas grimaced. "I've grown past that, Dad. Now, we got three times what you paid for it and it's certainly in worse shape than you found it."

The trucks to replace the freighting teams and wagons had cost considerably, and Thomas hoped to cover the difference from the land sale.

"The freight," Cartrell informed him, "is the only stable investment you have at the present. We've never borrowed from the ranch to pay the freight's way, nor did we ever do that with the orchard. Each must support its own. I hope that, with what you've done, you'll be in the clear before you begin raising a family or you'll have nothing to offer them."

Beneath a hot August sun, Thomas smiled secretively. "Then we'd better hope for a miracle, because it's due in five and a half months."

Cartrell smiled, not surprised. He studied the younger man. "With a baby coming, do you think you and Nell would want to live alone, away from your parents' home?"

"Where? There's nothing here but decaying old houses."

"McAllister's house," Cartrell suggested. "I know it's the oldest, but it's the best one here. It can be renovated, you know, before the winter if you'd like." Meeting Thomas' eyes, he added, "It might be better for Nell with the baby, and quieter for your parents."

The sturdy log structure which had been built by the trapper and the Indian, Two Way, soon became the comfortable home of the younger Llewellyns. Albert seemed unaware at times of Nell's condition. When he had been informed, it did not appear to register with him.

Thomas joked with his wife, "Now, if you were a cow or mare, wearing a brown hide with the Skaha brand on it, he'd sit up and take real appreciative notice."

15

At Christmastime the Cartrell daughters arrived at their father's home, having travelled from the Fraser Valley. Jennifer, now twenty-five, and her husband, William Brown, brought their two-year-old son, Jason. Karen, twenty-three, was joined by the young man, George Wood, to whom she had recently become engaged. It was an exciting, happy time for the family.

Winter imposed the normal hardships of drifted snow, blocked roads, icy fields and freezing temperatures. Still, Dick Foderow was able to get a team up to Skaha with gift parcels, barrels of food supplies and grain for the cattle, horses, other farm animals and fowl. He also delivered the first mail received in a dozen days.

Nell was exuberant over news from her sister-in-law, now settled on the family farm near Williams Lake. "Listen Tom, it's from the Dietrichs."

Sydney looked up from her needlework, her eyes wide. "Dietrichs?"

"Yes, in 150 Mile House near Williams Lake."

Glancing in Thomas' direction, she told him, "We know a Dietrich. Helga's brother."

In the lamplight, Nell read the letter. "Joanie says they had a baby boy last May. They call him David Ryan, family names apparently, from Rick's father, David, and his great-grandfather, Rayne, who was an Okanagan trapper. They turned it into Ryan, more modern. She thinks they may move to Prince George."

Sydney rose and quietly left the room.

Cartrell passed his grandson to his daughter, and followed Sydney. Nell glanced awkwardly toward Thomas, but noticed that he remained still, his eyes cast upon the patterns of the rug as though waiting for something to move there.

The door to Sydney's room closed as Cartrell reached the top of the stairs. Without hesitation he opened it and entered. Sydney fumbled to light the lamp, but Cartrell took the match from her and reached out, drawing her close to him.

"Her letter brings it all back," she whispered. "I never loved David in the same way I do you, nor like I did Albert, but it does make the heart ache a little to hear of his family."

"The man she speaks of is David's son, Richard. I knew Anna married a fellow named Dietrich. The name meant nothing to me."

"We came over the mountains to Kamloops together," Sydney told Cartrell. "Anton went to a place called Barkerville, leaving Helga alone. She married Gus Volholven and never kept in touch with her brother. The four of us, and the boys, came down here."

Cartrell brushed the loose strands of hair from her face, and in so doing, touched the tears which had silently fallen. "You're crying? Whatever for, dear heart?"

"Oh, Ian, there's just so much waste to life." She took the large handkerchief he offered and wiped at her eyes. "So much has happened over the years. Nothing seems in balance anymore. Look at you and me. But for the fact that Albert still breathes, we might be wed, not taking our moments together like fugitives. And that's confusing, too. I don't want Albert to die. I loved him so deeply once, just as you loved Belle. I know life is nothing for him now, and hasn't been for so long. He sleeps most of the time. Sometimes he doesn't even know us."

Cartrell smiled at her. "We all have our memories, Sydney. I miss Belle, as you will miss Albert. She was the mother of that family sitting in your parlour and, when I look at them all, I see her there."

Sydney drew a breath and sighed wearily. "We should go back downstairs."

The festive season was an exhilarating, exciting time for all at Skaha Ranch. Brilliant winter sunlight sparkled across the drifts of new snow and the younger set chose to be outdoors. The sound of sleigh bells and laughter broke the cool, still air as Thomas reined a splendid team of Percherons along the snow-packed passages through the draws and atop the ravines.

A feeling of true happiness seized Thomas and he suddenly felt very good about his life. He reached out and cupped Nell's hand in his. She leaned against him, feeling safe and secure with his nearness. Bundled warmly in great coats and thick blankets, they all enjoyed the crisp, fresh air of a countryside wonderland.

Sydney and Mrs. Davies watched from above the yard, through the binoculars. "We are surrounded by youth, Alma," Sydney whispered in a sad voice, "and when I watch it in action, I wonder where my own years went and why they passed so swiftly– and that I did not really notice their passing."

Alma's matronly smile registered understanding, as well as indulgence of Sydney's mood.

It began to snow once more, large, star-shaped flakes tumbling in whirling flurry. Cartrell entered the house, carrying his grandson upon his shoulders. The two-year-old tugged playfully at his grandfather's thick fur hat, as Sydney reached up and lifted him down.

"My, my, Jason, snowflakes everywhere!" she teased.

Mrs. Davies' voice called to them from the parlour. "They're returning now, across the flats!"

"Marvellous!" Sydney chirped happily. "We have a fantastic New Year's dinner waiting for everyone. Imagine, it's 1922 already." She spun merrily from the hallway into the dining room, her long wool skirt swaying. Cartrell watched her and she saw his open admiration. Her smile was brilliant. Behind him the door opened. Everyone crowded into the hallway, allowing the snow and cold to enter with them.

Nell pulled off her woollen mitts, hat and scarf. Patting her swollen body where her child moved restlessly within, she exclaimed, "A lovely sleigh ride. Even the little fellow enjoyed it, bunting me all the way."

Thomas entered then, smiling broadly. "Got him started on the outdoors already. He'll take to ranching easily. I'll see to that."

"You're counting on a boy, then," commented Jennifer's husband, William.

Thomas glanced backward as he passed Cartrell in the parlour doorway, "What else?" he asked them all, seemingly appalled at any other thought. Cartrell raised a brow at Thomas' words.

Laughter filled the rooms, echoing to the upstairs landing where Albert watched from his wheelchair.

Looking up, Thomas called to his father, "Be up in a minute to bring you down." Hooking his coat upon the rack, he nodded to Cartrell. "Give me a hand, Ian?"

Sydney's gaze followed the two men for the moment and noticed that William Brown and George Wood went up the stairs with them. She turned quickly and led the others into the dining room. She wished not to be witness to the humiliation which she knew Albert must feel, of such dependence upon their son, and more particularly upon Cartrell. She spoke almost absently to her daughter-in-law, "Are you sure you're feeling well after that ride? You look a little pale and awfully tired."

Nell, who was still four weeks away from her time, glanced with surprise at Sydney. "I'm quite alright, everything considered. Oh look, it's beginning to snow in earnest now."

Sydney saw the thick wall of tumbling flakes, but she heard only the sounds of the men behind her shifting Albert into place at one end of the long table. Tears of regret threatened to fill her eyes, as her glance fell upon the sturdy table and the two rows of beautifully carved chairs. What a long time it had been since Albert had presented these magnificent pieces of craftsmanship to her. They had been created with the love he had vowed to her always. Strong had remained the furniture, but wasted had become the marriage.

Sydney watched their guests seat themselves and lamented for a moment, that it was not Harrie and Bronwen who sat together with Thomas, herself and their father, instead of Ian with his daughters and their menfolk. We are a family gathered here, she thought, but mostly of all the wrong people.

Abruptly, Sydney was drawn from her reverie by Thomas' gentle hand at her elbow. "We're ready," he told her, smiling. "Just waiting on you to give the blessing, and dinner is getting cold."

Sydney responded to his humour with a warm smile, while her misty eyes met the questioning gaze of Cartrell. He reads my every thought, she cautioned herself, and quickly stepped toward the chair which Thomas held aside for her. Reaching for Nell's hand on her left and that of Cartrell's little grandson on her right, Sydney spoke in a voice barely audible, "Dear Lord, we are thankful for the life we share together. We remember loved ones you have called from us and ask that we may continue to walk in your care. Bless the bounty upon this table. In Jesus name, Amen."

The snow blew down from the mountains, a thick, swirling mass engulfing the ranch in a mid-January storm. It drifted against buildings and fences, and hung on the trees like great white weights. The flats became a rolling series of impassable roads and hidden fence lines. In the white January night Thomas Llewellyn prepared his horse for the trip to Penticton. An appalling emergency had occurred at a disastrous time of year.

In the freezing temperature and howling wind, Cartrell hovered near. As he watched Thomas thread the cinch strap through its ring on the saddle and felt his own fingers freezing, he wondered that Thomas had any life left in his at all. The man had a long ride ahead through a bitter night, and Cartrell worried. Cartrell had made a similar trip to Fairview in bad weather many years before and he realized the perils of haste. He silently cursed the fact that the Buick was completely useless in such a storm.

"Above all," he warned Thomas, "keep your head. A collected mind saves a man, you know. Nell's only been in labour a short while and by all I've heard, it can go on for several hours. So you've time to take things carefully and not freeze to death or kill your horse."

"She's been in a bad state for too many hours already," Thomas reminded Cartrell, "and Mother and Alma seem helpless at this point."

"Probably that boy you want. Boys rush things until they've grown old, and then wonder why they hurried so much." He smiled wanly.

"I'm not in a joking mood right now, Ian," Thomas snapped as he placed the bridle bit into the gelding's mouth. He led the horse out of the barn into the freezing winter. Positioning the stirrup, he placed his foot firmly into it, and swung into the saddle. He looked down at Cartrell, huddled against the barn, and called loudly, "Stay close to them. Without your help my wife may die before I get back with a doctor– if a doctor will come out on a night like this."

Cartrell reached up to Thomas' gloved hands cupped over the saddle horn, but before he could offer reassurance, Thomas had lifted the reins and moved off into the wind and swirling snow.

Keeping to the higher levels among the trees where the drifts were lighter, he rode at a pace not tiring for his horse. As he wound through the mountains toward the valley floor, his thoughts never left the drama taking place that night at Skaha. A terrible foreboding crept over Thomas, and he feared for the lives of both his wife and their child.

The blizzard continued. Snow caught on his hat. It packed against his chaps and saddle and clung to the horse's mane and face. Finally he crested the hill above the town and cautiously eased his horse onto the flats.

The kitchen in Harold Stobie's small house was a welcoming harbour. When Thomas entered, the ice began to melt, dripping from his hat, coat and boots. Hanging them with his chaps above the wood box near the stove, he explained his emergency to the doctor. Stobie immediately went to the telephone mounted on the wall and turned the handle to ring the operator.

When he was finished the call, he said to Thomas, "We have two good young men here in town now, and one will go out with you. Name's Lord, Jonathon Lord. Now, you get this hot tea into you. Lace it a bit," he ordered as he reached into the cupboard for a bottle of brandy. "Keeps the chill out. Too bad you couldn't have used the car."

In her husband's absence that night, life did not deal fairly with Nell Llewellyn and, when Thomas reached Skaha, he found that his wife had slipped away from them twenty minutes before. The tiny bundle cradled in Sydney's arms was asleep.

Thomas fought to get a grip on himself. He could not believe she had died; not Nell, his wonderful wife, his love. Death resulted from other causes, he thought, not childbirth. He held her hand, gently touched her face, listened for her heartbeat, and pinched his eyes closed against the finality of their happy life together. The sadness Thomas felt was deep and profound. This was the second time in his life he had lost a loved one to death; both times, because of a baby. He could not grasp a reason, a meaning.

Finally, he turned to view the baby, to discover it was a girl, not the son he had expected to see there. As the doctor reached for the baby to carry out examination, Thomas turned away from everyone and left the room, crossing the hall to his father's den.

The wide corner windows of the room presented the calm, white world of a winter morning. Only snow drifts remained of the storm which had passed through the night. Thomas listened to his father's laboured breathing. Did he unconsciously resent the fact that his weakened father still lived, while Nell– Thomas hung his head. Sweet, gentle Nell had ceased to live, for whatever reason the doctor would soon come in and give him. And, what about the baby? He cursed silently. It's the cause of the dying. Thomas knew he was being morbid, but had not the will to resist the mood.

He spoke to his father. "I have something to tell you, Da," he said softly. "Listen– are you listening?" When he was satisfied that Albert was paying attention, he said, "Nell is dead. The baby is a girl and it's alive; no boy to carry on your name." Thomas peered closely at Albert's seemingly emotionless, pale face. He remained at the bedside until his mother went in to get him.

"Will you come, Thomas?" Sydney asked. "I'd like you to see the baby." The air in the room was oppressive and still. "She needs you."

There was a long pause during which Thomas seemed to assess his feelings. Sydney waited patiently. "It doesn't need me at all," he told her harshly.

Sydney's mind reeled. The implication of his words were too clear. Behind them she closed the door to the den. "There is no time nor room for a nasty attitude in this house, Thomas," she told him testily. "A terrible tragedy has occurred tonight and your loss is great. But Thomas, you have a responsibility to your baby girl, and you'll not be shirking it." Sydney descended the stairs, aware that Thomas remained on the landing.

Cartrell looked up from the doorway of the parlour. Reaching for her hand, he offered, "Come have a cup of tea, then lay down and get some badly-needed rest."

Sydney sank onto the sofa. "To think that barely two weeks ago we all sat together and asked God's care. Ian, in this day and age there is no reason for such a death. Medical science has advanced–"

"Not as far as you imagine," Cartrell interrupted. "There is little to be done to halt massive haemorrhaging and other complications, especially in the dead of winter with no doctor for a neighbour. Not that he could have saved her, all things considered."

After several minutes they became aware of Thomas' presence in the doorway. Cartrell leaned back against the sofa cushions. Sydney wiped at the tears which had begun to fall.

Thomas said quietly, "I'm going home." And, putting on his coat and hat, he left the house. Upstairs, the baby cried. Mrs. Davies' footsteps could be heard as she padded about the bedroom in care of the infant. Thomas Llewellyn had not gone to see his daughter that day. Nor had he entered the bedroom of his youth where his wife now lay in death. His grief was overwhelming, and he wished only to be alone.

The babe was named Sydney Alexandra. Cartrell sat at the narrow desk in the hallway and recorded the birth in the Llewellyn family Bible. Below those lines he penned the sad entry of Nell Llewellyn's passing.

Late that night Thomas entered his mother's room and looked into the cradle. From where she rested against her pillows, Sydney let her novel fall aside and watched her son with deep concern. The faint lamplight cast shadows across the weary lines of Thomas' face. She saw with dismay the visible lingering disappointment.

"Thomas," she ventured. "We all suffer private hurts, but there are also joys in living. Your daughter is one of those joys. She's beautiful, Thomas. She is part of Nell, a child in her likeness; and part of you. She is alive and she's healthy. She can be just as rewarding as a son would be if you give her the chance."

Thomas had no reply. The room was still.

Sydney continued. "Her name is Sydney Alexandra. Ian chose Sydney; he felt that you would approve. I decided on Alexandra, Nell's middle name. She needed to be named, you know. Dr. Lord took all the information with him to register her. He will also advise the coroner about Nell and contact Rev. Glass." She raised her book, leaving Thomas to his private thoughts. In a few moments he left the room. When she heard the door close at the entrance downstairs, she knew that he had returned to his own home.

As Thomas followed the snow-packed trench toward the old McAllister log house, he thought of Cartrell. The man had known only daughters, yet appeared satisfied. But then, Thomas considered, he has me. How often I am reminded.

Once Two Way had told him, "Often men leave no sons, but their lives are greatly enriched by the women in it." Glancing up into the clear, star- speckled sky, Thomas asked, "Well, you old philosopher, who are my women now? I have no wife–" and as though the Indian Two Way had heard him, it came to Thomas Llewellyn, you have Sydney Alexandra.

16

Ian Cartrell stood before the side window of his office and watched the activity of winter-feeding on the distant flats. Cattle, bunched together against a late February storm, began to spread out as the team and sleigh arrived. Thomas forked hay in long lines among the herd while Bud Smith managed the Percherons.

His gaze turned to the Llewellyn house. Half hidden by enormous snow banks and the snow-laden branches of the shade trees Albert had planted twenty-five years before, the house appeared solitary and deserted. A cold loneliness surrounded it. Inside, Cartrell knew, nothing much differed.

While it was milder on the valley floor, it was definitely still winter at White Lake. As Cartrell considered the lengthy season, he recalled his wife's objection to living on the flats. Life was, indeed, much more comfortable down below. But below, there was not the quiet beauty nor sense of peace that one could feel in the hills.

He knew he could never move away from the ranch. Nor could Sydney; not even Pickle Bill and the hired hands. None of them would go. Well, perhaps Thomas, he considered. Cartrell smiled and turned his eyes to the pasture where Thomas worked. That man's body is full of restless bones and no one knows where they will take him.

As Cartrell turned away from the window, an approaching vehicle caught his attention. He waved as Dick Foderow brought the truck to a stop before the steps.

Cartrell opened the door. "I don't believe you managed that road without an accident."

"Easy. I don't drive like Tom," Foderow joked, "and I got a good set of chains rattlin' underneath."

"What brings you?"

Foderow banged his snow-covered boots against the step and entered Cartrell's office. "Well, I kind of like it up here. Could easily live here, and Fern doesn't care where she lives as long as it's with me." He grinned at Cartrell. "Here's a paper about next month's bull sale, some letters for you, and medicine for old Albert, if he's still alive over there." He glanced through the window toward the big house. "Maybe I'll take it over myself and see Sydney."

While Cartrell sorted through his mail and commented on a note from his second daughter announcing her marriage, Foderow watched Thomas in the field. "These girls of mine seem bent on eloping," he heard Cartrell say, but paid no mind.

"You know Ian, Tom has done some talkin' about this freighting business we have."

"What kind of talk?"

"Sellin' talk."

Cartrell stared at Foderow, then sank into his chair. "I'm not surprised. He's waiting on Albert over there, who is weakening every day."

"Well, I'll drop this parcel off to Sydney. See you later." Foderow left the building, knowing that Cartrell would be deep in thought for a long while.

Death was approaching Albert Llewellyn on a warm evening in May. At his bedside was Sydney, huddled in her husband's large chair with a knitted wrap about her shoulders. Outside, the world reflected spring in glorious colour and gentle breeze. While the weather was warm, Sydney felt chilled and insisted that Thomas set the fireplace.

At nine o'clock Cartrell entered the parlour, alone. "Any news?" he enquired swiftly.

"Dr. Lord left a half hour ago. He says it's only a matter of hours." Thomas' mood was cool, indifferent and almost resentful of having to include Cartrell in this emotional family time. "Ian, could you leave my mother and I alone tonight?"

Cartrell rose from the chair, feeling shut-out of a family that he had spent a lifetime protecting. Without a word, he placed his hat firmly upon his head, buttoned up his coat and left the Llewellyn house.

Looking up, Sydney smiled as Thomas entered his father's room. She reached for his hand, drawing him near, to sit on an arm of the chair. "This is the end. Tonight. Now." Gazing intently up at him, she spoke softly. "Here we are, Thomas, you, your father and me, truly alone now, waiting–"

Words escaped Thomas as he looked away from her, around the room and along the shelves containing his father's memorabilia and the empty gun cabinet. Then he turned toward the bed.

Sydney continued, "Your father is waiting for death to take him from a world which has been nothing but years of lonely emptiness. And I wonder about myself. Am I waiting for my freedom? How quickly do I want to put unhappy memories behind me?" She touched his arm lightly. "And you, Thomas? Are you waiting for the inheritance that will be yours? This ranch and more? He's never changed his will, you know. Refused to the end to include me and

112

couldn't avoid you."

Thomas shrank from the meaning of her words.

"What will you do with it? Everything that will be yours is what we gave our marriage to," she whispered sadly. "It cost us that."

Thomas moved away from her hand, the chair and her depressing thoughts. They were meanderings unwelcome to him. Outside a full moon brightened the countryside. With his forehead resting against the cool windowpane, he told his mother, "This place cost me something too, only you can't see into my heart to know. Life has been next to nothing for me without Nell."

A faint gasping sound from across the room returned Thomas' thoughts to the moment, and drew Sydney's attention to the bed. The slackened mouth, the open eyes told Thomas that death had finally, mercifully come to his father. The house was suddenly still.

After a long while Sydney rose from the chair and, laying aside the shawl, crossed the room to her husband. She placed a steady hand upon his chest and waited. "His heart has ceased to beat," she whispered calmly. Reaching out to gently lower Albert's eyelids, she said to her son, "Thomas, I wish to be alone with your father."

Thomas watched his mother kneel at the bedside, the long, full gray skirt of her dress falling in soft folds upon the rug. His eyes followed the length of the still, wasted body of his father before her; saw the face, soft and pale in death and finally free of pain and resentment. As his mother lowered her head upon her hands formed in prayer, Thomas quietly closed the door, leaving his parents together.

The legacy of Skaha, which had run down the McAllister line was now handed down to a young Llewellyn, and seemed slated for no better fate than that of earlier times. What had begun with an inspired Indian and an ambitious trapper, was inherited by a second generation, and willed to a third. It was bought up and improved by an enterprising Welshman, and due once more to go on the block. Where young David McAllister had sold his holdings to keep abreast of personal debts, the younger Llewellyn was inclined to dispose of most of it, for no better reason than a lack of interest in the businesses which were not of his personal preference.

Where reluctant agreement had been struck between both Thomas and Cartrell in the sale of the orchard to Kennedy and the over-grazed range to developers, disagreement ensued when the issue of freighting arose.

On a hot summer day, Thomas faced Cartrell in the office and stated boldly, "I never liked the business right from when I was a youngster. I tried, but I just couldn't like it."

An outraged Cartrell confronted him, "You're selling it to spite your father! He's dead! Dick is running those trucks constantly. The freighting can continue in this manner for years, or at least until Dick leaves it. You don't have to go near the place."

"We need the sale to improve the ranch," Thomas told him.

Thomas' refusal to reply sensibly to any accusation so infuriated Cartrell, that he picked up his hat, plopped it carelessly upon his head and stomped angrily from his office.

The summer months quickly passed into autumn. Thomas negotiated the sale of the freight business and trucks without further intervention from Cartrell. Now depleted of both the orchard and transport business, Thomas was left with only the ranch which, in Cartrell's eyes, was the least lucrative of all Albert's initial ventures.

Cartrell refrained from further intervention. He had voiced his mind enough as it was, he decided. He simply kept the books for Thomas, which were becoming increasingly difficult to balance, and was thankful to be relieved of the overall responsibility which had once been his lot. At times he found it difficult to look Dick Foderow in the eyes. Llewellyn's freighting service had been the man's life.

With incredible foresight, Cartrell had purchased shares in construction companies, mining endeavours and lumber mills through the years, which he now sold quite profitably. He could relax in relative comfort at the age of sixty-two. Similar investments had been made on behalf of Albert Llewellyn, with Sydney as a beneficiary. The value realized afforded Sydney the independence from Thomas she longed for.

Eventually Cartrell, angered by Thomas' dwindling interest in the future of the ranch, voiced his opinion without tact, in the presence of Foderow. "It appals me that you cannot see where you must invest, Tom. You have a tendency to believe in cash in the bank. I am not saying that concept is wrong, but good business is better. It was premature, to say the least, to sell the trucks. I know that we've hashed this issue over and nearly worn it out, but it's that I feel the transport business has not yet come into its own here." Glancing at Foderow, he saw the other man nod agreement.

"Ian--" Thomas responded impatiently, "The railways are taking over, and we'll always have the boats on the lakes. Think about that."

"Time will tell on that, too. I predict that there'll be more transports on our roads than rail lines and boats. The automobile is truly a fascinating invention and will be used to its fullest advantage. Ranching will not always be our major industry. The orchard and trucks that you sold, will be." Cartrell sighed wearily, reached for his handkerchief and blew his nose as discreetly as possible. He had developed a head cold which plagued his sinuses mercilessly. The others waited.

Cartrell shrugged his shoulders in a helpless manner. "I suppose I should say to you, don't be discouraged by my words, that they're simply the ramblings of one from an earlier generation. The old, you know, never quite understand the priorities of the young. I'm sure the situation wasn't much different when my father wanted me to remain in the east, and I went west instead. The difference was, I had only myself to think about. You Tom, have your mother and young daughter to consider."

Lately, Thomas had taken to leaving the room when faced with a disagreeable conversation, thereby abruptly closing the subject. This, he did now.

Cartrell watched him leap down the steps and cross the yard to his mother's house. "Rumour has it," he told Foderow, "that Tom has a lady-friend in Oliver. I wonder if he's tiring of everything here, including the ranch. Young men are moving about these days, it seems." He placed a hand on Foderow's shoulder. "You *will* move up soon, I hope, Dick."

Foderow nodded. "Before winter sets in; the Carmichael place 'till somethin' better comes up."

Cartrell smiled and heaved a sigh of relief.

17

As Sydney Alexandra toddled her way through babyhood into childhood, she brought joy and laughter into the lives of those around her, an ingredient too long absent. Her coquettish, enchanting ways commanded indulgence from the very beginning. A pretty four year old with a crown of golden curls and sparkling hazel eyes, she captivated everyone. With an inquisitive, sometimes sassy nature Sydney Alex followed Thomas everywhere, often getting thoroughly in his way.

Like her grandmother, Sydney Alex showed a keen interest in horses, and would become a competent horsewoman. She and her friend, Janet Foderow, roamed the fields, picking wild flowers, and hanging around the barn with the horses. Rivalry between the girls would never be an issue, for at an early age, little Janet seemed aware of who was going to be the leader. Sydney Alex fascinated Janet, for she was daring in their games and much more mischievous. That Sydney Alex was taller, prettier and one year older mattered little to Janet. They had no choice but to be friends. They were the only children living on the ranch, since the Foderows had moved up to Skaha and all the others had moved away.

As the sun broke over the mountain ridges and spread its warmth across the land one brilliant September day in 1926, little Sydney Alex' future was unintentionally determined in an idle conversation between her father and Ian Cartrell. They watched the girl's horsemanship from the steps of the office, as she took some riding advice from Bud Smith.

"By the way, Tom," said Cartrell, "your mother and I have talked about being married soon."

"Where will you live? Here in her house, or over at yours?"

"No doubt, we'll build our own. Your father's been gone two years now. It's time for us."

"Whatever," Thomas mumbled. He could hardly bother himself about Cartrell and his mother these days. Their unconventional relationship was known about the ranch and no longer continued to embarrass him. He was weary of it; of many things lately. He had a new relationship of his own to occupy his mind. He turned into the office and began a search through the file drawers. "You'll keep Sydney Alex with you, of course," he called back. "That way she'll be brought up properly."

"Of course. What are you looking for?"

"The brand registration forms."

Cartrell strode into the office, reached into the drawer and drew out the forms without hardly a glance at the folders within. Thomas snatched them from between the accountant's thin fingers.

Cartrell smiled. "How many head are you taking? It's early, you know."

"Eighty, in a week's time, and hope for the best possible price. We'll drive them. I can't afford to send them by rail, nor keep them through the winter." Thomas turned and looked directly into Cartrell's dark eyes. "I feel a little desperate," he confessed. "Can you understand that?"

Cartrell failed to understand it. To him the whole business of a cattle drive seemed ridiculous in a time when barge and rail transport was as close as Penticton, and had been used to get the bulls to Kamloops. At least the cowboys seemed set on the trip and were almost happy to do it. He felt relief in that.

Dick Foderow, John Strickland, Bud Smith and Thomas left Skaha, driving a herd of eighty head, a mix of Skaha's oldest cows and two year old steers. They departed at early dawn while a light rain fell. Ahead of them lay well over one hundred miles of tiring days and cold October nights.

The four cowboys formed an excellent quartette, for they were good horsemen and enjoyed the rugged, outdoor way of life which they now had to share as a close unit. With them were two extra riders from Penticton, eager to experience something of a way of life long past. They rode one man in the lead, two at each side and another in drag, thereby holding the herd well together. At their evening campfires they relaxed in easy camaraderie, each man taking his turn at watch.

To break the monotony, Bud Smith often pulled a harmonica from his pocket and blew familiar tunes. Unmarried and thirty-three, he was content with his place on the ranch and, as the youngest of the Skaha men, admirably put up with their jokes about his cooking when he helped Pickle Bill. He was not tall like the others, was quiet by nature and saw no profit in disagreeing with their fun of him. He knew they all liked him.

The rain ceased the second day on the trail. It had been welcome relief in a season that was hot and dry. Thomas lamented, "If we don't get a good snow pack this winter, the hay– I get tired of battling the elements. Aught to sell the place and be done."

Dick Foderow shifted uneasily across from them. He lamented what he had just heard, for he had been around many years and watched the ranch develop. "It was a big place once. Your dad's dream. In the beginning it was Dave's life, but your dad never slept nights until he got hold of it all."

"I know, I know," Thomas replied, embarrassed. "I've heard it all."

Thomas watched the nostalgic expression on Foderow's face in the dancing light of the fire. He recognized that Foderow knew more than anyone about everything concerning Skaha, for he was there even before Cartrell.

After the rain, the sun rose and warmed the countryside. White clouds lazed about a clear, blue sky. Before them stretched the rolling hills between the Okanagan and the Thompson River, and the trail used by the early fur brigades.

Kamloops was crowded with cowboys, cattle and horses, buyers and spectators. It bustled with activity and exuded energy. John Strickland enjoyed the camaraderie in the cattleman's world and felt a great pride in his occupation. It was ingrained from the days of rough, tough cow-camps and the trail rides of his Montana youth. At fifty-six he revelled in the distinction of being a true cowboy of his time.

"We're different," he told Thomas, who was perched upon a post beside him, at the stockyards. "We represent the strength of our country and man's basic values in life; the old nitty-gritty of real western living. It's a hard way of life maybe, but a world that others on the outside envy."

Thomas stared, astonished, at the man. He had never viewed cowboying in quite that light. "You really get wrapped up in all this, don't you. Well, it's good for me that you do."

"You're right!" Strickland agreed, without looking around at Thomas. "It's what got your cattle here with all head accounted for."

From his perch on the fence Thomas watched the C.P.R. engine pull ahead, hauling the cattlecars, flatcars of lumber from the Shuswap region, and coal cars loaded in the Kootenays. It would travel along the Thompson River west to Spences Bridge, and on to Vancouver. Cartrell was wrong, Thomas was convinced, and he was right in selling the freight business; the railway had definitely taken over transportation.

Given the rise in the valley of other types of farming, he pondered the fate of his ranch and the cattle business. During the two previous decades cattle ranching had taken on a different look, as ranges became depleted of sufficient grasses to sustain large herds. As well, he realized, so many settlers had moved into the Okanagan Valley that ranchers were forced to fence their rangelands and define leaseholds. The days of large herds and land held in the grip of only a few owners was gone.

Strickland leapt to the ground, the rowles of his spurs jingling as he landed. He was a heavy-set, taut-muscled man of five feet eleven and did not land as easy on his feet as the younger ones did. "Come on," he waved. "Let's go get ourselves a drink in this town."

"No, I don't think so," Thomas replied seriously. "I'm goin' along to the hotel and look up an old construction man, and visit awhile."

"Uh huh!" Strickland grinned. "The girlfriend's daddy, eh?"

As they walked along the hard-packed street parallel to the riverside park, the discordant sound of their spurs broke the still late afternoon air, and Thomas wished that he had removed his. Whereas John Strickland was happy in his occupation, Thomas Llewellyn remained in sombre conflict with the choices in his world. There was little conversation between the two and they parted at the Patricia Hotel.

Thomas entered Terrance McGovern's room and shook the man's hand in greeting. Their conversation centred at first on cattle, for McGovern's passion was watching cattle sales. Thomas stood before the room's long, narrow window and stared down at the street below for several minutes. "I've heard," he began, breaking the silence, "that in the early days this place was the hub of the fur trade, a capital. Now, it's a divisional point for the railway."

"And," McGovern added hopefully, striking a match to his deep bowled pipe, "it may well become an important centre of construction. The area has vast possibilities for industry of all kinds. A town like this one up here in the interior should pursue all potential avenues, and reach right out and grab them in." He stood beside Thomas, held his pipe in one hand, while propping an elbow in the other. "Oh, to be young in times like these. We're on the verge of a revolution in construction; in engineering, equipment, and achieving the end result." He puffed at his pipe, blue smoke curling out into the small room. "Roads, you know. Logging, some mining, dams--"

Presently, he turned away from the window to the round table beside them, opened a bottle of whiskey and poured two small glasses. He handed one to Thomas and raised his. "Here's to the workin' man." They drank. McGovern enquired with a smile, "Are you interested?"

When Thomas did not immediately reply, McGovern tossed the remainder of his drink down his throat, coughed, then clamped his teeth against the stem of his pipe. "I venture to suggest," he said from one side of his mouth, "that you are at a crossroads in your life right now. I don't know you very well, Tom, but perhaps the war left you a bit unsettled, or you're still afloat from the loss of your wife." He watched Thomas' expression. "I know about both. My time was spent in the Boer War, and my wife died ten years ago when my daughter-- when Mary was seventeen." He drew on the pipe. Smoke once more filled the air. "I'm sixty-one now and wishin' I could start all over. Oh, I've not been unsuccessful, as you know, but the time for real construction with heavy equipment is just around the corner. It's your time now. Mine has passed."

Without moving or taking his eyes from the scene beyond the window, Thomas said to McGovern, "Terrance, I want to marry your daughter."

"You know she has a husband who will not grant a divorce unless the grounds are provided by her, and that is adultery."

"We've talked about it." Thomas placed an arm against the window frame and leaned his forehead against it. "We'll provide the grounds."

Beside him, Terrance McGovern fell quiet.

"I'm sorry, sir, but sometimes a wrong does make a right," Thomas offered soberly. "This will be one of those times. Two years from now, who even remembers." Turning, he set his empty glass upon the table and asked McGovern, "Can we have supper together downstairs?"

McGovern smiled. "Certainly. I hardly know you, but I do like you. You are, at least, honest and straightforward with me, and I appreciate that." They left the room together, stomping noisily down the stairs and into the dining room.

Rain began to fall, lightly at first, then suddenly bursting into a heavy downpour from a sky quickly darkened by black clouds. Evening seemed to fall early with the rain and it was not long before Thomas retired to his own room, with a mind no more at ease than before he had begun the visit.

18

The sporadic bursts of rain which had fallen upon the camps of the Skaha cattlemen during their trail drive were the last the country would know for a long time. Wintertime left an insignificant snow pack in the mountains. March winds had blown down from the valley ridges, sweeping across the benches and flat bottomland with dry fury. Regular April showers which the country depended upon were few. Grass and shrubs dried out. Flowers, planted in hope, failed to mature.

In June the alfalfa fields lay wilting beneath the blazing summer sun, and were almost beyond recovery by July. The creek was barely a trickle, the dam nearly empty, and the flumes unused. The only reliable source of water was Mercy Spring, and some private wells which served the households.

Daily, Sydney stood before the window of her kitchen, watching spiralling funnels of dust leave barren patches across the land. Sometimes with the wind the dust rode high, blotting the landscape. It banked against buildings and seeped into every corner of the houses. Some of the rocky banks along the hill to the White Lake bench occasionally loosened, sliding across the road, hampering transport.

To reach his office each day, Cartrell fought the dry, swirling, gray air with a handkerchief held over his nose in an effort to breath properly.

On a day that Sydney watched him walking bent into the wind, her thoughts were broken by Sydney Alex' call from atop the stairs. "Gran, may we play in the big room?" She referred to the den, a room used for storage since Albert's passing. "With your old clothes from the trunks?"

"We're going to play theatre, Mrs. Llewellyn, so get ready to watch us!" Janet called cheerily.

When Sydney entered the large room much later, the two girls pranced prettily before her in a fashion parade of abandoned dresses. They had turned the four trunks on their sides, for the rounded lids did not serve as a stage. As Sydney sat down to watch their performance, her gaze was drawn to a shiny object nailed to the bottom of one of the trunks. She knelt before it to discover a small, rusted key held fast to the wooden braces by two bent nails. "My goodness," she whispered in revelation. "I have finally found it. Why

121

didn't I think to look on-"

Sydney Alex hurried to kneel beside her. "What is it, Gran?"

"The key, child. All this time the key was right there. Only Rachel knew-" She rested against the heels of her shoes, her long skirt bunched around them, while she contemplated her find.

"Who is Rachel, Gran?" Sydney Alex plagued her.

"Hush, child, and go get a hammer for me. Quickly!"

Sydney Alex rushed down the stairs, calling for Mrs. Davies and a hammer. Janet Foderow crept close to Sydney. "Can I watch?"

"Yes, darling, you can watch."

Sydney Alex returned with the hammer, followed up the stairs by a curious Alma Davies.

"I'm almost afraid to touch it," Sydney whispered reverently, glancing up at Alma. "This trunk came from Rachel McAllister's house when Ian cleared it out after she died." Then to her granddaughter, she explained, "You never knew this lady, Sydney Alex. She was born a long time ago."

Sydney carefully removed the nails so as to not damage the rusted key, and soon the lid was slowly lifted against its hinges.

The past leapt out to them. The articles, dried and creased from their confinement, unfolded a heritage; a time and place and way of life which was foreign to most who lived in 1927. They spoke of an illustrious and mysterious past; a collection made by a woman who, in her youth, felt the need to preserve her time in history.

A profound emotion seized Sydney Llewellyn. She reached for the top article, a wedding dress yellowed with age. It was followed by another, much older wedding dress, accompanied by a string of large beads. A small oval sketch of a young Negro boy was unwrapped. His particulars had at one time been printed on the back, but were no longer legible. His clothes were creased, but intact. Beneath them, Sydney found a deerskin bag which emptied out several differently-shaped knives. They lay upon a white fur robe.

She glanced at the unusually quiet girls and Alma Davies. "I think," she told them, "we'll just leave all of this until Ian comes by tonight." Getting to her feet, she steered Sydney Alex and Janet from the den, while Mrs. Davies closed the door.

In the late evening when Sydney Alex had finally fallen asleep, Sydney and Cartrell climbed the stairs to the den. Stuffy, oppressive heat hung in the house and did nothing to lighten the stale odour in the room. Raising the lamp so that they might move without incident, he enquired with an indulgent smile, "Now, what is this great discovery of yours, my dear?"

Her hand on his arm cautioned him. "Mind your step, now. Some of it is spread out on the floor. Oh Ian, you can't imagine how I felt when I lifted that lid," she whispered. "Through all these years I believed it was just full of old clothes that meant nothing. I thought the key was lost."

Cartrell set the lamp upon a table and smiled at her. "Why are we whispering? Is someone listening?"

"Stop making fun of me and look at this!"

Cartrell leaned forward, adjusting his glasses. "Indeed! This is quite a discovery. One could start a museum with such quality leftovers."

"And in the trunk," Sydney indicated with her hand, "are robes and a large hide. There's a bag of some kind of animal hide, and knives."

"Which must have belonged to that trapper who became a legend in this part of the country." Cartrell straightened up and replaced his glasses in their case.

"Really? A McAllister?"

"It was always held by Two Way, that he was one of the first fur men to remain in the valley and begin farming for a living," he informed her.

"My goodness! Possibly David's grandfather?" She looked around at the articles on the floor and those still in the trunk. "And these are his family's things?"

"Well, Rachel was his daughter-in-law."

Cartrell held the lamp above the trunk while Sydney lifted the robes. Beneath them were wooden utensils, baby clothes and small wood carvings. It was a valuable link to a time at Skaha which they had until now, only guessed at.

When all had been returned to the trunk and the key put in place once more, Cartrell took up the lamp, closed the door behind them and followed Sydney down the stairs. As he did so, he decided the time was right to discuss a date for their marriage.

Once in the parlour Sydney sank into the sofa, dabbing a handkerchief at her neck. The heat had become unbearable and Sydney despised it. Her clothes held fast to her body in an unhealthy stickiness and the threat of suffocation seemed constantly with her.

"Sydney–" Cartrell began. "I want to be serious for a moment." Their affair, which had lingered much longer than he had imagined it should, must be brought to marriage. "It seems that I have loved you all my life, at times in vain, but always in hope. Are we waiting for somebody's permission to marry? I don't think so."

Sydney smiled as she waved a fan before her face. "Then let's do it."

Cartrell's chin dropped in surprise. "How long have you waited for me to say this?"

"Forever, darling!"

He stared down at her for a moment, smiling. "Then we'll obtain the necessary license. Do you suppose you could get together some flowers, a cake and plan a luncheon in celebration?" He leaned over her, brushing aside the damp strands of hair clinging to her ear and neck. "I believe that little church beside Willow Creek could be opened for this occasion." Pulling Sydney to her feet, he drew her close, pressing her head against his shoulder. Turning her face toward his, he lifted her chin with gentle fingertips and touched her lips with his.

The wedding of Sydney Llewellyn and Ian Cartrell took place in October, 1927. Cartrell, breaking with his traditional suit of black in favour of brown, waited at the entrance of the church with Dick Foderow beside him.

In a moment of amusement, Foderow, as tall as Cartrell, leaned sideways, smiled and remarked, "That suit is quite a switch for you, Ian. Sure that Sydney will recognize you?"

Ian smiled but did not reply.

The car arrived, bringing Sydney, Thomas and Sydney's longtime friend Helga Volholven. Cartrell and Foderow turned toward the dark interior of the church and, with Reverend Allan Glass who had travelled up from Oliver, walked up the aisle past a dozen guests. Cartrell's family was present and had seated themselves with Foderow's wife and daughter, and Sydney Alex. Gus Volholven was beside Alma Davies.

Perfection in soft, flowing green chiffon and velvet, a regal Sydney entered the little church on Thomas' arm. Soft curls were loosely held by a clasp of silk flowers.

Cartrell's heart raced. Forever, it seemed, this woman's femininity and beauty had captured him. As she moved toward him, Sydney seemed now, more than at any other time, to truly belong to him.

No bitter memories flooded Sydney's mind this day. The harshness of what her life had been, the disappointments, the sorrow over her losses had all been put behind her so that she may begin anew in an uncomplicated love.

As they left the church amid cheers, Cartrell grasped Sydney's hand and got into the car.

Suddenly Thomas' arm reached toward his mother and he called, "I'd like you to meet someone." A hopeful look came into his eyes, a seeking of silent approval, as he introduced them. "Mother, this is Mary McGovern. Mary, meet my mother." Grinning while meeting Cartrell's dark eyes, he added, "and Ian, my step-father."

Nodding, Cartrell replied, "Pleased, my dear. Thomas was not right to keep you hidden from us; but, no longer, I trust."

Sydney's smile was bright and encouraging. "This makes me very pleased," she said softly. "Mary, come into the car with us. Sydney Alex, hurry now. Lunch is waiting for us at Skaha Place."

Cartrell's head swung around. "Skaha Place?"

Enchantingly, Sydney informed him, "Of course, Ian dear! As soon as we've built a new house for ourselves, I'll put my plans into action. The Llewellyn house will become Skaha Place. I have been inspired by the discovery of the contents of Rachel's trunk."

"A place for what?"

"Ian, darling, for people to stay in. By turning it into a holiday lodge and displaying those old artifacts, a visit to our area will be very informative and interesting. Please trust me and let us enjoy the best meal hereabouts today." Sydney's enthusiasm for this special occasion never faltered.

Thomas had come to realize that Cartrell would not, at any time, let her down. In fact, he concluded, I have done that more than anyone. He recalled many times when Cartrell's presence was needed and had always been provided.

Eventually Cartrell and Thomas were alone on the wide veranda.

"I commend you, Tom, for your gentlemanly way in giving your mother to me." Looking across at Thomas, he suggested, "It could not have been easy for you."

Thomas was amused by their circumstances. "Was this deliberate? To finally make me your son?"

"Of course it was! I must say, Tom, I am impressed with your friend."

"From Oliver, at this time. She's teaching there." There was a moment's hesitation before he volunteered further information, but eventually he confided, "She is not yet divorced, although that will soon be done. She's already gone back to her maiden name. Her father is Terry McGovern of the construction company."

Ian nodded, recognizing the name. "Shall we go back in? Quite possibly our brawn is needed to restore the place to order." He opened the screen door and they passed through.

In the early evening Sydney and Ian left the house and got into the car, where Thomas and Mary waited to take them to Penticton. A room had been taken at the Incola Hotel. In Penticton they would board a rail coach in the morning for a honeymoon in Vancouver. The cool evening air enveloped Skaha and a growing darkness enclosed its occupants as Thomas drove away from the ranch. He saw his mother's new marriage as not only a beginning for her, but the closing of an era at White Lake.

Dawn of the following day saw the start of construction on Cartrell's new home. Arrangements had been left with Foderow. The selected site was near Mercy Spring, named for the young Negro, Mercy Bright, who had lived in the trapper's time at Skaha. Tall Ponderosa pines and firs lent a calm, protective atmosphere to the area. The site, uncultivated and private, signified a new beginning for Ian and Sydney.

19

Sydney Cartrell's enthusiasm for her Skaha Place project found, not development and prosperity, but a world substantially dampened by the declining economy of the country. In the aftermath of the stock market crash in October, 1929, Canada was deep in an unimaginable depression.

As Sydney and Ian listened to news through the noisy static of their battery radio, they learned that some of the Similkameen mines were closing. Men laid off, found work in the building of the Hope-Princeton road, a portion of the highway linking the Okanagan and Fraser valleys. Government relief camps were being set up, and what work was available for full time employees would be divided between the various camps located at points along that road. As the number of unemployed rose, Ian and Sydney sat back in their chairs, aghast. Each new day brought more devastating news. How could the situation possibly get worse?

But, it did.

Drought began its destruction of the west.

In April, 1933 Sydney and her granddaughter, now a tall, slim eleven year old, stepped out of the Buick into the warm sunshine of a Friday morning, and onto the path crossing the churchyard at Okanagan Falls. Brushing at the wisps of golden curls over young Sydney Alex' shoulders, Sydney suggested through tight lips, "You might look a little brighter. After all, child, it isn't the end of the world, you know. Confirmation is one of the highlights of a young girl's life, and you need to study for it."

The white clapboard exterior of the United Church reflected the morning sun as the door was opened by Reverend Allan Glass. When pleasantries had been exchanged, Sydney Alex left them for the lesson held in the small classroom at the back of the building.

"I am struck each time I come here," Sydney said to Reverend Glass, "by the fact that this church was collapsed by a dynamite blast, gathered up and brought here from Fairview, and is so perfectly rebuilt."

Allan Glass was proud of that accomplishment, which had taken place in 1929. He now conducted services in both Oliver and Okanagan Falls.

"Might I have a serious word with you, Reverend?" Sydney

suggested.

"Anytime, Mrs. Cartrell. This door is always open and so, may I add, are my ears." A short man of five feet six, he barely had to tilt his head to look across into Sydney's face. He had been in the service of the church for twenty years and, at forty-five, held his small congregation solidly together with a sprinkling of tactful wit and humour, which was also injected into his interaction with the community.

"And I daresay," she mused mischievously, "that you've heard many a tale under the cloak of secrecy."

He led her along the aisle beneath a ceiling of polished pine board and offered her one of the two chairs beside a small table on the dais.

"Well, this is not a confidential matter. It's everyone's problem, which must be dealt with," Sydney began.

From across the desk Allan Glass' eyes widened in curiosity. "It sounds as if you've hit upon a plan to save the country from its economic crisis. Or reorganize our little parish when, I can assure you, everything's running tickity-boo."

Sydney stifled a giggle. "Oh, to be blessed with the power to do both! But seriously, it has to do with Skaha."

Reverend Glass leaned back in his chair, pondering the active and imaginative mind of the impeccably dressed lady across from him.

"My intention, Reverend, is to turn the Llewellyn house at Skaha into a lodge."

"A lodge? For what reason, located where it is."

"Two months ago, Dick brought a young man to us who was desperate for help. He was alone and without work, without food or any other provisions. We took him in. He keeps the wood bins filled, and helps Thomas and Dick with renovations to the old house. All that he asks is a meal a day. We give him three. He has a room of his own, and I have given him some of Thomas' old clothes."

Allan Glass nodded approvingly. "That's very generous of you."

"That boy is an example of what is going on all across our country. I know about such matters. I hear it on the radio and read it in the paper. Just three weeks ago Ian brought another young man home, whom he caught stealing bread down here at Hicks' grocery. He had hopped a train in Vancouver and fractured his ankle. He's still with us, mending well and, of course, living in the old house."

The Reverend leaned cautiously forward in his chair. "Well, fine examples they are, indeed. Now Mrs. Cartrell, you're telling me all this for a reason. Am I to raise some assistance from the congregation for you? The congregation is barely feeding and clothing itself."

Sydney's back straightened. Allan Glass saw this. The dye is cast, he told himself. I'm in it now.

Her smile was winning. Her soft blue eyes never wavered under his steady gaze. "What I ask from you, is that you request old blankets, clothes, footwear, even furniture and dishes, anything to share with the residents of my old house. There may only be two there at the moment, but word gets around, you know." Sydney rose to leave.

"I will do my best—"

"Actually Reverend Glass," she interrupted, "people are not really interested in whether they'll go to Heaven or to Hell, but more in how to stay alive and avoid both."

Glass was astonished. He followed her down the narrow aisle. "An interesting point of view, Mrs. Cartrell."

Reaching for the door nob, she said quietly, "I'll let myself out. Thank you for your assistance. The Lord smiles upon good deeds. But then," Sydney turned, glancing back at him coquettishly, "I don't need to tell you that, do I?"

Allan Glass watched Sydney walk along the grassy pathway, the hem of her skirt swaying above her stockinged ankles. He shook his head in wonder. An indomitable woman. Is there one who could say no to her?

Help arrived as a result of Allan Glass' impassioned plea, and before the renovations were finished, the old Llewellyn house was well furnished. True to Sydney's prediction, as one month passed into another, Skaha's number of impoverished occupants increased.

Cartrell muttered impatiently from his chair in the living room of their new home, as the fury of a September thunderstorm struck outside, "The place is getting like a relief camp."

"Well, Ian darling, that's exactly what it is already, only the support is coming from us and the community, not the government. After all, when you brought home the young man who had the broken ankle, did you believe for a single minute that you would turn him back out to hop onto another train and smash the other foot?"

Thomas, who had joined them for the evening meal, dared to comment, "I have almost more men working for me than I have horses to look after."

His mother replied curtly, "Look at it this way, Thomas, you've more help than you've ever had and you need it. Instead of employing three or four men steady on full wages, you're giving a home and good fare to many— including some women and children, and getting more jobs done. The cost amounts to the same. Also," she continued, "we have a teacher in one of the ladies. We can open the school and eliminate the daily travel to Kaleden."

Cartrell looked up from his newspaper and across the room at Thomas to catch his reaction. To his wife, Cartrell said, "Your sense of logic always manages to put a strain on one's imagination."

"We are simply keeping people alive who might otherwise have got themselves thrown in jail, been left to freeze to death, or die of starvation." Rising from the sofa, Sydney stood authoritatively before them. "We have an enormous garden this year despite a drought. As a result, the root house is full. The woodshed is full, and logs wait for the saw. We have eggs, milk and butter and extra vegetables to barter with. We are not living in the lap of luxury ourselves, but neither are we dependent upon anyone else's generosity."

"Undoubtedly, my dear, you are headed for martyrdom." Cartrell spoke quietly, smiling toward his wife, who remained unsmiling before him, in wonder of his statement.

The current activities at Skaha pressed young Sydney Alex into action in an area unfamiliar to her; work. The idea of employment in her life and its necessity in her future was making itself felt for the first time. The hours of her day, when not given to studies, were spent learning to sew her own clothes, preserve foods, separate milk, and collect eggs. Her protests went unheard by her grandmother. Cartrell, as well, had an unsympathetic ear. To her father, Sydney Alex confided nothing, for he was seldom at home and did not live in the same house anyway.

On a warm October afternoon Sydney Alex complained to her best friend, Janet Foderow, "Life is dull, dull, dull!"

"I agree, 'gree, 'gree," replied Janet, "but your Gran rules the roost, so to speak," mimicking Cartrell, "and there's nothing you can do about it."

The girls convulsed in giggles over Janet's ability in mimicry, and sat upon the grass near the stream at Mercy Spring. Pessimism reigned in Sydney Alex' thoughts and she murmured forlornly, "No one exciting ever comes here. All those people who live at the big house are old men and skinny women with whiney brats." She sat up abruptly and pulled idly at the dry grass.

Janet glanced at Sydney Alex from beneath long, dark lashes. "You mean, no boys ever land here; boys our age."

"The youngest one here is twenty-five and that's old already."

"What about school? There's some smart ones there, and cute-looking, too." When Sydney Alex did not reply, Janet suggested, "Maybe they're not smart enough for you."

Sydney Alex ignored the remark and flopped back against the ground to stare up at the clear October sky.

Sensing the dangerous ground on which she had nearly tread,

Janet leapt to her feet. "I'm going to run all the way home and hope I lose some of this awful baby fat. Coming?"

"I don't need to run. I'm not fat," Sydney Alex replied smugly.

Janet stared at Sydney Alex a moment. "Well, see you later then," she called as she dashed off at a quick pace along the dusty pathway.

Sydney Alexandra lingered, walking slowly, kicking unhappily at the twigs and pine cones littering the trail. A deep craving for excitement burned within her. Her world seemed to be shrinking and, instead of developing into the alert, exciting, interesting and mysterious young woman she craved to be, she feared that she was becoming an insufferable bore. Such natural pains of growing up were difficult for Sydney Alex to bear.

Autumn disappeared beneath winter's cold and snow. The occupants of the old Llewellyn house bonded together as if they were a family, and prepared their home for the approaching Christmas season. The residents were living several to a room and were crowded with children, but nonetheless happy for a warm hearth. The pantry, the smokehouse, and the root cellar built into the hillside, held ample provisions for the year ahead.

On a crisp December morning one week before Christmas Day, Sydney Alex accompanied Cartrell up the wooded hillside behind their new house, in search of two nicely tapered firs. With a pale sun peeking over the far mountain ridges, she hurried along behind the tall man.

Through the years Sydney Alex had become quite comfortable with him. She had shed her old fear, and a bond had developed between them.

The relationship which she had dreamed would never end with her father, had drawn to a close when Mary McGovern entered their lives. Horse races along the old fur brigade road, cattle drives out to spring range and fast trips to town in the ranch's light delivery truck had abruptly ended. Sydney Alex felt as though she suddenly had no father at all.

"I miss my father, you know, Papa," she suddenly blurted. "I should be doing this with him."

A man sensitive to others' needs, Cartrell quickly picked up on young Sydney's troubles and listened attentively.

"I don't think he loves me much anymore." Stumbling alongside Cartrell, she hastily added, "That is a secret, Papa."

Cartrell smiled. He had raised two daughters of his own and lived in worlds in which they had woven their magic moments and shared their secrets with him. "Well, it is safe with me. Now hold tight while

I saw this tree." The saw handle kept catching on the pocket of his wool coat, irritating him until, after a few moments, he began to wonder why he was out there at all.

"Thank you, Papa. I love you very much, you know."

He smiled. "I hope so. I'd hate to be feeding an extra mouth at the table that didn't give a damn for me."

As Cartrell and Sydney Alex dragged two trees homeward, the sun disappeared and a light breeze came up to play amongst the branches of the pines and huge firs towering near them. On the rise behind the new house they rested in the snow.

Below them Thomas' car entered the clearing, bogging down in the soft snow at the garden gateway. Sydney appeared on the veranda, extending her hands in welcome to Mary McGovern as she took the steps to the house. Their happy voices drifted on the air.

"I don't like Miss McGovern," Sydney Alex confessed.

Cartrell was hardly surprised. The girl's disappearance from the room during the rare times that Mary was with them, told him that. "Do you know why you don't like her?" He returned his gaze toward the yard below them. "Is it because you feel the competition of her love for your father? She does love him, you know, and he has strong feelings for her. The loss of your mother has been very hard for him. Mary brought him out of his shell, so to speak."

Sydney Alex remained silent.

Cartrell touched her shoulder lightly. "Come," he said. "There's no point in my telling you that it will work out for the best. It may not, unless you are willing to look within yourself for some understanding."

They slid on the snow as they travelled downhill, and the trees glided with them. Cartrell's raised voice was carried on the air as he attempted to bring her back from her reverie.

"There are a lot of people worse off than you, girl. They would consider themselves blessed if all they had to worry about was whether they liked one another or not. Think about it!" he called back to her.

Sydney Alexandra Llewellyn willed her ears not to listen to his reasoning, for she knew his every word to be the truth, as always. Soon she would be twelve; old enough to recognize that it was time for her to begin growing up emotionally, but the process seemed agonizing to her. Oh, dear Lord, if only I could become a young woman overnight!

The shapely tree that Cartrell had taken to his own home stood proudly in the corner dressed in colourful bulbs and silver tinsel, but it was bereft of gifts beneath it. The true spirit of Christmas, Sydney explained, was in making others less fortunate feel included, and her unselfish nature insisted that their gifts be placed with those under the tree in the lodge.

Everybody had one gift. A small tub of homemade candies and biscuits was brought out for the children. The group, numbering twenty-three adults and seven children, sat down to a dinner of roast turkey, vegetables and preserves from the cellar, and hams from the smokehouse. Carrot pudding with the traditional plum sauce and a large fruit cake covered with a thin layer of rich almond paste completed the dinner.

Afterward Thomas harnessed a team of horses, eased them into the traces of the sleigh and the hay rides were on. There was skating on a small pond created near Cartrell's new home and a bonfire lit for warmth. In the evening when everyone had returned to the house warm and happy, Sydney sat to the piano in the parlour, signalling the commencement of carols.

Darkness had descended upon them by several hours and the snow began. Throughout the rooms, gas lamps were hung from the ceilings, their circles of light lending a cheery atmosphere as the day drew near its close.

Cartrell left the group, put on his hat and coat, and quietly left for a walk. As he strolled along the road past his old office and the new livery barn, the snow crunched loudly with each step. Flakes dampened his face, blurring his vision through the glasses he wore, so he removed them, carefully stowing them away in a pocket case.

Nostalgia gripped him. The sound of rich, ringing voices followed him from the distance, the lyrics echoing across the yard through the crisp December air. But somewhere ahead of him along the old fur brigade road, from another lodge, from another time, Cartrell heard the plaintive wail of a harmonica and the soft strum of a guitar; a vision of a table in the corner of a smoke-filled room, cowboys holding their cards within the small circle of the dull, yellow glow of a lamp toward which curled the smoke from their cigarettes; a scene from yesteryear. He could see, again, young David McAllister slumped into the chair before the blazing hearth, his crutches resting beside him, when Dick Foderow entered the room on a chilly October evening to tell the man of the birth of his son; and Albert Llewellyn barking orders over at the livery barn to the stubborn blacksmith, Holinger, who listened to no one but himself.

Ian Cartrell could not know of a past more significant to Skaha than that of his own time there; the winter evenings when the trapper, Rayne McAllister, and the young Okanagan, Two Way, walked this same road from their lodgings to the tack shed. There they had spent their evenings by a lighted oil-wick mending harness while Two Way's sister, Nahna, stitched deer hide tunics and moccasins.

It was not of Cartrell's time, the sound of three hundred pack horses, the brigade bugler sounding the departure in the early morning mist. Water, fresh and cool splashed from the yard pump into the long trough as tired, dusty men of the fur trade were welcomed to what comfort could be offered at Skaha Crossing. He knew of it only from Duncan McAllister and Two Way. He had learned from Rachel McAllister and Horace Whiteman of the wagon train that brought the Hackett, Whiteman, Willemeyer and Bean families to settle in the White Lake basin.

The familiar sounds that Cartrell's memory drew on that night were those of freight teams and creaking wagons crossing the flats; the bawl of cattle being herded into the mountains of summer range; and, of course, the unforgettable rumbling of water which had flooded Skaha.

Cartrell returned to the big house. Through the falling snow he saw the carollers beyond the windowpane, grouped about the piano with his wife, who was a marvellous combination of encouragement and strength to them. She will always be, he knew, beautiful, youthful and caring. He was very proud of her.

As Cartrell returned to the house and stepped up on the veranda, the odour of tobacco drew his attention to the far corner.

Dick Foderow sat alone, a trail of smoke from his cigarette drifting away. He said to Cartrell, "I believe this to be one of the finest evenings I've ever spent up here, Ian. How about you?"

"Indeed," replied Cartrell. "A few folks missing–"

"Uh huh."

"Old Two Way shuffling through the snowdrifts to the livery for his daily visit with that grouchy Holinger; people we took for granted. And things like a townsite full of lighted houses at night and fiddle music from the community hall. A bit different now, Dick."

Foderow replied in a soft tone, "But the feeling's the same, Ian. It's here on this place. Nothing about the feeling of tonight is much different from then."

"Of our time here," said Cartrell, "only Sydney has known it all, helped build it and live it, then watched as a town dwindled to just a ranch. Did you know that she and Albert arrived here in 1891? She has told me about the ship they came on to Canada, the railway and the wagon trip across the prairies, the mountain trail and rivers. Real hardships not entirely unlike some of my own, but things are more difficult for a woman; especially a woman with children."

Foderow asked reflectively, "Is there a McAllister alive anywhere these days? Does anyone know of them? People seem to disappear somehow."

"Well, yes. I believe there is still McAllister kin up north somewhere. Nell knew one of them." Cartrell smiled and sighed. "Founding residents might disappear, but Skaha shall never die if Sydney has a say. She holds an ace up her sleeve - a trunk full of memorabilia from the past, the legacy of Rachel Hackett McAllister."

Inside the house the music had stopped. The night had fallen quiet and snow ceased to fall.

In the dark of the veranda, Cartrell said to Foderow, "Do you realize, Dick, that in only seven more days you and Sydney and I begin the year 1934? Do you remember the night we met– the time Llewellyn's hay barn got on fire? It was in 1896, I believe. We've come a fair mile together."

Foderow rose to his feet and met Cartrell's steady gaze. "And there's never been a cross word between us. Let's shake on that, Ian." Reaching out, their hands clasped for a moment before they entered the house.

20

On a mid-February morning in 1934, Sydney Alex travelled to Penticton with her father to meet Mary McGovern, arriving on the eastbound train from Vancouver. Mary was returning from a two month leave of absence to care for her father who had suddenly been taken ill; a matter which hardly drew Sydney Alex' interest. She was simply along because she had been told that she should spend more time with her father and get better acquainted with Mary. Clad warmly in a blue wool coat and a muff which had been given to her grandmother long ago, she was well-insulated against the cold weather, and the chill which she knew would emanate from Mary McGovern.

That day, which began uneventfully, would set in motion the destiny of Sydney Alex Llewellyn.

Thomas and his young daughter waited wordlessly together. Silence between them seemed to have become an unexplained habit. Occasionally, as if seeking reassurance of her presence there, Sydney Alex glanced up at her tall father, studying the stern features of his face. She wondered if he could feel her uneasiness.

As the Canadian Pacific engine braked to a stop amid the hissing sounds of steam and screeching wheels against the rails, they caught a glimpse of Mary as she stepped through the doorway of the coach. For a brief startling moment, Thomas was struck by the resemblance between this woman and his deceased wife, Nell, as she had been when he had met her at the Winnipeg depot.

Long, dark hair spread from beneath Mary's ribboned hat, partly hiding her face and lending an aura of mystery to her appearance. Tall and slim, as Nell Windsor had been, she wore her clothes well, the style in keeping with the trend and season.

Standing on the platform, Sydney Alex reached out and tugged at her father's jacket sleeve. "Is she to be my mother? Is that why I'm here?"

Startled out of the reverie in which Thomas watched Mary, he frowned at his daughter. "You're here because I decided that you should be here. There doesn't have to be a reason."

Rebuffed, Sydney Alex dropped her gaze to the rough planking of the platform, staring through the spaces between the oily boards to the snow patches which had drifted and dried beneath.

Suddenly something dark moved under the boards, over the dirty snow. Sydney Alex looked away sharply, up to her father's face and back to the planks. It was still there. In fact, she discovered, the patch of snow was now completely covered by it.

Sydney Alex noticed the broad smile which broke across her father's face as he stepped off the platform and swept Mary up in his arms. He's forgotten that I am here, she decided, and leaned forward once more to peer between the boards. Nothing moved now, but Sydney Alex' curiosity had been piqued. Carefully watching the crowd, she stepped toward the edge of the platform and deliberately dropped her small handbag alongside the steps. Hastily she moved to retrieve it, kneeling to the ground to linger near the opening beneath the platform.

Wide brown eyes watched her from the darkness within, warning her into silence. Catching her breath in astonishment, she whispered, "Who are you?"

"Get away!" hissed a voice full of desperation.

Her attention completely caught now, Sydney Alex intentionally dumped the contents of the purse onto the crusty snow and, with an eye upon the figure lying before her in the shadows, she methodically began to replace them. "Tell me who you are. Are you hurt? Tell me or I'll scream that you snatched my purse."

"Get away! Go on!"

"No. I'm going to scream now." A surge of excitement gripped her.

"Alright! My name is Ryan. Now beat it, kid."

"You sound very young. Why are you here?"

"Because I ain't got no place else to be."

"You're hiding from someone."

He quickly realized that if he aggravated this girl, she might deliberately give his position away, so he replied cautiously, "The constable, and if you stay here he's bound to find me. Now get lost." He cursed himself for having got into such a situation by illegally hopping the train. However, these were hard times and he had no money for transportation.

Sydney Alex rose to her feet as Thomas and Mary joined her.

"Now that we're all together," Thomas was saying, "Let's go and get your luggage, Mary."

"Daddy, I'll wait here. You won't mind, Miss McGovern?" Composed now, Sydney Alex held her ground, thereby shielding her discovery from view of the passengers milling about and the constable pacing the railway tracks between the platform and the waiting train. "I want to watch the engine puff its steam when it leaves," she added cheerfully.

Thomas tapped her shoulder with a warning,. "Don't you move then."

"Don't worry about that. Thank you." She held her position firmly.

As the constable passed by her, he queried, "Have you been left behind, young lady?"

"No, sir. I'm waiting for my father, Mr. Thomas Llewellyn."

Nodding, for he recognized the name, he cautioned, "Righto. Don't move then."

Sydney Alex stifled an amused smile. Quickly dragging an abandoned crate toward the steps, she sat down, carefully smoothing her coat over her knees. Through long blonde ringlets which fell over her face as she turned her head to the side, she spoke to the boy behind her. "Everybody's gone now. You can tell me why you're being hunted."

"I'm not being hunted. I'm only hiding."

"It's the same thing."

"How old are you anyway?" he queried suspiciously.

"I'm twelve, last month. Are you much grown up? I mean, you don't sound like an old man."

"It's a little tough to sound grown up from underneath here on the ground."

"Well, you can come out now. There's no one around. I want to see what a fugitive looks like."

"I'll be fifteen pretty soon. And– I'm not a fugitive! In fact, I'm cold and hungry and wet, and the only thing I own is this blanket I got wrapped 'round me."

Into Sydney Alex' view came her father. "I'll tell you what you can do," she offered quickly. "Tonight you sneak out of here and go to a place called Skaha. It's up in the hills south of here at White Lake. My grandmother will look after you. She looks after everybody, and everyone knows her. I'm leaving now. My father's coming." Without a backward glance, Sydney Alex rose to leave the railway station with Thomas and Mary.

That evening Sydney Alex went to her grandmother's sitting room next to her grandparents' bedroom, to share the news of the young man beneath the railway platform. When she entered, an unhappy scene greeted her. Ian was leaning anxiously over his wife, who was slumped in an awkward manner into her chair, pain etched upon her face. Sydney Alex shrank against the wall as fear seized her.

Cartrell turned to her. "Run and get your father," he commanded calmly.

"He's not here, Papa. He took Miss McGov–"

"Get Dick then!"

"Yes, Papa. Is she dying, Papa?"

"Run!"

With fear gripping her, Sydney Alex fled through the doorway while screaming for Mrs. Davies.

Out of the ravine she ran, over the wet, slippery weeds of the trail, across the flats, the flashlight bobbing in the dark, until she finally reached the steps of Foderow's house. The door opened and Sydney Alex stumbled into the kitchen, breathless and, for a moment, she stared wordlessly at Dick.

"Please, please– Gran–"

However, Foderow, at first sight of Sydney Alex, had reached for his hat and coat. He stepped around the girl and left the house.

Cartrell had moved Sydney to their bed, placed a cool cloth upon her forehead and now waited. A feeling of utter helplessness and despair engulfed him as he felt for Sydney's pulse. Her breathing came with gasps of pain. Her lovely bright complexion was drained of all colour. Her body was weak.

Sydney Alex entered. Through tears which spilled over her cheeks, she whispered to Cartrell, "He's gone to get the car, Papa." She choked back a sob. "I used the short cut home. It's so dark out–"

"Come, child," Cartrell said, reaching for her hand. "Sit here with me. Gran'll be alright. She needs the hospital."

Sydney Alex stared tearfully into Cartrell's dark eyes, saw the worry there and felt something of the hurt he suffered for her grandmother. His hair is more gray than black, she noticed. As he leaned over the bed, he seemed like a tired old man. Her eyes rested upon her stricken grandmother, and Sydney Alex moved from Cartrell's side to kneel upon the floor close to the bed.

Gone was the bright smile, the lovely complexion. Her lips were pale and pinched against the pain flooding her chest. Lying over the pillow were the long strands of golden locks, loose and unbrushed. It seemed as though it was not her beautiful, lively grandmother who lay there, but a tired, old lady filled with great pain, who may die on this night if Dick Foderow did not soon arrive with the car.

Sydney Alex whispered, "She looks so old–"

"Shush, child– she can hear you," Cartrell admonished with a smile. "And when she gets better you'll get a smart swat for that remark!"

Foderow entered the room and gently carried Sydney outside to the vehicle. In as many seconds as it took Sydney Alex to blink back her tears, the car had disappeared into the dark night.

The girl turned away from the empty doorway and sought the solace of Mrs. Davies' comforting arms. "I wish Daddy was here," she wept forlornly. "I feel so lonely right now."

Mrs. Davies rocked her tenderly against her bosom, and laid her face against the top of Sydney Alex' head. "Your Gran is in the best possible hands–" she comforted. "She has the Lord on her side."

21

The sun was warm the following day, melting the snow and sending little rivulets of water rushing toward Willow Creek and the white alkaline lake. Slush and mud filled the unpaved road into Skaha, causing Dick Foderow to bog down in the half-frozen mire as he drove the light delivery toward the gate. He jumped out to get his shovel and noticed someone walking in the distance.

Foderow watched him pass through the wide gateway, pause briefly beneath the huge sign, SKAHA RANCH, and look up to study it. He was tall for his age, with the stride of the self-assured and unafraid. He carried no possessions and wore a torn denim jacket with a battered black cowboy hat sitting upon a thick mat of dirty, dark hair. Foderow did not know him, yet there was a certain familiarity about him. He leaned against the shovel.

Suddenly recognition registered in Foderow's mind, for when the young man turned to look at him, he knew his hunch was right.

The eyes of the man and the boy met.

"Name's Ryan McAllister. Call me Mac if you like," the newcomer stated with a broad smile. "Can I give you a hand there?"

Foderow shook his head. "I'll manage."

"I'm lookin' for a lady called Mrs. Cartrell."

A moment passed, during which Foderow gathered his thoughts. He lifted the shovel to continue digging. "Yup, everybody's lookin' for her alright. Well, she's in the hospital. Seems her tired heart gave out under the strain of everyone findin' her."

Ryan McAllister straightened and stilled, staring across into Foderow's eyes. "In other words, you mean for me to git my tail back on outta here and not bother the rest of you."

It took Foderow a moment, while he shovelled the mud, but he made an assessment and gave his instructions. "Naw, you go on over to the big house there and ask someone to give you some clothes. Then you get out back in the porch, stoke up the stove, haul some water from the creek and have a bath. And wash that hair. After that, you take those rags you got on your hide and burn 'em in that pit you see yonder. That gets rid of any bedbugs you might be packin' around."

Young McAllister grinned at Foderow. "There ain't no bugs on me, but I won't turn down a good scrubbing and some clean duds, and maybe a big plate of vittles, eh? I'm willing to work, you know." He stared openly at Foderow. "I don't take nothin' free," he added proudly. He reached out and, with a firm grasp, vigorously shook Foderow's hand. "Mighty glad to pump yer paw, cowboy!"

Turning, Ryan McAllister swung down the old brigade road that, unknown to him, his great-great-grandfather had cleared. Tossing his tattered hat high into the air, he leapt up to catch it, yelling out huskily, "E-ya-hoo!" sufficiently loud enough to bring a dozen residents from the house to watch, like a family of curious gophers.

Foderow smiled in amusement. As he watched the young McAllister stride along the roadway and heard him whistling a familiar tune, Dick Foderow sensed a new pulse, something akin to the feeling of a new beginning at Skaha. It was similar to when Ian Cartrell first arrived in old Dogtown. What he had glimpsed that day in Ryan McAllister told him there would be no putting the lad down, for there seemed to be a positive attitude not easily discouraged in this McAllister, which would be well worth hanging onto.

Did Ryan McAllister know that his roots were buried at Skaha? What had brought him to the Okanagan? How had he heard of Skaha? And where had he come from? Foderow could only await answers, as he watched Ryan enter the veranda of the old Llewellyn house and disappear into its depths.

He took up the shovel and began digging once more at the mud packed before the wheels of the truck, glancing occasionally toward the house. Eventually a thick curl of fresh smoke wound skyward from the chimney at the back. Across the yard McAllister ran to the creek with buckets for water. Foderow had dug his way out of the mud and loaded the delivery with the wood of a fallen pine before he noticed the lad walk across to the burning pit and drop his worn-out clothes.

When it was established that Sydney's condition would remain stable, although she would stay in hospital, Foderow received a message to return Cartrell to Skaha.

Soft, wet flakes of snow fell heavily against the windshield of the car. Watching them, Cartrell remarked, "Strange weather. Just when you think you've got an early spring coming, you find that winter's set in again." Turning to Foderow, he asked directly, "Did he say how it was that his name is McAllister? Could be only a coincidence, you know."

"I feel it in my bones. He said his name was Dietrich, but he found it didn't belong to him, so dropped it. He's pretty independent looking."

Cartrell informed him, "Dave's wife married a German fellow, Anton Dietrich who, Sydney says, came over the mountains with her and Albert. In fact, he's Helga Volholven's brother. And Tom tells me that when he came home from the army he met Richard, Dave's boy that Anna had before he died. The boy took the name Dietrich, not McAllister. Nell was Richard's sister-in-law."

Foderow blinked his eyes. Peering through the windshield kept clean by worn rubber wipers scraping noisily back and forth, he muttered, "Confusing, as hell, but somehow I followed you. It's sure a small world when you think of it."

"Well, Sydney tells me their name was Dietrich and Thomas says the same. My legal mind tells me that Dave's son was never adopted by the stepfather and McAllister still remains the family name." Cartrell glanced across at Foderow. "Also, that this lad and his parents have had a falling out. He's a long way from home. You know, Dick, these are hard times and here we have a fifteen year old boy out on his own in a country that's starving to death."

Ryan McAllister quickly became settled at Skaha. His easygoing, congenial manner endeared him to everyone, even Cartrell. He adapted to ranch life readily and, as the weeks passed, took over chores without hesitation.

At the barn one morning as they readied their horses for the drive to summer range, Foderow remarked to Thomas, "I like him. It's good to have him about the place. There's some life in that boy."

"Suits me," Thomas replied quickly. "You'll need him."

Foderow turned to watch Thomas, and Thomas looked across at Foderow. There was sudden silence in the dull interior of the building.

Foderow enquired bluntly, "You got somethin' in your craw, Tom?"

"I'm leaving the ranch," Thomas replied calmly.

Foderow was stunned. "What the hell makes you say that?"

"It's a long story."

"I'm listening!" Foderow angrily flung a bridle with broken reins into the nearest corner and reached another from off the wall, checking the bit. "I'm fifty-five years old and I've been workin' for this outfit one way or another since I was twenty, and I never thought I'd see a day here without a Llewellyn on the place." Foderow reached for Thomas' arm. "Come on outta this barn. Clear your head and tell me you're only joshin' me a little."

"Dick–" Thomas held back. "I'm not joshin'. I've given it a lot of thought for a long time and I've finally made a decision."

"A decision! Well, dammit–" Clearly, Foderow was beside himself with the news, and strode out of the barn into the bright May sunlight. He paced the yard and pounded his hat angrily against his leg. "You are crazy!" Looking across at Thomas, who had followed him outside, he asked bluntly, "Have you considered exactly what you'll do, where you'll go? There're no jobs. Hell, you know that. What happened?" A smile crossed Foderow's face. "Did Mary hit a windfall?"

Thomas looked down at the braided leather rein between his hands. "If it wasn't the truth, Dick, I'd hit you for that."

"The truth! What truth? And– hit me?" Astonishment flooded Foderow. He began to chew impatiently at the edge of his mustache, while he fumbled in his pocket for his cigarettes.

"Mary's leaving the school next month to teach in Vancouver, and I'm going with her." Thomas' voice was steady, controlled. For the first time in his life he felt he actually knew where he was going and what he was doing. "Her father has a construction company as you know–"

"Did I know that? Nobody knows that! I don't remember hearing that."

"You were with me in Kamloops when I met him. That's what I want to do. Machines are where the money will be in the future– heavy duty construction." Thomas turned into the dark hollow of the barn.

Foderow was incredulous. "Well, I don't goddamn well believe you!" he called after Thomas and stomped angrily down the road and across the flats to his house.

The place was empty. He supposed his wife must be down at the Cartrells or at the lodge, as the old Llewellyn house was now called. He dug furiously among the dishes in the dining room buffet and found his whiskey. Reaching for a glass, Dick Foderow poured himself a generous portion and, taking the bottle with him, went outside onto the porch and slumped down upon the wooden steps. This was, of course, another one of Thomas' whims or, he hoped, just a stupid dream. He remained on the porch a long time, while the cowboys waited and the morning wore on.

That same morning Cartrell had taken Sydney driving in the Buick and, having just returned to the ranch, they stalled as they were approaching the main yard. The Skaha cowboys rode away from the corrals to begin their cattle drive to summer range. In the distance the herd was milling restlessly, sensing the move.

Sydney, dependent on a cane, was confined to the surroundings of her home. Her damaged heart would not allow a great deal of activity and she remained unsteady on her feet. She saw little of anyone. Her special enjoyment was going for a drive with Ian.

Shielding her eyes against the sun's bright glare, Sydney enquired of Cartrell, "Who is that young man on the gray horse?"

"He's the McAllister boy I told you about." She turned her head and he met her eyes. "You're wondering of course, and justly so," he noted, "how it is he's not been to pay his respects at our house."

"I should say!" She sounded miffed, but Cartrell ignored that.

"Well, dear heart, you were in the hospital for nearly three months. I'll tell you, that boy works twenty out of twenty-four hours and sleeps the rest. And– he doesn't stay at your lodge. He lives over at the old log bunkhouse. Fixed it up to suit himself. Likes to be alone, he says. He bought a harmonica from his meagre wage and stays out of earshot of everyone. Dick insists on paying him a dollar now and then– he works longer and harder than ten others put together."

Sydney set the cane aside and settled herself more comfortably against the seat of the car. "Might I meet him?"

"I suppose– when he's ready for that. When he comes back from the drive." Cartrell got out of the car, turned the crank handle at the front and sat back in. "We are soon going to replace this antique with a car that does not require a crank to get it started!" He watched Foderow leave his house and walk across to the waiting cowboys, and wondered why they were leaving so late in the morning.

Ryan McAllister had not remained unaware of Sydney's presence in the car parked on the roadway, and he realized she must surely be enquiring about him. He had gleaned enough information from Dick Foderow to appreciate her curiosity respecting his residence at Skaha. As he rode within viewing distance of Sydney, he leaned forward in his saddle and touched a forefinger to the brim of his hat in greeting, then kneed his horse on by.

Sydney fell back against the seat of the car in astonishment. After a moment of reflection, she smiled in amusement and pleasure at his attention and sense of courtesy.

Three more weeks would pass before their meeting happened, for Ryan stayed at Skaha's cow-camp with Strickland and Smith. Upon his return he confessed to Dick Foderow as they travelled toward the Cartrell residence, "I got booted out for complaining about Smith's cookin'."

When they arrived, Alma Davies led them to Sydney's sitting room. Foderow watched as McAllister stood before Sydney and Cartrell, expecting him to feel uneasy under her careful scrutiny.

He nodded politely, "Ma'am" to her.

He is David all over again, Sydney saw, closing her eyes momentarily in thought. Contrary to the calm composure she presented, her heart seemed to pause for a second without her knowing why.

Ryan stared into Sydney's blue eyes, captivated. He decided, she is not as Grandma said she was. She's the most beautiful person I've ever seen. He realized that for Sydney's attractiveness alone, his grandmother Dietrich would dislike her.

With silver strands lacing the soft rolls of her hair which lay bound loosely about her face in familiar fashion, Sydney, very thin, showed the strain of her ordeal. Faint creases furrowed thinly across her forehead and about the corners of her delicate mouth. On this day she wore no cosmetics, and yet she was still beautiful.

Sydney snapped out of her reverie, moved slowly toward Foderow, and extended her hand to him. "Dick, dear friend, I apologize for taking you from other pursuits, but I understand this young man you've brought is someone I should have met weeks ago." Her light eyes smiled warmly at Ryan. Turning toward him, she said, "I'm curious to know how it is that your name is McAllister and not Dietrich. I'm told that you are from Prince George. That's a long way from here."

Although he stood somewhat in awe of her, Ryan was not uncomfortable in Sydney's presence. "My father has a hardware store in Prince George."

"That doesn't tell me why you are here."

"I didn't get along at home, so I was sent to my grandmother's near Williams Lake." He looked up from his hands clasped about the rim of his hat and into her eyes. "But my grandfather kicked me out," he added quite openly.

"Why?"

"He said I was lazy and he wasn't feeding the mouth of a slacker for free. Grandma told me to use my real name and go to Penticton. Somebody was bound to help me there."

"Well," Sydney sighed, "it seems that her intuition has been born out. My granddaughter just happened to be in the right place for you." Leaning on the cane, she turned toward a comfortable arm chair. "Come," she motioned, indicating the chair beside her, "sit here and tell me all about yourself and your family. McAllister is a very old name here, you know. Ian, dear--" she reached a hand affectionately toward Cartrell's arm. "Would you ask Alma for coffee and some of her little cakes. And Dick, it's Saturday morning, so Sydney Alex must be loitering about the house somewhere."

"Sure--" Foderow grinned, quickly snatching the door open to reveal the girl standing conspicuously there.

Sydney Alex moved impatiently away from Foderow, nodding almost timidly in Ryan's direction. Ryan smiled knowingly at her, realizing her embarrassment at having been caught eavesdropping. Briefly their gazes passed over each other. Sydney watched this with a curious eye, noting a new sense of awareness in her young granddaughter. Then McAllister's attention was again drawn to Sydney. "Did you know that when Sydney Alex found me, I was hiding from the police?"

"No." Sydney smiled. Was he attempting to shock her? Or was he simply being truthful. "You stole some food from somewhere, perhaps? Everybody's stealing food these days." It was a firm statement presented to show that she was unimpressed by his confession. "You can set your conscience right with a visit to Reverend Glass downtown."

"I hopped a train," he said.

A surprised expression crossed Sydney's face a moment. "I think you knew about Skaha before you met Sydney Alex."

"From Grandma," Ryan admitted. "She told me about this place. She doesn't like you, but she sent me here anyway." He glanced up at Cartrell, who had come back into the room and now stood quietly near the window.

Cartrell watched his wife's face, but she did not look up.

Young McAllister half whispered in apology, "My grandmother is very bitter about life."

Foderow excused himself from the room and the conversation in which he had been no more included than Cartrell. The two men stepped outside onto the veranda, where warm rays of sunshine danced between the vines climbing over the structure.

Cartrell glanced toward the clear sky and the hazy-blue mountains in the distance. The forest beside them had become very dry during the past month and appeared lifeless. Typically Okanagan, he reminded himself. Each year seemed to be drier than the last. Still, he felt a certain pride in the valley, despite the obvious affects the drought had on it. "He's Dave's grandson, you know."

Foderow nodded.

"We cannot avoid keeping the boy. Certainly there's no sending him back now. He's fallen out of favour all way 'round, it seems."

"Ian--" Foderow's husky voice was serious, which drew Cartrell's instant attention. "Has Tom talked to either of you lately about his plans for the future?"

"Plans? Thomas never has any plans for the future. Don't beat around the bush, Dick. Something's been bothering you for weeks."

Foderow met Cartrell's dark, knowing eyes. "Perceptive of you, Ian," he remarked, unsmiling, while rolling a cigarette. "He has told me that he's leaving the ranch in July."

Cartrell was suddenly still, but not completely surprised. Removing his glasses, he drew out his handkerchief, meticulously wiped the lens clean and replaced them, hooking the thin wires carefully over his ears. The entire process of methodical fussiness took Cartrell a full minute without a word spoken.

Beside him, Foderow cleared his throat impatiently.

"I know, I know--" Cartrell told him. "I'm expected to be shocked."

Foderow fitted his hat upon his head, running his hands along the thick felt rims, keeping the traditional curl in perfect form. "I didn't delude myself for a minute, Ian, that you'd be shocked, disappointed or even hurt by his desertion."

A hawk circled and dipped lazily in the sky above them. Cartrell's eyes followed it as he considered Thomas' thoughtless actions over the years. "He is always running away from something. The only stable, or what seemed like a stable period in his life, was the few years that Nell was here. I often wonder, if his brother had survived, what the difference might have been. Or, if Albert had been a better family man." Raising an inquisitive brow in the foreman's direction, he enquired, "Where is he going?"

"Old McGovern's construction company has moved to the coast and is taking on Thomas whenever he and Mary get there. He's been very ill with some kind of stomach trouble."

"Well, he has yet to inform his mother."

"What about the ranch?"

"Unfortunately," Cartrell sighed wearily, "Albert saw fit to leave it all to that wilful individual, but I shall soon rectify that. He'll not sell it out from under us like he did the freight."

Foderow swore. "Lord God, I hate being at his mercy! You and me– we raised him, you know."

"We're not at his mercy," Cartrell smiled. "Thomas is not smart enough to consider fright, on our part, a possibility. Leave it to me and don't mention you've told me. Forewarned is forearmed, so it is said, and I shall simply present Thomas with the documents of transfer one day. Under the threat of having both his knees shattered, he'll give Sydney the security which was Albert's obligation in the beginning. My God, the irresponsibility of some men appals me!"

Buttoning his sweater against the chance of a chill, Cartrell walked down the steps with Foderow, toward the truck. "Thank you, Dick. I'm much obliged for your confidence. By the way, young Ryan in there will get back to work by noon." Raising an arm, he waved briefly as Foderow departed the yard in the light delivery.

For the first time in his life Ian Cartrell felt as if he were growing old, and it was not a comforting feeling. The burden that was Thomas Llewellyn seemed never to cease. He wondered if Thomas had given consideration toward his daughter's future when deciding to make a move farther afield. He made a mental note to have a paper drawn up declaring the girl a legal ward of Sydney and himself.

During the summer of 1934 several arrangements were made which would help stabilize the ranch's years of faltering and lend hope that, despite the lingering depression, prosperity might come to Skaha.

Sydney became a shareholder in Skaha; Ian, its manager once more; and Dick, the ranch foreman. Ryan McAllister fit somewhere in the shuffle, but exactly where, no one was sure.

True to his word, Cartrell soon saw to it that Sydney Alexandra became his ward. Thomas viewed this as protection of eventual inheritance; but he was reluctant to let go completely, and caused Cartrell considerable trouble and delay. He realized that he was being deliberately cut out of a family enterprise, but it had never held his heart and will from the beginning anyway.

Of the struggle between himself and the accountant over withholding the controlling share in the ranch from his mother, Thomas told Cartrell, "To lose the controlling share means giving up my soul to you, Ian, and I just can't do that and live with myself."

"Soul, be damned," Cartrell stormed miserably. "It means giving up that footloose lifestyle of yours and using your head in a sensible manner. That's an exercise in earnestness entirely foreign to you!"

Following a long, tense pause during which he smarted angrily over Cartrell's words, Thomas told the accountant very meaningfully, "I won't give up the place, you know. You can throw all the legal angles you want my way, Ian, but I won't give it up to you. And– because you have Sydney Alex in your custody does not mean the ranch goes with her. You don't own anything. Remember, I have the controlling share."

Cartrell's black eyes snapped. He paced the room, furious that Thomas should have been awarded such control. "That's only a matter of time!"

Thomas did not reply. There was nothing further that he could add without deteriorating a situation that was already out of control. He did not want to argue. At this point he wanted to reach out for Cartrell's hand, and thank the man for his years of loyalty to his family; more particularly the role which Cartrell had played during the years of his rebellious youth. He hesitated, and soon the moment had passed.

The encounter between Sydney and her son would fracture their relationship for several years. There were no words of comfort to offer her, no explanation that she would understand or accept, nor any hope of a return promised. He noticed that there were no tears in her eyes, no tightening of her mouth, and that prompted concern over her recent illness.

He told her carefully, "You have Ian. You've always had Ian, Mother."

"I need you, Thomas," she said to him with a new coldness in her voice. "I have always needed you, but you've always been running away from me, much as your father spent his life doing. Was I so wrong for you both?"

"Not from you, but from life here. Please don't ask me to explain that, because I know that you remember how I used to like the ranch and Sandon's cow-camp. But I was a kid then, and they were an escape for me– the freight from the orchard, the ranch from the freight, and cow-camp from home." Thomas covered his eyes with his hand in an effort to hide his impatience. He heard her move across the room, her steps halting at the doorway as she leaned on the cane beneath her trembling hand.

"Perhaps that's the truth, but the fact that you would withhold one additional share from me, Thomas, especially when you don't want the ranch, angers me."

"Mother, I withhold it from Ian, not from you."

"In other words, you're saying that you believe me to be a doddering old woman who cannot make responsible decisions. Well, Thomas," she warned him through clenched teeth, "Ian will run this ranch the best way possible in these struggling times, and he and Dick will have their say no matter how many shares you own!"

"I know that will be so, but this ranch, by my one share, remains intact to become Sydney Alex' in the end, not Ian's."

Sydney turned, staring wide-eyed and amazed at her son's statement. "Why then," she whispered forlornly, "are you fighting him, when you both want the same thing? It is quite possible that in the end you will have lost everything, even your only child." Sydney's back straightened as she faced him directly. "Thomas, don't ever say that you were not warned!"

Sydney did not accept her son's decision well and fought his departure to the end. That he should turn away from his roots, his heritage, his daughter and the ranch which she and his father had given their lives to, was unbelievable to her.

That evening, in a moment of self-pity, she whispered to Cartrell, "It is unthinkable and inconsiderate, not to mention embarrassing." Lying back upon her bed, her eyes pleaded with him. "Whatever have I done to make him so irresponsible?"

"You've done nothing, though I know I'll never convince you of that." He placed the light coverlet over her. "The more you dwell on this thing, the slower your recovery will be." Gently brushing aside some loose strands of hair, Cartrell leaned down and tenderly kissed his wife at the corner of her soft mouth.

"I love you," she murmured, her blue eyes meeting his. For a moment Sydney watched his face, his dark eyes and his hair now graying at the temples and thinning at the brow. She noticed also the firm set of his jaw and felt a sense of protection in that. How handsome he is. How very capable in everything. Her gaze fell away, and soon Sydney rested.

Since Sydney Alex was ten, her father had ceased to be the focus of her attention because, she claimed, Mary McGovern had entered their lives and changed everything. It remained a mystery to Sydney Alex that Miss McGovern could relate successfully to her students each day of the week for ten months of the year, yet not allow a hint of affection toward her as a daughter.

The ordinary needs in Sydney Alex' life without her mother were adequately filled by the care and love from her grandmother. Nonetheless, whenever anyone reminisced about Nell, the longing to have her mother there surfaced. Her friends in school had both their parents, whereas she did not have even one memory to recall. Life, at times, felt empty and confusing to her, and was often very lonely.

Early in her life, Sydney Alex had learned of her father's sorrow at the loss of her mother and disappointment in not having a son. She could not ease that hurt for him, nor change Mary McGovern's possessiveness toward her father.

There was no tender farewell scene shared between Thomas and his daughter. As he held her, she felt little warmth in his arms around her. Although Sydney Alex remained resentful of this parting, she hugged him with strength.

Thomas recognized that a wall had been building between them for a long while. He recalled a similar wall between himself and his own father. That wall began with Harrie's sudden death. He knew his father never recovered from the shock. He wondered now, what his own reason was. Was it the untimely passing of Nell? Had he blamed his daughter for his loss, as he felt his father had blamed him? She was an innocent girl who never knew her mother and only asked for his recognition and love.

It was difficult for Thomas to reconcile his emotions and the tragedies in his life for which he felt blame. In recalling the loss of Marjorie Spencer, who drowned while carrying his child, he wondered if it would have been a boy. What kind of difference would her life and child have made to his? He knew no answers.

Thomas carried out his farewell with Cartrell and Foderow in easy banter, as sometimes men can do. As they stood in the yard at the livery where he stored his car, he wanted to thank them for trying to raise him right and to say he was sorry for the disappointment he was to them, but the words would not come.

Looking at the resentment that had festered inside him all his life, he finally recognized the short-sightedness he shared with his father in not appreciating what they had. He had lived with a rebellious nature in a world of adults who did not understand him. Did he understand himself? He doubted it; for in his life was Mary who, for reasons still unknown to him, could not embrace his daughter any easier than he, and he continued to allow it. Thomas had developed a love for Mary, deeper than he had felt for anyone and admitted to a twinge of fear of losing her if he complicated it with a family.

As Cartrell took Sydney Alex' hand and, with Foderow, left him, Thomas hung his head a moment. The warmth of the early morning sun broke over the countryside as he turned toward his car.

From the veranda of the old Llewellyn house, Sydney Alex watched her father back his car out of the livery. She felt the resentment of abandonment welling inside her and bit her lower lip to stifle a cry. It hurt to see him leave; but soon, she knew, she would be able to set it aside in turning her attention to the new hand at the ranch, who was her grandfather's obvious favourite.

Sydney Alex made no effort to hide her interest. She had found Ryan, had brought him to this place and, in her mind, he owed her his life.

22

Thomas Llewellyn left Skaha, putting behind him the forty-three years of his life spent there, in favour of a completely new beginning in the Fraser Valley. His sentiments were left unspoken, his feelings stifled and his personal heartache at last, buried. A feeling of freedom washed over him that warm, July day. He stowed his belongings in his Chevrolet and turned onto the same road over which his father had brought him by horse and carriage to Skaha Crossing in 1891, when he was only just a year old.

From the long narrow window on the top floor of the granary, Ryan McAllister watched Llewellyn's quiet departure. A sudden stillness settled over his tall, lean young frame. His contemplating gaze remained intent upon the dry roadway long after Thomas disappeared from the flats. It was as though the last sight of the car in the early dawn sent a message back to him, a forecast of his own destiny.

The sound of steps on the wooden stairway leading to the small room at the top, stirred his attention. In a moment Ian Cartrell was behind him at the window.

Cartrell, standing at ease with his hands in his pockets, looked over the rims of his glasses and across at young McAllister. "No surge of excitement racing through you?" he enquired curiously. "Are you not wondering about your future on the ranch now?"

"No, sir."

"You're that positive about its security?"

"Yes."

"How is that?"

McAllister turned away from the window and looked deep into the other's penetrating eyes and replied, "I got a feelin' about it, that's all." He stepped across to the work counter and began assembling the pieces of the separator, placing one into the other with care. Then he lifted a pail of fresh milk and slowly emptied it into the metal container. He stood back, watching without particular interest in the process, as the streams poured from their special spouts into the large glass jars on the stands beside him.

Cartrell assessed the youth for a moment. When he spoke again, his voice held a positive warning. "I can only say to you that, if you ever lose touch with the feeling you have that provides you with such assurance, you might as well pack your bag immediately. It is your good fortune, or if you choose– your misfortune that, as a McAllister, I feel you could become my successor here. The prospect bears watching. That is something I do very conscientiously– watch.

As Cartrell turned and quickly stepped through the doorway into the brightening daylight, he felt McAllister's gaze sweep his back. Without glancing back, Cartrell knew he had set the wheel of ambition in motion.

McAllister was so late leaving the dairy that morning, where his confused thoughts had kept him pondering the subject long past the normal separating time, that he nearly missed the breakfast of his free board. When he finally emerged into daylight, it was not with the usual purposeful stride interspersed with his much practised heel-kicks in the air which entertained everyone so well; but, as he crossed the field to the lodge, his gait was more that of the troubled, wondering mind of an unsettled young man.

With Ian Cartrell in control once more of ranch management, Skaha took on the appearance of brighter prospects, regardless of the nationwide depression. Receiving the offer of three dollars per ton for hay, Foderow had felt a little cheated, for he had wanted to hold out for four. But Cartrell wished to keep the price for hay in line with the general prices paid for cattle. He allowed a range of two dollars a ton for rain-damaged hay and three dollars a ton for better quality. However, as the drought persisted, Skaha remained lucky because they were able to irrigate by flume and ditch for most of the summer. Therefore, their hay was in demand. When the winter was nearly over, they found themselves perilously short in their own supply, as it was too soon to turn the herd onto spring range. The horses were simply left loose on the pastures and nearby hills to forage for what new growth there might be beneath the light snow cap in February and March.

Shipments of beef from Skaha to Vancouver and Calgary markets grossed the ranch twenty-three dollars a head for calves, forty-nine dollars for yearlings, and the two year olds went at ninety-seven. Foderow willingly agreed to work at half-wage and moved into the old house built by the trapper. Cartrell drew no income at all. Ryan McAllister continued working for little more than room and board, as did John Strickland and Bud Smith. Additional assistance to run the ranch was drawn from the residents of the lodge, where everyone, but Ryan, lived.

For the second year, the gardens yielded abundantly, once more filling the larder to its limit. Rows of tall bottles filled with eggs packed in waterglass (a substance composed of silicates of potassium), stood beside pickles, jams and fruit preserves. Cabbage and onions hung from ceiling rafters above bins of potatoes, pumpkin and squash. Carrots, turnips and parsnips remained in their earthy beds until the early frosts.

Once again at Christmastime the residents of Skaha considered their celebration feast the finest in the land. They were grateful for provisions in a country where near starvation walked with many.

The boundaries of Skaha Ranch were considerably smaller in 1935 than during Albert Llewellyn's reign. The property toward Fairview had been sold before Llewellyn's passing, and only a small portion of rangeland near Twin Lakes was retained by lease with the Lands Branch for a fee of seven cents per head per acre. Skaha Ranch continued to own the land of the original McAllister holdings, including the benchland above Skaha Lake.

For the present, these were firm boundaries, and Cartrell considered it vital to retain this acreage if a successful comeback was to be made. Throughout the years of the depression, he remained determined to meet, in his usual unwavering manner, the challenge of reviving the ranch and bringing it new status. Utilizing every measure of thrift and good husbandry, he kept expenses to a minimum and in stride with its income. He constantly preached about that important balance to Foderow and Strickland, during conversations which he insisted that young McAllister be party to.

Cartrell's plans for Ryan were real, not just wishful. While the nightmarish depression relentlessly continued, Cartrell chose to ignore the threat it presented of a continuing shattered economy. Instead, he placed his confidence in a future that would evolve from the ruins of the disaster.

His common sense told him that it could not continue forever. The country would return stronger than before. He envisioned not just a return to reasonable employment levels and stable markets, but a prosperity which new foreign trade might bring. Certainly the country was showing the signs of hideous deterioration. He read it every week in the newspapers and heard it every day through the radio. It was not difficult to envision a monumental rehabilitation program which would lift stricken areas out of poverty.

In the back of Cartrell's mind Ryan McAllister figured heavily in the upswing at Skaha.

However, not even Cartrell's admirable perception could predict the conflict that was beginning to ravage another continent. Before his startled eyes, pictures appeared in the newspapers and magazines to which he subscribed. He leaned closer to the battery radio in his living room to hear, in detail, events that were jarring the world, awakening fearful possibilities put behind them twenty years before. The Great War was to have ended all possible clashes between nations.

Nonetheless, the warning, discerned from the news broadcasts, of Germany's continued advancement in Europe, caused an uneasiness in Cartrell not readily set aside. He could ignore the call of the Defense Department for volunteers should Canada participate once more in a world conflict but, if ever conscription was exercised, he reasoned, McAllister would be lost to him. Cartrell began to fear the worst.

As Sydney Alex matured from girlhood into a young woman, her interest in Ryan McAllister deepened. This did not escape Ian and Sydney. Cartrell saw McAllister as a potential leader who may be encouraged by the fact that in Skaha lay his roots. Sydney also recognized the link with the past which Ryan represented. She hoped, as well, that he would be the one to settle her often fickle granddaughter into the stability necessary for Skaha to survive. But, should the young man be called to overseas duty and not return from action, who would fill the shoes which were being polished for him?

McALLISTER

"Those wild horses, they were a magnificent sight. They had such a freedom."

Sandy Brent
Okanagan Pioneer

23

Ryan McAllister crested the hill overlooking Twin Lakes and gazed appreciatively upon a snow-dappled landscape of rolling hillocks, gullies and water. The two lakes, with a narrow passage dividing them, were dotted with small blocks of melting ice. Patches of snow in the mountains meant a lingering winter. Sitting back in his saddle, relaxed and comfortable on the eight-year-old gray gelding Dick Foderow had given him, young McAllister felt a wonderful sense of peace in his life at Skaha.

As he looked upon the calm countryside, he could appreciate Foderow's sentiments, "If you're upset or lonely, the quiet in the mountains and the smell of the pines soothes your soul."

McAllister was neither sad nor lonely that morning. He had saddled Dobbyn and, out of curiosity, rode into the mountains of Skaha's rangeland, keeping to the higher, sunnier slopes.

When his horse had rested, McAllister was on the move once more, crossing the narrow winding road between the Okanagan and Similkameen and rode up into the open country of Marron Valley. The valley, where wild horses roamed, was named 'Marron' by the early traders and settlers for the chestnut colour of the tough mustangs which formed great bands.

From above, the clear April sun warmed McAllister; great flocks of Canada Geese migrating north signalled springtime. Raising an arm against the sun's glare, he squinted his eyes in search of their formation. He enjoyed the sound of their loud squawking. It meant a new season on the ranch.

Skaha had become his home and, after four years, he loved it as if he had been born there. Ryan realized what a good friend he had in Dick Foderow. However, Ian Cartrell– he smiled now as he sat atop his horse and thought of Skaha's iron-fisted manager - ah well, he sighed, I'll get used to him. He's dumped a heavy load on me.

Suddenly his body stilled in the saddle. His breath caught. Dobbyn's head turned, his ears forward, as if listening for something. A little surge of anticipation took hold, and McAllister raised himself up in the stirrups, leaning over the horn as if to see better. The sight below captured his gaze and stirred his imagination. Reaching into his saddlebag, McAllister quickly pulled out his binoculars, placed them against his eyes and scanned the valley beyond.

"My God, look at that," he whispered under his breath. Dobbyn's ears flicked anxiously. He moved restlessly beneath McAllister.

"Magnificent! You feel them too, Dobbyn, old fellow?"

There, in the range of hills between Skaha and Marron Valley, roamed the great band of wild horses. Led by a big white stallion, the band of nearly two hundred grazed the countryside in freedom. McAllister lowered the glasses and relaxed once more against his saddle. He was stunned by the size of the band. Several times he had questioned Foderow and John Strickland about them, but had learned little except that such a herd still existed in the mountains.

Reining Dobbyn around, McAllister followed the trail down the mountainside and cut across the rolling hills to the west. Eventually he rode up on a rise near where the horses grazed and paused to watch. They pawed beneath the lingering patches of snow to reach the new growth of spring grass, and moved restlessly amongst themselves. Nipping at each other, occasionally kicking out, they jostled for position within the group. How can it be, McAllister wondered, that no one has bothered to round them up, break them for use and sell them? We live in poor times and a few of these horses would bring a fair income. Resolving to talk to Dick Foderow about the possibility of such occupation, he attempted to complete an accurate count, but their constant nipping and trotting around prevented that. An hour later he gave up and reined Dobbyn homeward.

Cornering Foderow that afternoon did not prove easy. He eventually had to go over to the foreman's house in the evening and invite Dick over to his own lodgings for a discussion. While Foderow relaxed in a chair near the original table built by the trapper, which was scarred with a century of use, young McAllister paced about the room in anticipation of being on the edge of something big. He lowered his tall frame onto a chair, sitting on it backwards. He leaned over while he talked about his plans.

Foderow was a patient man. He idly stirred a cigarette butt in the ashes of the metal tray on the oilcloth-covered table. He listened attentively to the younger man exclaim his discovery and outline a plan to catch the horses. He smiled, remembering stories told by old Two Way, of times, as a boy, chasing wild mustangs around the higher hills above Lac du Chien, as Two Way had called Dog Lake.

Foderow said, "Your grandfather and I used to see them once in awhile up there when we'd lose a few cows an' have to go lookin' for them. Sometimes they roamed right over behind our range."

"And you didn't try to catch them?"

"A lot of them got rounded up and sold for cavalry use during the war. Army Remount buyers came around lookin' to purchase any horse that had good teeth and eyes and four sturdy legs under it. A few fellows hereabouts gathered them in and brought them down to holding pens where they were shipped out by the Army. There were many more runnin' on the east side, but they were caught, too."

Foderow's voice sounded nostalgic and McAllister tipped his head slightly to better see the foreman's face in the dull lamplight. He looks almost sentimental, McAllister decided apprehensively. He might not go for this deal after all. I know he has a soft spot for horses and their freedom.

"Well, hell," McAllister said quickly, "that was then– for the Army. This is now!" Up and pacing about the floor once more, he outlined, "There's no reason why we can't bring in a few at a time and sell them–" shrugging his shoulders, "as we need to. You should see them! Hell, there's at least a couple hundred in that bunch. And they don't look like scrub, either. I can hardly wait to get started." Pouring Foderow more coffee, he suggested impulsively, "Hey, I got a bottle of rye hid away here– found it in a cupboard," and laughed, "whose, I don't know. Nobody lives in this place but me and the dog and the mice. But we should have a drink on this deal, eh?"

Leaning back in the chair, Foderow smiled indulgently. Ah, he sighed, remembering a time of his own, youth knows no bounds. "Lord, but you're an anxious one. Who're you goin' to sell them to? And for how much?"

McAllister slipped back onto his chair and leaned over the table. On the oilcloth he scribbled figures with a stubby pencil as he talked. "How much did they sell for during the war?"

"Oh, five dollars a head."

"Worth more now. No doubt about it. Just think– green broke, only ten of them, just ten head could bring us one hundred dollars!"

Although Foderow smiled and nodded in consideration, he was truly tired of the idea already. "Well, I suppose," he grumbled good naturedly, "you're gonna be a burr in my side now, about this."

McAllister grinned, elated. "If it'll get me on track, I'll be the biggest, meanest burr you ever had there! You'll have to do it to get rid of me. You want that drink now?" he offered once more, rising from the chair.

Foderow looked up at McAllister. "A deal, lad, is not a deal until it's a deal. But– I'll have a drink with you, Ryan."

McAllister's smile was broad, his attitude positive. "I get your drift. It's okay." He reached into a lower cupboard, pulled out the bottle of rye and poured two small glasses. "I ain't got a lot of time I can wait on though."

"You got nothin' but time." Foderow raised his glass. "Good luck!"

The wild horses of Marron Valley were not the only bands roaming the hills of the Okanagan. Across Okanagan Lake on the east side, a few small herds still lived in the mountains between Penticton and Kelowna. The place had become known as Wild Horse Canyon and, like those running on Wild Horse Mountain in Marron Valley, the horses were descendants of sick or lame animals abandoned by the early fur brigades travelling the Okanagan trail. As well, many early ranchers lost good horses to the bands. As they roamed the hills, their lead stallions would steal mares from unattended herds.

Nonetheless, what was often one rancher's loss was another's gain. Settlers would comb the dry, brown hills during the summer months and catch the tamer horses to begin their own ranch herd, or to introduce new blood as they increased their stock.

Young Ryan McAllister learned the history of the wild horses and, by tracking their movements, became familiar with their habits. His yearning to capture some of them burned deeper. But first, he would wait for the mares to foal, the foals to strengthen, and the herd to venture southward, nearer Skaha range.

Meanwhile McAllister involved himself in ranch activities as he had each year, allowing time to work on his plan.

Two Way's old cabin was alongside Willow Creek. Contemplating its strategic location, he decided to carry out a few repairs to the building and move in. It was close to the creek, and a large corral could be put up beside the cabin. Having the horses right at his doorstep, he determined firmly, would allow constant watch over the precious herd. He approached Dick Foderow about the matter and, once granted permission, planned construction for mid-May, immediately after the cattle had been turned out to spring range.

On a warm May afternoon during one of his first work days, he was suddenly jarred from his reverie by the voice of Sydney Alex, who had unexpectedly turned up beside him. Her eyes took in the array of tools, a stack of peeled poles, and a set of sawhorses over which Ryan McAllister now laboured beneath the hot sun.

"What on earth is all this? What are you doing over here?" Sydney Alex asked in astonishment.

"Hello, there!" he called above the scraping, squeaking sounds of the handsaw. "Not in school today?"

Sydney Alex scowled. She loathed the word *school*, feeling it represented immaturity. "Well, it's Victoria day, a holiday– so, of course, I'm not in school!" The continuous scraping sound of the saw wore upon her nerves. "Really Ryan," she snapped impatiently, "must you keep on sawing while we talk?"

The noise ceased abruptly. McAllister brushed the sawdust from his pants and grinned across at her. "Sorry."

"What're you building?"

"Well," he began walking about the yard, waving his arms in explanation. "I'm goin' to fix up this old cabin and move in."

"But all those poles?"

"To build corrals– from down there, over the creek, right up to the cabin." He looked across at her. "For my horses."

Sydney Alex' head swung around. "What horses?"

"Well, for heaven's sake!" McAllister exclaimed. "Horses that I'm goin' to round up." He stood before her, hands on hips, amazed that she had not heard of his plan. Then suddenly realizing he wore no shirt, he glanced quickly about for the garment, caught it off the log pile and pulled it over his sweaty body.

"Round up from where?" Sydney Alex persisted, reaching a hand to flip her long hair away from her shoulders, for the day was getting warmer and her neck felt damp.

He did up the buttons of his shirt, put on his hat and said to her, "Come– come on– I'll show you from where." Reaching for her hand, he pulled her alongside him and they walked to the barn together. "We'll saddle up and you'll see them if they're still where they were a week ago."

She halted her steps. "But I'm not dressed for riding–"

"You got slacks on and shoes," he replied and caught her hand once more. "Wild horses don't give a damn about jodhpurs an' boots, and quirts 'n other junk." He was laughing as he entered the tack room. "Neither do I!" he called back to her.

Ryan and Sydney Alex rode along the ridge above a quiet meadow behind Skaha's range. Below them the band of horses grazed contentedly on the new green grass. Sydney Alex' breath caught. She glanced across at McAllister.

"See what I mean? Wild horses," he told her as he reached into the saddle bag for the binoculars. The strap caught awkwardly against the rifle in its scabbard and, while he shifted in the saddle to untangle things, he explained his plan to her. "I intend to cut out a few now and then, take 'em down below, break 'em if I have to, and sell 'em." His smile was broad, his eyes alert, his expression confident.

Clearly he was excited about it, Sydney Alex realized. She enquired curiously, "How? If they're wild, you just can't ride down there and hand pick them out."

"I know that!" he replied impatiently. "I've spent a lot of time up here lookin' for them and watchin'. The first time I rode down there they took off, but the mares are in foal right now, so I don't run 'em. I want them to get used to me near them, easy like, so they don't panic when the crunch comes."

Sydney Alex sighed. "I don't believe this!"

McAllister looked across at her. She sat tall, almost elegantly upon her magnificent-looking Anglo-Arab gelding. The light May breeze which played along the ridge, tossed her hair about her neck and collar. It gave her features, which were so like her grandmother's, a childlike, curious expression. He saw that her face shone with sudden excitement. Could it be the same kind of excitement which he felt every time he thought of the horses?

"Lord," he half whispered to her, "I can hardly sleep nights for thinkin' of them."

Sydney Alex turned to look at him. Her hazel eyes were wide and stared straight into his, bright and challenging. "I want to go down there."

McAllister hesitated a moment, then decided. "Alright then, but we can *not* scare them."

Together they galloped their horses the length of the ridge and cut down the slope, winding through the trees until they rode out onto the open flat of the meadow. When they were less than a mile from the band, the white stallion trotted away from the others, toward them, and stopped; watching, alert, and waiting.

"He's beautiful," Sydney Alex whispered to McAllister as he rode up beside her.

"Yes," he agreed proudly, almost possessively. "But we won't trust him. They're his mares. It's his band." Reining Dobbyn in, he warned, "We stop here, or he'll come after us."

Sydney Alex smiled. "I doubt it," she said calmly, pressing her knees firmly against the gelding.

Suddenly McAllister felt apprehensive. "Come on, let's go back," he ordered and reined his horse around. But Sydney Alex had already bolted away from him.

"No, Sydney!" he called after her, fighting to control his own horse. "You don't know—"

But Sydney Alex was galloping toward the herd, flying across the clearing. McAllister tore after her, pressing his own horse into full gallop. He saw the white stallion rear up and paw the air with his front legs. His shrill warning rode on the stiff breeze across the meadow.

Suddenly the stallion's massive chest heaved and his forelegs dropped to the ground. His nostrils flared. He tossed his head wildly, fiercely. His scream of fury pierced the air once more. Then without further warning, the great white horse leapt forward, his pounding hoofs flinging the earth up behind him as he thundered toward Sydney Alex.

Galloping hard, McAllister managed to lean back and pull his rifle from the scabbard and, charging directly between Sydney Alex and the powerful stallion, he raised the gun skyward, released the safety and pulled the trigger. The shot echoed noisily around them. The stallion turned, kicking and screaming, proclaiming his dominance and territory, while he raced away from them. Their horses fought to keep their footing as they turned and galloped toward the mountain.

Behind them in the meadow, the white stallion pranced majestically while gathering his band together, then led them out of the green valley.

When McAllister and Sydney Alex were once more on the ledge, he turned to see the wild horses leaving the meadow, then be lost from sight amongst the high trees in the distance. His heart fell. Nearby, he listened to the snorting of their horses following the gallop, and the sound of Sydney Alex' frightened breathing as she slid from her saddle and sank wearily upon the ground. Returning the gun to its scabbard he, too, stepped down from his horse and looped the reins over Dobbyn's neck, allowing him freedom to graze.

"Are you alright?" he asked through clenched teeth. Anger threatened to choke him.

Her reply was weak, "Yes," as she fell back against the grass and dead leaves.

McAllister sat down beside her. "I can't bring myself to ask why–Sydney Alex, I told you we couldn't–" he stammered, his eyes searching the empty meadow below them. "What a stupid thing to do!" He reached up, yanking his hat from his head and flung it to the ground, emphasizing his frustration. "You had more sense when you were six I bet, than you do at sixteen!"

Sydney Alex remained silent, her thoughts and embarrassment kept to herself. She turned to lay back and stare up at the clouds moving across the sky. She could not answer him. There was no explanation for her impulsive chase, nor the danger she had carelessly courted.

They remained silent. When McAllister turned to look at her, his anger was gone and he could now rationalize. "You know," he said softly to her, "we're very lucky neither of us got hurt down there."

"I'm sorry, Ryan," she whispered between fingers held over her trembling mouth, "I'm truly sorry." She turned her eyes toward him. They were full of tears.

"Aw, well–" He watched her, shook his head, and finally smiled. "You know, Sydney Alex, this may come as a shock to you," he began slowly, "but old Cartrell and your Grandma have been makin' plans for the past while for us to marry. Now, if that's somethin' that's goin' to actually happen," he teased, "you'll have to learn to listen to me a little better than you did today." He pulled idly at the grass beneath his raised knees. "I'd rather that you didn't challenge fightin' stallions or any other renegade. Wild horses are for men to handle."

Beside him, Sydney Alex clambered hastily to her feet, caught the reins to her horse and prepared to step into the saddle.

Across the space between them, McAllister could feel her instant anger.

"How can you marry someone you don't love," she snapped

sorrowfully, "and whom you've never once kissed." Swinging up into the saddle, Sydney Alex reined the gelding around and trotted off into the trees.

McAllister lay back, his head cupped against his clenched hands. He closed his eyes and his body relaxed. That little oversight, he vowed, will soon be remedied! For the moment his loss was not Sydney Alex and a kiss left unstolen, but the absence from the meadow of his herd, as he had come to feel about the wild horses of Marron Valley.

As the weeks slid toward September, Sydney Alex saw Ryan McAllister only at a distance, keeping space between them. Feeling embarrassment over the incident of the wild horses, she confided in her friend, Janet Foderow, and then only briefly.

"It's out now," she breathed a weary sigh. "And I feel better for having told someone." She and Janet walked the pathway from Janet's house, along the creek and up the rise toward Skaha's graveyard. In passing, the girls barely glanced at the weathered crosses, and continued in conversation. "I trust you, Janet," she added, for Janet had remained very quiet as they walked. "There's no one else I can talk to, not even Gran. Besides, I doubt that Gran would understand how a girl feels at my age."

Janet smiled discreetly. The friendship between the two girls seemed very solid. There were differences, as there were bound to be, for Sydney Alex sometimes acted like the spoilt young lady she was, while Janet's quiet, unassuming nature was often put to the test by her friend's varying moods.

Janet enjoyed the friendship of many others in school. Her classmates looked up to her maturity and friendly manner. Her appreciation of the wonderful life she shared at home with her parents showed in her happiness. At fifteen, she was becoming an attractive brunette who had a natural interest in boys, and a confiding relationship with her mother. Her father had become an idol, someone by whom she felt she could measure all men, for Janet knew he was well-respected by all who knew him. Having grown up in the romantic environment of ranching, a cowboy with a steadfast and honourable nature in all his rugged appearance was bound to be the dream in the girl's future. And into that ideal category and Janet's fantasies, fell Ryan McAllister.

Sydney Alex shared few of Janet's redeeming qualities, but she was, as she often noticed before the long mirror in her bedroom, prettier, taller and slimmer. Her naturally wavy hair and evenly sculpted profile inherited from her grandmother, were outstanding when compared to Janet's regular features crowned by dark, straight hair which had to be tediously curled every morning with hot, metal tongs. Her conceited, sometimes petty nature did not attract others readily, but nonetheless, unlike Janet, Sydney Alex need not search for the idol of her dreams. After all, she reminded herself regularly, it is as good as cast in stone that Ryan and I will marry, for it's convenient and Papa will decree it.

While Janet was content to dream, Sydney Alex became determined in her quest for McAllister's attention. She developed little interest in other young men in the area, and shunned any which came her way when in town with her friends.

It was this intense, resolute purpose of mind made obvious by Sydney Alex throughout the summer, that caused Ryan McAllister to think seriously about his growing attraction to her.

24

McAllister failed to capture the wild horses, for during the summer months they roamed north behind Summerland, and had often been seen west of Peachland. His loss was a constant aggravation to him, and an embarrassment. He had talked of nothing else for a long time, and even elaborated on how he was going to do it. Failure at anything was hard for McAllister to bear. He was sorry he had taken Sydney Alex to the meadow that day, and resolved to start all over with the horses the following year.

In the spring of 1939, when calving was over and branding time finished, the Skaha herd was gathered together for the push onto summer range. Ryan trailed the long column stretched across the flats to the western slopes. The air was cool in the hills.

John Strickland dropped back to ride beside him. "Cooler up here," he noted. "Glad for a coat now. 'Course it's not sunup yet," he said and pulled up the collar of his jacket. "The higher we get, the later the spring."

The morning breeze tugged at McAllister's wide-brimmed hat and he reached up and settled it tightly over his brow. He, too, pulled his collar up around his neck. The discomforts were minor. Every year McAllister felt an unexplainable thrill at being a part of the ride, and a part of Skaha. Five years before, as he lay in the dirty snow beneath the railway platform in argument with Sydney Alex, not a thought of such perfect peace as he knew this day, had crossed his mind.

To have made a friend in Dick Foderow was precious reward itself. For McAllister, as he worked beside the ranch foreman daily, there was no finer boss man, no more skilled cowboy, or gentler man with animals. That was especially true with horses. McAllister had great admiration for Foderow and longed intensely to be as responsible and knowledgeable as the foreman.

The cowboys rode out of the trees, across the sagebrush bench and into the rolling hills. Armed against cacti, rattlesnakes and prickly greasewood and ticks, the men were protected with high boots and leather chaps. Four pack horses trailed the herd loaded with supplies for the line cabin, and salt blocks for the cattle. Steam rose from the mass of brown backs as, warmed by the rising sun, the cattle moved along the open draws and into the hills.

The line cabin, nestled in its secluded grove of trees beside a narrow creek, came into view by mid-afternoon. Foderow left the herd to gallop back to the end, the metal shoes of his horse thudding heavily upon the ground. He reached Bud Smith who led the pack horses toward the camp and, reining alongside the seasoned veteran of many Skaha drives, called out, "Well, young fella, how're you doin' there?"

Smith's smile was testy. "Well, I'll tell you true-- I'm damned sick of this dust back here!" he grumbled. "I don't know how I got behind, when I started out in front."

"Come on, I'll help you get these horses in and unpacked." Jigging the reins slightly, Foderow urged his horse onto the trail toward the cabin. In passing Smith, he reached out and took the lead line from him.

At the creek, he dismounted, removed his hat and joined Smith on the bank. While lying over the ground, they drank thirstily of the cool, clear mountain water which had its origin from natural springs higher up. Behind them in the distance, the cattle fanned out across the meadows where the new grass was fresh and green. They were followed by two of the ranch's Border Collies.

Foderow sat back against a rock, replacing his hat. He looked across at Bud Smith. "We've ridden this range a few times, Bud."

Smith undid the checkered kerchief at his neck, dipped it into the cold water and mopped it over his dust-covered face. "Kinda miss that old Pickle Bill, though. He taught me the harmonica. Could always put a restless man to sleep with that sound, he could."

Foderow laughed. "Well, I think young Ryan's got one in his pack. I hear him now and then practising down there where he lives."

The door of the nearby cabin squeaked on its rusty hinges as McAllister pushed it open. The familiar sound of it caught Foderow's attention. In a sombre moment he told Smith, "When I first came here, Bud, it was with that boy's grandfather. Two other young fellows rode for him, and stayed here through the whole summer. The last time that Dave rode out here, I came with him. He had a hunch about some rustlers." Idly twisting a dead birch twig, he frowned in remembrance.

Foderow looked up, his eyes scanning the sky, but not really seeing the small fluffy clouds racing each other across the vast blueness. Dropping his gaze to Smith, who rested against the rocks beside him, Foderow told him solemnly, "Every time I come up here, Bud, I have a hell of a fight with myself to go into that damned cabin. We shared his last meal in there, played some poker-- he never, ever won anything. We told some jokes and talked about his being best man at my wedding. I packed him out over this trail, and he died on me along the way." Foderow snapped the twig between his fingers, stared a moment at the broken pieces, then tossed them idly to the ground.

The shuffling of a boot in the dead leaves caused the foreman to glance up into the eyes of the young McAllister, who had been listening with intense interest. Speaking to no one in particular, Foderow mumbled, chewing at the edge of his full mustache, "He was like an older brother to me. I was twenty when I met him and he was around thirty. Quite an age difference, but I know I was the best friend he ever had."

Looking up once more, he contemplated the McAllister who stood before him. Wide rays of sunlight streamed through the branches of the trees over the creek. Outlined in its brilliance, the young man stood tall, lean, tanned and clean-shaven in a circle of mustached men. He knew that McAllister's brown eyes measured him intently and that he had hung on every word spoken of the grandfather he never knew.

Smith cleared his throat. Foderow rose to his feet, asking McAllister almost curtly, "Well?"

"I came to help you unpack, that's all," Ryan replied quietly and turned away.

Although Foderow's story had gripped the young man's imagination, he reserved questioning of it for another time. The softer side of Foderow often allowed for unguarded, mellow moments and there would be another time, he knew.

The pack boxes were unstrapped and removed, saddles were hung over their posts on the outside wall of the cabin, and the horses brushed down. McAllister led the animals across the creek into the trees where corrals had been built, and McAllister turned the horses loose inside. Returning to the hitching rail, he gave his attention to his own horse. Removing the blankets, he spread them over his saddle on the specially constructed rack which was built under the roof many years before and acted as a shield from the weather. He loosened the bridle, pulled the bit from Dobbyn's mouth and looped the apparatus over the saddle horn.

Pondering what Dick Foderow's life with his grandfather must have been with freight wagons and teams, rustlers and guns, young McAllister now vigorously brushed over the gelding's back, down the legs and around his chest. Continuing this circuit, he remained lost in contemplation of his own role with these riders and the ranch at Skaha.

He was jarred from his beleaguered reverie by John Strickland's hoarse voice. "I don't s'pose you'll be happy 'till you get the hide rubbed right off 'im." His chuckle was friendly. "Come on in here and get some vittles."

McAllister leaned against Dobbyn and pulled idly at the loose hair trapped in the brush. The afternoon sun was warm and he felt good at being up in the higher hills.

"What's eatin' your mind, lad?" Strickland asked beside him.

"Just a mite sad that I never knew my real grandfather, that's all. I heard Dick talkin' to Bud about him. I can tell you, I've never known anybody like them– cowboys, I mean. My Dad ran a hardware and grocery store in Prince George." He glanced across at Strickland. "I guess you an' Dick are the only real cowboys I do know."

At that unhappy moment the pains of his youth and the constant feeling of inadequacy, of not quite measuring up to his step-grandfather Dietrich's expectations gripped him. Lack of interest in taking over the hardware business also weighed upon him now. He wondered if he would ever measure up to what the tough, dependable men of Skaha expected of him. That he may, in time, become head of Skaha Ranch was a secret ambition he harboured only unto himself. When he looked across the space into Strickland's smiling, understanding eyes, McAllister realized his moment of speculation had been detected by the other man.

Strickland nodded reassuringly. "You'll be alright, lad." Turning to unsaddle his own horse, he told McAllister, "Dick and me 'ave been around here a long time. Mind you, Dick a while longer, of course. It seems like Cartrell's been here forever, but Dick was hauling freight for old Llewellyn before Cartrell arrived."

McAllister reached for Strickland's worn saddle. "Here, I'll do this for you. It's been a long ride."

Strickland nodded appreciatively. "Thank you, son." Patting a hand against the boards of the saddle rack, he said, "A good setup, this rack. Keeps the rattlesnakes out of the blankets at night and gets rid of the wood ticks at the same time." He coughed, cleared his throat and spit to the ground. "Well, see you at the grub board."

McAllister threw back his dark head and laughed as he swung the saddle up onto the rack. "Now, that's different! I never heard the dinner table called that before?"

"The learnin' never stops!" Strickland called back.

McAllister smiled as he brushed Strickland's roan. The feeling inside him was good. For the first time in awhile he wanted to run across the flats, kick his heels together and call out to the world his pleasure at simply being alive.

The line camp served as home to the three Skaha cowboys who remained for the season. When Foderow had ridden out two days later, the cabin seemed suddenly lonely to McAllister, Strickland and Smith. A bit of that loneliness seized McAllister as he lay on the hard, lumpy mattress on his bunk, close to the rough board ceiling. A branch from a tree beside the log structure scraped annoyingly against the roof over his head. Then, as if the exhaustion of the day's ride and ensuing chores had suddenly caught up with him, he pinched his tired eyes tightly between his fingers to rest them. With the soft hum of the men's voices below him as they played poker and drank coffee laced liberally with brandy, Ryan McAllister turned toward the wall, closed his eyes and fell asleep.

Life in a cow-camp could be either mildly interesting or absolutely dull, depending on what the cowboys made of it. But in either case, there was no denying that it was a lonely existence. The work of a line camp rider was monotonous and wearisome. McAllister discovered anew, as he did each year, just how tedious it could really be. In all manner of weather the cowboy must be in his saddle, keeping a constant check on the cattle. Repairing fence that stretched miles over rocky terrain, across flatlands and through forested gullies was the never-ending, thankless job the cowboys disliked the most. Ryan was no exception to this feeling of futility, but reserved complaint. His hours of work were long, though his sleep amounted to little, for a certain loneliness kept company with him even when his eyes were closed.

Entertainment was limited to learning what constituted a good poker hand, lariat practice or a game of horseshoes. Often McAllister took leave of the other two to seek out a quiet place along the creek where he sat alone listening to the soothing sound of the water. It was always a place where he could practice his harmonica out of earshot of the others, avoiding their friendly jokes about his lack of talent.

On the range the cowboys' diet was sometimes as monotonous as the daily work, depending on the cook. In a deep iron pot hung from a tripod over a fire, all manner of food became stew. Into this enormous black cauldron, Bud Smith tossed everything edible. Sometimes McAllister's stomach threatened to rebel. Food stuck in his throat when Smith told stories of skinning out rattlesnakes for a good stew or cougar meat for a good rump roast. Although it was all in fun, McAllister found the jokes sometimes hard to take.

"A queasy stomach, lad?" John Strickland enquired one evening while dishing out a plate of rabbit and vegetable stew. "If you think this's bad, you ought to've had old Pickle Bill's slumgullions! We were never sure what he had in there, but he boiled it well. It always tasted good and never killed us."

McAllister smiled. Don't worry about me, he wanted to say to them. I've toughened up to you old fellas!

Personal care was of limited privacy. McAllister carried out his laundry chores at the creekside with a large bar of lye soap in one hand and a stiff brush in the other. After scrubbing his pants and shirts against the rocks, he pulled a thin rope through the belt loops and sleeves and secured them all together from a branch leaning into the rushing water, so that while he worked in the hot sun all day, his laundry was automatically rinsed.

Strickland observed the results of McAllister's innovative nature. "Clever, clever– At this rate, you won't need to go back to the ranch at all this season!"

McAllister froze at such a thought. Not go back? "Altogether, that's five months," he blurted in hurt astonishment.

"Roughly."

"I can't stay out here for five months! The longest I've ever stayed is three weeks."

"Seems, Ryan, like you're puttin' up a good fight for it," the old cowboy continued to tease.

Thereafter, young McAllister resolved to slow down his attempts at comfort in the camp. But, he asked himself, how can making life as good as possible work against you? Damn, he cursed, these guys do this to me every year!

To the west of the camp, heavy thunder clouds were forming and moving northward, rapidly darkening the evening. Aware of the threat of sudden storm, Ryan hurriedly went about his chores and got himself inside before it broke.

The storm that unleashed itself that night upon the valley, had moved up from the high mountains of the Cathedral Range to the southwest. Sheeting rain, accompanied by shattering rolls of thunder and fiery lightning, fell heavily upon the quiet camp and the enormous herd of cattle.

Uneasiness crept through the herd. The bulls bawled and moved restlessly around, bunching their groups together in the meadows and groves. Strays took shelter beneath huge pine and firs, which afforded little protection from the persistent force of the storm. Lightning drove its electric forks to the land in spectacular brilliance, its silent power followed by the cracking rumble of thunder. It seemed as if the earth shuddered from the magnitude of the storm.

McAllister leaned his elbows against the window sill and stared out into the awesome activity of the storm.

"It wouldn't be good," Strickland warned, "if you was to be sittin' there and one of them big bolts of electricity came your way."

McAllister shuddered, the personal disaster of it prickling his mind. Nervously, he cleared his throat. "That's only an old wives' tale!"

"I'd say it was an old cowhand's experience," Strickland persisted. "Been known to happen, you know. Mind you, the guy I knew about lived to tell the tale, but that don't hold for everyone who gets hit." Amused by his own teasing, he winked in mischief toward Bud Smith, who rested on his bunk.

After a moment's contemplation, McAllister said, "This is the first summer I've been up here in a storm like this. Doesn't all that thunder 'n lightning spook the cattle at night?"

"Well, I guess Zane Grey's penned a word or two 'bout that alright, and they're pretty fond of runnin' the hell out of a herd in those western movies, but in real life, the cattle sort of 'climatize to the elements and reserve panic." Strickland watched the interest on young Ryan's face. "In the old days, seems like there was more to spook 'em than now. It wasn't always the weather. Sometimes just a falling rock will do it."

"I read about those long cattle drives– in your books."

"That was different. Where're they goin' to stampede to now? They're all fenced in good 'n tight. Mind– there's nothing' like a cow for gettin' through a piece of barbed wire."

McAllister pushed himself away from the open window.

John Strickland glanced past McAllister, to stare once more into the black night. "We'd be in trouble with all that lightning if we don't get the rain, with the weather being hot like it has."

In an effort to feel reassured, McAllister asked, "Doesn't it seem worse than it really is when you're up in the mountains, like now?"

"A little closer to Nature's fury here, that's all," replied Strickland as he rose from his chair and tossed his tin cup into the metal dish pan.

Not consoled by the conversation, Ryan crawled up onto the mattress of his bunk. Lying in the sudden quietness of the cabin, he watched over the edge of the bunk at Strickland as the man now concentrated on the pages of a Frontier Times magazine, his eyes straining in the dull light provided by the cabin's only coal oil lamp. He wanted to question the man about experience with fires. What happened to the cattle when the flames swept across their range? How would they ever stop a fire in such wooded country, if one got started? However, he held his curiosity in check and left the old cowboy to his reading.

McAllister turned on the bunk, facing the wall, and pushed his head deep against the feather pillow. In the distance the thunder sounded almost relaxing as it moved northwest away from Skaha into the North Okanagan and Nicola valleys, leaving the dry night silent.

Through the following weeks intense heat parched the land, forcing the cattle to move to higher range. The cowboys, weary of it, complained amongst themselves and wished for rain.

On a hot July night, while walking across the meadow with McAllister, Strickland suggested quietly, "Well, Ryan, I think you'll get your chance to go down to the ranch. How about tomorrow? You take the pack horses an' get supplies. Leave at dawn."

McAllister grinned. Looking across at the old cowboy, he chuckled, "Well, I've been workin' hard, and that's puttin' up a good fight for it!"

The two laughed together and Strickland slapped McAllister good-naturedly on the shoulder. "You got fixin' to do for the horses after supper. Now let's go eat."

In the early morning, McAllister placed the wooden frames of the pack saddles on top of the blankets stretched over the horses' backs. Strickland joined him. "Maybe next year they'll have a bulldozer in here buildin' us range fellas a good road. Sure would help to have a truck do all this packin' in."

"The way I see it," McAllister replied thoughtfully, "is if we can get a truck in, we won't need a line camp here at all. You know what I mean?" He glanced at Strickland. "Just truck the horses in every day, check the cattle, do the fencin' or whatever and drive back out."

Strickland looked into the guarded expression in McAllister's brown eyes. "Well, I don't think you'll see the day when a cow-camp's not needed on any range. But, you can suggest that to Dick, even Ian." He smiled with optimism.

Once away from the open meadows, the trail was twisting and narrow. McAllister rode steadily with the four pack horses in tow. He whistled cheerfully as he threaded his way among the trees, until he reached a familiar watering hole. At this point he was over half the way to Skaha, having been gone from the cow-camp by two hours. The July sun rose, hot and drying. The sky was clear.

He was near the ranch when he noticed smoke. Emerging from a small grove onto an open flat, the smell of it suddenly penetrated his nostrils, causing fear to seize his mind. He twisted in the saddle in search of its origin, his eyes peering alertly from beneath the wide hat brim. The sight of the massive white cloud building on the western horizon behind him, shocked him. Without hesitation, he grazed his spurs lightly against Dobbyn's side and, with the string of pack horses clambering clumsily behind him, McAllister galloped over the rise, then settled to a trot down the hillside and across the flats toward Skaha.

Behind him a great cloud of smoke was growing gray and heavy, spreading along the blue horizon. Each time he glanced back at it, he felt greater apprehension for the men and cattle he had left behind. Nearing the main buildings of the ranch, he called out. Men came running from the yard, questioning McAllister's news. The smell of smoke had not yet descended upon the lower basin. In fact, the developing dark cloud was barely visible at the ranch.

High up and many miles away at a small forestry lookout, the widening screen of smoke was detected and news of the fire dispatched to the Penticton-based forestry fire suppression headquarters. Men and machinery were already being moved into the mountainous area to build access routes and fire guards.

At Skaha, Foderow emerged from the equipment shed to focus his eyes west and hear young McAllister's story. When, in haste, the men began packing, the horses became difficult to manage. The sudden activity excited them and they were jittery and suspicious, but eventually bedrolls were tied behind saddles and pack horses were loaded with fire fighting hand equipment, food and other camp provisions.

In the melee of men and horses dealing with the sudden business of the hour past, Ryan failed to notice the presence on the scene of Sydney Alex. When he did, it was to see her standing near Cartrell's office building, not far from the corrals of the livery. He finished saddling Foderow's horse, glancing occasionally in her direction. When he was done, he turned the animal into the stall to feed on a handout of oats, and crossed the yard to where she waited.

Sydney Alex kept her smile faint, though she was pleased at Ryan's attention. Attempts to quell the excitement within her failed and she was positive that he could hear her heart beating. Watching her eyes, he smiled warmly, the lines of his mouth soft and sensuous. His dark brown eyes were searching. My word, she thought, he is so handsome! Even after he's ridden all day and is tired and dusty, and as brown from the sun as the colour of his shirt, he is a marvellous sight.

"I've missed you," she whispered suddenly, surprising herself with her impulsive honesty.

He pulled his hat brim lower against the bright sunlight and nodded slightly. "I missed you, too." After a pause, he added, "More than I thought I would."

The wonderful sound of those words thrilled her. "You've changed. You look older, more grown up–" she faltered.

"Probably you've changed, too."

"Do you have to go back?"

McAllister glanced toward the saddled horses standing near the corrals. "Soon," he replied quietly.

"Aren't you too tired?"

"Not really. I want to go."

"I wish you didn't– I mean, have to leave."

He looked down into her face again, then let his glance fall on the toes of his dusty boots. A bit guiltily, he replied, "Well, I want to."

From the distance of the barns, Foderow called. McAllister waved an arm in answer without turning, and continued to remain beside Sydney Alex. Reaching toward her arm, he told her, "I'll see you when I get back."

Their hands joined, clasping tightly. Sudden real awareness, a feeling not entirely new to them in each other's presence, swept over Sydney Alex and Ryan as they stood alone, away from the crowd in the yard. Their eyes explored the depths of each other's. What it was they sought through that intent gaze, neither was sure in that brief, wonderful moment of their youth.

The instant passed. The electricity of the moment was gone. In its infancy, their unspoken desire for one another was quelled by virtue and circumstance.

Foderow's voice jarred McAllister's mind and he dropped Sydney Alex' hand gently. "Goodbye, Sydney Alex," he whispered, creasing his brow as though questioning another time.

Sydney Alex did not speak, for to do so would have prompted tears, which threatened to spill anyway, so she clamped her mouth tight. She was hurt that he did not stay. Smiling, she watched him turn away from her and walk determinedly across the yard to the corrals where Foderow waited.

The men were mounting up, ready for the ride. Foderow leaned over the horn of his saddle and told McAllister, "Ian has received word that the forestry knows and the chaps are on their way out now."

"Where is it?" McAllister enquired. "I couldn't tell."

"West of Penticton, and if it jumps the road, it's on our range."

A horrified feeling assailed McAllister. "Oh boy, oh boy– John and Bud–" he muttered to no one. Then he remembered the band of wild horses, possibly grazing at that very moment in Marron Valley, and felt real fear for them.

The foreman of Skaha smiled pleasantly down at the young cowboy wearing a worried expression on his tanned face. Foderow pitied his youthful sensitivity to the inevitable in range life. "Ryan, go and get cleaned up now. As much as I'd like you to stay here and look after things, I know nothing would keep you from following us. Besides, i really need every hand available up there, and I'll leave you in charge of the stock. Go on now– clean up and get a good meal. You'll catch up to us. I'll see you out on the trail."

Serious consequences of a quick, dry lightning storm were taking place in the mountains, and McAllister wanted to be immediately quit of the ranch and back at cow-camp with Strickland and the others.

Foderow reined his big bay horse to the side and joined the men residing in the lodge, as well as neighbouring riders now gathering at the Skaha gateway. Above them the sun blazed, its glare almost blinding.

In the quiet shade of the veranda at the lodge, Ian Cartrell waited for McAllister to cross the dusty yard. Sydney Alex had walked away toward White Lake where a covey of quail searched the grass for seeds.

When McAllister stepped up onto the boards of the veranda, he immediately sensed Cartrell's presence in the shade. Pausing briefly, he stared boldly, openly into Cartrell's dark, compelling eyes. Then, touching the brim of his weathered hat lightly, McAllister greeted him, "Ian--" and passed on by.

Cartrell did not reply, only nodded. He smiled with satisfaction and a measure of respect.

In a moment McAllister had disappeared into the coolness of the building to eat and later change his dusty clothes for the return trip. It was where he craved to be at this time-- a part of the action, feeling at one with the other men. To be confronted face to face with danger and decision was an exciting struggle between courage and common sense. It was a dramatic moment for him. To imagine that his presence was desperately needed out there on the range rather than at the ranch, was a natural, if youthful reaction, and Ryan McAllister was just as vulnerable to such vanity as any other young man of his time.

Within the hour he was gone from Skaha, once again atop his own gray gelding. A late summer afternoon breeze was developing at his back and, as he rode steadily along the trail, he could feel its warm tug and hear the soft whisper of it in the trees. The fact that the breeze would probably blow into a strong fanning wind, gave McAllister hope that the fire would be blown back over its burnt-out area and eventually snuff itself out in its own smoldering ash.

Ahead of him in the mountain ravines and narrow valleys, the fire was growing stronger, fanned by the wind of its own flames as it roared through the canyons, leaping furiously from one tree top to another. Intense heat filled the air. The smell of burning timber drifted with the downdrafts.

McAllister rode into it with a growing sense of fear. The struggle within himself that had calmed for awhile, rose once more to a feeling of panic. He hurried his horse along the trail. His searching eyes scanned the distance ahead. The cloud was moving closer, thicker and more frightening. Along the forest path he could hear the scatter of fearful ground creatures. Now and then dark shapes of panic-stricken deer and coyotes bobbed frantically between the trees in their race to safety.

When McAllister came upon the camp, the ominous sight of advancing flames astonished him. For a moment the stark reality of the situation overwhelmed him. The fire, he saw, was at their doorstep.

It had jumped the road and spread so wide that it seemed as though it would sweep directly down upon them. Men were everywhere, running, calling orders, building fireguards and pumping water from their back-tanks into the flames, for individual patches of fire had sprung up from flying debris.

McAllister leapt from his horse and undid the packs, tossing them onto the cabin step. Then hurriedly he removed the bridle, hooked the stirrups over the horn, loosened the cinch of his saddle and ran the horse quickly into the corral at the creek. In a larger, separate corral the horses of the remuda (a band of spare saddle horses), raced madly about in panic. Their eyes rolled fearfully.

John Strickland appeared from behind the cabin, ashen-faced and dirty from the job. The weariness of the day showed clearly in his tired eyes. Despite the threat behind him, he smiled as he welcomed the young man and clapped a hand firmly upon McAllister's arm.

"It's under control already, they tell me," Strickland informed him, but McAllister, in glancing along the slopes, doubted it.

"I wouldn't say a damned thing's under control," he replied caustically.

"The pessimism of today's youth!" bellowed Strickland and, reaching up, he yanked McAllister's hat down over his brow. "Don't look at it then! Simple as that!"

"Cut it out, John! I'm serious!" Ryan snapped, readjusting his hat. "This's awful! Where is everybody?"

Strickland waved an arm, barely covered by his torn shirtsleeve, toward the wide blaze topping a far rise. "Where else?"

"Well, I'm goin' out there—"

Strickland quickly caught McAllister's sleeve, spinning him around. "To do what? You damn well stay right here! These horses are your responsibility now, and so are those cattle we got run down below. The night's upon us and we ain't goin' to get the wind in our favour like we thought, so all's calm if you'll stay calm and behave yourself."

McAllister was astonished and stared hard at the old cowboy. In that moment's glance Strickland felt the young man's hostility and knew that McAllister was embarrassed and resentful of the reprove. He would get over it, Strickland knew, for the young always came to respect the decisions of the old. In light of that, Strickland half smiled at McAllister, whose only response was to walk away toward the corrals in an outward show of defiance.

McAllister felt crushed, deprived of being out in the thick of things and stripped of the opportunity to prove to the men, Foderow above all, that he would not let them down. His body and mind, filled with anticipation, craved such action.

A cracking noise at the corrals returned his attention to the stark reality of the moment. He saw the gate give way against the strain of the anxious horses. The boards split, falling away at all angles. The restless animals charged into each other in their bolt for freedom. Before his disbelieving eyes, the horses sped out of the compound, galloping frantically through the forest, darting between the trees. Their hooves pounded against the hard, dry earth, tearing up the dirt and grass in their wake. Beside them in a small corral, his own horse whinnied, pranced in agitation and pawed the ground.

McAllister's feet came alive. Without caution, he leapt toward his horse, caught the halter, bridled him, tightened the cinch, dropped the stirrups and mounted, and was off through the woods behind the others, in what seemed a single moment. He rode as one with his horse, galloping between the trees, weaving through the thick brush, and finally out onto the open bench. Wild now in their charge to freedom, the horses leapt ahead, crossing the meadow; a moving wall in a pounding gallop.

McAllister choked on the smoke-filled air as he angled his horse along the wooded hillside. The brush scraped noisily across his leather chaps, and dead branches tore at his clothes. He could feel and hear the animal beneath him heaving with exhaustion, but still he urged the powerful gelding on. At the top of the rise he spotted the herd in the distance, though it was difficult to see in the growing darkness.

Then suddenly, a piercing cry echoed from the cliff above him. He glanced up and saw that a cougar paced nervously along the ledge. Ahead of him, the horses bolted. Having turned, it was as though in their panic, they were now heading straight into the fire. McAllister raced alongside them, whistling shrilly.

Then, by the sheer force of heat and smoke and by McAllister's presence outlined ahead of them in the awesome brilliance of the fire's light, the band suddenly thundered to a halt. Swirling in the dust and stomping the ground with fearful impatience, their whinnying pierced the evening air beneath the great descending roll of smoke. The call was answered by the distinct cry of another band.

McAllister's senses were suddenly jarred to greater alertness. He and Dobbyn plunged down the slope toward the band, sliding dangerously among the rocks and loose gravel, through the sagebrush and young fir, leaping over decaying pine. The terrorized horses wheeled and spun away across the meadow. He followed them, forcing them to remain ahead of him. His gelding fell into a comfortable trot as darkness descended upon them.

A strange silence prevailed. The horses were safe. The cougar had disappeared. McAllister shivered in the cool night air. He listened for other sounds: the wild ones– he sensed they were close by. Halting his horse, he held his breath and searched the darkness for sign of them. He thought of the great white stallion and let out his breath. He knew he could not fight him in the dark, if he came. Beneath him Dobbyn's sides heaved and McAllister reached out to pat his neck, then pressed his hand reassuringly against the rifle in its scabbard beneath his knee.

He dismounted, allowing Dobbyn to rest while they walked together. McAllister listened to the horses continue their race across the flats ahead of him and into the trees, through which he knew they would come upon other meadows to the south. There, their frantic energy would finally expire.

Common sense told him they would still be there in the morning and, with that consolation, he dropped to the grass. Lying there, he breathed deeply the sweet smell of wild hay and listened to Dobbyn's breathing. In a moment he turned over on his back and stared toward the sky.

Nighttime was upon them. The dark spirals of smoke appeared almost white in the blackening night. Red licks of flame dotted the distant mountain ridges, like candles placed indiscriminately upon a cake. A late evening wind blew gently over him. He smiled. The force of disaster had been averted. The inferno would burn itself out with the night and within a few days would leave nothing but a charred, smoldering landscape.

His body ached all over. The hours of this day could not be measured. Strength of muscle and mind had been tested. Aware of his own exhaustion and that of his horse, McAllister rose from the ground. Taking up the reins, he banished from his tired mind the threat of the cougar's presence in the valley, concentrating more on the white stallion which he felt had, by this time, collected Skaha's horses into his own band. In the dark he led the gelding across the meadow and into the trees, threading between the tall black outlines, to finally break out onto the long high ridge that benched the range south to Fairview.

Quietness surrounded him as he walked, leading his horse. Only the soft, steady thumping of Dobbyn's hooves on the grass and leaves broke the silence. All the birds had flown. No deer waited hidden in the thickets as he threaded his way southward. Finally McAllister came upon the grazing horses. He mounted and rode down the slope.

Only the faintest odour of burning forest reached him now. He had travelled southward far enough to be away from the holocaust. As he dismounted and unsaddled, the gelding nibbled wearily at the dry grass. In the darkness McAllister had no way of knowing if and when he had crossed the boundaries of Skaha range. He recalled no fences, and yet he knew there must have been at least two. If so, he reckoned realistically, there would be some injured among the herd, and Foderow to face when he returned in the morning.

Uncoiling his lariat, McAllister tethered the gray at length so that he could feed, contrary to the usual nighttime snubbing to a tree. Spreading the sweat-dampened blankets over nearby bushes to dry,

McAllister lay back upon the ground. With his saddle for a pillow and his rifle at his side, he pulled his jacket over him and closed his eyes against the dark shadows of the forest. The restless sound of the band reached his ears from the distance. While they grazed, Ryan McAllister slept beneath a dark sky.

25

Dick Foderow walked about the soot-covered camp in quiet agitation. They were all on foot now and his frustration of that fact was very clear. Only a handful of forestry recruits remained at the camp, the rest having been left at the fire. Bulldozers had cleaned an access to within a mile of the camp.

With the driver of one of the trucks leaving, Foderow relayed an assessment of the situation to Cartrell: that a road had been pushed into the area and the fire was under control, but all the horses were gone.

"Hopefully, by God," Foderow cussed, "with a lot of luck and his brain in the proper gear, that young bugger will turn up leadin' them all back!" His concern grew over the condition of the camp and the cleanup which must be employed. Most of the trees about the place had been burnt and stood like ugly, black sentinels against the bright skyline. Repairs would have to be made immediately to the cabin roof and corrals.

"All I needed," he fussed, "was one empty-headed cowboy to lose all our stock for us." His irritation continued in the nervous slapping of his gloves against his thigh as he prowled forlornly around damaged corrals, to and fro across the dusty yard, and in and out of the soot-filled cabin. Ashes covered the ground, puffing up from beneath his boots to settle stickily against his dust-caked clothes. Occasionally he paused to peer from beneath his hat brim and scan the horizon for the slightest sign of an advancing band of horses.

John Strickland watched, waited and wondered. He could see that the noise of hammers and saws at the corral site grated against the foreman's frayed nerves. Clearly, Dick was not in good form, so he disappeared toward the cabin to help Smith repair the roof.

It was near dusk before McAllister arrived. The sun had set, casting long, gray shadows across the blackened valley. Foderow had almost given up waiting.

Sitting astride the new poles of the mended corral, Dick's eyes trained eastward, when Strickland's shout drew his attention to the cloud of dust drifting from the south. He rose slowly, straddling the poles, and squinted into the growing darkness and distance. His mouth suddenly pinched tight in slight amusement. "He's back," the foreman breathed with relief, "and with the horses to boot." Then, startled by the size of the advancing herd, Foderow's expression registered astonishment. "By God," he half-whispered to Strickland, who had come back outside, "He caught his wild ones."

Strickland grinned widely, nodding confidently. "Well, shave my whiskers," he exclaimed, "the little devil actually did it," and leaned against the rails to watch.

Foderow leapt to the ground. "Form up, boys," he called to the men, "and don't let a-one slip by you!"

Slowly, patiently, as he had led them all day, Ryan McAllister brought the horses closer to camp. He had kept them bunched together, their pace consistent. So far, he prided himself, he had managed to control them, keeping an eye out for the stallion. He had allowed them to feed, eased them carefully along the trail, and refused now to let excitement or premature confidence bring him to ruin.

There was no rushing, no hard galloping, yelling or whistling to keep them bunched together. Instead of a wild and scattered herd thundering into the repaired corral, McAllister brought a quieted and unscarred band of horses home to Foderow.

As he rode past the ranch foreman, McAllister glanced confidently into the face of the tall man. Foderow nodded slightly, his mouth unsmiling, but his eyes full of admiration and relief. Strickland watched, discerning that in the brief exchange he had just witnessed between the man and the boy, the bond that had slowly been developing during recent years had just received a generous sprinkling of cement.

No words were needed between the two. Despite his frustration over the fire, Foderow accepted that McAllister had done what he must, and had done it well.

McAllister unsaddled his gelding, let it in with the others and strode toward the creek. Downstream among the boulders, he stopped at a small pool, threw off his clothes and jumped into the cold water. Although the initial plunge chilled him to the bone, he luxuriated in its cleansing, and allowed the water to swallow him momentarily while he floated, staying in the darker depths near the rocks.

Then suddenly a noise onshore caught his attention. He squinted his eyes open, peering through their thin slits to see Foderow approaching the rocks with a towel and bar of soap in hand. Tossing the articles near the water's edge, the foreman called, while retreating, "You leave with me for the ranch at five in the morning! Don't drown in the meantime!"

26

Their arrival at Skaha was heralded by the sharp clanging of the dinner bell hangin on the veranda at the lodge. The huge iron piece, carefully moulded for Albert Llewellyn by the blacksmith Holinger, sent its clear, resounding toll echoing across the flats.

The residents living at the lodge anxiously ran out to greet them, but Foderow shunned any waste of time in recounting the past days' events. Instead, he got himself and young McAllister into the light delivery and drove immediately to the Cartrell residence.

"Get word to my wife that I'm home," he ordered brusquely from the truck to anyone who cared to take it along, as they disappeared in a great cloud of dust across the flats of Skaha.

Ryan McAllister's mind was not preoccupied with details of the fire or its resulting devastation, as Foderow's was. He had mentally detached himself from the present and filled his thoughts with images of Sydney Alex as she had been days before when he had impulsively clasped her hand, and momentarily drowned in the light green pools of her searching eyes.

"Dick," he said suddenly. "Can you let me out here?"

Foderow slammed a foot at the truck brakes.

"I think I'll walk over home, take a look around." Glancing across at the older man, he faltered in his explanation. "Maybe do a little more work outside. I feel a little keyed up. You know– well, I'd like to be alone for awhile."

"Sure, sure. We all like that." Foderow brought the truck to a quick stop and young McAllister leapt over the running board, striking across to Two Way's old cabin. Behind him, he heard the truck pull away and bump along Cartrell's ravine road.

He knew she was there even before he touched the handle of the door. How, he could not explain; he simply knew.

Soft streams of afternoon sunlight poured through the small window, the rays interrupted only by leafy patterns of the vine growing over it. McAllister's eyes searched the dull interior for her. The scent of her was in the room; gentle whiffs of lavender came to him. Oh Lord, he thought, how I need to see her right now; hold her, feel her close to me, where she has never yet been.

Sydney Alex moved toward him. The moment longed for, dreamed of, this precious moment that she knew would eventually come, was upon them. Their youth had nothing to do with it. It was all in their hearts, kept alive by dreams and the memory of the gentle clasp of their hands that day in the yard, when nothing else had mattered but their being together.

His hand came up into her hair, held her head to him as his mouth covered hers. He kissed her eyes and ears, and allowed his senses to wander in the soft curve of her neck, the warm slope of her throat. She bared her shoulder to him, leaning back, sighing, bracing her body daringly against his in a way which she had never been with any boy. But this is no boy, she reminded herself in a rush of feeling. She felt his mouth move sensuously onto her breast.

Then suddenly, as swiftly as it had begun, it was halted. She fell back against the wall, clutching at her loosened blouse, staring widely into his astonished eyes. He was left aching and perplexed by her sudden move. He tried to catch his breath and wondered what was wrong.

"Sydney– what the hell– I'm sorry if I–" he frowned, his hurt very evident. And for the first time, he wondered what had brought her to his house on this day. She could not have known he was coming home.

"Oh, my," she whispered, "what must you think of me– think of me for this." Hastily she began doing up the buttons, turning away from him, her pretty face flushed despite its tan. "I've never acted so–"

"So, what? Bold? Honest? Normal? It just got out of hand, that's all," he said uneasily, confused. "It was right, or it wouldn't have happened." He crossed the space which she had put between them. "Well– Sydney, I think I love you– if I know what love is at all."

Embarrassed, Sydney Alex sank down to rest against her heels, crouching beside the wall. He knelt beside her, placed a comforting arm about her as she hid her face from him, refusing to meet his searching eyes.

No one had taught her that the longings she felt were wrong, she reminded herself, but the other girls called it shameful acting. Their words, while they gossiped, echoed now in her ears. She looked up at Ryan and admitted to herself that she had wanted him to take her across the room to his bed. Hadn't she always loved him from the very first day he had arrived at Skaha? Was she too young, too naive to know what these feelings were and would lead to? She knew all about it actually; had read countless books while hiding from her grandmother, with only a small flashlight. And she had exchanged information with the young girls at the badminton club. She had not been without boyfriends who had tried to touch her. She was, Sydney Alex realized, no longer a silly girl, but a perfectly normal young woman ready for the experience of love with the right man, yet fearful of it.

Beside her, Ryan gently asked in a wondering voice, "Why did you come here?"

"I just wanted to feel near you. Sometimes I come here-- just sit in that chair, to be alone and think of you." She was near tears and he sensed that.

"Come on, Sydney, let's get out of here," he whispered near her. "I'll walk you back to the house." Gently he held her arm as she rose with him.

Sydney Alex stifled her tears of embarrassment at the sound of his words. Protest rose in her throat, and died in realism. Obediently she left the cabin.

For a long while that evening Ryan McAllister strolled the paths of the ranch with a troubled mind and unsettled body. He did not want to see Foderow or bump into Cartrell and, least of all, meet Mrs. Cartrell somewhere. He wished that Sydney Alex was with him, then, at times, was glad she was not. He knew his own feelings. Did she? His were easily sorted. It was all very simple. He loved Sydney Alex Llewellyn.

He accepted control of their behaviour. He could not allow irresponsibility to complicate their lives. Yet, it was bound to happen, was it not? He wished he could have asked her that. With or without the wedding ring, he was certain it was going to happen.

Eventually McAllister returned to his cabin beside Willow Creek. Throughout the night he tossed restlessly in and out of sleep. His thoughts filled with Sydney Alex, vowing each time he woke, to not again allow that soft smooth skin of hers to tempt him into corners from whence it was difficult to retreat - until he had asked Ian Cartrell for her hand in marriage.

In the dull, early morning light McAllister smiled ruefully over the matter and wondered how he might go about doing that. Asking for the hand of the heir of Skaha was like saying outright, I'd appreciate it. Ian, old boy, if you'd hand over those reins of control you more or less promised me.

Swinging his feet over the edge of the bed to the floor, he stood before the washstand and the mirror on the wall above it. Nodding to his reflection, he talked aloud. "You won, Ian Cartrell. I want her. I want the ranch and everything that goes with it." He lathered his face ready for shaving. So you won. But, what did you have to fight? He poised the razor above his cheekbone and grinned at himself. It was, my friend, your granddaughter who got me for you, and my own ambition; not your planning, nor your power. "Ha, ha!" he exclaimed triumphantly and swished downward with the sharp razor against the stubble of his beard. McAllister thought further, more seriously, as if making a final commitment to his future. Without Ian's prodding and with or without Sydney Alex, I want Skaha!

It was easy for McAllister to concern himself with the daily tasks of ranch life. There was always something awaiting his attention. What was getting difficult for his mind to handle was the news of war every time he turned on the small battery radio on his kitchen table. He realized, as everyone did, that any week now, Great Britain would declare war on Germany. At the thought of such a decisive act, a wave of patriotism gripped him. While the feeling was full of anticipation, it was nonetheless mingled with fear of the unknown.

When, on September third, 1939, the announcement was finally made by England and France, followed by Canada on September tenth, McAllister was once more installed at cow-camp in the Okanagan mountains.

John Strickland brought the news out to McAllister and Smith. Upon dismounting his saddle horse, he simply stated, "We are, once more, at war."

27

They brought the cattle and horses down to Skaha the first week in November. McAllister rode at one side of the herd, while Foderow took the lead, with Strickland on the other side. Two young men who lodged in the big house at the ranch rode with them. Bud Smith led the pack horses out.

Ryan huddled deeper into his mackinaw and pulled its collar up around his neck. The air was cold. Frost covered the ground like a thin, white film. In chilled precision, the men of Skaha rode alongside the herd in the late afternoon light.

Comfortable upon Dobbyn, with the cattle in control beside him on the new forestry road, McAllister's mind dwelt upon his hopes for the future. He was at home at Skaha, even though he constantly felt as if he were fighting some kind of silent battle with Ian Cartrell. He mentioned this once to Dick Foderow, who had knowingly smiled and replied truthfully, "You're one among many, son."

McAllister realized that not only was his youth against him, but he lacked a complete formal education as well. This often led to a feeling of inadequacy, especially in the areas of veterinary and business management. He always listened with avid interest when Foderow and Cartrell discussed ranch matters. They never objected to his presence.

Riding alongside the range-fattened red and white Herefords and the sprinkling of Black Angus amongst them, he contemplated the consequence of war insofar as he, a Canadian, would be affected. The thought of enlistment was scarey; however, he considered quickly, with Sydney Alex off to stay with her father in Vancouver and attend nursing school, and the war not likely to last more than a year, maybe he should get away from the place for awhile. He pulled his bandanna tighter around his neck and adjusted his hat against the stiff fall breeze blustering around them.

I'm trapped in a vicious circle, he told himself wearily. I'm not yet what they call a real man around here, but no longer a boy. My life is full of anxieties I do not need - Sydney Alex, who left for Vancouver without telling me until at the last, and Ian, who has my life mapped out for me. Then there's Strickland, who keeps one eye trained on me as if I might falter in my obligation to the ranch. An amused smile creased the corners of his mouth. I can, of course, he decided on impulse, willingly go off to war and leave it all behind for awhile.

Two days later, McAllister rode in the truck beside Foderow on their way to Penticton. He studied the foreman's profile carefully in an attempt to discern the man's mood.

The day was windy and cold with the threat of snow in the air. Foderow talked of bad weather and feeding cattle during the rough winters of the old days, but McAllister hardly heard him. His mind was preoccupied with war news. In fact, there was seldom anything else in the news. Over 50,000 volunteers signed up almost immediately, and the First Canadian Division was preparing to leave Canada for England any week now. An overwhelming feeling of patriotism seized him and, glancing across the cab at Foderow, he wondered about mentioning his intentions.

However, Foderow broke into McAllister's troubled, churning thoughts before he could speak of the matter. "You're awfully damned quiet. Somethin' wrong?"

Staring down at the scarred toes of his cowboy boots against the floorboard, McAllister blurted impulsively, "I think I'll join the Army, Dick. I mean– I feel–"

Foderow grinned indulgently, his amusement over the statement obvious. "You'll do no such fool thing."

McAllister looked up, "I'm serious."

"Of course you're serious. The first blast of a gun goes off and you young'uns figure you got to get over there right away and set it all straight. Well, I'll tell you, son, I think we need you here more." Foderow reached out to give the younger man an encouraging pat upon his shoulder. "The feelin' will pass. Give it time. It's a bit of loyalty to the Crown that we all know, comin' out in you, that's all. You're young."

"Well, I think I'll join anyway." He chewed nervously at his lower lip while staring at the winding dirt road ahead of him. A frowning, disagreeing image of Ian Cartrell loomed before him, but somehow he felt he would overcome argument with the man. "Besides," he added candidly, "it may be decided for me anyway, by conscription. I've read about that." Although the magnitude of the word escaped him, McAllister did know what it meant. "And it may not last very long."

Foderow grimaced. "Well, everyone thought the first one wouldn't either, but it did– it did. I think this one will be worse. The news is horrifying." Foderow fell silent. Well, the boy might be right. There may be no choice left to him. At that moment, he felt sympathy for young McAllister. He wanted to tell him how he had personally come to feel about him, that he admired the way he handled himself with the other men, especially Cartrell, and was pleased about his care of the stock. The extra money garnered from the sale of ten of the fourteen wild horses, which McAllister had turned over to him, had paid for the load of grain stockpiled for winter feeding. However, Foderow remained quiet, his thoughts and admiration for McAllister kept to himself, for it would be like saying, I'd like you for a son-in-law, and he could not barge like that into the life of his wonderful daughter.

Sydney Alex returned to Skaha two weeks before Christmas with her father. Thomas was pleased to be back at the ranch to see his mother, Ian and his old friends. The bitterness between Sydney and himself over his departure had lessened and Sydney welcomed him home. Time, it appeared, had healed emotional wounds.

As Sydney studied her son during the visit she noticed a new confidence in him, gained, no doubt, through his success with his father-in-law's business. She smiled when she remembered how quickly cars and motorized machinery caught his attention. Thomas is obviously happy with everything in his life, she thought and sighed with relief.

Sydney Alex had hardly slid her suitcase through the doorway of her room, when she hastily changed from her travelling clothes into a warm sweater and wool slacks and left the house to visit Janet Foderow. She also hoped to catch sight of Ryan McAllister. "Lordy!" she said aloud as she walked through the fresh snow on the ravine road. "How I've dreamed of this homecoming– thought of no one else but him!" Her steps quickened and soon she was at the ranch site.

Sydney Alex heard the activity at McAllister's corrals before she knew what it was all about. As she neared them, she noticed Janet and her father perched upon the corral railing with several others who lodged at the ranch. Nearest to her were Strickland and Smith, watching with wide smiles. She approached them and leaned against the rails beside John Strickland. Peering into the corral, she was astonished to see McAllister bobbing wildly atop a black horse, who bucked furiously around the arena in a concentrated attempt to unload him.

"My word," she whispered. "What's going on?"

Strickland grinned down at her. "Well, he got himself some more wild ones, and now he's set on breakin' them."

Sydney Alex caught her breath. "He'll get hurt!"

"I doubt it," Bud Smith interjected with obvious confidence in McAllister. "He's as wiry a little bugger as you'll ever see!"

Sydney Alex leaned over the rails in the direction of the Foderows. Janet was standing now with her parents and, as the ride ended and McAllister leapt out of the stirrups, she saw that Janet clapped her hands in exuberant applause. McAllister removed his hat, held it at his waist and bowed deeply before her in acknowledgement of her praise. Laughter filled the air. Good humour prevailed. Everyone had enjoyed the performance, and McAllister enjoyed everyone's attention.

As McAllister chased the horse from the arena into the second corral beyond his cabin, his gaze shifted toward Strickland and Smith. His step halted. She's here! He was surprised. When did she come home? How could it be that the car got past here without my seeing it? He closed the gate securely and, forgetting all others hanging around the corrals, strode swiftly toward the end of the arena where Sydney Alex waited. Both Strickland and Smith did a tactful retreat.

Sharing an emotional gaze, he took her arm and led her from the corrals. They crossed the road to Cartrells and walked along a narrow deer path toward the snowy hillside. Once into the trees, McAllister clasped Sydney Alex to him, and held her tightly in the circle of his arms, savouring the wonderful moment of having her near. He heard the faint whisper of his name and cupped the back of her head and her soft honey-coloured hair, turning her face to his, touching her warm lips with his own. They allowed their closeness to envelop them. Their kiss was deep; the deepest, most searching they had shared, and it led them to sink upon the cold ground beneath the trees where they lay quietly together. The moment needed to linger for memory's sake.

They began to talk. In hurried sentences she told him about the exciting big city and the hospital. He talked about the horses. It was stalling the inevitable. When they rose, for the winter afternoon was wearing on and growing colder, little had been left unsaid. Between them was expectation of a new familiarity and promise.

War news and the Commonwealth's participation filled the radio broadcasts and motion picture news continuously; McAllister felt he could no longer stall his decision. Striding his long body across the snow-covered yard to Cartrell's office, where Foderow often met with his men, McAllister slumped down into a chair before the ranch foreman and said abruptly, "Dick, when Sydney Alex goes back to Vancouver, I'm goin' up to Prince George to see my folks. I also got my grandparents near Williams Lake to see. Then I'll come down to Vernon and sign up. So many others are already gone, and I've never been anywhere, and I'd feel foolish if I didn't—"

"And what have you said to Ian?" Foderow interrupted, as he shifted around in the chair. He reached into the cupboard near his knee, suddenly feeling the need for the rye that was kept there.

"Nothing. I thought I'd leave that up to you," McAllister replied warily.

Remembering Thomas Llewellyn's decision to leave, Foderow stated in an agitated manner, "As others have before you." He poured two shots into the glasses, handed one to McAllister and raised his own. "Aw well– Seems once I toasted to your success with the wild horses like this. Now, it's to your safe return home when this war's done with."

"Home," McAllister repeated, trying to smile. Their glasses clinked and they drank.

Foderow smiled ruefully. "This is different occupation than collecting wild horses, lad. Very serious–"

"I can handle it," McAllister assured him confidently, "just like you, no doubt, handled a lot of things in your life so far," recalling a rumour that the foreman had once killed an American outlaw.

"War was not one of 'em. That was Thomas' lot." Foderow waited, watching the young man across from him. "Ian and I held the ranch together, like I thought you might do during this latest round."

McAllister crossed a leg over his knee and sat turning the glass between his hands. He found it hard to look at Dick at the moment. "It's just something I have to do, Dick. It's been on my mind, you know."

"And Sydney Alex? I know that you two–"

"I have to do this, Dick."

Quietness prevailed for several moments. McAllister concentrated on the toe of his boot laying across his knee, and Foderow focussed on McAllister.

The foreman broke the silence. "Well, Ryan, it's not like I don't understand. Lord, I had some indecision in my life at times, too, but I guess I'm just thinking of the ranch first."

"This isn't indecision, Dick. I know what I'm doing." He emptied his glass and set it on the desk.

"You're puttin' a lot of space between you and the girl, which doesn't hurt. You're young yet, Ryan, and–"

McAllister looked across at Foderow and smiled. "You sound like a father. I've never talked to anyone like this before."

Foderow sighed. "Well, I guess I'm a little like Ian. Never had a boy of my own." He set his glass on the desk. "I'll worry, you know."

McAllister dropped his boot to the floor and stood up. Extending his hand, he grasped the other's. "It'll be good to know you're doin' that, Dick."

As the time drew near for Sydney Alex' return to nursing school, and Ryan's enlistment, their moments alone became more passionate. Strained by the thought of lengthy separation, one night between Christmas and the new year, Sydney Alex left Janet's house and stopped at Ryan's cabin.

From his window where he waited, McAllister watched her walk the snowy pathway to his yard. As she neared, he blew out the light from the lamp and opened the door to her.

He was everything Sydney Alex had dreamed of; and she was all that he had imagined her to be. The interlude, begun with a certain awkwardness, ended with longed-for fulfilment. The experience of such intimacy, new to Sydney Alex, had been known to Ryan only occasionally. Still, he understood gentleness and patience, and enjoyed a warm and loving feeling toward her. Huddled beneath the quilt over his bed, he held her close to him while they rested, confident in the love they shared.

Although McAllister did not know what his future held, for he was only nineteen years old and would soon be in another field, he realized that his time with Sydney Alex, as he lay with her that night, would sustain him through the months, or years ahead as he thought it might now become. He savoured the scent of her, the feel of her soft breasts against his chest and the wonderful thrill of her mouth as it gently teased his. I will need this, he thought, all of it, every day of my life. Curving his neck to glance down at her face in the darkened room, he wondered, what will she remember of me? That she found me underneath a dirty platform? That I caught wild horses? Or, how I touched her, how she came to me, how we were together? How much deeper our love for each other will be now. He closed his eyes and held Sydney Alex a little tighter.

McAllister smiled in the dark. I will not back out of my decision, he vowed. Because of this night in this bed, and because I can see little beyond it right now, I feel I have the best possible reason to fight like crazy over there and get back home. Men have always fought for dreams, he reminded himself; dreams of land and honourable occupation, of promise and hope for a rewarding future, and for the life and love which he held now, so close in his arms.

Although his physical rest through the night was peaceful, McAllister, nonetheless, slept with a sorrowing heart.

28

The deep gorges of Coquihalla Pass, spanned by the high wooden trestles of the C.P.R., were cloaked in the darkness of night. Ian and Sydney, accompanied by Dick and Fern Foderow, travelled over this nightmarish pass from Penticton to Vancouver. Aware of the treacherous depths of the great canyon and the mighty Fraser River below them, they rested uneasily in their sleeping car as the train sped along the canyon walls and through long black tunnels, threading its way like an enormous snake, to the Pacific city. Always passed in the dark, the awesome scenery was never seen by travellers.

In the cool, gray dawn of the early May morning the passengers stepped down onto the C.P.R. platform at Vancouver and mingled with others in the waiting room. At once Thomas Llewellyn was beside his mother, taking her hand in his, wanting to scoop her up in a rush of feeling, but not daring to. Sydney appeared frail. He noticed that she continued to use her cane.

It was a friendly greeting, free of strain. Thomas had been away from Skaha for eight years, with only brief annual visits to his old home. He had reached toward his own goals in his father-in-law's construction company, McGovern & Watt. He no longer suffered the terrible inferiority that Ian Cartrell's imposing presence caused throughout his years of life on the ranch. He was especially pleased to see Dick Foderow again. While Mary, now Thomas' wife, stood quietly by, Thomas spent a moment with Dick to enquire about the ranch.

Running along the length of the platform, Sydney Alex and Janet burst into the waiting room with giggles of excitement, throwing their arms open in embrace. It was an important time in the lives of the two young women. Although their vocations differed, for Janet was already working as a hairdresser at Kamloops and Sydney Alex was to graduate from nursing school this weekend, they had remained close friends and were pleased to be together again for this celebration.

When the racket became too much for Cartrell, he raised his voice and said authoritatively, "Enough is enough! This silly screeching will now cease!" Then more calmly, he instructed, "Let's proceed to the hotel and get ourselves settled in," whereupon they divided themselves into the waiting vehicles. As Sydney Alex stepped toward a car that held a young man, Cartrell enquired, "Are you not riding with your grandmother and me?"

Sydney Alex halted her step. "Why no, Papa, I'm with Dennis in his car. We'll take Janet and her–" she faltered, failing to impress Cartrell. She met his dark eyes. "Papa, he's not Janet's boyfriend." The statement, with all its implications, hung on the air. Her hazel eyes watched the dark pools of his.

With reproach, Cartrell stared into his granddaughter's face - almost as beautiful as her grandmother, and obviously just as independent. He noticed the blonde hair shining in the early morning sun, curled loosely around her face. With her mother's height, she was stunning. He knew she waited for his response. Ian Cartrell felt his stiff reserve slowly slip away. Why, he wondered, did I expect her not to have a boyfriend.

Nodding slightly, he conceded, "So be it, child."

Sydney Alex' shoulders dropped in relief. She smiled warmly. "Papa– it's wonderful to see you again. Truly–"

"Go, go–" he replied impatiently. "Our time to talk will come."

A forlorn, unhappy feeling crept through Sydney Alex and her attempts at shrugging it off were futile. How was she going to explain her real feelings? Would he accept her reasons for turning to someone other than his choice, altering his plan? With the same reasoning which her father had often exercised, she wondered– why must I account to him? But Sydney Alex knew - because he cared, and in the role of grandfather, he had been a mentor to her, a companion through her youth.

Sliding across the seat of the car, close to the young man waiting there, Sydney Alex rode toward the tall majestic, green-turreted Hotel Vancouver in silence, eyes downcast in thought.

The gray dawn of the city skyline gave way to the brighter light of day. The streets were busy and noisy. Sydney looked out at the buildings and bridges; several years had gone since they had been in the city.

Presently Cartrell returned to their suite. Crossing the room, he placed his arms around his wife's slight shoulders, drawing her back against his chest. "What are you thinking, dear heart?" His smile was warm, thoughtful and he looked around expectantly at her face.

"That it is all very huge and too noisy. I've hardly been past the gates of Skaha in fifty years," she whispered, disbelieving the passage of time. "Have you ever thought about that? It has not struck me until this moment, to wonder if I've missed something in life by not travelling. There was a time when I felt I had journeyed far enough."

"Are you sad about that?" He waited. "I, too, have been locked more or less, behind the same gates for nearly as many years. When I reached Skaha, it was time to stop." He trailed his lips along the length of her neck, "Perhaps a trip to Banff and the sulphur springs?"

Sydney glanced over her shoulder at him. "To see the Rocky Mountains again-- oh my!" Then, frowning, "Tell me, Ian, who was that young man with Sydney Alex?"

Cartrell pursed his lips. "I believe he might be the rival of our Ryan, who's lost somewhere in Europe, and the disruption of my plans." A rueful smile passed over his slightly creased face. "An enquiry to Thomas gave up that this Dennis has obtained a degree in animal care and will take a place in his father's veterinary. How he has escaped the eye of the army puzzles me. However, you mustn't bother your lovely head about it, my dear. Mine will be plagued enough for both of us." Turning Sydney around to face him, he smiled, "Now, shall we go down to breakfast? We've a long day ahead."

Throughout the graduation ceremonies and the social hour that followed, Cartrell was acutely aware of the presence of the young man, whose only name so far was Dennis.

Careful to remain as distant as possible, Dennis Michaels kept an eye on Skaha's tall, dark-eyed, pencil-straight manager, who had kept himself in remarkable physical condition and left no doubt about his capabilities or sense of perception. He knew that when he least expected it, he would find himself face to face with Cartrell. His fight for a life with Sydney Alex would not be an easy one, he sensed, but he was willing to give it all he had.

Two years older than Sydney Alex and barely the same height, Michaels was a bright young man, well-educated, with a promising future. A car accident had left him with spinal injuries which would remain a painful reminder of carelessness. Quiet and conservative, with a romantic nature, he was bound to appeal to Sydney Alex, who felt acutely, the pangs of loneliness since the departure of Ryan McAllister. Sandy-haired and brown-eyed, Dennis' easy-going disposition had captured her heart from the start. It was a new beginning for the country girl from Skaha whose only romance in the past two and a half years had been occasional letters from the war front, until even they, after a time, failed to arrive in her mailbox.

Cartrell suggested to Sydney Alex that she return to Skaha with them at the end of their visit and, if not now, then after she cleared her things from her room at residence and her father's house. Also, she was to return alone.

Avoiding Cartrell's eyes until his final word, Sydney Alex ignored the warning in their dark depths, and spoke up. There was a new rebelliousness in her, Cartrell noticed, startlingly reminiscent of her father's years before.

"Papa--" she began, clenching her hands nervously. "I've been waiting for the chance to tell you about Dennis."

Cartrell waited.

"He is my boyfriend and–"

"I'm capable of perceiving that much." He stood near the window with arms folded across his chest.

"Well then," she sighed. "There's only one way to say it. Papa, we are going to be married."

He began to pace the floor. His expression had turned to stone and the chill of his mood reached her. She willed herself to remain positive about her choice. "Papa, I know you had plans, but it's really my life we're talking about. And I am entitled to my choices."

Cartrell refused to look at her and stared out at the tall city buildings as though they held greater appeal at the moment.

"Really, Papa, you make people say things that they don't want to."

Cartrell's eyes swung around to look at her. "I make people say things?" He waited a moment. "Are you telling me that I am making you say that you plan to marry this schoolboy?"

Sydney Alex hung her head in exasperation and leaned against the wall. "You force words from my mouth before I'm really ready to say them, and then you're upset because I don't say what you want to hear." Clamping her teeth together, she added petulantly, "And, he's not a schoolboy!"

"He is nothing more."

"Just because he's not like Ryan, because he doesn't run around in cowboy boots and a big hat, and ride bucking horses, you're picking on him!" Sydney Alex' face flushed. Despite the apprehension which flooded her, she spoke with earnestness, "I'll not have you put him down like that, Papa. I really won't."

For a brief moment Ian Cartrell held his breath in tolerance of her childish outburst. Then he spoke to her with the same sense of earnestness. "And, I'll not have you marrying him until you've given the relationship more serious thought. You are an educated woman now, with a good future before you."

Her hazel eyes clouded. Impulsively Sydney Alex leapt away from the wall. "I'm going to marry him, Papa, with or without your blessing."

With a single searing moment passing between them, during which their eyes met in stubborn clash, Cartrell spun on his heel and left the room. Sydney Alex collapsed angrily into the nearest chair.

"Oh, why can't you help me through this," she wept bitterly, "instead of making me fight you." Burrowing further into the big hotel chair, Sydney Alex covered her face with shaking hands against her hurt, as tears of disappointment fell unchecked.

When he returned to his suite an hour later, Cartrell found the girl gone, as he had expected. A strong will reigned in Sydney Alex. And a stubbornness familiar to all who knew him, prevailed in Cartrell.

Sydney Alex consistently refused, when coaxed by Thomas, to

return to the hotel to say goodbye to everyone. She talked to her grandmother and was grateful for Sydney's patient understanding. Her father chose to remain as far from argument as possible, leaving her alone at his home while he took the group to the train.

Cartrell was visibly shaken at the girl's absence from the depot, pacing the platform boards. He could not believe that Sydney Alex had developed the strength to defy and ignore him in such a manner.

The incident continued to nag fiercely at Cartrell's conscience. When Sydney Alex and Dennis arrived at Skaha three weeks later, the first thing he did was draw her aside and inspect her left hand for a ring– and there it was, a plain gold band shining defiantly in the noonday sun, pressing the marriage into his mind. It suddenly seemed to Cartrell that his fifty years of preserving the ranch had been carried out in vain.

Cartrell spent the afternoon walking the pathways of the ranch, staring for long moments toward the distant blue mountains. He mourned, prematurely, the demise of Skaha which now appeared imminent to him. He realized that any attempt at persuading the Canadian army to release the young soldier from active duty would get no further than the paper on which it was written. Furthermore, Cartrell suspected that McAllister may be missing in action, although that fact had not yet been confirmed. It had been nearly a year since anyone had heard from him and, thinking rationally about it, Cartrell could hardly blame Sydney Alex for turning to another. Had not he and her grandmother done the same?

29

With surprising interest, Dennis Michaels settled into a prolonged visit at the ranch. The size of the ranch astounded him. In the coastal valley he was accustomed to visiting farms of ten to fifty acres. To imagine thousands of acres in one family's control was awesome. He began to show enthusiasm for the work and it appeared as though he might stay.

In conversations, Foderow and Strickland found his knowledge of animals extensive and his training impressive. The serious side of Dennis' nature was always present and his veterinary skills academic.

Riding with Dennis to cow-camp was not the comfortable journey through the mountains Foderow had felt with Ryan McAllister. However, Foderow gave Dennis credit that, while not born to the saddle, the boy did outlast the trip and its accompanying discomforts without complaint.

Michaels viewed the great herd of cattle with an appreciative eye, but failed to fully grasp the vastness of Skaha as a working unit. It was not that he turned aside approaches to consider the ranch his future and its rugged comforts his home, but more that his goals had been planned to a smaller scale. Nonetheless, he was not adverse to adjustment, even though he preferred veterinary for small animals.

Foderow refrained from comment, for he had overheard Dennis express that sentiment to Cartrell, and did not wish to pass judgement. Although he had come to like the young man and admire his ability with animals, he secretly agreed with Cartrell that Ryan would have been a better match.

Cornering the foreman at the barn one day, Cartrell explained, "You see, Dick, what happens to the ranch in the end, really depended on who that girl married." Smiling disconsolately, he added, "Sydney's right when she says I've become a little like Albert was with Tom over Skaha."

At that moment, as if she had planned the timing, Sydney Alex entered the driveway of the ranch and trotted her horse along the grassy edges of the hardened roadway to where the two men stood. In typical riding dress, she appeared relaxed and happy and seemingly oblivious to the disruption her marriage had caused.

It was not difficult for Sydney Alex to be home at Skaha, for she had long ago grown accustomed to Ryan McAllister's absence. What *was* upsetting at times was that it might continue and she would never actually see him again. More interested in her own situation, she had failed to recognize how difficult the transition was for her husband.

Dennis saw exactly what was expected of him and wondered if he would ever measure up to Cartrell's expectations. At times he questioned the potential of a move to the ranch. He knew it would be a challenge, but until he actually arrived and realized the enormity of the place, he had no idea how great the challenge would be. While Sydney Alex rode her horse about the hills taking sentimental photographs with a new Brownie camera, Michaels struggled with the demands of daily ranch life at Skaha. Living under the same roof as Ian Cartrell lent nothing but further anxiety. Finally, in August, the newlyweds moved into Cartrell's old rooms above the office and exulted in the privacy it afforded.

On that bright sunshine morning when Sydney Alex returned from her ride, she called greetings to Foderow and Cartrell. Stepping down from the saddle, she began, "I hope Janet will be home to visit soon. I have some exciting news to tell her. I haven't seen her all summer."

Foderow reached for the reins. "It takes awhile to get settled in a new job, and Kamloops is a full day's ride by bus to get here," he smiled. "I'll look after this for you," he offered, and led the horse to the corral.

"Thank you. Papa, I'm going along to talk to Gran. Coming? I've something to share with you both." A coquettish smile played about her mouth.

Cartrell smiled and noticed the light flush across her cheeks. "Well child, you can tell me here. I'm a busy man these days."

"But Gran is only over at the old house," she informed him. "We are putting plans together for that place, you know, now that it's nearly empty."

"I know well enough where your grandmother is and she's always putting plans together for something. I've no time to waste in idle talk."

With a mischievous grin, Sydney Alex glanced quickly at the foreman who unsaddled her horse. "Oh, okay! I'm going to have a baby, that's all." Swiftly then, she turned on her heel and strode down the road toward the old Llewellyn house. Little puffs of dust billowed about her boots with each firm step, and the soft sounds of a tune hummed in youthful contentment drifted back to the two men.

Foderow, who had been smoking, now tossed his cigarette to the ground. He lifted the saddle from the gelding and strode with it into the dark interior of the tack room.

Cartrell remained rigid, his hands fisted in his pockets, the smile wiped from his astonished face. The August sun momentarily dipped behind a cloud as though avoiding the man's dampened spirits.

Foderow emerged from the doorway behind Cartrell to drape the saddle blankets over the rail and turn the horse loose. "Are you alright, Ian? Did you think it wouldn't happen?"

"Oh, I've survived worse news!" Cartrell snapped glumly.

"I'll leave you then," Foderow told him. "I promised Bud I'd be in cow-camp with supplies and you know how impatient he can get."

To Cartrell, the blow had come. The announcement by Sydney Alex had fallen like a yoke upon his neck. He was becoming weary of the ranch and its ponderous responsibilities. He lapsed momentarily into troubled reverie where the crushing effect of Sydney Alex' words reeled about his brain.

Sydney Alex, revelling in her marriage, exhibited a carefree, unconcerned attitude toward the ranch and her eventual inheritance. Dennis Michaels was careful to remain apart from the agitation between his wife and her grandparents, and often wondered where, in all the mapping of their future, did his father-in-law, Thomas Llewellyn, place?

One evening as he and Sydney Alex strolled through the woods in the gathering dusk, he told her, "I'd sure like to get back home and talk to Dad. It seems like your grandfather has cast a shadow over me, and nowhere can I get away from it to decide about my life."

"I think that's been a curse for many." Sydney Alex sympathetically took his hand in hers, pulling his arm through the loop of her own. "Honey, it's just that Ryan was such a damned good cowboy, born to the saddle as they say, and friendly with Mr. Foderow and all–" When she looked around at Dennis, he was frowning, his mouth pinched tight in decision and concern.

"It's not that I don't want the place, Sydney Alex. At first I thought I wouldn't, but–"

"You have to take a decent stab at it, Dennis. It's all ours in the end– yours, all of it under your control. It's huge, Dennis." She watched his face for sign of consent. "Papa means well. He's stern, but he means well."

Michaels looked across at his wife. How could he refuse her? He never refused her anything. It might work, he decided. "We'll go back to the coast for awhile. Soon."

She tossed her blonde curls away from her shoulders, leaned across and brushed her lips gently over his cheek. "I love you, you know," she whispered and saw the unhappiness in his expression, even though he was smiling. After that, Sydney Alex walked just a little closer to him, her body touching his in provocative ways as they strolled.

For a long while Foderow refrained from any intervention, feeling that it was not his place to persuade. But one day, when opportunity presented itself at the barnyard, he cast resolve aside and mentioned to Cartrell, "When a man's not born into this mould, it's a little unsettlin' to his whole way of thinkin'." As he talked, he trimmed and filed at a front hoof of his horse, then nailed the metal shoe against the smoothed surface. With patient stance, the gelding kept balance despite the hundreds of tiny flies plaguing his belly and legs.

"You can't just take him into the barn, Ian, and remind him that he married into this great opportunity," Foderow continued, "and that it's his privilege to make the change to our way of life. You know what I mean?" He set his tools aside and allowed the horse's leg to drop. "It didn't work with Tom and it won't go far with this boy, either. I think he'd like to try it here, but he has a mind of his own and just needs time to think it through." He straightened his back, carefully working his body forward, then back to ease the pain of strain. "At times I miss that young McAllister– like now."

From his shirt pocket Foderow drew a pouch and began rolling the thin paper and tobacco together into a smokable cigarette. Cartrell remained quiet. Beside him the gelding stomped in the dust against the insects. "You're pretty damned hard on him, Ian. Dennis doesn't deserve that."

Cartrell stared through rimless glasses. "I know all about rights, and infringements on another's decision," he responded impatiently.

Foderow struck a match to his cigarette. "Well, he's an independent cuss. Not like young Ryan was. Ryan wanted to be here, wanted to learn. Dennis had his own family and plans, and came to us with an education behind him, not out from under a railway platform in the middle of winter." Foderow waited for a reply.

Tiredly, Cartrell leaned his length against the wall of the shed, shoved his hands deep into his pockets and allowed his aching eyes, which had known little sleep of late, to search the clear summer sky. It was completely cloudless and blue, typically Okanagan. "Of course, you're right, Dick, but the tremendous investment here and what it could eventually come to mean for him seems to me might be carelessly thrown away." Cartrell cleared his throat and murmured, "I don't think he'll stay."

As Sydney Alex assisted her grandmother in converting a portion of the old Llewellyn house into a display for the contents of Rachel McAllister's trunk, Dennis Michaels took careful stock of his life and what it might become at Skaha. He was being asked to change course and choose a pathway completely unknown to him; to fall in line with a stranger's domineering nature concerning Skaha. It was a place which he had not even known existed until he met Sydney

Alex Llewellyn.

Dennis had dreamed of a veterinary practice of his own and had worked hard toward that goal. He had made his parents proud by following along in the family profession. Still, he enjoyed the idea of a challenge and the ranch presented that. Nonetheless, at the end of August 1943, Dennis and Sydney Alex were preparing to leave Skaha to re-evaluate.

One morning when Sydney Alex and her grandmother met at the old Llewellyn house, they set a plan into action. They discussed how to turn the ranch into an adventure in tourism, instead of just a bunkhouse as it seemed to have become.

"This war can't go on forever," the older Sydney stated. "Soon the boys will all be home, the economy will change and people will begin travelling again, perhaps more than before." She laid the papers out upon the floor and began drawing a sketch of the hallway and parlour. "For instance, we are planning a trip to Banff next month. There are those who would plan vacations to the Okanagan. We have the whole winter to prepare Skaha as a suitable guest ranch."

"You know, Gran," Sydney Alex said suddenly. "Papa's very put out with me. I can feel it. It's been following me for two months now."

"Nonsense!" Sydney admonished lightly. "He loves you deeply, child. Your baby will make him just as happy as his own grandchildren do."

Sydney Alex placed a hand against her abdomen. "Gran, when will I first feel the baby move? Maybe something's wrong." She knelt on the floor above the plans, and felt a reassuring hand upon her shoulder.

"When it begins to kick, it won't stop. Take my word for it!"

Sydney Alex reached up and gently grasped the hand between her own. "Sometimes I feel really close to you, Gran, like now." She looked up, meeting the blue eyes watching her. "When I opened the lid of that trunk, it was like when we played upstairs, just Janet and me."

Sydney's voice was nostalgic. "I remember so well the lady who filled that trunk."

"What was she to Ryan?"

"His great-grandmother."

Suddenly the room was still. The sound of their breathing, the ticking of a clock somewhere in the house, even Sydney's slow movement across the floor seemed extraordinarily loud.

Sydney Alex sat back against her heels and asked carefully, "Gran, do you suppose Ryan is alive? Sometimes I can't help but wonder."

"And if he is, will he return to us? Well, of course he'll come here. He believes that you are here waiting for him, dear."

Sydney Alex' shoulders slumped. "Gran, I really didn't want to hear that," she murmured forlornly.

"I'm sorry, but it's true. He has no way of knowing differently."

"He could've written," Sydney Alex mumbled petulantly.

"Perhaps that's not possible, child. Circumstances of war–"

Leaping quickly to her feet, her cheeks suddenly flushed. Sydney Alex blurted impulsively, "I'm not concerned with circumstances of war!"

Sydney looked aghast at her granddaughter and frowned reprovingly. "Dear, dear, dear!" she mourned aloud.

There was no further ground to be gained by remaining together. The talk had invaded the closed corners of Sydney Alex' mind and her memories hidden there. She kissed her grandmother good-day and left the house, just as Ian arrived to take Sydney home.

Doubts began to plague Sydney Alex' mind. In her subconscious lay the reasons, which seemed feeble now, for having forsaken those precious memories. Questions pressed into her conscience. What of the love she had felt a long time ago for the boy who had become a man, and then a soldier? What of the few moments they had shared together, tender and intimate? Could she push aside completely, that bond shared with her first love?

A troubled Sydney Alex walked the pathways of the gardens, by the shore of the small pond near the Cartrell home. Of course she was happy with Dennis. Was he not divinely good to her? Did he not truly care about her? Here she was, carrying his child nearly three months, quite happily anticipating the role of motherhood.

Sydney Alex felt a pride in being a young, married woman. All her girlfriends at the university were either engaged or married, and that was something these days in a country suffering a shortage of available young men. Except Janet, she reflected. Sydney Alex was certain Janet would be an old maid. Everything pointed to it.

She sighed. The world is crazy, Sydney Alex decided - war, separation, responsibilities, and the necessity of education for women. The chill of the evening mountain air pricked her skin and she wished she had worn a sweater, so she returned to the house.

The following Saturday Dennis and Sydney Alex packed their belongings to leave. Ending a two-month stay at the ranch, they loaded their suitcases and boxes into the car and drove out through the gate above which hung Albert Llewellyn's imposing sign, SKAHA RANCH.

Cartrell, watching the car disappear in the brown swirls of September dust, whispered to the empty room, "McAllister must return. This has gone on far too long," and stepped outside his office into the fresh air.

30

The white, calcimined walls caused an unrelenting glare against Ryan McAllister's eyes; sunlight shone through the unshaded window directly into them. It hurt to open his eyes, so he kept them closed. Images of the past and present mingled and swept across the visionary plain of his mind. He knew it was 1944 and that he was in a hospital somewhere in England. When he attempted to lift his head he became dizzy, and people seemed a blur. He soon succumbed to medication and sleep.

McAllister's mind was in turmoil as he moved in and out of consciousness. At times, he heard the sounds and saw again the bright flashes of explosions and soldiers running, shooting, screaming, dying; in other moments, a magnificent white stallion with flaring nostrils, galloping across a wide green meadow. And Sydney Alex, tossing her golden hair with a flip of her hand as she laughed merrily into his eyes; then, the urgent call "Stretcher! We have a soldier here with no knee left!"

When he could walk without the aid of crutches and was released from hospital for transfer to Canada, McAllister, while elated at returning home, began to feel an inward loneliness accompanied by a sense that he was, in some way, deserting. Guilt dogged him.

It was difficult for him to shake off the feeling that he should not be going home; that, instead, his place was at the front, not on a sleek liner crossing the Atlantic. As he stood, day by day, staring across the vast ocean, hearing voices in the silence, he finally accepted that he had to rebuild his life.

The train sped across the Canadian prairies to Calgary where he would overnight before continuing to Vancouver. McAllister listened to the rhythmic clickity-click of steel against steel and watched the moon rise over the vast, glimmering flat land. He began to count his blessings; first, that he had lived, and secondly, that he bore few scars from his ordeal. Medical science had provided him with a new kneecap and, therefore, the ability to walk again.

At Calgary an unfortunate accident occurred. McAllister was careless and tripped over someone's kit bag, falling hard upon his injured knee. He was forced to spend the next week in hospital. Consequently, when he once more boarded the train, he was again on crutches. He cursed his bad luck. Were it not for his clumsiness, he told himself, he would be lying in Sydney Alex' arms already, and later, travelling with her to Prince George to meet his parents. Now, so close, he became impatient to be done with the trip.

When the Canadian Pacific engine chugged into the Vancouver station, drawing to a steamy, hissing stop, McAllister flung his kit bag across his back, stepped down onto the platform on his wooden crutches and immediately located a telephone. With his heart racing, he held his breath as it rang.

He tried to stay calm. "Sydney Alex Llewellyn, please?"

"Sydney– Llewellyn? You mean, Sydney Michaels. She is not here," the crisp voice of Mary Llewellyn replied.

His throat tightened. "Michaels?"

"I'm sorry, Sydney and Dennis live in New Westminster. I can give you Dennis' office number. This is her father's home."

A long pause ensued, during which McAllister attempted to collect his reeling thoughts. "Tom Llewellyn's home?"

"Yes, yes. Who is calling, please?"

McAllister sensed the woman's impatience. He was bereft of words. Had he heard her correctly? New West, did she say?

"Thank you," he murmured against the mouthpiece, and carefully hung the telephone in its cradle on the box. He stepped out into Vancouver's damp spring air. His mind refused to settle. *Michaels*, he wondered. There had to be some mistake!

However, as McAllister stared at the gray skyline with its uneven contour of distant hills, tall buildings and great expanse of water, he began to assemble priorities. Suddenly he felt desperate to be home at Skaha, feel his roots, be with everyone there and, though now impossible, have Sydney Alex close to him. He needed to be reassured that what he had left behind four years earlier still existed.

Following demobilization, he wandered alone in the parks, slept fitfully against his kit bag on the damp grass and ate little. Being alone, being hungry and being a wanderer was not new to him. It amused him to remember, as he lay upon a park bench, how he had found his way to Skaha the first time. Now, while he ached to return there, he also felt desperate to remain away from old memories.

Finally he realized that he could not return to Skaha because Sydney Alex really was not there. Nor could he linger in the park much longer. His uniform was becoming untidy and he had developed a miserable cold. McAllister brushed the grass from his uniform, located the Greyhound depot, changed his clothes and bought a one-way ticket to Prince George, in the Cariboo country, where he had lived as a boy. The need to see his mother again grew as each hour passed. Four years had gone by since his enlistment, the last time he had visited.

The Greyhound bus carrying Ryan passed through the town of

Hope and along the mighty Fraser River; the night darkened and became cooler with the rain. Most of the passengers slept, as did McAllister, while the long, blue and white bus crossed over the wide Thompson River and headed north.

McAllister awoke with a start. The lights in the carrier had been turned on. The driver was announcing the time - midnight. They would soon be in Cache Creek and could stretch their legs or get something to eat. McAllister cautiously hopped down the metal steps, holding onto his crutches for balance, and breathed deeply of the rain-freshened country air.

"I'd forgotten," he said to the man who stepped down beside him, "just how wonderful clean air smells!"

"Well, you're in the Cariboo," the other drawled. "No air like Cariboo air," he grinned sideways at McAllister.

The soldier was surprised to notice how young McAllister was. When he had boarded at Chilliwack, his first glimpse of the soldier huddled in his seat with crutches, left an impression of a man in his late thirties, nursing old war wounds.

McAllister nodded. "You're from here?"

"Oh yes-- 100 Mile House to be exact." He offered his cigarettes to McAllister, who declined. "And you? Where're you from?"

"Family at Prince George." He stared across the flats darkened by a moonless night. He knew what the country looked like and did not need daylight to show him. He had been raised to know it well and respect its environment. For a wonderfully nostalgic moment it was as if he could hear the lonesome call of the Common Loon across a wilderness lake, see a deer at the edge of a meadow, or watch a moose on a marshland. He had thrilled to it all as a boy while following his Grandfather Dietrich through high wooded mountains, learning, as a young fellow should, about hunting and survival.

Leaning now against the motionless bus, Ryan pulled the collar of his khaki tunic around his neck against the chill of the spring rain. With lowered eyes, he listened to it fall and contemplated his shiny, black boots beneath the straight cut of his pants. He sighed unhappily and closed his eyes. I have missed Sydney Alex, and I've been so homesick for this land.

The two soldiers talked as they sat in the midnight quiet of the depot restaurant.

"Name's Manny Anderson."

"Ryan McAllister. I got on at Vancouver. You?"

"Chilliwack."

"I didn't see you. Must've been sleepin'. Wounded? I guess so, like the rest of us home this early." McAllister smiled, eyes on his plate.

Anderson said, "My family's got a trucking business throughout these parts," and wolfed down his sandwich.

McAllister nodded. "At least you know where you are. I'm somewhere between a retail business and cattle ranching."

They laughed lightly together, but the statement held a serious jest.

"Well," furthered Anderson, "I grew up wishing I was an only child and my old man had a ranch. Instead, he bought a couple of trucks and had four sons."

"I am an only child and it's pretty lonely," McAllister lamented. "And– I don't really want the hardware business."

Anderson leaned back in his chair and contemplated McAllister as he watched him eat. At thirty, Manny Anderson had what was sometimes called 'been around a bit', meaning that, as the eldest in a family of four boys he had assumed responsibility early in life, learned to drive a truck and get out on the road in it at sixteen. He had enlisted at the outbreak of war to allow room in the trucking world for younger brothers during harsh economic times in the country.

He was a man of average height, five feet nine, and of husky build. He suffered an injury to his spine and was subsequently discharged from the Army. He was passionately loyal to his country, and true to his friends.

McAllister found Manny Anderson comfortable to be with and fell into talking about the Okanagan and Skaha Ranch.

Anderson suggested, "Why don't you lay over awhile with my folks. See what kind of work's goin' on up here. That is, if you don't want to go into the store or back down south."

The offer was a good one, McAllister knew. He would need a job somewhere, doing whatever possible. He decided quickly. "Might as well check here first. I want to get home to the folks, though. It's been a few years since I saw them." He was reluctant to linger.

Anderson pushed aside his cup and plate, shoved the chair back and rose to his feet. "Another hour and we'll have this trip licked." He pulled his jacket into place at his waist and waited for McAllister to get started on his crutches.

They were called to board and once more the long carrier turned north onto the highway following the old Cariboo wagon road of the early gold mining boom. The rain had slowed. McAllister opened the small window beside him, breathed deeply of the fresh air, leaned back against the seat and fell asleep.

31

Anton Dietrich drove the highway between his ranch near Williams Lake and Prince George, cursing the unfortunate circumstances which called him out at such a time. It was pouring rain and the frayed rubber wipers could hardly keep the windshield clear. He lamented the shocking news he received only hours before. When reaching the city in late afternoon, he presented himself at the police detachment, a stooped, tired and angry old man in his seventies who had run out of patience with a lot of things in life.

Dietrich's lot had been a lifetime of very hard work: all the labour in ranching without benefit of machinery, and bending for hours to fit metal shoes, which he made himself, onto horses as difficult and stubborn as mules. His hair had whitened and been allowed to grow, hanging over his collar. His face, clean shaven most of the time, was deeply lined and tanned.

He carried within him a bitterness toward this harsh life. His dream of gold and riches had been abandoned long ago in favour of a marriage to gain property and a place in community life, and the realization that a man could starve while looking for gold.

He was ushered into an office where he might find a comfortable place to rest.

"I don't need a chair," he grumbled. "I just sat the last four hours and I need to get this business over with!"

Dietrich was briefed on the details of the accident and the resulting charges against the driver that careened through an intersection and took Richard and Joan Dietrich to their deaths on the stormy night before.

The young uniformed officer who stood across the room from him seemed almost an affront to Dietrich's own stance. Dietrich took his time at shaking raindrops from his slicker, then loudly blew his nose.

The officer cleared his throat to draw attention, and Dietrich looked up. "I am sorry, sir, about your family. I tell you, I detest moments like this when I must ask someone to identify a body." Noticing that Dietrich's expression had not changed, he decided that the old farmer was a seasoned veteran of his time and that he need not apologize further. "You'll have to come with me." Shrugging into his own raincoat and hat, he reached into a drawer for keys to a police cruiser, and led Dietrich outside toward the car.

It was explained to Dietrich, "An autopsy was ordered and carried out this morning, as you allowed by telephone. You'll have to sign the paper for that."

At the mortuary, Anton Dietrich succumbed. "Richard, Anna's only son. The daughter died many years ago. By God– this is a terrible thing that has happened." He felt very sad indeed. The boy had caused him no trouble, he remembered; had even been an enthusiastic companion at times. "Never liked farming, though. Joined up young in the First War, he did. Brought his wife from England. Her name is Joan."

"Did they have children? I'm sorry– you see, I don't know them, being with this detachment only two months."

They left the building as Dietrich explained. "Oh, a son overseas. Nobody's heard from him for a while. He wrote to his mother sometimes. When he was little, he hung around our ranch a lot. A good kid, but didn't get along with his folks. Anna, my wife– she sent him down to a ranch she knew about in the Okanagan, but he joined up from there and disappeared. May be dead, too."

The young officer shook his head in wonder that a family could be so loosely knit, and each member so isolated as to not know who was even alive. He said, "I'll put you in touch with a notary in town who will help you in clearing up the affairs of the deceased, and any assistance you may need in arranging burial."

Anton Dietrich left the police station no more at peace with the circumstances than when he had entered. He looked toward the sky, growing darker as thunderclouds moved up from the south, then down at his calloused hands between which he absently bounced the keys to his truck.

He stood on the wide step in a moment's contemplation of his life. His thoughts were drawn to his sister, Helga, whom he had not seen in fifty years. She had gone to the Okanagan, he remembered, with the Dutchman who had lost his wife and child in crossing a river and whose name he could not now recall. He had heard of her briefly from his wife, Anna, who had been married to a McAllister down in the Okanagan.

Dietrich crossed the street to his truck, refusing to further allow his mind to wander back to a time when he had known kin of his own. Stupid memories, he scoffed silently. Who needs them!

Within a week of arriving at the Anderson residence, Ryan was once again aboard the Greyhound carrier toward Williams Lake. There was no work available for him anywhere in the area, and he could no longer sit at another man's table without contributing to its fare.

When Anna Dietrich answered the knock at her door she was shocked to see her grandson. He gazed into her tear-filled eyes as she explained the tragedy of his parents, and stood before her in disbelief. He could find no words and fell quiet.

As Anna shuffled across the polished wood floor to prepare their lunch, she appeared to Ryan a tired, defeated, unhappy woman who had long ago given up the fight for an easier life. She was trying to make her sad news easier for him, but had an awkward way of doing it.

"Nothing is ever free– not even your own life," she told him. "Just when you think you have been successful with it, somebody comes along and takes it, just like your Ma and Pa had done to them." Her shaky voice held bitterness and hurt. She seemed on the verge of tears and he wished she would stop talking about it. He was fighting to control his own sense of loss and did not need to deal with hers as well. However, Anna did not cease her chatter and McAllister was trapped there in the kitchen chair unable to get away. Crestfallen, he tried to concentrate on her words.

"Some bone-headed idiot– maniac behind the wheel of a car had to come along and put an end to a couple of real fine, hard-working folks who never did nobody no harm." Now she was crying. Tears ran over her cheeks and fell into the collar of her sweater. Her hair was almost as white as his grandfather's, he saw. The skirt she wore had been mended with a large unmatched patch near the hem, and her black sweater was too small, clinging in an ugly way to the rolls of her thick body. "He was my son–" she whispered.

"Grandma," he said softly. "You don't need to talk about it, you know. I understand how you feel. They were my folks and I haven't seen them in a long time. I wanted to get home–" He was infinitely sorry now, that he had lingered at the Anderson residence.

Anna Dietrich hastened toward the chair, wrapped her arms around her grandson's head and cradled his face against her ample bosom, murmuring words of consolation. Ryan wished only to be outside, to walk alone across the field into the woods and think in privacy. He nonetheless responded to her sorrow and placed his arms about her waist, remaining still in the chair. She had always been a good grandparent to him and he loved her.

Anton Dietrich entered the house, scuffing his boots loudly across the veranda platform, and the embrace between his wife and her grandson was broken. While Anna set the table for the noon meal, the two men greeted each other in a detached way and talked about the weather. Dietrich was not a man who invited a lot of conversation, and had developed a concerted dislike for the sight of openly displayed sorrow. He did not wish to discuss the accident which caused the deaths. Nor did he enquire about the war. He heard about it every day on the radio and that was enough. Germany was the country he was from and it taxed his mind to listen to news and criticism.

The weeks which followed McAllister's arrival at the ranch were filled with advice from both grandparents about what he should be doing with his life. They told him that he must make an effort to get off his crutches.

He worked with the young calves at branding time, putting his knee to the test. His grandmother's sometimes sharp tongue echoed in his ears. He would never again complain about not having roots, he vowed, for she had cut him down with, "Don't whine to me about no 'roots', young man. All your roots were planted in the Okanagan over a hundred years ago!" Then struck him further to the quick by admonishing, "Forget about that girl. Go back down there where there's everything for you. Here, there's nothing. We'll sell this ranch soon and go live in town. Where will you go then?"

Each time her lectures became intolerable, McAllister got himself out of sight for awhile. He realized she cared about him and knew what was best for him, but he felt so alone.

In the cool spring northland evenings, Ryan walked along the familiar trails of his youth, sometimes with his grandfather who had, like his grandmother, grown old and very grumpy.

While alone, his thoughts wandered to Skaha and the time he had first spotted the band of wild horses. He remembered Dick Foderow, and recalled Tom Llewellyn saying that Dick had killed an outlaw. He did not dwell on memories of his parents. On rare occasions he allowed his mind to recall Sydney Alex– tall and beautiful, with skin as smooth and soft as silk, her mouth so warm and seeking. Oh God, he cried inside, how I feel the loss!

When he thought of the war, which had gone on much longer than anyone expected, he wondered, where was the glory? What was the satisfaction, now that the battle was over for him? He had begun the journey into the unknown full of pride and passion and a burning patriotism. Ready for the challenge, he had carried the dream of returning a hero to the woman he loved; but the fighting, the misery and the dying had been unimaginably real. His mind and body had been assaulted by the agonies of war. The death and destruction, and realism of conflict had touched his soul. It was imprinted forever in his mind and left him much loneliness. His youth had passed quickly and, he wondered, now, about the man in its place.

On Dominion Day McAllister borrowed his grandfather's truck and drove to the annual stampede at Williams Lake. The grounds were located on a flat stretch near the river where a cloud of dust was rising into the clear summer air. Someone on a tractor was harrowing the arena in preparation for the rodeo. He parked the truck and watched the activity; riders herded stock into the pens, horses squealed, bulls snorted and young steers kicked at each other. Men called out orders and gates slammed.

The town was busy. It was full of people, vehicles, horses, and noise. Situated on a wide slope above the long lake, shimmering brilliantly beneath the summer sun, the town was home to ranchers, loggers, mill workers, and business.

The stampede seemed to have grown considerably. The lure of horses and rodeo pulled McAllister to the action. "I can see," he said in the direction of several cowboys hanging over the bucking chutes, "that this is where it's all happening. If you need a hand at anything, I'd be willing."

"We can use you this afternoon," one man called out. "Everything's volunteer."

"I can't jump, that's all. Knee injury, just healed."

"Look after the calves then, around three o'clock– with Manny down at the end there."

McAllister's head swung around, catching sight of Manny Anderson. He smiled, pleased, and crossed to the holding pen for the calves used in roping events.

Manny Anderson stepped up beside McAllister. "Ah, I see you're without your crutches," he commented as he adjusted the brim of his hat against the bright July sun.

McAllister smiled, "One day I hung them on Grandma's coat rack and said to myself, 'Now, why don't I go south? Why am I up here, instead of down there?'"

Anderson looked at the horse beside them, who nuzzled McAllister's arm. "Your horse?"

McAllister looked across the arena and nodded toward a rider, "His. He's into steer-wrestling, I think." Staring out across the flats from above the railing of the chute, he said almost regretfully, "The summer will go fast, you know, then soon it will be autumn." He looked across at Anderson. "I can't help thinkin' of Skaha," he admitted solemnly, reaching out to pet the horse. "My grandma tells me she's selling the ranch, that there's nothing here for me now." In a moment, he added, "She's right, now that my folks are gone."

Manny Anderson was surprised by McAllister's sad news but would wait for him to talk about it when he was ready. Ryan's the type that gets lonely easy, Anderson realized. On impulse, he asked, "Do you want company?" - and could not believe he had made the offer. "I've never been to the Okanagan."

The steer wrestler arrived back at the corrals to get his horse. He swung into the saddle and rode off to join others in the arena forming up the parade. The opening ceremonies began. The crowd cheered and the announcer introduced dignitaries, flag bearers and pick-up riders. The stampede had begun.

As the day wore on, it became very warm. Anderson and McAllister walked away from the arena. Anderson lifted his hat to mop his brow with his bandanna. "I rode a few times in this stampede when I didn't believe that bones actually broke. Things weren't so professional as now. It's the biggest stampede in the province, you know."

At the river's shore, McAllister dipped a hand in to splash water up into his face to feel cooler. "Did you mean it? To go with me?"

Anderson shrugged his shoulders. He was at loose ends. His brothers had settled into the family business. "Yeah, I meant it. Might as well be out of place there, as here."

The two men sat in silence at the water's edge. Across the expanse a dog barked and chased after something in the tall grass along the shoreline. McAllister watched the dog play. "Did you ever wonder what it was like here before our time? A hundred years ago. Life is so bloody serious for us. Look at that hound, not a worry in the world, just playin', lazin' around, got someone to look after him proper." He glanced across at Anderson. "I'm goin' to get me a horse, Manny, to go south. Don't want no more of this bus ridin'. Cowboys oughtn't to be travellin' in a carrier with a long, skinny dog painted on the side! Besides, I'd like to live awhile in the hills. You can find peace in the mountains."

"What about your grandparents' ranch? And your folks' estate?"

"Let my grandmother have it. I think it was hers in the beginning, anyway."

"I've heard a bit about Anton Dietrich, you know. He'll have it all."

McAllister thought for a moment. "Naw, she'll get some of it, don't ever worry. Grandma looks after herself okay. I'll trade Grandpa my share for a couple of good horses for us, and some tack and chaps n' things. He's got a barn full of saddles and bags and such. I don't care about anything else."

"You think your knee and my back'll put up with all that ridin'?"

"Oh sure! We're tough. Who's to beat us?"

The two men laughed together and shrugged their shoulders at their situation. "Come on," Anderson suggested. "Let's find somethin' to drink and get rid of this weighty matter of travellin' before we have to wrestle those calves into their chutes."

McAllister held back. "No, I'm serious." He looked out from beneath his wide hat brim, across at Anderson. "Serious."

Anderson laughed again and patted McAllister's shoulder. "Well, so am I, Buddy. Now, what d'you think about that?"

The mountains of the valley beckoned to McAllister. The distant blue hills were the most welcoming sight about the Okanagan. They had been his home, and had afforded him the most stable period in his life.

He said to Anderson, as they rode, "My grandmother told me that life is full of challenges; go out and meet them. I wonder why it's always grandmas who give you the encouragement." He smiled. "My dad would just say, 'Bring that box over here, boy. Empty that crate on those shelves.' And Grandpa, well it was, 'Hurry up with that hay. You're wastin' time!'"

Glancing skyward, then across the rolling hills over which they rode, McAllister was thoughtful. "I wonder what's in store for me at Skaha."

After three weeks, their nomadic journey ended when they topped a ridge and looked out upon a stunning view of Okanagan Lake. Anderson glanced across at McAllister. "And you tell me this is desert country? Look at that lake!"

"Oh man, this is home!" McAllister looped the reins of the bridle around his saddle horn and leaned against the cantle.

"Where's the desert? Not that I'm anxious for it, full of black widows and rattlers. I had in mind some dry, wasted sand dunes." Rising in his saddle, Anderson stepped down from the stirrups and spoke to the black gelding obtained in the barter with Anton Dietrich. "Come on young fella, we'll find you some water, and let this dreamer admire the view."

Ryan McAllister smiled. He felt glad at last, to be home.

32

The two riders crested the hill above Skaha and trotted their horses down the trail to the bottom, galloping beneath the SKAHA RANCH sign swinging squeakily in the wind on its rusted links. Dust blew in little swirls around them. The sky to the south was dark with summer thunderclouds.

Anderson and McAllister reined their geldings in at the barn. A quick glance about the corral brought a smile to McAllister's tanned face. "I see they still got old Dobbyn," he commented, looping the reins over the rail. They strode off across the yard toward Foderow's house.

As they stepped up on the veranda, a light delivery truck was brought to a stop behind them. Foderow got out, swinging a hand against the dust he had created. He looked up at the two young cowboys. Astonishment flooded his face. "I'll be damned! Lord, if I'm not dreamin'!" he exclaimed as he stared at Ryan.

McAllister leapt over the single step to the ground and reached for the foreman's hand. "Hello, Dick."

"Good God, young man, we all thought you were gone. We never heard a word." Foderow banged his hat against his knee to rid it of dust. "Come on in here and have a drink on this day!"

"Dick, this is a fellow vet, Manny Anderson. From up Cariboo way, near my grandparents." They removed their hats as they followed Foderow up the steps. "Came along for the same reason I did. We're both lookin' for work."

Foderow and Anderson shook hands in a friendly manner and they entered the house. "Got plenty of that around here alright." He turned and stared directly into McAllister's unwavering brown eyes which met his. "You know, Ryan, Ian never gave up on you. Always said you were out there somewhere; down maybe, but not for long."

McAllister smiled and sighed slightly, glancing across at Anderson. "There's no accounting for it, his name can still raise a little fear in me."

All three laughed together. Foderow took a bottle from the cabinet and poured them each a shot. "Here's lookin' at you," he offered, and raised his glass to theirs. "And to a new tomorrow!"

As Foderow and McAllister talked, Anderson glanced about the room. This was a very old house, he could see, built by someone who knew how to cut logs to fit forever. On the mantle above the stone fireplace, he noticed a wedding photograph of Foderow and his wife, who was, at the moment, absent from the house. Beside it was another of a young woman beside a horse. A set of shelves contained books and keepsakes. In one corner stood a Marconi battery radio, and beside that, a rocker filled with brightly covered pillows. It was a comfortable room, and told him much about the family who lived in it.

The following day, while Anderson walked about the ranch with the older cowboys, Foderow and McAllister saddled their horses and rode off in the direction of the dam. Above the sound of hooves gnashing against the rocky terrain, Foderow called, "There's much to tell you."

McAllister replied quickly, "There's much I want to know."

"I drove down and told Ian last night. I knew you wouldn't go there right away, with Sydney Alex just gettin' home and all."

"No, no–" McAllister murmured thoughtfully. "I need some space between us. I feel things are different, but just how different–"

"I know you're hurtin' some, and it ain't from your knee; those kind of wounds heal fast." Foderow reined his horse in and swung down from the saddle. "The heart takes a little longer, that's all. A few years've passed. Lots has happened." Leading the bay toward the creek trickling over the rocks, he rolled a cigarette and let his horse drink.

McAllister put his horse alongside the other at the creek. "I could see at a glance yesterday, that the ranch needs young muscle, but what I wonder, Dick, is there really room for me here? You say there's a veterinarian in the family now, who must plan his life around this place. And the big question I guess, is– can I live here with him as the boss? I always had it in my mind that someday I'd be runnin' the place after you. Also knowing that every night of his life he sleeps in the same bed as Sydney Alex–" Glancing over his saddle across at Foderow, he admitted, "I always thought her and I would get married, you know. I lived every day with that dream." Bitterness registered in his voice.

Foderow smoked awhile, then tossed the cigarette into the mud of the creek's edge. He wiped his bandanna across his brow. "What you don't know is that they aren't gettin' along. She lost a baby the first year they were married. Cord around its neck, I think. And miscarried the second one this spring. Ian brought her home a week ago."

McAllister's eyes widened in surprise. He turned away from Foderow to stare into the forest beyond the creek. A familiar place this is, he thought, for he had ridden there many times to either raise or close the dam gate. At first he found it hard to believe Foderow's words, and tried to comprehend what they might mean in his life. He gathered up Dobbyn's reins, stepped into the stirrup and swung into the saddle. His injured right knee had begun to bother him and he straightened it, bending and straightening several times. Finally, he mounted up and urged his horse forward to follow the foreman along the trail.

McAllister's meeting with Ian Cartrell was no less formal than all other meetings had ever been. The word *confrontation* came to McAllister's mind, but he smiled and shrugged the gloom away. He could feel Cartrell's dark eyes upon him, assessing him now, friendly though their greeting had been. Sydney had got out of the car to give him a welcoming hug. Ryan felt a special affection for Sydney. She was still very beautiful, he saw, and showed few visible lines of age. He was proud to introduce her to Manny Anderson.

Beneath the summer sun, which warmed a land refreshed by the previous night's rain, Cartrell looked out from beneath eyebrows that matched the gray of his thinning hair and said, "Shall me meet at my house or over in the office?"

McAllister cleared his throat and replied calmly, "Actually Ian, I'd prefer the dairy. I'm on my own ground there."

Cartrell nodded and walked with McAllister toward the dairy as Anderson accompanied Sydney to the lodge.

When they were alone Cartrell placed a hand on the other's arm and said, "I don't need to tell you, Ryan, how pleased your return makes us all feel. Sorry to learn about your knee, but physical injuries have a way of healing. I'm certain it won't hold you back any."

McAllister smiled. "I can't say enough, how glad I am to be here." If there is a genuine feeling of affection for me, he decided, this is the closest I'm going to know it. Ian looks old and tired. He's surely eighty by now. McAllister reached out and brought a chair forward. "Have a seat, Ian," he offered, feeling respect for the man and what he meant to the welfare of Skaha.

"And you?"

"I'll stand." McAllister leaned back against the counter on which eggs were candled and milk was bottled. He crossed his arms over his chest. "When I'm face to face with you, Ian, I like to have both feet planted on solid ground, or boards in this case."

"Well, I'm not as indomitable a creature as reputation has me."

"And I'm not generally a pessimist. I have gained some confidence through the past few years." The statement was meant to create awareness in the other man, of strengths gained from war service.

Little humour ran in Cartrell's veins. Life had always been a series of major concerns for him, and with each passing year he became more aware of a leaderless Skaha. There had been many changes to the ranch as a working enterprise; not all of them to his liking, but some, including Sydney's venture into tourism had proved to be quite profitable.

"First off, I'd like you to know, Ryan, how sorry I was to learn about your parents. I knew your grandmother years ago, and my wife travelled west with Anton Dietrich." He drew out his handkerchief to wipe at the lens of his glasses. "Now, I know that Dick has told you Sydney Alex was married while you were away," Cartrell began without hesitation, "and that they lost their son at birth. That does not mean to say there will never be other children. I doubt this present separation will last."

McAllister stiffened, braced his mind against hope. "Ian, should they come back to live here permanently, the question would arise, whether I stay or not." He paused a moment. "Well, I laid awake all night last night thinking about it. I stay. It's where I belong. My ties with this place go back a hell of a long way. It's only fair to tell you how I feel."

Cartrell's mouth tightened. He rose from the chair, stepped around it and leaned his hands against the back of it. His brow creased in deep thought. Although he understood what McAllister must surely be going through, he was reluctant to put it into words. After a long pause, in which the quiet of the room pressed upon them, Cartrell spoke. "Ryan, I have always had it in mind that you would become Skaha's manager someday. But there's a ladder to climb to—"

"Not just manager," McAllister interrupted boldly. "More, Ian."

Cartrell straightened and smiled. "Strangely, a little voice inside me tells me that your wish and mine, although we have opposite ways of expressing it, remain about the same." He peered over the rims of his glasses. "I'm sure that you will not leave this place. If that were a possibility, knowing what you learned the minute you telephoned Tom's house in Vancouver, you would not have returned. Dick told me about that." He cleared his throat. "Skaha was a prominent centre in the south valley once, and can be again."

McAllister remained silent as he turned to look out across the yard from the dairy window, thereby unintentionally placing his back to Cartrell.

Cartrell stared hard at McAllister's broad shoulders and straight back. "Apparently a little soul searching has brought you face to face with what you really want for yourself, Ryan, not face to face with me, as you put it earlier."

"I don't want to work all my life here for just wages."

"Can you say that Dick has worked for nothing all his life on this place?"

"What does he own? What can he leave his family when he goes?"

"He leaves them the security of a home on the ranch and a pension which has been set up, in that event. They will be looked after, on or off the place. While he lives, when he can no longer work, that provision stands for him as well. That is considerable these days, I might add."

McAllister nodded acknowledgment. "Yes, I suppose it is, but I see all that as your personal provision for them, a return for lifelong loyalty. No ordinary cowboy is left so well off. This is a different time we're talking about, Ian. I doubt I would be in such good favour with Sydney Alex and her husband, or her father." He turned away from the window and looked into Cartrell's eyes. "Both you and Mrs. Cartrell are getting on in years. The way I see it, any one of them can walk in here and throw me out on my ear before you're in your graves." His voice had risen and he was not happy with the way the conversation was going.

"Would you not give us credit for providing a clause in our wills to prevent that? Certain circumstances considered, of course."

"Ian--" McAllister raised a hand in protest. "I'm just keeping in mind, that I once heard that Tom held the controlling interest in Skaha. I don't want a handout in your will. I want ownership and I'm prepared to work at it. Sort of getting back what my family built and lost."

"Yes, well–" Cartrell was thoughtful a moment. "Tom's interest has recently been acquired by his mother. With the recent passing of his father-in-law, he now owns a construction company. The possibilities here are unlimited for you, and you have a right to them in a way, but it will require considerable effort on your part."

"I'm up to it." McAllister's mouth was set.

The rough board walls of the dairy seemed to close around him. He heard Cartrell's shoes scrape against the floor as he walked toward the doorway.

"Young man," Ian Cartrell said softly. "I've talked to you on what you referred to as your own ground, while you had your two feet planted firmly upon this floor. Now then, it's obvious that this place will not come into your hands by way of marriage, as I had initially hoped. And perhaps that is a good thing. In other words, you'll have to work for it."

"I have just said–"

Cartrell raised a hand against further interruption. "I can offer it to you– that controlling interest. But it will not come easy. Every aspect of management must be studied. Every square foot of this ranch must become known to you. The respect of every employee, now and in the future, must be earned by you. You will have to become known in the valley and outside it, in cattlemen's associations and at sales, and learn everything there is to know about a cow, a bull, a horse and all else that walks on Skaha land; and that includes veterinary. Responsibility is heavy. I hope those shoulders you presented to me a moment ago are broad enough to carry it." He paused a moment. "The minute you drop your guard, Ryan, I will be there to remind you of this day and that I have the power to change the situation."

McAllister was speechless.

"When next we meet it will be in my office, not your dairy. An office is a place of business and managing a ranch is business." He turned the handle and the door creaked open. Cartrell paused without glancing back and added, "And, young man, do not ever turn your back to me again." He left the dairy and Ryan McAllister, to step out into a typically warm Okanagan summer day.

From the window McAllister watched Cartrell join Sydney and the Foderows on the lodge veranda. He could not help but admire the man for the self-assurance he possessed and the staunch faith he held in Skaha. When he had gathered his thoughts, he recognized the worth of Cartrell's plan. It was, indeed, an enormous offer.

That evening McAllister left Manny Anderson where they were temporarily lodged in the small apartment above the ranch office, and walked across to the creekside where his old log cabin still remained. It had been Two Way's home, built in the 1830's. However, it was five years since anyone had lived in it, and it was now in poor condition with a leaky roof. He placed a boot against the bottom rail of the corral and leaned his arms on the top. McAllister smiled, remembering how much he had enjoyed living there.

Into this corral he had driven the small herd of wild horses from Marron Valley, and had ridden them, trained them and sold them from there. He could see them yet, snorting and whinnying as they tossed their heads in defiance of his intentions. They were always pawing and prancing in their unnatural confinement. It had been with the greatest sense of pride that he had handed over to Dick Foderow, his first cheque for one hundred dollars. Personal achievement had been something new to him then. It all seemed long ago now. A sense of loneliness gripped him.

There were five original buildings still usable at Skaha - the granary; the original McAllister log house to where Foderow moved from the Carmichael place; the Carmichael's, which would soon be occupied by a couple named Pye who would work at the lodge; Two Way's cabin; and Cartrell's office. The original lodge used by the men of the fur brigade, which had been Ryan's housing when he first arrived, had collapsed at one end. The trapper's tack shed lay in a heap of broken boards. The church, school and community hall, all built much later, had been boarded up for several years. The more recent Llewellyn two-storey house had, McAllister could see, received a complete face-lift and been renovated to accommodate Sydney's plan for a tourist hideaway.

McAllister smiled. "Dude ranches, they call them", he muttered and found he did not dislike the idea. The whole endeavour must, he supposed, have a lucrative side, or Cartrell would not have allowed it.

McAllister left the corrals to follow the path along the creek, past Cartrell's old house that had been built by Lenny Parr. Now abandoned, one glance told him that with the next severe wind it, too, might collapse. Grass and noxious weeds surrounded the site. White baby's breath flourished everywhere. Purple lilacs crowded against the walls. In the distance a small cabin had fallen in, that of the Negro boy who he'd heard had been murdered there years ago.

As McAllister walked along the paths from one building of Skaha to another, an image began to form in his mind. Once these crumbling structures had been homes; a lodge, which was the stopping house of Skaha Crossing; a store, demolished by a flood; a community hall, a school and a church beside Willow Creek. A life had pulsed upon these flats well before his grandfather David's time. At the small graveyard, he passed markers recognizing his family, and wondered what their lives had been and what had happened to change it all. Time, he told himself; time alters everything.

As he walked, McAllister began to realize he needed a good plan of action. Cartrell's words were taking hold. He smiled. His brain had come alive. He was planning with excitement. What is needed, he decided, is one of Tom's bulldozers to clean up these flats. "Then we can start anew." His words hung on the stifling August air. What is this? Am I actually planning something here? Anticipation gripped him.

Suddenly he stopped. He was standing in the middle of the flats. A vision of new barns, increased cattle herd and long hay sheds beside wide, green fields raced through his mind, testing his imagination. A decent irrigation system would be the greatest advantage. Roads into cow-camps. A proper bunkhouse and a machine shed housing modern equipment.

When he passed the livery he paused at the corral to admire the four Percherons which Skaha had always kept. As if they could read his mind, know his plans, they plodded across to where he leaned against the boards. McAllister petted them affectionately. "Now, I promise you old folks," he vowed, "to let you pasture your days out here."

McAllister turned, leaning backward against the corral, allowing an old mare to nibble at his shirt collar.

Contemplating the yard activity, which was slow in a warm evening holding none of the freshness left by the previous night's storm, he watched a young couple stroll hand in hand near the white lake, followed by a ranch dog racing along the shoreline. His heart ached for the romance which should belong to him. He knew Sydney Alex remained out of sight with her grandparents. He had not yet seen her and realized that he would not see her during this visit.

On the ridge above White Lake a string of horses trod the worn trail toward the ranch, taking their riders home. The enormous ridge, rocky and mountainous at its base, but smooth toward its final outcropping, was dramatic against the brilliant red skyline. Ryan decided that it resembled, in a disjointed manner, a hog's back; then, as he studied it further, he saw it was a perfect Indian head complete with plumed headdress, lending a proud, majestic appearance as it faced west. It was bathed in a magnificent glow of colours from the sinking sun. Upon the great crown, the eight riders paused to savour a view of the basin and surrounding hills before proceeding down the trail to the bottomland.

McAllister was impressed. He waited as the group returned, watching and listening as the riders dismounted. Some immediately wandered off toward the lodge. Others lingered to assist the wrangler in unsaddling. The evening had become quiet, settled.

The horses trotted out from the barn into the corral, to roll in the dirt and vigorously shake away the dust and black flies which plagued them. To McAllister it was a beautiful sight. The sound of their snorting and squealing as they chased out to pasture, gave life to the drowsy atmosphere of evening and the ranch. I am so lucky, he reminded himself, to be alive with all this around me. He enjoyed the rush of pride that filled his chest.

When he stood the following evening with Foderow and Cartrell near the window of the ranch office, Ryan said, as tactfully as he knew how, "I'd like to suggest something I think should be done here, Dick-- Ian-- and it won't cost any money."

"That is?" from Cartrell with a wary voice.

"Set fire to those old buildings, sheds and outhouses and such, that're crowding the hay fields. There should be a water system on those fields, but it won't run around buildings. It needs a clear path. They're nothin' but firetraps and if we don't get to them, the lightning eventually will."

Ian had been sitting in the chair with his hands crossed over his chest, listening. He rose slowly now, to look out. His throat had suddenly seemed to fill and he cleared it several times, sending sharp, raspy sounds into the stilled room. He turned to fix his eyes upon McAllister's serious expression.

Foderow shifted where he leaned against the office wall, feeling a little discomfort with the conversation. He could remember worse tensions rising in this room, for less reason. He turned a sombre gaze upon McAllister a moment, then glanced beyond Cartrell to the outlying pastures and abandoned structures.

Cartrell said in a quiet voice, "Well, we'll let you be the one to toss the match. I doubt either Dick or I will have the heart for it."

"I reside in the oldest building," Foderow murmured, "in this whole White Lake valley." He left the office then, standing for a reflective moment on the wide step.

Foderow's gaze took in all the buildings; the lights of years gone by. He could see them yet, on a cold winter night when he had ridden up from old Dogtown with news of the birth of this boy's father. Set fire to them? Foderow shrank from the thought. Burn up all those memories? He recalled Sydney Cartrell and the community's social buildings and life she had created.

Foderow pulled his hat low over his forehead. Out of habit, he chewed at the middle of his full mustache. Perhaps it takes the young, he admitted reluctantly, to come along and make the necessary changes after all, and decided that he needed a shot of good whiskey to mellow his troubled mind.

In his office, Cartrell was explaining, "You'll be burning up our lives here, young man. Granted, you'll clean the place up. Nonetheless, we've lived here amongst these few unsightly ruins, tolerated them, and I suppose, even revered them."

Ian Cartrell left the office and got into his car. As quickly as he could speed the vehicle up, he departed the Skaha yard, leaving a long funnel of dust behind as proof of his heightened emotions.

McAllister was aware of having touched a nerve. Nevertheless, he was determined to get rid of the eyesores and create a new beginning. As the dusk of evening fell over the land and a settled quiet prevailed at Skaha Ranch, he felt an impatience to begin.

33

The burning of Skaha was an awesome sight and went on for ten hours. Rolling gray plumes filled the air as Ryan torched the derelict buildings. Foderow was reluctant to come out of his house which, standing in the middle of Skaha, was now shrouded in smoke and flying cinders.

The necessary steps had been taken to carry out the burning, for September was still a dry time in any year. The local Forestry branch had been consulted. Barrels of water were placed at strategic locations. Help was hired to patrol for possible spreading fires.

As evening fell, Cartrell watched the burn from the second floor of the lodge, where Albert Llewellyn had always overlooked Skaha. He silently commended Foderow for the patience with which he had accepted young McAllister's dedication to destroying all that was of no use to the future of the ranch.

He lowered the binoculars and sank into a chair to stare absently across the room in the direction of Albert Llewellyn's pinewood gun cabinet. Now used as a display case, it contained rifles, pistols, holsters, powder horns and ammunition belts. All had been meticulously arranged by Sydney in her bid to preserve the history of Skaha. How ironic, Cartrell thought now, that while his wife sought to preserve the little things that Rachel McAllister had saved, her great-grandson saw fit to destroy all but five of the original buildings which had housed the artifacts. The den was filled with memorabilia of Skaha and nearby places, all of which served to remind him how fast life marched on.

The binoculars fell gently upon Cartrell's knees as he rested in the chair. Outside, the call of orders between the patrols reached his ears. He closed his eyes, feeling weary. The offensive smell of smoke filled the house.

Throughout the day the flames had shot skyward; then as the evening air cooled, a thin blanket of smoke settled over the ranch. Buildings tumbled inward, reigniting. The glow could be seen for several miles, drawing spectators who offered help. Among them were the younger Whiteman generation. Jason and Jonathon were now in their nineties and still lived on their father's large farm north of Skaha Ranch.

The fiery spectacle lent an eerie atmosphere to the region.

McAllister and Anderson organized the cleanup of the charred debris allowing the piles to smoulder down to ash to be carted away.

As the men worked, Ian Cartrell drove his car out of the ravine of his home, across the flats of the ranch and stopped before his office, disappearing into the building. McAllister leaned against the shovel, his eyes rivetted in Sydney Alex' direction as she arrived with her grandfather. She gave no indication that she was aware of his presence on the road.

Raising his eyes heavenward, McAllister said aloud, "Lord Almighty– I'm bound for feeling guilty about everything." She's leaving, without having once come out of that ravine to speak to me. And now, he saw, she could not even glance at him standing where she had just passed so closely. He pursed his lips together as a feeling of anger crept through him. Was she feeling some guilt? Did her heart ache, as did his, when memories were drawn upon?

When he was satisfied that Sydney Alex would remain resolute in ignoring him, McAllister raised the shovel over his shoulder and turned his back to her. He strode across the field to where his great-great-grandfather's lodge had once stood in wait of the fur brigade, which now lay in ashes on the ground.

One week later, it was as if Skaha had not enjoyed a one hundred year history. The first house built there, now Foderow's residence, stood as a reminder that once a lone trapper had passed this way and stopped to live awhile beside the white alkaline lake.

34

One morning in October, when fall was in the air, Ryan McAllister saddled his horse and rode out to the range camp in the Okanagan hills. Leading two pack horses, he followed the trails he knew so well. He was glad to ride alone.

Twice during the past month he had escaped the short weekend visits of Sydney Alex and Dennis to Skaha, by volunteering his labour to a group of ranchers who were reconstructing stockyards at Okanagan Falls. He cared not to meet the man, nor see Sydney Alex with him in their presentation of a happily married couple.

The dry, pine smell of the forest at its lower level, and the danger of a season lingering without rain in the mountains was all around him. The sound of crackling, crumbling grass and weeds underfoot brought to mind the blazing inferno which had razed these mountains during an earlier year at camp. The devastation was still evident. He broke out of the woods, onto the wide meadow.

The cowboys spotted McAllister in the distance. Waving their hats, they called and whistled. Manny Anderson, astride his horse following a long day of riding, galloped out to meet McAllister, taking the rope of the pack horses.

"Good to see you, Buddy," he called. "Just got in myself." Anderson sat his horse well. He was comfortable around the cattle and seemed to enjoy his occupation. Moreover, he got along superbly well with Strickland and Smith. McAllister nodded to Anderson and fell in beside him.

Anderson had not been raised in ranch life but could see a future for himself at Skaha. It was evident that able men were needed at the ranch as well as on the range. Disrepair was everywhere. Horses, which should have been broke and in use long ago, roamed idly about the pastures. And, there was a lack of dependable ranch machinery.

McAllister dismounted and began unsaddling. When the horses had been unpacked and turned into the corral, the men washed up at a bench beside the cabin, then filed inside to fill their plates.

"Stayin' long?" Anderson asked, dishing out their stew at the stove.

"Nope." replied McAllister. "I got Ian waitin' on my tail back in his office. Got some book-learnin' to do. He says we can never trust any accountant quite the same as 'ol Llewellyn trusted him."

In the morning they rode west in weather that was sunny, yet early morning cool. Autumn was evident in the mountains, and so was the horrible infestation of grasshoppers. Morning dew lay heavy upon the ground. A rangeland which had been abundant throughout September, now appeared brittle and depleted by October.

"I can tell you," Anderson began, "the sons-of-b's were everywhere. Just as bad as at the ranch before we burned them out. Between grasshoppers and mosquitoes, and those damn deer flies, life wasn't worth a pinch of anything here for a few weeks."

"I can see."

"The old boys an' I went out and hauled windfall into piles and made smudges. Finally, with all the smoke, the horses settled down. The cattle moved a little closer. Even the deer came in." Anderson smiled. "We had an old cougar hang around for awhile, just to keep us on our toes." He noticed that McAllister raised a brow in thought, but offered no comment.

They topped a rise above Yellow Lake, west of Twin Lakes, and dismounted, allowing their horses to graze awhile. Movement in a distant meadow caught McAllister's attention. He put an arm outward as if to halt his companion's steps and held his breath, listening.

"Am I to stop breathing, or what?" Anderson chided.

McAllister smiled, pleasure filling his concentrated gaze. "I don't believe this– it's the horses," McAllister half whispered. "The wild ones."

Anderson looked across at McAllister and grinned. "Well, you can speak up, you know. It's not as if you'll scare them– I mean, they're at least a mile away from us."

McAllister sank down against a fallen log and allowed Dobbyn to graze. He glanced up at Manny, then across the meadow below. "The first time I ever saw the wild horses, they were ranging in Marron Valley. I looked for them, hunted 'em out, you know." McAllister paused. His voice became nostalgic. "They were led by a big white stallion, a magnificent creature. When I saw him, got to know him after awhile, it became a challenge to steal some of his mares and young colts. My God, what a drive was in me to do that!"

"Did you?"

McAllister's smile faded. He looked down at the scuffed toes of his riding boots. "Yes. Yes, I caught some of them. I was just a kid then and it was important to impress the old fellows on the ranch, especially Dick." He laughed slightly. "They thought all I knew what to do was eat and play the harmonica. I have always looked up to Dick, you know; wanted to be like him." He paused a moment. "Oh, I green-broke 'em and sold them. The first lot brought a hundred dollars. The next, two hundred. I gave the money to Dick for the ranch. Times were tough and they took me in without question."

Near the end of the meadow, the stallion gathered his band of mares and offspring. At a precision-like trot, he led them out of the valley, as if on parade before the cowboys watching on the hill.

"Well, I'll be damned!" McAllister exclaimed. "The boss is a black one!" He rose to his feet and pulled in Dobbyn's rein. "You know, Manny, I got lots of plans for Skaha. I feel real good about the place, like there's something here for me now."

Anderson flipped a stirrup over the saddle horn and tightened the cinch that had loosened. His horse grunted in protest. McAllister came to stand near him, leaning against the rump of Anderson's horse. Idly twisting Dobbyn's reins, he looked into Anderson's tanned face.

"Just for a minute, Manny," he asked, "try to imagine things. There's more for Skaha than what we see there now. You know, that Mrs. Cartrell's got a quick mind. She wouldn't be doing things the way she is with those dudes if it was all wrong. Ian wouldn't let her."

Anderson dropped the stirrup into place and took up the reins. "It ain't the ranch or the changes that bother me, Buddy. It's you." Reaching out, he clamped a gloved hand over McAllister's shoulder. "How you're goin' to feel about things when that girl keeps coming home, like she does. You may feel like runnin' from it all after awhile."

McAllister's pensive expression did not change. "I don't expect to see her, Manny. It's that simple. I've made up my mind. When she's here she'll stay at Cartrell's, and I'll go to cow-camp; but I'm not running from this ranch. I want it, with or without her."

"There's no cow-camp during wintertime," Anderson reminded quietly. He slipped his boot into the stirrup and mounted up while he watched McAllister swing into his saddle and jig Dobbyn's reins. Above them the sky was clear, the autumn sun just comfortably warm.

"I've been down to the Falls a bit lately," McAllister called back as they rode along the trail, "Some of the fellas remembered me. I got a good feeling from that."

He had been told and now related to Anderson that, in 1942, local cattlemen formed the Southern Interior Stockmen's Association and built the stockyards at Okanagan Falls. "The next year they had their first sale."

Ranchers travelled from the surrounding area to join local cattlemen on the flats along the Okanagan River, to build the first yards from locally milled lumber. In 1944 the yards were reconstructed, to lend greater organization at sale time. It was the only facility of its kind south of Kamloops and it accepted livestock from the Okanagan and Similkameen valleys, and the Boundary country.

As they rode back to camp, McAllister's mind continued to mull over plans. "Damned if I don't someday get a road pushed all the way in here–" he vowed.

It was time to move the cattle down from summer range. As the grasshoppers had made a meal of the forage, there was no purpose in keeping the herd there further. John Strickland agreed and, allowing McAllister the final word, began preparations to have the herd and horses out by the end of October.

In the bunkhouse at the camp, McAllister told the men, "I'll ask Dick about it."

Strickland suggested, "He's waitin' on your decision."

McAllister stilled on the edge of his top bunk. "He's testing me, then."

"Just like old Ian used to test Tom Llewellyn," added Bud Smith solemnly. "Testin's good for ya!"

Roundup was underway throughout the gullies and ravines of the range; two extra riders had been hired to assist Anderson, McAllister and Strickland. The cattle were gathered by the end of October and collected into small groups brought in each evening to the holding area near the camp. Each man took his turn at night watch. The yearling steers and heifers, and a few dry cows, were sorted for sale. Skaha's herd, which had once again been increased to the size of earlier McAllister-Llewellyn days, was now comprised mostly of Herefords, with some Black Angus, but no Shorthorn. Despite the hoards of grasshoppers which voraciously consumed the rangeland, the cattle destined for sale appeared fattened sufficiently for marketing.

The morning turned cold. At daylight, they moved the cattle out of the mountains onto the flats south of Skaha, and along a little-used wagon road that would take them to the Okanagan River crossing. Rain began to fall in heavy pelting drops and the cowboys pulled the collars of their slickers under the shelter of their hat brims. Before long it turned to snow which, within twenty minutes, blew into a stiff blizzard. The cattle bunched together, reluctant to move.

Beneath the western blue ridges of the Okanagan, snow-capped and beautiful, the riders kept the herd of one hundred and twenty head moving. The snow drove against them. Shouts and whistles from the cowboys, and the bawling, protesting cattle filled the narrow valley. The ground soon became soggy and slippery. Nonetheless, they moved without incident, riding out the storm, and stopped near a small lake at four o'clock. They bunched the cattle together.

Then without warning, a scream pierced the air and echoed across the lake, sending a chill along McAllister's spine. He had heard the cry before. That cougar, he remembered soberly, when he had found the horses after the fire! He swung his head around, looking up behind him.

There on the bluff, poised magnificently against the cloudy skyline, was the tawny old mountain lion. Her four feet bunched together, the feline balanced perfectly on a rock slab, her muscles taut, tail still, ears out, and her mouth wide, hissing a warning.

"Well, you old lady! You're lookin' thin!" he called out to her, "Bound to have your day, aren't you!" Then surprise and fear gripped him.

He saw the cougar leap in an unprovoked attack on Manny Anderson as he rode below the bluff. Her scream bounced on the air. Anderson's startled horse skidded and fell. The man was yanked from his saddle in one swift, vicious stroke.

Instantly McAllister pulled his rifle from its scabbard and placed it firmly against his shoulder in careful aim. He pressed his boots in their stirrups tight against Dobbyn's flanks for support, and fired. The cougar rolled off Anderson, grunted, coughed and fell still. He leapt from his horse, favouring his right knee, while tossing the rifle to one of the cowboys, and ran to where Anderson attempted to get up off the ground.

Visibly shaken by the experience, Anderson shook his head, and pulled at his jacket. He looked down at the rivulets of blood running through the clothes at his waist. His back began to pain with an intense burning. McAllister gently removed the torn shirt from Anderson's shoulders to expose the deep claw marks.

Anderson's senses reeled. Dizziness threatened to overcome him, and he quickly pushed the shirt beneath his face as he rolled over on the cold ground. McAllister sat back against his boots and studied Anderson's torn skin. In the distance he could hear the cowboys catching Anderson's horse, for it had recovered from its fall and frantically bolted.

The young man with McAllister's gun rode alongside Dobbyn, replaced the rifle in its scabbard and picked up the idle reins. Stepping down from his own horse, he glanced briefly at the dead cougar, then gathered all the reins together and waited for the rider leading Anderson's horse. "How is he?"

"It'll take awhile," McAllister replied quietly. "In my left saddlebag is a first aid kit." When the kit had been brought to him, he rolled it out upon the snowy ground. "Manny? You okay now?"

"I'll live," Anderson grunted. "Do what you gotta do and let's get back on the trail."

Within ten minutes Anderson's open wounds had been swabbed with a disinfectant, padded and wrapped. When he had inspected his gelding's legs, Anderson stepped once more up into the saddle. He did not look back at the dead cougar being hauled off into the trees. He could not understand what had motivated her into attack, but accepted that all cats are unpredictable.

Beside him, McAllister said, "That old feline's been hanging around us quite a few years, you know. We finally had our last say on her."

"Sort of made herself a companion of the cow-camp. Heard her lots. I won't miss her," Anderson replied curtly. Trotting over the slope toward Green Lake where the others held the herd, Anderson whistled and waved. "Move out!" he called and the cowboys took up the order.

They held the herd alongside the Okanagan River at the meadows north of Vaseux Lake and set up an overnight camp. A young cowboy who had picked up some last minute advice on campfire cookery from Bud Smith, produced a fair meal from vegetables, meat and bannock brought along in his saddlebags. The welcome aroma of strong frontier coffee, boiling in a billy-can over the fire, soon filled the air. As McAllister began to redress Anderson's wounds, the others gathered close.

"You'll have to see a Doc, you know," one of them suggested.

"Naw," Anderson scoffed from where he sat on a stump. "I got one tendin' things now."

"I'm serious. I've seen gashes like these and you need some stitches." He stepped back, glancing around at the others self-consciously, "Sutures, they call 'em."

Both McAllister and Anderson looked up at the young man. He was a new hand hired only for the drive, but was the youngest of them all at twenty years. He had been the one to catch Anderson's horse. McAllister studied the tall, fair-haired cowboy who had blurted out his advice.

"Caverly, right?" Anderson queried. "What's your first name? Ahhh," he winced under McAllister's ministrations.

"Allan. My dad's a doctor in town."

"Well, Allan, I thank you kindly. When I need one, I will know who to see." Anderson rose from the stump, moved his shoulders back and forth several times and declared himself almost healed, while he looked out toward the herd. Nearby the camp, the horses stood quietly, their noses deep in grain bags. The cattle exhibited restlessness while night fell upon the land.

As Anderson watched the milling of the herd, he called to McAllister, "They need the sound of your harmonica, Buddy, screechy as it is." He smiled to himself. "I know you can't play worth a damn, but give it your best. Cattle like music. Might save us a bit of trouble tonight." Pain played tiresome patterns over the muscles of his back and he dreaded crawling into his bedroll in an attempt to sleep. "I'll take the first watch," he offered in self-defense.

Overhead the sky had cleared. The night air held the distinct chill of winter. McAllister leaned back against his saddle and blew gently on the harmonica, while the others huddled beneath their blankets.

35

Waiting on the east bank of the Okanagan River, Dick and Janet Foderow watched the riders get the cattle into the water at the crossing. The river was wide and reasonably shallow. Alongside and behind the herd, the cowboys whistled and yipped, urging them easily into the water. Having trucked their horses down from Skaha, Foderow and his daughter had ridden south to meet them. They now assisted the others in driving the cattle onto the flats and toward the stockyards. The day, though cold, was pleasant.

As her father reined his horse into lead position at the head of the herd, Janet stayed at the side. Shortly McAllister galloped alongside her. He smiled broadly and nodded a greeting. She looked very attractive in a dark blue denim outfit, cowboy boots and hat.

McAllister could not help but notice. "By golly now, it's been awhile since I saw you!"

"Four years," Janet chirped, clearly glad to meet Ryan again.

"About that. You don't come home to visit very often. I've been back since August, and I never saw you at the ranch."

"From Kamloops, the bus takes a full day." Janet smiled smugly as though hiding a secret. "However, I put that to rest. I'm moving down to Penticton." She looked McAllister full in the face when he turned a startled gaze.

"Penticton? When? I heard nothing."

Janet kneed the mare forward. "Come on, I'll ride with you. It's good to see you again, Ryan. I've known you were back. Dad, of course–"

"I surprised him some." They rode together, catching up on news, until they reached a creek that emptied into Okanagan River. Janet left to ride with her father while McAllister whistled and urged the cattle across the bridge. Once over, Anderson galloped toward him.

"Who was that?" he called.

"Dick's daughter."

The young girl in the photo, Anderson remembered, that day in Dick's house when we first arrived. He smiled. "An old flame? You do believe in complicating your life."

McAllister slapped the reins gently over Dobbyn's rump and called back, "She gave up on me long ago! And– you better go to Penticton and see a doctor about those scratches!"

They drove the cattle into the pens at the stockyards. Half an hour later, both Anderson and Janet loaded their horses into the truck.

With Janet behind the steering wheel, Manny was chauffeured back to Skaha where they left the horses, and from there to Dr. Caverly's office. His wounds were redressed, for they had been aggravated by exertion and had soaked his shirt.

Dr. Martin Caverly, a short, stocky man who wore a kindly expression, advised wisely, "In future, when you get mauled like this, you'd best not be playing around with infection. I know you cowboys like to prove up your stamina, but it's not worth it. I got a son who fancies the life, too."

"He's a good boy; works hard," Anderson complimented, carefully pulling his shirt over the medicated bandages.

"Well, he's on his way to becoming an accountant." The doctor placed the instruments into a metal sterilizing container and snapped the lid tight.

"Cougars leave you alone in an office."

"One can only hope that things turn out okay. Allan suffers mild epilepsy." Dr. Caverly looked around at Anderson. "You did not detect any sign of it?"

Anderson placed his hat on his head, fitting it comfortably and stepped toward the doorway. "Not once," he replied with a smile, "and I was there all the time." He and the doctor shook hands, then Anderson left the office.

Across the street, Janet waited patiently in the ranch light delivery. Confusing emotions bothered her. Twice on this very day, she considered, I meet men I could easily fall in love with. How is it that I should live so many years hoping, with nothing happening? Then suddenly Ryan shows up! Janet smiled as she stared absently down Main Street toward the dark, choppy water of Okanagan Lake. And, he brings along somebody probably more suitable than himself. Lowering her eyes, as if hiding from someone reading her mind, she admitted to herself how she felt about the new man on the ranch. She looked across at Dr. Caverly's office, and felt good about moving back home.

Manny Anderson stood for a few moments on the narrow veranda of the office to gather his thoughts about the turn of events and, more particularly, of Janet Foderow. Riding in the truck together had been a pleasant experience for him and, he hoped, for her. He had been instantly attracted by her cheerful nature, and impressed by the way she had her life in control when she talked about her plans. And how she had talked, he thought now. His quiet nature allowed room for her chatter and genuine enthusiasm for life.

"I'll move to Penticton as soon as I can secure a lease on the salon," she had told him. "There's an apartment above it, just fine for me." Janet had then turned to face him, her eyes smiling into his from beneath the bangs of her short, bobbed hair and, there in the truck that Autumn day, completely captured his heart.

Anderson stepped down onto the sidewalk, crossed the street and got into the truck beside her. "Can't say I'm sorry that visit's over with," he winked across at her. "How're we doin' for time?"

"I would love a cup of coffee, if I could interest you in that. However, there's not a lot of time to linger. Sydney Alex and Dennis are due home in a few hours, and I haven't seen her in simply ages." She looked across at Anderson, tilting her head slightly as if seeking his approval of something. "Every minute counts, don't you think? When you're best friends?"

Janet started the truck and steered it jerkily out into the traffic. Anderson leaned forward, for he dared not lean back, and braced himself with a hand against the dashboard. He forced his mind to think of the fine Skaha cattle being taken to the yards for auction the following morning. He estimated the time needed for his back to heal, which at the moment seemed on fire. He had yet to return to cow-camp and drive the remaining cattle down to the ranch. He even contemplated how long it would be before McAllister would actually manage Skaha. Or would it be Dennis Michaels?

In the end, he gave up dodging the inevitable and asked outright, "I would like you to go out with me, Janet– Jan. May I call you Jan?"

"I would like that."

"Maybe to a movie, or a dance– well, I don't dance, but something like that."

Janet braked the truck to a mean stop before a restaurant.

Anderson looked over at her and quickly offered, "Tell you what– if you'll teach me to dance, I'll be glad to give you some tips on drivin'."

Her merry eyes met his, as she extended her hand to him. "It's a deal!" she exclaimed. "Oh, you're buying the coffee, you know, even though I did suggest it."

As he nodded, Manny Anderson's heart capitulated. He knew he was falling wonderfully in love.

When Anderson and Janet Foderow returned to Skaha, they noticed some activity near the barn. Foderow was bent over examining a foreleg of McAllister's horse. McAllister stood beside him, hands braced against his hips, a pose which Ian Cartrell often termed the stance of impatience, and frowned in great concern as he watched Foderow bathe a warm saline solution over the deep cut below Dobbyn's knee. From a bowl of Epsom salts mixed with glycerine, Foderow spread a thick layer of paste over the wound and covered it with gauze padding.

"There– that ought to ease things a bit." Foderow motioned to McAllister. "Take this bandage now, and wrap it up - not too snug.

We'll change it in twenty-four hours." Foderow straightened. His back pained and he rubbed a hand firmly along his lower spine to ease the ache. "We could use that veterinarian husband of Sydney Alex' right about now," he mumbled as he walked into the barn.

McAllister stooped to kneel on the ground, and began wrapping. His expression had gone cold. His heart suddenly felt as heavy as stone. He dared not look in the foreman's direction, for he knew the resentment which surged within him would be there for the other to see. Face to face with one of his inadequacies, it seemed to McAllister at that moment, as it had at other times, that the transition toward a place in Skaha's management might ascend to a silent war with somebody he had yet to meet.

In a few minutes he got to his feet, hung an arm over Dobbyn's bowed neck and said close to him, "You're a good old fellow, you know." Taking up the lead rope, he led the horse into the barn, selected the largest stall and enclosed Dobbyn for the night.

Anderson and Janet appeared in the doorway. "What has happened?" Anderson queried and smiled. "Just leave you alone for an hour--"

McAllister returned the smile. Anderson's humour was refreshing. "You're a fine one to talk!"

Janet broke in. "Tell us what happened." She glanced the length of the barn where her father was hanging bridles on the wall.

McAllister explained, "Your dad and I rode up over the hill from the river and the old fellow here took a bad stumble. Threw a shoe. Gashed his leg open on the rocks." McAllister gathered up his saddle and blankets.

Janet caught her breath for only a moment, before blurting, "Well, Dennis will be along shortly, thank heavens!"

McAllister turned slowly and stared long into her brown eyes, while he undid the ties of his leather chaps. She looked quite pretty, he noticed, in her blue denim suit and white kerchief at her throat. Her short, dark hair was styled with soft curls over her ears. There was a new sparkle in her eyes. From the corner of his eye he caught a glance of Anderson turning Foderow's horse out to pasture. "I doubt," McAllister replied coolly, "if he could improve on your dad's work."

Janet's startled expression registered the abruptness of McAllister's remark. She stepped toward him, as he hung his chaps on a wall hook and started to leave the barn. "I'm sorry, Ryan," she spoke up, following him. "I didn't mean it the way you took it. You'll have to come to terms with his presence on this ranch, you know. He'll own it someday. It's obvious that you still care for Sydney Alex. Get over her, Ryan. Find somebody new. There's a happy life out there waiting for you." Having spoken her mind, Janet Foderow turned on her heel and strode with an impatient gait across the yard.

Anderson, who had returned to the barn, raised a questioning brow when McAllister glanced across at him.

"She's as bossy as her dad can sometimes be," McAllister muttered out of earshot of Foderow. "You might keep that in mind if--"

"Naw," Anderson interjected quickly. "Just sees things as they really are, that's all." And, he too, left the barn.

When McAllister took up the fork and climbed the ladder to the loft to toss hay down into the stall for Dobbyn, the sound of an approaching car drew his attention. He stooped down and glanced through the open doorway and saw that it was, as Janet had said, the Michaels driving by. "Well, there's your saviour, Dick," he called down to Foderow, while his heart fell. He disconsolately returned to his work.

36

In Ian Cartrell's small office, McAllister laboured over plans and accounts far into each night. Discussions with Cartrell had been encouraging. In his aim to leave a qualified servant to Skaha, Cartrell exercised an unexpected understanding of McAllister's lack of formal education.

In a light-hearted way, he reminded McAllister, "You might ride like the wind and be a whiz with a branding iron, but you've a definite aversion to wielding an ordinary pencil on accounting books. If your ambitions aspire to ownership, you will require a qualified accountant, so his salary must be figured into your budget, and it will be considerably more than mine."

McAllister leaned back against his chair and stared across at Cartrell.

"My days in this office are numbered, you realize." Cartrell's lined features and the tiredness they showed were accentuated by the circle of lamplight, and McAllister became aware of the man's advancing age. "I've quit this office twice already and been dragged back out of necessity. I point this up to you, for I do not believe for a minute, that bookkeeping is one of your strong suits."

"No more than veterinary is, but that, I will learn from Dick," McAllister snapped.

Cartrell glanced suspiciously over the rims of his glasses, focussing a direct gaze into McAllister's brooding brown eyes. "That can't be jealousy, surely. Sydney Alex has been home a week now, and there's not a chance that you've run into each other, I suppose."

"Skaha is a big place."

"Oh, I don't know--" Cartrell removed his glasses, clamping one arm of them between his teeth in thought. "The entire world can be quite small when one person seeks out the attention of another." The room became close in the silence.

In the morning Foderow, Strickland, McAllister and Anderson saddled their horses and rode away from Skaha along the trail to cow-camp. The air was cool. Small patches of snow were crusted beneath the trees. They were greeted by Bud Smith and young Allan Caverly.

Strickland was astonished to see Caverly. "What the dickens are you doin' up here?"

Caverly reached for the reins of two of the horses. "Oh, just thought I'd get a few cooking lessons from old Bud here." Everyone laughed and began unsaddling their horses.

"Well, we're closing camp in two days," Foderow informed him. He handed the lead rope of his horse to Caverly. "Good to see you, lad."

Anderson walked beside Caverly, leading his own horse. "One foot in the door is as good as your whole body in the room." He glanced up at the tall young man.

"I guess you'd know," Caverly smiled without looking back, and stretched his stride toward the corral. He called over his shoulder, "Your cat scratches made the ride okay?"

"Your dad wraps a tight bandage!"

The herd was gathered the next day and cow-camp was closed.

Across the meadow, through the trees and out of the mountains rode the five cowboys, with Smith ahead, leading his pack horses. Caverly kept the small remuda together. The remainder of Skaha's herd moved toward the ranch.

Foderow wore a pleased look. He was comfortable with life in the saddle and enjoyed the camaraderie of the other men. McAllister was relieved to be away from the ranch for few a days and hoped that the Michaels would be gone upon his return.

Anderson rode close to Allan Caverly. His mind constantly wandered to Janet Foderow and, because it had become a real struggle to get his thoughts away from her, he chose to keep his distance from her father.

Heavy clouds blew across the western horizon and by noon, the sky was dark and the air had become very cold. "Snow by nightfall," Strickland predicted, as the men shared a small campfire and lunch.

However, the winter weather did not wait on them. The storm blew out of the mountains with a vengeance not seen in several years, circling the riders and cattle in great swirls of sleety-snow. The ground became slippery and in some places, treacherous.

Foderow brushed at the snow collecting on his horse's mane. His horse had begun to limp and he decided to fall back. Dismounting, he lifted a back leg as Anderson rode alongside.

"What's up?" McAllister called through the trees as he urged a cow back into the herd.

"I think my horse has got himself a bad foot," came the worried reply.

In a moment McAllister was beside Foderow. "I'll trade you mine if you like, Dick," he offered. "I'll get one of those broncs from Allan up ahead." Glancing across at Foderow, he shook his head in disbelief. "We don't have a lot of luck lately with our animals."

"Oh, I'll just take it slow. We'll be alright." Giving a reassuring pat to the gelding's neck, he brushed at the snow piling up in his saddle and mounted up. "Just a bruise, I guess." But soon it was evident that the horse was becoming lame. The gelding stumbled continuously on the mucky trail and eventually Foderow dismounted to inspect the hoof once more. McAllister stepped down beside him.

"By God, my old eyes ain't missin' anything here, I hope," Foderow muttered, scraping a gloved thumb across what might be a tender spot.

"I'll have a look for you." McAllister dropped the reins of his horse and took up the foot of Foderow's, holding it tightly between his knees. With his pocket knife he gently scraped away the caked mud and saw the large sliver of rock imbedded in the sole of the foot. "Picked it up smack in the middle. Deep," he informed the foreman. Throwing his gloves aside McAllister hooked onto the rock with the narrow end of the knife, and worked it out of its bed. "Kind of a thin-soled boy, this horse of yours." He let the leg down. "You take Old Bob, Dick. He brought me all the way down from Williams Lake without trouble. I'll get another and lead yours home."

When a horse had been cut out from the remuda, their saddles exchanged and the men mounted once more, Foderow turned toward McAllister to speak.

McAllister put up a hand to halt him. "Say nothin'. I'll be okay. May be a bit slow, but we'll get home." He took the lead rope of Foderow's horse and fell in behind the others.

The wind subsided; however, snow continued to fall so that the backs of the herd glistened with it. The cowboys were chilled and weary, and thankful to catch sight of Skaha in the darkening late afternoon, as they crested the benches above the White Lake basin. Nowhere, now, was there a trace of the powdery, dry dust of the grasshopper-ravaged terrain.

Ian Cartrell drove across the flats to meet them, and greeted Foderow as he alighted wearily from his saddle. From the cab of the truck he produced a thermos of hot coffee and poured a lid full. "You're later than we expected."

"Bigger herd, bad weather."

It was a tired, impatient voice Cartrell had just heard. His sharp eyes roamed over the cattle now bunching together in the open field. He watched Smith and Caverly ride by with the spare horses. "Where's Ryan?" he enquired. A slight frown creased his face.

"Leadin' my horse that got a rock in its foot."

Before long the single figure of a man, followed by Foderow's black horse, topped the rise above the flats and edged down the hill onto the trail to the corrals. Allan Caverly rode in, taking up the reins of Old Bob, so that the foreman could travel with Cartrell.

As they arrived at the barn, Dennis Michaels stepped off the veranda of the lodge and strolled across the yard toward them. The cowboys rode in and dismounted.

242

A stillness settled on the air. Only McAllister noticed it.

Foderow introduced Michaels and McAllister as quickly as possible, wishing to get the uncomfortable moment over with, and took the lead rope of his horse from McAllister. Ignoring McAllister, Dennis Michaels lifted the gelding's leg, placed it firmly between his knees and inspected the injured sole.

McAllister took up the reins of Old Bob, on whom Foderow had finished the ride, and stepped with noticeable ease into the foreman's saddle. With question in his expression, Michaels looked up at him and stiffly enquired of the cause.

"I pried a rock sliver out of the frog. It was badly swollen," McAllister replied carefully, looking directly down into the other man's eyes. "He's all yours now." There was no sarcasm in his voice, only a desire to be away from the scene.

It had not escaped Dennis Michaels' attention, the total ease with which Ryan had conducted himself during their unexpected meeting. The slight nod of the man's head as he touched a finger to the brim of his black hat in acknowledgment, had immediately presented to Michaels the confident side of McAllister. The steady gaze of his dark brown eyes firmed up the veterinarian's belief that, beneath the calm exterior there was likely a strong, competitive nature. He had not been kept in the dark about his wife's friendship before the man's enlistment.

In perfect image of the modern young cowboy, McAllister sat in silence atop Old Bob, reins held loosely in hand as he leaned comfortably against crossed arms over the saddle horn. He waited now for the educated diagnosis, and Michaels could feel it. As he addressed the situation to Foderow, his glance took in McAllister as well. He saw the wide hat with its perfect curl at the sides, the slicker over a sheep-lined denim jacket, the leather chaps, and boots that fit into the stirrups as if they had been crafted there.

Not only is he tall, Michaels concluded in a downcast way, but tanned and good-looking as well. Without a doubt, he's at one with his horse, completely in tune with the ranch, and probably more at home on the range than anywhere. A vision of McAllister in full gallop across the meadow at cow-camp, flowing in easy motion with Dobbyn or Old Bob, reminded Michaels of how he trotted or walked his own horse and tended to keep one hand clamped over the saddle horn.

People, he lamented sadly, as he meticulously cleaned the gelding's damaged foot, have somehow come to regard cowboys as the toughest of men, yet the gentlest. Women adore them in their western wear. He had not missed how Strickland, Smith, Foderow and McAllister, even the late-comers, Caverly and Anderson, wore their hats low over their brow, leaving one guessing what might be read in their eyes. As they dismounted only a few minutes before, they had gone about their unsaddling with great jocularity amongst themselves, their spurs jangling in a sort of threatening tone with each step they took.

Cowboying and ranching, Michaels had once been told by an old-timer from Alberta who had visited his father, was a salt of the earth occupation. Well, there's no doubt about it, he concluded sorrowfully, Ryan McAllister's certainly in the right mould and he's got everything going for him, including the favour of Ian, the friendship of Dick and no doubt, the love of my wife.

It stripped Dennis Michaels suddenly of self-esteem and nerve. The fact that he was well-educated and knowledgeable in his profession, fell short of the bearing and confidence which McAllister presented from the saddle.

Turning away from the men, he led Foderow's horse into the barn where McAllister's Dobbyn had spent the past week. The realization that eventually he must deal with his fragile relationship with his wife, and therefore his future at Skaha, settled over him like a depressing dark cloud.

37

During the previous year the lodge at the ranch had taken on the appearance of a country inn. Upstairs, Albert Llewellyn's private den had become a place to relax, read and admire artifacts from the past. The walls were lined with bookshelves and glassed display cabinets. Framed photographs told of the pioneers who had settled the area. The room did what Sydney Cartrell had intended - tell the story of Skaha.

Through the past strolled Sydney Alex on the eve of her departure from Skaha. It had been a good holiday, even though she recognized the widening gap between herself and Dennis. They were becoming more like comfortable old friends, she mused, than husband and wife. Had the loss of their babies caused that? Or were she and Dennis not suited to one another. Had they both married out of loneliness, in a time when the world was being torn apart by war and people struggled to keep together through love? Why could romance in her life not have been as easy to enjoy as it seemed for Janet? Sydney Alex had not missed the attention paid Janet by Manny Anderson, nor the enthusiasm, so open and uncomplicated, in Janet's response to his overtures.

Sydney Alex sat alone that November afternoon in a comfortable chair, and thought of the recent days of pleasant visits with Janet, horseback riding with Dennis in the cool morning, and quiet times strolling through the woods. McAllister and Llewellyn memorabilia was all around her. The windows allowed expansive views of the ranch and surrounding mountains. It was a quiet room and Sydney Alex felt at home in it.

 On the distant eastern horizon the thin line of waning daylight hovered above the mountains. Late afternoon shadows cast their lengths across the yard of Skaha. Suddenly, noises on the veranda below drew her attention. She lifted the window and looked down. The ranch pickup was parked at the steps of the house and Foderow was helping three men unload their gear. Hunters, she determined. Then her eyes widened. McAllister stepped from the front of the truck to lift groceries out of the back. The others were already in, and she heard Foderow explaining that McAllister would see them settled.

The house suddenly felt chilled. Sydney Alex pulled her sweater tighter about her shoulders against the coolness. A light breeze blew through the open window and she quickly pulled it shut, causing it to slam with her haste.

At the bottom of the stairs McAllister heard the noise and looked up with curiosity. Quickly, he leapt up the stairs. The door to the den was ajar and he cautiously pushed it further.

"Come in," he heard Sydney Alex say from the window.

He was surprised to see her there. "I heard a slam–"

Hunching a shoulder, she said guiltily, "I was watching."

McAllister stepped into the room, closing the door behind him, and leaned against it. In the den, where a sense of the past engulfed them, they were now face to face with no place to run. The room became very still. Across the impenetrable silence McAllister looked into Sydney Alex' guarded hazel eyes. Her hand clasped the neck of her sweater nervously, while she searched for something sensible to say. So much time had passed, and too many avoidances.

"Ryan, I'm so sorry–" she whispered with a voice so full of feeling, it stunned McAllister. "Sorry–"

He raised his hands defensively against her unexpected remorse. "The last thing I need is sympathy for being left. I'm getting over it." Glancing idly around the room, he added, "What I never understood was, why?"

She watched his expression in the dull light of the room and noticed a tightness about the corners of his mouth. Without further pretense, Sydney Alex offered, "He was there, Ryan, and I was so alone. I never heard from you. I didn't know if you were even alive. I don't know anything about war. Ryan–"

"Those are excuses," he told her coldly, "not reasons." When he looked at Sydney Alex again, his expression had become cold.

She could not answer him.

"I don't think you love him."

"Yes, oh yes I do!"

McAllister's brow shot up. Sydney Alex could hardly be surprised at the disbelief in his eyes, and she wanted to bite back her words. A rush of feeling welled inside her, and her love for Dennis found no place in the magical moment that was now happening between herself and the man across the room from her.

The anticipation of this avoided moment swept through them both. To see her framed against the window, tall and beautiful, returned the image he had held through his overseas duty. It was the memories and dreams during the weeks in hospital, and the part of his heart which he believed had died that day in a Vancouver telephone booth. His arms ached to hold her, and he knew that all he had to do was open them and she would be there. It was in her eyes for him to read. Just then Sydney Alex reached up to toss the sweater from her shoulders in a bold move toward him and the gold wedding band caught his eye. The sight of it jolted him back to reality.

"My mistake," he whispered.

"Maybe we can talk sometime, Ryan," he heard her say with a shaken voice. "Please think about it."

"It's difficult for me to– I can maybe forgive, but I can't forget." He looked across at her. "Somehow I don't think I can do one without the other. I can't explain that, except that your ring there–"

"So much has happened, so much that was wrong." Her voice was calmer now. The electric moment was passing. "We need to be friends."

He reached down and picked up her sweater.

"Ryan, could we try?" she asked, close to tears.

"Just friends?" He handed the sweater to her.

"Yes, it's possible."

"I don't think so. I can't forget that it's him who holds you every night even though I can see the feeling hasn't changed between you and me." He raised her arm and touched the ring upon her finger. "It's only this that got in the way a minute ago and I won't respect that forever. So you see, being just friends doesn't stand a chance."

McAllister left her then, with a greater heartache than when he had arrived, and leapt hastily down the stairs. The noise of his boots echoed throughout the house. Below her, the outside door slammed.

Sydney Alex remained at the top of the stairs contemplating her troubled life and the terrible uncertainty of her future.

McAllister left the lodge, crossed Willow Creek and entered the barn. He lit the lantern and hung it on its peg. Over the gate of the stall, he patted Foderow's horse, talking to it and consoling it, allowing it to nuzzle his shoulder. Behind him he heard someone enter the barn, and thought it might be Manny. He was surprised when he saw Dennis.

Michaels walked along the passageway to McAllister, saying, "I guess we're here for the same reason." His voice was even, but not unfriendly.

"Well, I was over at the lodge and thought I'd drop by on my way home." McAllister opened the door, went in to check the feed bin and returned. The door clicked loudly behind him. "You're leavin' soon?"

"Is that what you're waiting for?" Michaels opened the gate, entered and lifted the horse's hoof.

"I heard someone mention it, nothing more. After all, it *is* your ranch." McAllister threw up his hands in resignation and turned away. He could sense the other's agitation and did not want an argument.

"And you want it," Michaels snapped involuntarily.

McAllister looked around at Michaels. "I've made that clear to Ian."

"And now to me." Michaels' body was rigid with expectation. He had not expected to find McAllister in the barn.

McAllister tried to be cordial. "Well, I'm not goin' to fight you over it. I understand you have a bad back."

"I understand you have a bad leg."

Anderson's deep voice interrupted them. "And I understand you are both being fools. I saw you come in here tonight and thought I might referee." He noticed that Michaels began to pace the passageway in an agitated manner. "You're not contesting over the ranch, you know. It's the girl. It's she who has the ranch and neither of you has a say, at all."

"It's *not* about the girl, Manny. I think we know where we're at here." McAllister's temper rose. "This is my heritage, Manny. Over there by the creek, that's where it all began with that grave by the creek. I walk through the cemetery on the hill up there and see my ancestors, and that makes me want to keep the place in McAllister hands."

"You just came from the lodge." Michaels stated, shoving his hands into his jeans pockets. "My wife is there."

"Perhaps– Yes, she is." McAllister cleared his throat. "We talked."

Anderson was surprised and stared at McAllister. "Now Ryan, how d'you think that makes Dennis here, feel?"

"Stop right there," McAllister commanded, staring at both men. "The matter *is* the ranch. This is not about Sydney Alex. It's about control."

Anderson took McAllister's elbow, attempting to lead him aside. "Listen, I'm serious, Ryan. This talk will only end up with you both in the shavings here, and that is not what the ranch is about."

McAllister shook the hand away, but Anderson continued. "It's also not what control is about." He caught McAllister's arm again. "Now think about it. You have a goal and he has a goal. I honestly believe they are worlds apart." Turning to Michaels, he suggested, "Dennis, I think you really need to talk this out with your wife. And maybe with Ian."

McAllister pulled his arm from Anderson's grasp. "Manny, this is none of your damn business!"

"Yeah, it is. Come– take a walk with me. Talkin' helps, you know."

As Michaels watched them leave the barn, he reached up, turned down the wick in the lantern, raised the glass and blew out the flame. At that moment he sadly, reluctantly, decided to set Sydney Alex free of obligation to him. It was time to end their dreary, hopeless marriage.

38

Sydney Cartrell's desire to have a stable and paddocks constructed had required only the merest mention. When plans were drafted and the lumber was ordered and hauled out to Skaha, building began. Daily, Sydney rode with Ian in their new Chevrolet, to watch her dream materialize. When the building was completed in February, she arrived for a final inspection.

In response to her praise, McAllister teased her. "Now, you know I'd do anything for the attention of a beautiful lady." With a quick wink in Cartrell's direction, he leaned slightly toward her. "And for me, you've still got it hands down over all others." He offered to assist her from the car and into the long passageway. "This was a very expensive shack to build for a few old horses."

"Not just any horses! Look at them–" Sydney motioned toward the field beyond the stable. "Beautiful Arabs for the experienced riders and steady Quarter Horses for the less practised." Smiling up at McAllister, she said softly, "I've developed quite an interest in Quarter Horses, you know."

A quick breeze blew through the walkway and played about the hem of Sydney's long skirt, swinging with each step around her high boots. Her muskrat cape, wool hat and gloves proved stunning attire to be strolling through a barn. McAllister watched her with fascination. His glance fell on Cartrell, taking in the black great coat, fur cap and leather gloves. McAllister smiled in the pleasure of their company. Even in their old age, he thought, they make a remarkable couple.

Beyond the barn, new rail fencing stretched across the flats. Old posts had been pried out of the hard ground, and the strands of barbed wire rolled onto reels and put into storage for use on the range.

Dick Foderow joined them, pulling the collar of his jacket up around his neck against the February breeze.

McAllister was saying, "Next spring we'll put a new irrigation system on those fields out there," and, testing Cartrell, added gently, "using sprinklers."

"You have, I've noticed," Cartrell answered curtly, "a penchant for spending. Budgets, young man, are put in place for reasons. I tried for several years to get that through to one other McAllister." He nodded in Foderow's direction. "Good morning, Dick."

"Mornin' Ian," Foderow replied and smiled at Sydney. "Good to see you out, though it's a freezer of a day. I've brought your mail."

McAllister nodded a greeting to Foderow and continued talking to Cartrell as they stepped toward the open doorway of the stable. "Not only will we have enough hay for ourselves," he pointed out, "but once more Skaha will be able to sell it. I understand that's how it was when my grandfather owned this place."

Cartrell's gaze fastened itself on McAllister's serious expression and he stopped walking. Foderow leaned against the door and felt no concern with the sudden tension. He carried a letter delivered that morning by a rider from Okanagan Falls, with news he had heard only minutes before on the telephone recently installed in Cartrell's office.

Cartrell was saying, "If it had not been for a personal injection of funds by my wife lately, things might well have taken a stricter turn. The past year's budget was stretched beyond its limits for building, seeding and so on. As well, I hear you want a bulldozer to build a road into cow-camp." He cleared his throat, thereby commanding renewed attention. "I agree that the full house we generally have at the lodge shores-up the pocketbook; however, as I am still in control here, I order now, that no more spending be done beyond the renovations to the community hall for a bunkhouse." Cartrell stepped through the doorway into the slippery, snow-covered yard.

McAllister stared at Cartrell's back. "You came out here this morning to tell me that?"

"I came out in this abominable cold," Cartrell informed him testily, "to escort my wife on a stroll through this stable, and you happened to be here."

"Ian," Sydney broke in. "Dick has brought a letter. It is news of Gus Volholven's death."

Cartrell swung around to look at her. He was shocked. "From what?"

"Cancer. It was apparently discovered only three weeks ago." She looked up at her husband. "I must go to Helga as soon as possible. You understand, don't you?"

Cartrell looked down into his wife's soft blue eyes. Her colour had paled. Her hands shook as she folded the letter over and over so many times that he eventually had to remove it from her fingers. He nodded to McAllister. "Ryan, I'm sure you won't mind driving my wife down to Oliver."

Sydney glanced up quickly. "Not you, Ian?"

"Not today, my dear. I confess to a certain tiredness of late, and I think it wise if I were to rest. I'm sure you'll want to stay overnight and I know I'm not up to that." Cartrell opened the door while McAllister assisted Sydney into the car. He said, "We'll see that your hotel is covered, Ryan. I needn't remind you, young man, that the hills are slippery and the road around Vaseux Lake downright treacherous in this weather." As Sydney was now settled in the car, he closed the door and went around to his own side. "I'm eighty-three years old and, right now, not up to travel. Sydney will be ready by two o'clock."

McAllister and Foderow watched the green sedan disappear up the draw. "You know, if it wasn't for Alma Davies keeping house out there," Foderow commented seriously, "I'd be a might worried about those two."

McAllister buttoned up his jacket and said to the foreman, "I tell you what– if I have to stay in a hotel down there, I'm gettin' Manny to come with me. Might as well enjoy myself if I'm to wait it out next door to a bar." Glancing across at Foderow, he grinned mischievously. "Right?"

Foderow chewed out of habit, at the middle of his mustache and warned half-heartedly, "Stay out of trouble."

"Always!" McAllister called back as he walked across the snow-covered yard toward the apartment above Skaha's office.

Sydney and Helga greeted each other warmly. It had been four months since the two women had seen each other, so there was much to talk about. McAllister could hear Sydney saying, "I had no idea–" and Helga's choked reply, "No one did."

They quickly got Sydney settled with her suitcase and two boxes of bread, pies and a cake from the lodge kitchen. The lodge was now managed by Erin and Will Pye who resided in the Carmichael place.

Helga offered McAllister and Anderson room, but McAllister declined in favour of family.

Astonished at McAllister's suggestion, Helga swung her head around to stare at him. Suddenly he was unnerved by this tall, well-postured woman who frowned darkly into his eyes. "Family? What family? I have none," she snapped.

Sydney tactfully intervened. "Ryan means Anton, of course. He knows that his Grandfather Dietrich is your brother."

"A brother who abandons a sister is no brother at all." It was a sad statement, full of bitterness, and suddenly McAllister had no desire to remain in her house. They left for town and registered in the Reopel Hotel.

At the chapel the following afternoon, Sydney and Helga stood side by side, supporting each other. Ryan sat alone at the back, present only if Sydney should need him. He had been stiffly warned by Foderow to remember his obligations.

As he watched the two women rise to sing, McAllister was struck by the difference in their height. Both were dressed in black calf-length skirts, gray hats, gloves and pumps, with strands of pearls adorning their black blouses. Sydney wore her blonde hair in the more modern up-sweep tucked under her wide-brimmed hat, while Helga allowed hers to fall loosely from a feather cap. They made a striking, attractive pair. He envisioned Sydney Alex at the same age.

At the reception held in the Volholven house, Helga said tearfully to Sydney, "I do not want to stay here now. I have an offer for the place from our neighbour and I will sell it to him." She took Sydney's arm in a firm grip and led her into the bedroom where they could have a few moments of privacy. She pulled the long silver pin from her hat and set the accessories upon her vanity. Sydney did the same.

Helga said seriously, "My dearest friend, I want to return to Skaha."

Sydney sat on the edge of the bed. "I would love nothing better, Helga. How I have missed you and many times longed for the company of a close friend, like it used to be." She reached out and took Helga's hand. "Do you remember, Helga, the hiking we did, the horseback riding at Skaha; all the times Thomas hid from us in that old house down the field. And Harrie– Harrie– Well," she sighed, "that was a long time ago when we were all a family."

Rising, Sydney suggested, "We'll have to get a cottage built for you as soon as spring breaks. That young Ryan went about the ranch burning everything down. But do not worry, Ian will take care of everything. He always takes care of everything."

Allan Caverly strode confidently through the door of the hotel barroom, his eyes searching the crowded, smoke-filled room until he located the Skaha men, then joined them uninvited. "Heard you were down here," he told them casually. "What for? You're never down here."

McAllister told him. "And what're you doing in here? You're hardly dry behind the ears, let alone able to enjoy bar privileges."

Caverly recognized the kidding he was about to take from them and replied with a grin, "Well, I think it was twenty-one I turned this morning."

"Go on! Today?" Anderson chided as he waved for the attention of the waiter.

"Good reason, I'd say, for a celebration," McAllister decided. Then on a serious note, he said, "But, I think we better keep Sydney's welfare in mind and talk a little business."

Anderson's head swung around. "You're serious."

McAllister nodded. "Lookin' at Allan gives me an idea. We might chart a course for the future here tonight, over this barroom table, and make old Ian quite proud of us."

Anderson shifted his hat back and forth over a crossed knee and glanced in Caverly's direction. "How're you comin' with your book-learnin'? Accounting, is it? Veterinary, too?"

McAllister leaned back in his chair, waiting.

Allan Caverly was quick to seize an opportunity. "I could hire on tomorrow, permanently." Raising his hands outward to indicate readiness. "No problem here, but am I talking to the guys that hire?"

"No, you're not," McAllister admitted. He pushed his chair slightly, tipping it against the wall, balancing there while studying young Caverly. "Dick hires for the cattle," he said quietly, "but it's still Ian who hires for the office, and so far there's never been a hint that he's ready to do that."

"Well, I got time," Caverly sighed and sipped at the foam along the rim of the glass. "I'll push cows in the meantime-- even cook, if I have to." He then turned a steady gaze on McAllister. "I want up there, you know. It's the life I want, what I like to do."

Anderson sneezed suddenly and drew out his handkerchief. "Well, I've no authority up there," he began, once the interruption was over, "but I suggest, Allan--" glancing from one to the other, "that you just bring along your books and throw your bedroll in with Bud and John in the bunkhouse. Just take your chances." He ordered another round of beer, and stated, "I know for a fact that Ryan here, will appreciate your acquired knowledge of mathematics and veterinary. Could come in handy."

McAllister smiled dubiously, bouncing forward in his chair. "Damned if I'm not up against Ian for this. You boys put me in a hard place, you know."

Allan Caverly sat just a little taller in his chair, raised his glass just as high as the others, and drank his beer just as quickly. One foot in the door, he remembered Anderson saying, and was pleased that he had finally taken that giant step. Now, he smiled in a sober way, he must prove his worth; if to no one else, then certainly to the two men whom he drank with that evening.

As the weeks passed, McAllister developed a real respect for Allan Caverly. He was a young man of many capabilities. The first job he did was remodel the community hall into a comfortable bunkhouse of four bedrooms with a modern bathroom, a large sitting room, and a kitchen with a cold water tap at the sink. Upon completion, Anderson and McAllister moved in with the others.

On a day when calving was nearly finished, Cartrell drove his car over the bumpy road to the corrals. The men were hauling straw and moving mothers with youngsters out into the pasture. Stepping up to the rail fence, Cartrell motioned anxiously for Foderow's attention. The foreman quickly obliged, fearing the worst.

"Sydney?" he called as he strode toward the car where Cartrell had retreated.

"No, no– it's the war!" Cartrell appeared flushed and somewhat excited, a vision seldom seen of the man.

"The war?"

"Yes! Yes! That damned, horrible nightmare has finally been brought to an end!" Cartrell stuffed his handkerchief to his nose against the barnyard odours which he had never been able to tolerate, and placed a hand on Foderow's shoulder. "It's done, I'm telling you." They shook hands, although Foderow remained slightly confused. "And, God forbid that the world should ever again know another such holocaust!"

"How d'you know it's over?"

"We heard it on the radio– only minutes ago."

Foderow turned, watching McAllister as he carried a calf toward the barn, followed by Anderson who led the cow. How will they feel, he could not help but wonder. Looking back at Cartrell, he said with a smile, "I'll tell them."

Cartrell, glancing about the place and seeing McAllister and Anderson at work, remarked without sarcasm, "Gone are the days, I see, when men let Nature take its course. Where did that calf come from?"

"Down the creek, right at the edge of the water. Thanks, Ian, for coming out with the news. I should warn you," he called over his shoulder while walking away, "Don't expect those boys to be here in the mornin'! They'll be sleepin' it off somewhere."

As he spoke, Allan Caverly arrived on foot, received the news with quiet respect, and removed his hat for a moment, his blonde natural wavy hair shining beneath the bright spring sunshine. The war had touched his life only in small ways, in the use of food coupons and gas for their car. A shortage of doctors in the area had kept his father away from home much of the time.

However, in the barn where McAllister and Anderson were being given the news there was instant jubilation. Then in a calmer, more reflective moment the two veterans looked at one another and remembered their own passage of active service. In awhile McAllister looked down at his dusty boots as if disbelieving he had them planted on safe soil. Anderson absently rubbed a hand along his spine while thinking of the buddy he had saved while taking the shrapnel in his back. Where was he now? Where were they all at this momentous hour of peace?

Dick Foderow left the barn. He, like Cartrell, had never served in anyone's army. Although he rejoiced in the end of the conflict, he nonetheless departed the corrals in a downhearted mood. He knew nothing of the kinship felt by Anderson and McAllister. He could not share in the exaltation of having fought for peace. Kinship for him had been with David McAllister in freighting and on the range.

Together he and Caverly watched Cartrell's car disappear across the field toward the Skaha office.

"That's a very old building," Caverly commented, indicating the office.

Foderow looked across at him and nodded. "Yours I suppose, one day," he said, feeling weary of everything.

"You know, Dick," Calverly began, keeping pace with the foreman, as they walked, "I hope so. I certainly plan on it and study toward that end."

"You gotta learn from the bottom, like you are– being a good cow hand on the ranch first, a reliable cowboy on the range, and general jack of all trades."

"Well, I figure as I started out cooking on the drive last fall, I was at the bottom. Truth is, I hate cookin'. Where did you start?"

Foderow stopped walking. Caverly also. "Something wrong?" Caverly asked quickly.

"I started," said Foderow thoughtfully, "before the car was invented, before the railroad was brought in here and there were only barges on the lakes. I started in a time of freight teams and rustlers and guns." He looked across the wide fields of Skaha. "I did my share to settle this land, and I did my killin', too." Foderow began walking once more. "It wasn't a war that took my best buddy, but it was the killin' of him that made a man outta me."

"My God," Allan Caverly whispered in awe of Foderow's remarks. "I'm nothing compared to you guys."

"Aw, you've naught to be ashamed of in yourself," Foderow eased Caverly's mind. "You're a doer, and that counts for somethin' around here. You'll be alright."

However, later, when the business of branding put Caverly further to the test, he failed miserably at catching even one calf.

"Give him a hot iron and a sharp knife," Foderow growled. "He can't rope a calf worth a damn– if it was tied to a post!" It was true. The others watched while shaking their heads. Desperate to master the art of handling a lariat, Caverly tired out the calves and all but wore out his horse.

"Well, the advantage," Anderson ruefully pointed out, "is that they'll drop on their own and save us the trouble of ropin' 'em." However, Anderson's humour failed to amuse Foderow, and young Caverly was removed from his horse to the ground, to help Strickland with the branding.

Nonetheless, Allan Caverly felt proud of his accomplishments. Somehow, he knew, Ryan had parlayed with Ian Cartrell in favour of his hiring-on. Although remaining aloof, never showing approval or disapproval, Cartrell was always pleasant upon meeting him. Caverly interpreted that aloofness as a warning to stay out of the office until specifically invited. It told him that his time there had not yet arrived and reminded him further, that Ian Cartrell still held fast, all the reins of Skaha.

There's no hurry, he convinced himself often as the weeks slid by, while he mucked out the barn and chicken pen, split wood and chewed dust in the branding corral. He studied late into the night, mastering his accounting through correspondence.

"At least I got a job," he had remarked to Anderson once, "when many others haven't." With that remark, Caverly won total respect from Manny Anderson.

39

In 1945, national celebrations and ticker tape parades in major cities signalled the end of World War II. Cathedrals and country churches were filled during days of religious thanks for peace. Families waited eagerly for loved ones to return home. Others mourned their loss. While it was a time of jubilation for some, it remained for others a period of sorrow.

At Skaha, Sydney planned a small celebration dinner party to be held at her house in the ravine. The cattle had been moved out to spring range where the countryside was lush with tall grass. Rain fell regularly, enhancing the terrain.

Anderson and McAllister led two pack horses loaded with salt blocks, bedding and food to the first line cabin where, in two days, Allan Caverly would accompany Strickland and Smith to the range. Dusk was falling when they returned to Skaha.

Cartrell met them. "I wonder, Ryan," he began right away, "how I can possibly teach you anything about management when you're still playing cowboy."

McAllister glanced at Anderson, grinned and replied to Cartrell, "Well, I just like to be sure everything's fine on the range." Tossing the saddle blankets over the rail fence, he gave Dobbyn a gentle pat. The horse trotted into the pasture, where he promptly lowered himself to the ground and enjoyed a good roll in the dirt. Turning back to Cartrell, McAllister enquired, "What did you really come to meet us for, Ian? Has something happened?"

"Perhaps you both would join us for dinner at the house tomorrow evening; a thanksgiving for the peace which the world at large might now enjoy."

"That's nice of you, Ian. No ulterior motives?"

"None." While Cartrell considered the statement a little out of place, he said calmly, "Perhaps a little shop talk. It won't kill you."

"I understand, Ian." McAllister really did understand the man's apprehension over expenses. There was much he needed to learn and the realization that Cartrell would not always be at everyone's elbow occurred to McAllister more often than Cartrell might have guessed. His main problem lately, lay with himself. Allan Caverly was openly readying for the key position, so it was therefore, easy for McAllister to let administration matters slide.

Cartrell left the two cowboys at the barn, returned to the office yard, got into his car and drove off at a faster speed than was normal for him.

"He's in a huff. It's real easy for him to talk money, you know, Manny," McAllister grumbled while tidying up his tack. "Ian likes numbers in books, but I like numbers on the range. He doesn't like riding a horse anymore and I'll bet he hasn't been on one in ten years. I could live in a saddle." His voice held a sad note. "There's fifty-five or so years between us and it's hard for us to get along." He slung his chaps over a wall peg. "He warned me, you know, that he'd be lookin' over my shoulder."

Anderson stood beside McAllister near the open doorway of the barn. "Well, setting aside all the books and horses and cattle, I have some news I'm finally going to share with you. Janet and I are getting married."

McAllister swung around. "You old sodbuster! Puttin' down some roots, are you? Well, I'm not surprised, Manny, but you hardly know her."

"Soon, Ryan. Probably September," Anderson furthered. "As to knowin' her, I knew right away last fall when she took me in to see old Doc Caverly." He winked at McAllister. "I want you to stand up with me."

"Of course." Then, more thoughtfully, "You are a lucky man, you know." His mood became reflective. "Janet will never let you down, Manny. She deserves a good husband."

As they talked, the sound of the ranch pick-up was heard near the Skaha gateway. Within minutes Foderow passed by the barn with Sydney Alex Michaels beside him. "Well, here comes the bridesmaid," McAllister murmured, a trace of bitterness lacing his words.

A shred of guilt assailed Anderson and he said apologetically, "I hadn't thought of that when I asked you."

"Oh, I'll live," McAllister assured him.

Nearly all of the Cartrell family returned to Skaha for their annual vacation. Jennifer Brown and Karen Wood arrived from the Fraser Valley with their husbands and took up residence in the lodge, which was now being referred to as Skaha Place.

On the evening of Sydney's special dinner, McAllister and Anderson walked the road to the Cartrells. They were passed along the way by the Foderow and left in a swirl of dust, which quickly settled upon the clean clothes they wore. They viewed Dick's speed with disdain, while they brushed at their shirtsleeves.

Anderson was at ease going to dinner at the Cartrells, for he was at ease wherever he went; whereas McAllister walked slowly and wondered where he would be seated in relation to Sydney Alex. They had both met Cartrell's family the year before and knew that Jennifer's son, Jason, was still in England, having enlisted with the

Royal Air Force.

"You're dragging your heels, Buddy, and I know it's because of an old flame," Anderson admonished in a friendly way. Slightly embarrassed, McAllister stepped out a little faster while trying not to scuff his highly polished boots.

"I was thinking about Jason," he said to Anderson. "I hear he wears a tunic full of medals now. Some kind of air ace." He spoke without sarcasm. "What do you and I have to show for our time there?"

"Nothing but scars and we're not alone and I'm not concerned. Get a move on or they'll eat without us."

McAllister sat between Janet and Karen. Opposite was Anderson, who had at his side a quiet, sad-looking Sydney Alex. They listened to the women chatter about their houses, their cooking, and the safe return of their children serving in various war zones. The men talked of business and war bonds. McAllister glanced toward Cartrell at one end of the table and Sydney at the other. He became acutely aware of their ages. Here I am, barely twenty-five and these two people are more than fifty years older than me. What were their responsibilities at my age? What will mine be, at theirs?

McAllister had developed a deep respect for Cartrell's astute judgment. He recognized in the accountant's dominant attitude how much was at stake at Skaha; that many people relied upon its success and, that as Skaha expanded its horizon into tourism, steadfast control was necessary. But, he wondered, when the time comes that Ian is gone, who then? He guessed that control would be divided between himself and Caverly, with Dick to lead them by experience. Would I have a voice among other cattlemen, older and more experienced? Would Allan be as capable as Ian has been, and stay with us as many years? Or, McAllister hung his head in deep thought, will Sydney Alex' husband return and throw us all out!

As he ate his dinner of roast beef and Yorkshire pudding, he glanced around at Cartrell, who was raising his wine glass in an impromptu toast to the safe return of his grandchildren. McAllister smiled and touched his glass lightly with Janet's.

"Don't you think," he whispered to her while glancing in Sydney Alex' direction, "that you should break your wonderful news to everybody tonight?"

Janet smiled at his mischievousness and, peeking out from beneath the curl of hair over her eye, warned in a low tone, "Behave yourself, Ryan McAllister, or I'll have you excused from the table."

Glancing across the table, he said, "Sydney Alex hasn't smiled all through dinner."

Janet leaned toward him. "You know, don't you? She and Dennis are in another separation."

McAllister sank back in his chair. In a moment, he met Janet's curious eyes.

"It's true. There might be a divorce this time."

McAllister grinned. "You know so much, lassie–"

"I know it all and I can read your intention in your eyes already." Janet turned her interest to the thick raspberry pies topped with generous scoops of homemade ice cream being served by Jennifer.

Throughout the dinner, his eyes had not once met those of Sydney Alex. She had been politely sociable upon his arrival and, thereafter, avoided him completely. He felt deserted by her and considered her aloofness unnecessary and unfair.

Meanwhile, Cartrell, in a convivial mood, was proposing another toast. Getting to his feet once more, he raised his glass briefly to Sydney. "To my beautiful wife," he began in a clear, sobering tone, then stared with challenge, in McAllister's direction, "and to the young man in whose care her welfare may someday be entrusted."

Everyone raised their glasses and sipped the rich, red wine. McAllister's eyes met those of Sydney Cartrell and he inclined his head slightly, raising his glass to her, thereby bonding his pledge. Sydney appeared regal and gracious, qualities which age had only enhanced. She nodded her acknowledgment.

Anderson was impressed with McAllister's manner. Ryan has come to know them both very well, he decided, and learned how to react appropriately. The table fell momentarily quiet until Janet prodded her father into making the announcement.

Cartrell responded by suggesting, "It is indeed an evening of surprises, wouldn't you say, Ryan?"

"'Tis indeed, sir," McAllister replied barely above a whisper, while attempting to comprehend the full extent of the man's earlier words.

When the dinner was finished and no talk ensued afterward of ranch management or other pertinent topics, McAllister and Anderson rose and left. As they walked the road out of the ravine, McAllister suggested,"Manny, let's go to town tonight and have ourselves a roarin' good time."

"How, by horse? They have the truck."

"Ian's old car is in the shed beside the barn and the key hangs on the wall in the office."

"I know the old man laid a heavy one on you tonight and, on top of it, Sydney Alex ignored you."

"The last time for you and me, Manny. You'll wow the ladies for sure with that full mustache you've grown. After this summer you'll be an old married man and all the fun ends."

Anderson shook his head and smiled, but understood his friend. Had he not just spent a fine evening beside the one he knew McAllister still loved? He had found Sydney Alex to be an intelligent, well-educated woman who could effectively carry a conversation to its conclusion despite the sadness he was aware she suffered. Certainly her physical attractiveness could not go unnoticed by any man, he rationalized, and felt a little sorry for his enamoured friend.

As they rode out of the White Lake hills in Cartrell's old sedan, Anderson pondered his future at Skaha. He held no particular ambitions about the ranch. He accepted what he had and expected to drift through his life comfortably. In that respect Manny Anderson likened himself to Dick Foderow. He considered the ranch his home now and, married to Janet, Skaha would ultimately come to mean more to him.

In deep thought, he rode quietly beside McAllister, absently twisting the ends of his new mustache. In a society of clean-shaven men, only he and Foderow sported mustaches, although Caverly was trying to grow one. Long ago Strickland and Smith had done away with theirs.

Anderson glanced across at McAllister, noticed the stern, set appearance of his jaw, the tightness at the corners of his mouth, and his concentration on his driving. "Do you think we can stay out of trouble?"

"We won't go lookin' for it, but if it comes our way, well?" He braked the car to a stop in front of a hotel across the street from where a regular Penticton Saturday night dance was getting under way. They sat in the crowded smoky barroom drinking draft beer with several others until it was deemed time by them all to cross to the other side and enter the dance hall.

It was as if by sheer appearance, trouble was incited. Only one dance had been played by the band of guitars and fiddles before McAllister had been laid flat by the fist of a powerful man well over two hundred pounds. He claimed McAllister had interfered with his girlfriend. While the statement was not the truth, the stage had been set. The girl had openly flirted. Anderson calmed everyone while McAllister got up from the floor. They left to stand on the outside steps.

However, the assailant was persistent and the two Skaha men soon learned that the man's fickle girlfriend had only been a ruse. Within earshot of both men on the step the aggressor launched a verbal attack on Ian Cartrell.

"Do I know this fool?" McAllister enquired graciously of Anderson.

"Watch your step," Anderson cautioned. "He's got a burr in his side, and you've had two too many beer."

Hateful words were aimed at McAllister. "That old man cheated me, you know. I traded him grain for steers and when I went to pick 'em up there's one missin'."

"You don't know how to count, Joe!" someone called out.

"It was all down on paper." The man stared at McAllister sitting on the step and flexed the thick muscles of his arms. "That Ian Cartrell is a sly, cheap, stealin' son-of-a-bitch. I'll bet it ain't the first time he fixed the books on folks. How d'you think they do so well out there, livin' like fat hogs!"

It was an unprovoked attack on a man most knew little about, but whom all respected. For only a second, McAllister pinched his mouth against his rising temper, then bolted up from the step, away from Anderson's restraining arm, to leap full upon the other man. They crashed to the platform at the entrance, smashing at each other, rising, wrestling until they had rolled down the steps and onto the ground.

Anderson quickly turned to face the others. "Nobody steps in here!" he warned in an ominous tone. They backed away to watch.

But soon the watching became too much for one bystander who jumped into the fight, fists flying, cursing that McAllister was killing his brother. Anderson took a blow to an eye while getting him out of it. It was only a matter of minutes before the noise drew a substantial crowd and the cheering began once sides had been established. To McAllister's quick reckoning there appeared to be support for only one side and it was not his. Amid the sound of thudding boots, scrambling bodies upon the ground and the acrid smell of blood from bruised and lacerated flesh, McAllister crawled across to Anderson who suggested they hastily leave.

They did, but not before Anderson placed two fingers between his teeth and sent a shrill whistle into the night air.

When everyone had halted, McAllister stepped alongside his opponent, who was being dragged away by his brother, and told him, "Ian Cartrell is the most honest man this country has the privilege to know. You owe these men who stood up for you tonight, an apology. So face 'em, pinhead, and give it to them."

Anderson's arm shot out, catching McAllister by the elbow. They crossed the street to Cartrell's car. Anderson's back began to pain him, and he wished only to return to the ranch. Beside him, McAllister wiped at his bruises and fell quiet.

In the morning beneath a rising sun, Dick Foderow entered the cowboys' living quarters in the old community hall, allowing a blast of humid air to accompany him. Viewing the swollen mess of their faces and hands, he declined his employees' invitation to linger.

"I can see that things did not go your way last night, so I'll let you lick your wounds in peace," he chided them seriously.

McAllister called from his bunk, "Wrong, Dick, everything in our favour."

Foderow did not smile. "You have ten minutes to repair and

recover. Then I want you, young man," he ordered McAllister, "to get over to my house as fast as you can move."

McAllister glanced at Foderow, then across the room to Anderson who lounged painfully against the wall. His gaze returned to the foreman. The consternation in his own eyes was no match for the annoyance in Foderow's, and McAllister carefully nodded his acknowledgment of the order.

Anderson bunted himself away from the wall and walked into the kitchen. "I'd say there was somethin' more important than the sight of us on that man's mind this a.m."

McAllister's chest tightened. He sensed disaster. To move from this bed, he considered now, means entering into the consequences of whatever had gone wrong overnight. He got to his feet and sat massaging his injured knee. At the washroom tap he splashed cold water against the bruises around his swollen eyes. Shrugging into a fresh shirt, he tightened his belt, then quickly pulled on his boots. At the doorway, he turned back to Anderson. "Thanks for backin' me up last night. See you in awhile."

Puffs of dust billowed up from beneath his boots as McAllister crossed the yard to Foderow's house. He hesitated about knocking his swollen knuckles against the screen door.

Foderow had seen him arrive and opened the door.

McAllister entered. The smell of fresh coffee brought welcome relief from the room's stuffiness. He frowned as he watched Fern Foderow nervously wind her hands into her long apron. In the tense silence that hung between them McAllister's brown eyes searched those of the foreman for explanation.

Reaching a hand toward McAllister's shoulder in a comforting gesture, Dick Foderow told him in a voice hoarse with humility and hurt, "Cartrell is dead."

40

The wide pinewood door of the church beside Willow Creek was opened by the elderly Reverend Allan Glass, and the family was led inside. Sydney paused briefly to notice the arrangements of garden flowers sprinkled with wild lilies and fern which banked the closed coffin. The church was full and some waited outside. This did not surprise her, for Ian had become very well known. In the third row the six pallbearers were seated; the cowboys of Skaha. A hymn which Thomas' wife, Mary, was playing on the Hackett organ, ceased. A veiled Sydney chose to walk alone.

In a comforting voice, Reverend Glass began, "I quote, 'This spot wherein I dwell, this home of mine lies, so it seems, upon the palm of God's dear hand - the fingers raised so we can see the tips, and not beyond. So I spend all my days within the hand –'"

Sydney bowed her head. She tried to listen to the words of a poem from a favourite book of Ian's, one that he had often read aloud to her. The words had meaning and reflected not just his, but all of their lives which had been lived within the cupped hand of Skaha. Her loss was more profound than many knew. She stared beyond the window to the lilacs in bloom along the creek, the distant fields of grain, and the pastures where colts and fillies frolicked beneath the summer sun.

Sydney heard Ian's voice as if he were there beside her, reading to her. "'It is so primitive, the toil we do, over and over in the season's turn; the land, the hay, the harvest time.'" Feeling the rush of tears, Sydney bit her lip against them.

Allan Glass read softly, "'The warm south wind that follows on the storm, the green flush on the pasture's sallow cheek...'"

It was sorrowful for Sydney to follow the casket out. I must at last, give him up, give him up– The soft blue of her eyes clouded and soon filled with tears left unchecked, as she watched the cowboys lift the coffin onto the wagon. Two groomed Skaha Percherons waited in their traces. Sydney impulsively stepped up beside Foderow and briefly touched the polished pine lid. McAllister took her arm and urged her back, holding her beside him.

Foderow climbed up on the wagon bench, took up the lines and released the brake. The team stepped out along the winding road to the graveyard on the hill above Mercy Spring.

For a long while McAllister remained near the gravesite. As everyone departed and Foderow looked across at him in question, McAllister shook his head and turned away.

As he walked the rows of markers he saw before him the story and struggle of Skaha; names he hardly knew, some he had never heard of, and those of his family. Stooping to read, he examined the name Rayne and, suddenly, he realized that his own name had derived from that of his great-great-grandfather, the trapper. A sentimental feeling washed over Ryan as he recognized the tie that bound him to Skaha.

He remembered reading a date of more than one hundred years before, on a cross that had been saved from the flood at the creek. That grave, Ryan had been told, belonged to the trapper's first wife, his great-great grandmother, and was the first burial at Skaha.

"My God--" he sighed in wonder, "what a long time in the making of a place."

The sun was disappearing behind the western hills, relieving the land of the intense daytime heat. To the south McAllister noticed heavy dark clouds moving over from the Cathedral Mountains in the Similkameen. He welcomed the possibility of rain. The land was dry. From the hill he looked out upon the sweeping fields of hay and grain, and pastures which held mares with their young. It was a refreshing sight, he felt, a worthy life down there.

Glancing back to where all the markers stood like vigilant sentinels, McAllister felt a great pride. You had something here to be proud of, Ian, he thought, you and the Llewellyns, and all those McAllisters before you. His breath caught a moment. Then in sudden grief mingled with fear of a future without Cartrell, Ryan sank to his knees, lowered his head into his hands and wept for the first time since his childhood. 'Boys do not cry,' he could hear his mother say when, as a small lad, he sustained a bruise. He had not thought of his mother in a long while. But this is no small bruise, he wanted to tell her, no small bruise.

Footsteps along the road before him drew McAllister's attention. When he looked up he saw Thomas Llewellyn. The ranch Collie ran alongside. McAllister rose and stuffed his handkerchief away, fit his hat upon his head and waited.

"Hello there. Didn't think anyone was around." Thomas smiled, knowing McAllister's reason for lingering. "Funerals always tug a little at the nostalgic side of a man."

"Well, it's for sure," McAllister agreed, "that this burial ground takes you and me back to our roots in a hurry."

Thomas smiled, remembering. "There was an old Indian lived here nearly all his life. He was called Two Way. His band buried him on the east bench across the valley where some of his family farmed. I always felt he belonged here."

McAllister seated himself on a log and watched Llewellyn walk among the markers. He doesn't look the fifty-six years Dick says he is. Some gray hair and only a few extra pounds on him. He smiled, recalling the conversation with Foderow. Sixty-nine, Dick claims to be and in excellent condition. When I'm Dick's age, I'll be happy to look like him. Hard work and good whiskey and a happy marriage, he says. Maybe that's what Tom has finally found. McAllister's smile disappeared and his thoughts were halted. A happy marriage!

When Llewellyn returned, he sat down beside McAllister. "I remember the day they buried my brother, Harrie. I know my father never got over it. It made him a bitter, critical man and, looking back," he glanced at McAllister adding with a grin, "which we should never do, I didn't make things easier for the folks; nor for my daughter. It seems us Llewelllyn men are short on understanding and long on blame."

He tossed several sticks for the Collie to retrieve, which only succeeded in stirring up a lot of dust. "Ian tried to make up for certain losses in our lives. A lesson in futility, he once termed me. Lord, how right he was."

McAllister murmured, "He was always right," and called the dog to lay quietly beside him. "Tom, this is not really the time to be talking business, but I thought if you had a bulldozer on a job up our way sometime, you could push a good road into the main cow-camp. The forestry pushed one part way in, but it's not enough."

"David– your grandfather, got killed out there," Llewellyn said, then shrugged his shoulders and added, "I heard that Dick tracked down the man they called the bandit, shot him, tied him to his saddle and turned the horse loose in the direction of Fairview. That's where the police were located at the time." Llewellyn hesitated a moment, as if recalling memories. "There was a bunch of them gave my Dad trouble with the freight wagon and gold one time, and later galloped through Skaha shooting and doing a lot of damage." Llewellyn looked down at the ground and his boots in an absent manner, thinking. "Ian knew. Dick never said. I waited for years to hear it from him."

"Well, I heard somethin' of the sort, but never put any store in it. Dick ain't the killin' type." After a pause, he continued, "A decent road to the main camp would let us in and out quickly with supplies and help hold the cattle together when we move 'em. We'll increase the herd over the years if we can lease more range. It's getting tight, though."

"We used to own it all. My father did. He followed Ian's advice and sold it because it wasn't being used. The sale kept our heads above water in the thirties." Llewellyn considered the request for only a moment. "Well, the road is long overdue. In October then."

266

"Can you give a rough estimate for me? We run on a tight budget."

Llewellyn replied firmly, "It's on the house. It's ludicrous to believe I'd have it any other way." They rose to their feet, shook hands on their agreement, and left the hillside together as the first drops of rain began to fall. Neither cared that, years before, a handshake between a Llewellyn and a McAllister was out of the question.

Foderow decided that it was important to get Allan Caverly into the office as soon as possible, while everybody tried to adjust to the sudden loss of Ian Cartrell.

Two months later, it was still painful for Foderow to wake each morning and face the emptiness which Cartrell's absence rendered by a heart attack. They had been a team for fifty years, starting the night of the fire when Llewellyn's freight shed and barns, and David McAllister's house, had all burned to the ground.

Every morning Foderow visited with Sydney and kept her apprised of ranch affairs. On his return from one meeting he parked the Dodge and waved to Caverly. Foderow's thoughts wandered. The boy oozes confidence. He'll need it. Many will criticize him along the way, but if he's worth his salt, he'll stand his ground, just as Ian did. The sound of the tractor which Strickland was using drew his attention. The three men met at the equipment shed.

"How does the hay look?" Foderow enquired.

"Not bad. Could be better," Strickland replied as they walked toward the barn. He raised the handle of the pump beside the long water trough. "A little of this stuff at the right time and we'd double the crop." Bending, he pumped water over his head and neck. "It's a hot one, today. That rain the day we buried Ian, was probably the last for this year."

Caverly smiled. "Ryan wants sprinklers out there real bad. He says that's one reason he's glad he's out at cow-camp. He doesn't have to look at dry fields and be frustrated."

Foderow squinted his eyes against the sun. "Well, it's hard to say why Ian never okayed that. We talked about water enough times. He used to test Ryan, I know, but I don't think he would do it to the detriment of the ranch." He glanced across at Allan. "Have you made head and tail of things in that office, yet?"

Caverly nodded. "I feel comfortable with it, yes. Are you asking about the sprinklers? Those big wheeled ones would cost a couple thousand for each field. They're using them up the other end of the valley."

"Well, let's get out of this damned heat!" Foderow said. They walked toward the office. Strickland left them for the bunkhouse. "This way," Foderow continued, "we're lucky to get a second cut, let alone a third. We should be gettin' three. I remember some years with rain, Dave got three cuts. You can do that in the Okanagan."

"Well, it's dry, dusty hay. I walked out there when John was cutting."

"Okay for cattle, but hell on horses," Foderow added. "Just let our Sydney hear one of her pets coughing, we might all be in trouble."

"On the other side of that thought," Caverly grinned across the room at Foderow, "we might get our sprinklers. She still signs the first line on the cheques."

Foderow stared at Caverly. He noticed how tall the young man was, the straight cut of the jeans he wore and the shine on his boots. But it's the chin, Foderow decided. He's not a rugged-looking kid, but he's got a stubborn set to that chin, which means that when something's fixed in his mind, it's there for awhile. In a moment, he reluctantly offered, "Yes, well, I'll get Ryan out there to see her. She cottons to him alright. But, Sydney's no fool. Never play games with her."

"Then," Caverly nodded, pleased, "she'll see the worth in water." With one finger he swung Cartrell's swivel chair around, and seated himself. "On days like this, I kind of miss the range. It's cool up there."

Foderow stepped through the open doorway. Behind him, Caverly called, "By the way, Dick, I passed my exam. Next is veterinary."

As Dick Foderow left the office that day, a weariness swept over him, leaving him pondering Cartrell's sudden death. Sydney had told him that Ian had felt weary after their victory dinner, had retired early to bed, and just went to sleep. His heart ached for Sydney. He had admired her all the years he had known her, for the loyal friendship and support she had always demonstrated toward him. He pictured again as he had many times during the past weeks, Cartrell as he had stood proposing his toasts when they were last together. I think Ian knew, he decided, as he crossed the road to the lodge.

When Foderow passed the stables, he saw Sydney Alex saddling her horse, an Arab gelding which she had ridden since it was five years old. He noticed the ease with which she swung into the saddle. "You take care out there now, you hear?" he ordered in fun.

"You know, Dick," Sydney Alex called back, as the gelding pawed impatiently at the ground and side-stepped around the yard. "I've not been out to cow-camp since I was little and went once with my father. Maybe I could ride with you next time you go?"

Foderow nodded consent. "I know your motive, young lady," he replied, though he doubted she heard him in her attempt to gain control of the horse. "You're feedin' that old hay-burner too much grain!" he shouted and waved his hand for her to be off with the group of tourists waiting for her.

Foderow and Sydney Alex arrived in cow-camp five days later with supplies. Dismounting, Sydney Alex presented a stunning appearance to the men housed there, for she looked very attractive in a pink checkered shirt, with the natural curls of her blonde hair tossing provocatively in the gentle mountain breeze. As she greeted the astonished cowboys, Sydney Alex' smile was as brilliant as the summer sun above them.

McAllister attempted to discern a sensible reason for her presence in their camp. Anderson, in an all-knowing mood, attended to resetting a shoe on his patient horse. While Anderson's back pained under the strain of bending, he considered himself infinitely more at ease than he reckoned his friend might be.

As expected, it was only a matter of minutes before McAllister and Sydney Alex strolled awkwardly together toward the creek. Along the trail, stalks of orange tiger lilies and brilliant red Indian paintbrush spread in a colourful blanket away from the dusty path. It led into the sunlit forest beyond the rippling creek where song birds warbled in melodious tones. It was a lovers pathway, but at this moment it was not lovers who trod it.

McAllister loosened his bandanna. "You caught us all at a busy time on a very hot day. We're not exactly fresh as daisies," he joked, refusing to be intimidated by her immaculate appearance.

"So this is where you hide out when you're not home managing the ranch."

"Dick manages the ranch and I hide out here to avoid you avoiding me." He pinched his lips together in a feigned smile.

"Not fair!" They crossed the creek, disappearing into the trees.

"Altogether fair!"

She sank down upon the soft ground and leaned against a tree.

"We have a thing or two to sort out," McAllister said. "In two weeks we'll be standing with Manny and Janet, so since you're here, this silent treatment can be brought to an end." He seated himself upon a fallen tree.

"I'm not free yet."

"Of course you're free. You and Dennis aren't together." He frowned and wondered aloud, "Why did you ride out here today, Sydney Alex? You've never come here before."

"Do you ask Jan why she comes here?"

McAllister raised his eyes heavenward. "Come on! We all know why she rides out here. Sydney, we're not talkin' about Janet. We're dealin' with us. You and me." Frustration gripped him. "How you test my senses! Look in my eyes, girl. It's all there for you to see."

With a voice edged with tears, Sydney Alex murmured, "Dennis and I have not come to a decision yet. It's so hard." Sydney Alex lowered her head to her knees. Tears fell over her face. "I always had

Papa to talk to; take care of things. Oh, how I miss him."

In an instant, McAllister was at her side. He took her hand in his. It was cold and he gently stroked it. "We'll be alright soon. Everything takes time." He cradled her head against his shoulder, wanting to bend down and touch her lips with his, but held back.

When there were no more tears, he looked into her flushed face. "Well now, we'd best be gettin' ourselves out of these trees," he advised wisely, "before we *are* in some kind of trouble." He tried to joke about the situation. "I'm ill prepared to follow temptation today, and what I don't need is your father after me with a shotgun."

She smiled while admonishing, "Oh, stop that!" and pushed away from his chest.

He caught her arm as they rose. "We've been there, Sydney. I know you remember. We both know what we are together," he whispered.

"I've never forgotten," she confessed at last.

They were words he had waited so long to hear. McAllister loosened his grip and Sydney Alex moved away from him, quickly leaping the wide stones across the creek to reach the other side. "It's very nice out here, you know. Cool," she called back, knowing that she was within earshot of the men unloading the supplies near the cabin. "You're lucky to be staying here."

In an upset mood, McAllister replied miserably, "I don't think so."

41

The marriage of Janet Foderow and Manny Anderson was held at Skaha. It was a warm September day, but a dark sky lent portent of ominous weather. As they left the church a stiff breeze was blowing up. In the distance a funnel of dust could be seen spiralling from the roadway. Out of the twisting cloud, a car sped toward the townsite, braking before the lodge.

Dennis Michaels stepped out.

A gasp escaped Sydney Alex. McAllister flashed Foderow an astonished look. Michaels leaned against his car and waited for the wedding party to cross the creek to the lodge to attend the reception.

As the group neared the lodge, Sydney Alex broke away and greeted her husband.

Foderow joined them. "A surprise, to say the least," he joked.

Michaels shrugged while keeping an arm around his wife. "Thought I'd come up and help, as it's soon time to bring the cattle down."

"Another month yet, Dennis," Sydney Alex told him. "But, it's nice that you're here." She was genuinely glad to see him. While she did not entirely put McAllister out of mind, she considered that the marriage must come first.

Foderow coughed and tossed his cigarette into the dirt. "Well, we can use every hand available when we make the drive. Come on in. We got a weddin' supper inside."

As the warm September evening wore on and the dinner remains were cleared away, musicians in the crowd brought out instruments particular to their talents and struck a lively dance band.

"At last," breathed Anderson, "I can take this choker off," and pulled at his tie, unbuttoning the collar of his shirt. "A man could suffocate in these clothes." McAllister did the same. Neither one mentioned the appearance of Dennis Michaels, who was dancing past them with Sydney Alex held tightly in his arms.

McAllister finally spoke up. "You know, I thought that marriage was done when she came out to cow-camp."

"Well, now you know. Remember that until there's a divorce, the ranch is basically his call. Ian is gone and, aside from Dick, he could be in charge. Now excuse me, I have a wife who's prettier than you and has no troubles. Much more fun to be with." He laughed slightly and disappeared into the crowd.

Everyone danced to the exciting rhythms of the fiddle, guitar and harmonica and sang old sentimental ballads. McAllister went across to the bunkhouse and got his own harmonica and joined Bud Smith, trying to ignore Michaels' presence. One of the tourists residing in the lodge borrowed two spoons from the kitchen and, bouncing them against his knee, added greatly to the music. The sound of the music brought poignant memories to Sydney and Helga Volholven, who was staying with Sydney. They went to sit beside Foderow and his wife.

"It's been a very long time since we've had such a night in this old house, Dick," Sydney said in an emotional voice.

"It has, indeed." He thought of a crisp Christmas evening when long ago he and Ian talked of old times on the veranda while Sydney played carols on the piano.

Before leaving, Anderson spoke to Foderow about the weather. "I wonder what's going on up at the camp. All but two guys, who don't hardly know that range, are down here tonight. We're not going far; just above the office. There's a storm brewing and I won't leave."

Foderow lit his cigarette and looked up at his son-in-law. "Appreciate that, Manny. Truly do." He knew Anderson planned to leave the next day for a week in the Cariboo, where his family still resided. He rose from his chair. "Well, ladies whenever you're ready, I am. Fern?"

Across the room McAllister watched. He sipped the wine from his glass, swirled it slowly between steady fingers, and sipped again. He suddenly felt very alone. He took notice of where the others were: Strickland seated in a corner with an old friend, Smith still blowing on his harmonica, and Allan Caverly dancing with one of Janet's friends. He thought of the weather blowing into a storm and wished there was a proper road into camp.

On impulse, McAllister set his glass aside. Passing the cowboys on his way out, he told them, "Stick close tonight. We'll find ourselves on the range, if a storm breaks." As if to reinforce his prediction, lightning flashed across the countryside. An enormous clash of thunder broke harshly over the ranch. McAllister paused at the door and suggested to Dennis Michaels, "You'll have to saddle up, you know. It's part of the job. I heard you say that's what you came back for."

Michaels stared, disbelieving, at McAllister. "You're surely not going out there in this storm! You'll never find your way around in that forest!"

"We'll leave shortly. You arrived just in time, as it turns out." Without smiling he added, "We need every man on deck." Settling his hat over his brow, McAllister nodded and left the lodge without looking at Sydney Alex.

Lightning struck with eerie force and thunder crashed in

shattering rolls. McAllister ran to the bunkhouse and saw Foderow step out of his house. In the yard they met Manny Anderson.

"We're goin' in to camp, you know," Foderow called. The air sizzled.

An hour later most of the horses were saddled, while others continued to be difficult in the storm. Men staying at the lodge held lanterns.

McAllister voiced his feelings once more to Foderow over the lack of quick access to their camp. When they were ready to leave, Foderow flicked his cigarette lighter to see the time on his watch. "Quarter to one," he noted aloud.

Finally, rain began to fall. Thunder continued to roll and crash ominously above them, the sound of it bounced catastrophically between the mountains.

As he looked up at the black sky, McAllister called to the men from the lodge, "Any of you fellas want to ride, you're welcome to join us if you think you can handle cattle." Two men stepped forward. "I trust the rest of you will see to the ranch if somethin' happens here tonight. We've not looked this storm in the eye, yet."

They rode into the mountains, keeping in strict procession along the trail. The rain had passed over, a mere shower compared to what had been expected. However, as McAllister had predicted, the worst was yet to come.

When the riders were little more than halfway to camp, the rain began to pour. It pelted the parched landscape, closeting the countryside in a great white sheet. Waterholes and bogs filled. Wild torrents formed pools in the meadows and hollows, and creeks soon levelled to overflowing. The trail through the woods became unpredictable and perilous.

Cattle could be heard bawling and running through the trees, crashing over windfall and spreading out in a frantic mass. The two cowboys who had been on watch followed, attempting to get alongside, but the trees and debris presented dangerous barriers. The Skaha riders scattered themselves to the flanks in an effort to bring the cattle under control. Lightning flashed, its long yellow forks dancing crazily above the herd. Once in the open, where there appeared to be a cleared ravine, they were able to gather and contain them in a gully.

From beneath the brim of his hat over which water ran onto his slicker, Strickland peered through the rain at McAllister. "There's about half of them here." Glancing around him, perplexed, he asked, "Where's Dick?"

"Not with me. He lit out with Manny." McAllister tipped his head to the side allowing the water to run off his hat. "Michaels. Where'd he go? And the others."

"Bud went into camp to fix up something to eat." Strickland told him. "We'll see what the morning brings." He reined his horse away to circle the front.

McAllister rode to the back of the herd. It was not long before he encountered Anderson riding out of the trees, leading Foderow's horse. The foreman was huddled over his saddle horn in a painful way, covered by his yellow slicker.

"He took a snag in his ribs. Got bounced to the ground pretty hard. Landed over a log." Anderson announced. McAllister leaned over, viewed Foderow's position, and dismounted. "Allan's behind us," Anderson informed him. "He could take Dick into camp and have a look at it."

"D'you want us to get you out of that saddle, Dick? I'll get my shirt off and wrap it."

"Naw, I'll wait for the boy." He held his arm tight against his side, for the pressure relieved the pain. "I'm under this slicker an' I ain't gettin' out till it's time!"

Allan Caverly appeared and without further wait, took the lead rope of Foderow's horse and urged his own ahead.

"D'you know where you're goin'?" McAllister called after them with concern that locating camp could be made difficult by any number of barriers.

Caverly inclined his head. "I don't," he replied with a slight smile, "but this old-timer does!" The two men disappeared into the night.

The storm was weakening as it moved northward. Nonetheless, it continued to rain. The thunder soon took on an empty, distant sound. McAllister stared toward the dark hole in the forest where Foderow and Caverly had disappeared. A sudden sense of aloneness settled over him. He looked up at the sky reckoning the time at nearly daybreak.

"Are we goin' to move 'em?" Anderson enquired, doubt in his voice.

"Very carefully," McAllister replied. "Yes, we'll move 'em– when this storm's gone. Manny, has anybody seen Dennis?"

"Not me." Anderson jigged the reins of his horse and the animal trotted ahead. Shortly he met one of the dudes who had ridden with them and questioned him. No one had seen Dennis Michaels.

As daybreak cast its faint light across the ridges of the distant range, bathing the sky in an orange glow, the men began to move the now-settled herd toward camp. About one hundred head were missing.

When the rain had ceased and the sun was fully up, McAllister brooded over the missing cattle, but more over the absent Michaels. An uneasiness gnawed at him as he sat alone on the cabin step. Behind him the others crowded around the breakfast table.

Suddenly he called out, "Manny! Allan! I know where the cattle are. Come on!" But, he worried, I don't know where Dennis is.

In half an hour's ride, they crested the knoll where once McAllister had found wild horses. The cattle grazed in the green valley below as if no storm had passed. It was now a peaceful rain-freshened valley basking in the warmth of a late September sun.

Dennis Michaels sat relaxed in his saddle and watched the herd.

As they started down the hill, McAllister suddenly reined in his horse. He put out his hand to ensure quiet from the others. In the distance he could hear the pounding of hooves. "The horses," he whispered, "The wild ones. They'll surprise the cattle."

They swept out upon the approaching band, galloping from the trees to turn them at the front, away from the cattle. The horses bolted away from the riders, scattering at first. Then the threatened stallion desperately gathered them together and they raced across the meadow toward the cattle.

Startled, McAllister spotted Michaels in the distance. The herd had begun to mill and bawl. Michaels grabbed up the reins of his excited horse, which danced and slid on the wet grass. As the horses neared, the cattle began to run.

Suddenly the stallion ceased to lead and turned abruptly toward Michaels. Tossing his head and mane wildly, he pranced and pawed the ground. Wheeling and kicking, he raced at Michaels, attempting to bite Michaels' horse.

Michaels lost control and fought to stay in his saddle. Beside him cattle and horses tore frantically past him, jarring his frightened horse. Clinging to the saddle horn as his horse bolted and kicked, Michaels was swept along with the stampeding band. They pushed him into the running cattle. The stallion kept after him, viciously biting at his galloping horse, bumping against it, leaving him loose in his saddle. Suddenly Michaels' horse kicked high, throwing him to the ground. Hooves trampled the ground around him, striking and stumbling over his body as he tried to get up. His world went black as he slipped into unconsciousness.

McAllister raced toward the stampeding herd in an effort to reach Michaels. He caught his breath as he saw Michaels' attempts to get up, then finally go down. His heart raced. Across the meadow Michaels' horse galloped with the herd.

With Anderson and Caverly, McAllister broke into the stampeding herd to where Michaels lay covered with mud and grassy sod.

McAllister leapt to the ground and carefully turned Michaels over. Horror flooded him at sight of the stricken man. Quickly he reached for his canteen. Using his bandanna, he dabbed lightly at Michaels' face. Sitting back against his heels, he closed his eyes and hung his head in despair.

In the distance the cattle crowded together as the wild horses raced on, leaving the valley quiet once more.

McAllister looked up as the others dismounted. In reply to the question in their eyes, he said in a worried voice, "I doubt that he will live."

42

October colours graced the countryside as Dick Foderow drove the winding road to White Lake. In a depressed mood, Dennis Michaels sat uncomfortably in the back seat of the sedan. He had extensive injuries. Surgery repaired his body, but his mind refused to heal. Resentment festered toward everyone at Skaha.

Sydney Alex had remained by her husband's bedside through the three weeks in hospital. Now, she attempted to cheer him with news of the ranch and the upcoming stock sale. Her efforts only depressed him more. She gave up and leaned into her corner of the car, retreating into her private thoughts.

The image of McAllister and their last conversation invaded her mind. She tried to push it aside. They had both crossed boundaries with harsh words that would stand between them for a long while. A tear stole over her cheek. "You did it on purpose!" she had accused. "You made him feel small and incapable! Shamed him into going out there."

Ryan had snapped coldly, "I can't help what happened. He either cuts it, or he doesn't. It's part of the job." His mouth had been pinched, his stare penetrating, almost hateful at being blamed. She could feel it yet. This was not the gentle man who had held her at cow-camp and respected their boundaries.

She had screamed at him, "He's seriously hurt! I think you hoped he would be dead! My God, how I hate you now!" She could never take back those words. She did not hate him. He was the one who had found Dennis, brought him out of the hills and stayed with them at the hospital until the critical stage had passed. Regardless of how he likely felt about Dennis, he had been their support. She knew that Dennis would return to his parents' home permanently now. Would she go with him, she wondered; would she have a choice?

By early November the herd was gathered and sale stock selected. Skaha riders, dressed against the first chill of the fall season, moved the cattle off the range over the trail to the Okanagan River where they crossed and were driven to the stockyards. In ten days, Thomas Llewellyn would have a machine arrive at Skaha to blade a proper, more direct route into cow-camp.

The stock sale at Okanagan Falls drew buyers from meat packing plants in Western Canada. Anderson and Caverly kept the cattle moving in small lots to the auction ring, while Strickland and

McAllister got them before the auctioneer. Foderow placed himself in a strategic position to keep a keen eye on the bidders.

This was Ryan McAllister's world and it appeared to be Anderson's as well. As Foderow watched the two work together, he was reminded of David McAllister and himself.

That evening the cattle were loaded into railway cattle cars. Across from Foderow where they were seated on the posts of the loading chutes, Strickland said, "I told Tom Llewellyn once, that cowboys were the toughest breed of men on earth. He thought I was being pompous, but watching those boys learnin' to be good with cattle, I don't think I'm far off." He smiled, reflecting for a moment on his own life. "Maybe a little prejudice tucked in there."

Foderow leaned over the chute to urge a stubborn cow into the car while guarding his fractured ribs. "Well, get your prejudiced ass off that post," he told Strickland, "and help get these critters in here!"

"Now, Dick, you know my back won't allow–" Strickland grinned.

"The state of your back 'as got nothin' to do with it. After all," he mimicked Strickland, "cowboys are the toughest breed of men. Didn't you just say that?" Foderow looked out from beneath the brim of his hat across the chute into the other's smiling eyes. "Ain't that what I just heard?"

When McAllister called at the Cartrell residence later that evening, he was met by Helga Volholven, who told him that Sydney would be right along. She left him alone in the hallway and the silence of the house. He leaned against the wall in contemplation of his relationship with Sydney Alex. Since the night of the storm his life was in turmoil. He could hear her in the kitchen preparing a tray for her husband. He dared not go in.

In crossing to a chair, his eyes caught sight of the Llewellyn family Bible upon the hall table. Its pages had been left open at the back. In the dull light he recognized Sydney's even handwriting, for he had seen records kept by her in the office. He leaned over to view the page and found to his amazement, a recorded history of her family dating back to 1887 in Wales.

The reality of the document gripped McAllister and, as he read, he was prompted to take up the long tapered pen. Dipping the nib into the inkwell, he began to write what it was he knew Sydney could not:

"On the night of 25th of June, 1945, the death of Ian Cartrell occurred at 84 years. He was Master of Skaha and no man could stare him down. Signed, R.McA."

Aware of its fragility, McAllister closed the lid of the Bible with care and tightened its gold clasp. He noticed a locked diary with the name

Sydney Llewellyn inscribed on its cover. As he looked down at the two books, wondering about the story they told, Sydney appeared in the foyer.

"Reading?" she enquired in a gentle way.

He smiled at her. He had grown very fond of Sydney and took the business of looking after her seriously. "I filled in the space that I know you could not."

She reached for his hand. "Thank you, Ryan. Are you not going to the stockman's dance?"

He shook his head. "Just making my nightly call to look in on you and talk about the ranch."

Sydney let his hand drop. "It's a lonely life you've elected for yourself, Ryan. You have my sympathy."

"Sydney, do you think Sydney Alex will leave here permanently? We said a lot of cruel things at the time of the accident."

Her blue eyes met his troubled gaze. "No. No, she won't, Ryan."

In the kitchen Sydney Alex heard her grandmother and felt a great relief flood her. The decision regarding her marriage and her life had just been made for her. In a moment she picked up the tray and, leaving her dour mood behind, delivered it to Dennis with a smile. One day, she now understood, this will all be over.

43

The remaining herd was brought down from the range, where they were turned onto the fields which had been harvested through the summer. During the autumn months horses raised on the ranch would be broke for riding. Older geldings would be used for trail rides, sold, or traded for younger ones, to round out the count in saddle horses needed at cow-camp. As Sydney owned an enviable number of beautiful Quarter Horses, Caverly was able to talk her into letting some of them be taken into the remuda.

In mid-December McAllister organized a meeting in the dining room of the lodge. A new direction for Skaha needed to be discussed. There was not yet a recognized head of management at Skaha, as there had been during Ian Cartrell's tenure; everyone expected that Dick Foderow, as foreman, would take the lead in ranch decisions.

While walking to the lodge on that chilly December morning, John Strickland spoke seriously to Foderow of the situation as he perceived it. "There's a new generation sittin' over there waitin' for us, Dick. New ideas, innovations waitin' to happen. Just like in our time. Only our time's goin', and it's theirs arriving. You know what I mean?"

Foderow nodded, shoving his hands deeper into his coat pockets, moving a cigarette back and forth between his lips while he walked. "Give 'em rein. It's what they need," he heard Strickland telling him. Foderow drew heavily on the cigarette while blowing the smoke out between his teeth. "You know, John, you're a wise old man. How come you never unseated me on this place?"

"'Cause you were always the best man with animals. And," he gave a lop-sided grin, "you were here first, so you had an edge."

They entered the lodge, helped themselves to coffee, and took chairs at the table. Discussion had waited on them.

McAllister enquired, "Where's Bud?"

"Oh, his gout's got his foot up," Strickland offered, "and he says there's nothin' goin' on here worth puttin' it down for."

Caverly sat at one end of the table. He was the only man hatless. That Allan Caverly filled that chair, lending authority to the meeting, did not happen by choice. The coincidence of it startled Foderow.

McAllister began by saying, "Pretty soon we'll be starting a new season here at Skaha and we've got to get a few things in place before another year slips by on us." He smiled across at Caverly.

"Now, Allan's spent a lot of time lately sorting out things with me over there in the office and we thought we'd put a few suggestions on the table."

"We need to discuss the hay fields and their possible yield," Caverly began with ease. "And sprinklers. We need to take a look at proper use of those fields and address the stock. Of course there's the matter of outdated machinery."

Good Lord, where did this boy come from, Foderow wondered and suggested, "Have you been going to another night school on us?"

Caverly grinned, accepting the kidding. He liked Foderow. The foreman had always been fair with him. "Just been nosing through Ian's notes. Lots of good horse sense hidden there." He drained his cup. "It's good to be out of debt and independent, but we are too much unto ourselves. We're without knowledge of change and know-how. No fault to be placed, but that's how the ranch was operated in the past."

Foderow felt a grain of guilt over those remarks. He and Cartrell were to blame if there was a falling behind. Why did Ian not get more involved, he wondered. He remembered that Cartrell had travelled the valley in search of new methods, practical innovations, and profitable moves to benefit Albert Llewellyn's holdings. Had Thomas taken the heart for the challenge out of the man? Or had Ian simply grown old and tired in wait for the injection of new blood?

Strickland leaned back against his chair to watch the others and admire a fresh attitude aboard.

Anderson sensed a congenial mood in the room. Foderow, he could see, had fallen still. Anderson removed his hat, hooking it over a crossed knee while watching his father-in-law. He's wondering where all the money will come from.

McAllister slouched slightly against the back of his chair, stretching his long legs beneath the table. It's time, he thought; this day of decision is long overdue.

Caverly had estimated the cost of sprinklers for the three fields to be five thousand dollars. "That includes everything necessary to get them up and working: pumps, pipes, wheels, everything plus a seasonal wage for a man to look after them."

"I think the one thing we have to quit is wintering the cattle on those fields," McAllister told them. "The hay we take off there is getting to be garbage. Weeds are taking over where there used to be healthy grass.

Anderson agreed. "Pick one field - the one with the creek running through it," he suggested, "and use it for winter feeding. Then put the horses on it through the spring and summer. With sprinklers, it'll hold up. When we start feeding the horses in the corrals, turn the cattle in there to clean up before winter feeding starts. Harrow it in the spring and start over. I can see a need for more cultivated land for hay if we increase the herd. It seems we barely meet the need now and, some years back, I understand you've had to buy. If we don't increase the cattle we'll be able to sell hay in two years because of proper irrigation."

Foderow shifted in his chair and dug in a pocket for his tobacco and papers. He did not offer them around, for, since Anderson had quit the habit, he was the only smoker in the room. "We're down on stock. In the days of Llewellyn and McAllister, the combined herds numbered over four hundred head. Right now we feed around two hundred and seventy through the winter, plus seventeen horses that belong to Sydney, and fifteen of our own. If you increase the yield, your method of haying has to change. With water you'll double the crop, maybe triple it."

"Which brings us to machinery," Caverly furthered quickly. "The first thing needed here is a baler. The major machine outlets have them. They're wire-tying balers and put out about thirty-five bales to the ton."

"It's water," McAllister thought aloud. "Water."

Foderow mumbled, "Water and a baler this year. The money?"

Straightening in his chair, McAllister furthered unflinchingly, "Water, a baler, a new mower and decent side rake, and one bull. Next year, one more bull, a new tractor and some more leased land." He looked at Caverly.

"The money? The bank," Caverly replied.

Silence followed that bold, disturbing statement.

Foderow cleared his throat and stubbed out his cigarette. "You got three old men ready to hit the rocking chair and only three young ones left to do the work of eight. Think about it."

"I have," McAllister said. "That's why we're talking to you. I know that with a little belt-tightening and hiring help only when we're in dire need, we can pull it off. Sydney's lodge and duding run nearly year round, paying for itself." He waited, but the room remained quiet. "Allan will be through his veterinary course soon."

Anderson rose from his chair, pushed it into place at the table, and said in a matter-of-fact way, "I'm in. I got everything to gain." Fitting his hat firmly upon his head, he soon departed the room.

Strickland rose to leave, offering, "Well, if you need the odd cow rounded up or any machinery fixed, you'll find me in the bunkhouse. I ain't goin' nowhere." He buttoned up his jacket. "I think I can speak for Bud."

When he had gone, Foderow leaned against his crossed elbows at the table edge. McAllister shifted upright in his chair. Caverly waited. He knew he had not spoken out of turn. He had done enough research to be positive about his suggestions. He was acutely aware of bank interest and loan agreement terms, and the debt which borrowing brought to any concern.

"You know, Allan," Foderow began slowly, "you're asking quite a lot from us, but it's us who let you sneak into that office. So I guess what I'm sayin' to you is that I'm goin' to do a lot of worryin'. Obviously you've done some homework. It's also clear that you're right about a lot of things, like draggin' our heels."

"Now Dick, I didn't mean that you and Ian–" Caverly attempted to apologize.

"I know. You're right about the place. Times are changin' and we have to change with 'em. It's just that the older you get, the less time matters to you." Foderow lifted his hat, smoothed back his thinning gray hair, replaced the hat and got to his feet. "All I can say is, don't hock us into the bank so bad that we can't get out. We're used to being free of unsettlin' things up here." He pushed his chair in place at the table. "I want to know if you have discussed this with Sydney."

Allan Caverly shook his head. "No, I have not. I wondered if someone other than myself should be doing that."

Foderow's gaze fell on McAllister. "It's your turn. My time for takin' any lead has gone. These modern days are yours, Ryan. Yours and Allan's, and that son-in-law of mine."

McAllister thought that the foreman's voice sounded a little sad, and hastened to correct him. "I think your time is still here, Dick. We need you at the helm and you know it. Even twenty years down the road, from that old rockin' chair over there, we'll need you in front of us."

Foderow turned back at the door. "For what? To recall old memories and spur on young hopes?" he asked quickly. "Naw, I'm grateful I lived in the time that I did, with old Llewellyn and your grandfather. I can remember with pleasure knowing a man like Ian," he looked over at McAllister, "and smile every time I think of what a sorry sight you were the first time I set eyes on you at the gate out there." Foderow did not close the door behind him.

Caverly and McAllister listened as his footsteps were heard going down the outside steps.

McAllister moved a hand along his brow and pinched his eyes closed for a moment. Finally he broke the long silence. "Well, it's really just you and me, isn't it?" he suggested, feeling it to be the truth. "They are all there for us, Allan, but it's really up to you and me to keep it figured out and working."

"Worried?"

McAllister looked into the other man's blue eyes. They were alert and confident, he noticed. "A little," he answered honestly.

"Me, too, but I will not admit that to anyone else." He pushed away from the table and stood up. "Coming? I got a bottle of hellish good

Scotch under my bunk. We could have a drink to the future."

McAllister laughed and rose from his chair, took Caverly by the elbow and steered him through the doorway. "Let's go dig out that Scotch."

As they walked across the yard toward the bunkhouse, McAllister was startled to see Ian Cartrell's sedan pass by. Anderson sat behind the wheel with Dennis Michaels beside him. He stopped, wondering. He noticed that Sydney Alex was not with them. Michaels' car had been left behind.

While he watched the sedan disappear, McAllister remembered a time when Thomas Llewellyn's car had left the ranch by the same road. Then, it was as if a new life full of excitement and challenge was opening to him. Now, he felt that another chapter was about to open.

Caverly frowned at him. "You don't know? Dennis is leaving. He's had enough of this life. Manny's taking him to meet his parents visiting in Penticton. He's left his car for Sydney Alex, part of an agreement, I guess."

McAllister fell quiet. He chose to ignore Caverly's news. "One time, when I was feeling a little down, I looked out across the flats from that big corner window in the den upstairs. I can tell you, Allan, the ranch was an awesome sight to my eyes." He fell into step with Caverly once more. "What I saw before me were miles of beautiful acres offering an unlimited bounty, the dream I'm sure the first McAllister envisioned when he sat atop his horse on some ridge here. It's beautiful. It's rich. And it's ours!"

Caverly looked around at him, perplexed, as they crossed the bridge over Willow Creek, their rubber boots pushing snow ahead of their steps. "Damned if I can understand you, Ryan. You sit there all morning without hardly a word and now I can't shut you up. You're a hard one to figure!"

"Don't try, Allan," McAllister replied with a solid pat to the younger man's shoulder. "That way we'll work very well together and stay friends."

44

The following year the green fields of Skaha basked luxuriously beneath a warm late May sun. Ploughed, harrowed and seeded, they took on a healthy, productive appearance. When the snow disappeared in March, McAllister's plans for the irrigation system soon went into effect with the arrival of big wheels, water pipes and sprinklers. It was a process that took Anderson and McAllister weeks to complete, so that by May, water swirled in wide overlapping patches. It was a beautiful sight.

During June the lodge filled with tourists anxious for a taste of country life. Occasional rodeos in the corrals behind the barn provided exciting entertainment. Horseback riding in the eastern hills was an inspiring meeting with Nature. Picnics were held in the quiet meadow near Mercy Spring. During Saturday evenings there was music and dancing in the large dining room of the lodge.

While prosperity finally seemed within reach for the ranch, harmony in McAllister's personal life continued to elude him. On friendlier terms with Sydney Alex since her separation from Dennis, he tried to pick up where their relationship had left off. For a while it remained out of reach, until late one Saturday afternoon at the corrals where he and Anderson leaned against the rails watching Caverly lead two of Sydney's Quarter Horses to the Skaha pasture.

Anderson said, "It's good to see some fresh stock in that string. Dick says that most of those old cayuses are those you brought down from the hills before the war."

McAllister's expression grew pensive. He turned to Anderson, while leaning his chin upon his arms over a rail, and spoke softly, "Just one more time I'd like to go up there and see if I can steal from that big black like I did from the white one." He heard Strickland nearby, grunting disapproval, but ignored it. "You know what I mean, Manny? Just one time. I want to do it while I can still ride like the wind." Glancing down at his dusty boot propped against the bottom rail, he reluctantly admitted, "Just a wish, that's all." He looked up and saw Sydney Alex watching him. How long had she been there? He nodded to her.

Sydney Alex smiled through the dust between them, as a daring young tourist was being bucked about by a tall roan. McAllister looked back at the rider, as the horse lowered his head to the ground and gave a great lift of his back legs, tossing the man against the railing in front of him. When he glanced across the corral again, she was gone.

Anderson said in leaving, "See you at supper. Big spread at the lodge for everyone."

Throughout the evening McAllister watched her, afraid to look away lest she disappear again. Finally, when the music began and he could no longer tolerate the distance between them, he crossed the floor and caught Sydney Alex up in a rousing polka. Wordlessly, he swung her into the hallway and down the veranda steps. In the camouflage of nearby lilacs, he pulled her into the dark depths of the branches, and allowed himself to drift with the pleasure of her mouth beneath his.

"No one must know we're together," he heard her say, her breath warm against his neck.

Leaning against the branches, he closed his eyes and held her close. "Everyone knows we're together now," he whispered.

"We must be discreet," she warned again, covering his face and neck with hurried kisses.

"Yes, yes. We will," he promised against her mouth. Lingering no longer, he pulled Sydney Alex from the cover of lilacs and away from the house. As if this night had always been planned, McAllister remembered that the apartment above the office was empty, and it was to his old room that he led Sydney Alex.

In the morning, in preparation for summer cow-camp, Foderow and McAllister gathered the horses of the remuda from distant Skaha pastures. Janet and Sydney Alex rode out to meet them. The small band broke into gallop across the ranch yard, toward the open gate of the corral. When they were in, McAllister leaned down from his saddle and swung the gate shut behind them.

Surprised to see them, he said, "Good morning, ladies. Sydney Alex, I thought you might be taking patients' temperatures at the hospital. And Janet, did you sell your shop?" He swung down from his saddle.

Janet replied seriously, staring at McAllister. "I thought I'd like to get at least one more chance at herding something before I settle for knitting booties and changing diapers."

McAllister fell still where he leaned against the rails. He wondered why Anderson had failed to mention such an important event to him. He looked across at Janet. "Well, that is good news; good news, for sure." He could not meet Sydney Alex' eyes at that moment, which he could feel were directed intently upon him. He walked out to where his horse had wandered to graze.

"Life," he told Dobbyn in a pessimistic voice, as he smoothed out his mane, "has a way, sometimes, of leaving you behind."

That evening when McAllister walked with Sydney Alex along the slope behind the Cartrell residence, he tried to find a beginning to conversation, an approach to the distress that her lingering divorce caused him. The ground beneath their shoes was dry from the lack of spring rain. At the top of the knoll they rested, sitting upon the pine needles and fern leaves.

"You certainly have a good remuda now, with so many new ones. Whatever you set out to do, you always come up a winner, it seems." She attempted to praise him, for he seemed preoccupied,

"Not always," he replied without looking at her. The tone of his voice was a dispassionate reminder of his continuing patience within the confines of their relationship.

When a long moment passed, she asked reluctantly, "Ryan, do you ever wish you had fallen in love with Jan instead of me? For a moment today, when she told you about their baby, you had the most regretful look on your face."

"I have to admit, there would've been less problems." He removed his hat, hooking it over a fallen snag, and leaned back against his elbows. "You are full of complications."

"Not last night," she smiled, trying to joke.

"All this wasted time. If you had been here when I came—"

"Well, I wasn't."

"—it wouldn't have turned out like this."

"But it did, Ryan, and you can't change that." Sydney Alex shifted on the ground to face him. "Ryan," she whispered tenderly, "I love you. I feel so much to blame for everything, but I'm not entirely at fault. It was the time we lived in that caused things to change. I know you understand that." She arranged her skirt under her knees against the prickle of dry grass.

"I just want to get on with life like everybody else has." He glanced across at her, noticing the soft curls of her honey-coloured hair which framed her face. He met her questioning hazel eyes. "Is that too much to ask?" He held her face and searched her eyes, as she leaned over him. "I want to marry you, Sydney," he told her in a gentle voice. Lifting his shoulders from the ground, his mouth sought hers, as he shifted from beneath, rolling over with her.

Overhead the sky was quickly darkening. In the trees beyond, a soft summer breeze played amongst the branches, casting concealing shadows over them.

45

In the mountains the warm July weather known at Skaha had not yet favoured the landscape. Mornings were clear and crisp. Lupin and sunflowers decorated the hillsides in splashes of yellow and blue. It was a fresh, beautiful world when the rising sun broke through the gray dawn.

The morning warmth was appreciated as the Skaha cowboys gathered strays from mountain canyons and ravines, grouping the main herd onto the lower areas of the range.

At the day's end, when the cattle could be heard, content in the meadow, a good campfire warmed them. Nearby their horses were settled with grain.

On the eve of Foderow and Strickland's departure for the ranch, the Skaha men gathered around their fire. A high wind rustled amongst the tall Ponderosa and cone-shaped alpine fir. Sparks flew up as the hot embers were disturbed, their glow against the darkness twinkling like tiny fireflies. The mountains enclosed them.

Getting to his feet, Strickland tapped Foderow's shoulder. "Time for us old boys to take ourselves off to our bunks, and let the young'uns keep the late hours."

Advice suddenly flew through the night air as they departed the campfire. "Keep your eyes open for old hungry cougars out there!" cautioned Strickland.

Yellow and orange flames danced up from the fire pit, throwing shadows across the ground and the men resting there. Caverly rose to pull several short logs into the fire bed.

McAllister was at peace with himself. Contentment filled him and he breathed deeply of the cool mountain air tinged faintly with the earthy smell of fallen needles and leaves which nourished the forest floor.

"I feel right, up here in the mountains," he told Anderson and Caverly. "Like being at home somehow."

"You sound like one of those early mountain men," Anderson chuckled. "They liked their solitude and unmolested earth. I think you were born a hundred years too late."

"Well, don't you sometimes feel that way, Manny? This kind of life is the best, don't you think, Allan? These hills are home." McAllister stretched out upon the ground, boots toward the fire and rested his head in his cupped hands.

A full moon sailed the sky above them and illuminated the

surrounding mountains. Yip-yipping of coyotes in the nearby hills filled the air. The rippling sound of the creek was soothing music to Ryan McAllister's sentimental mood. In the firelight, he smiled at Anderson, then looked over at Caverly. "Did you know that my great-great-grandfather was a trapper?"

Above them it was a starry night, a quiet and perfect evening in the blue Okanagan hills.

ISBN 141208400-8